ACKNOW

MW00399789

This b_k ___ _ot have been possible without the efforts of all the histc _ns _ esearchers who have written so many fine books on the s _ject _he Battle of Midway. There is a Further Reading section i_ the b_ _that lists some of these sources. I thank them all for their contribu tions to the knowledge base about this momentous battle. Any mistakes made in this novel are my own and do not reflect my research materials.

The members of the Battle of Midway Roundtable at www.midway.org are a fine group of individuals striving to study, discuss, and keep alive the memory of the battle and its participants. Some of the precious few remaining survivors of Midway regularly contribute and answer questions in this group. It was through this group that I met a man who I grew to love and admire in a very short time, Mr. Donald Hoff. Mr. Hoff flew in the rear-gunner position in an SBD and is credited with shooting down a Zero fighter plane during the attack on the Japanese fleet. He passed away in 2010. I miss him still.

Thanks go to a wonderful lady, Ms. Elsie Mobley, for graciously allowing me the use of her poem, "Going off to War", in Chapter 48.

Mr. Lloyd Childers, a veteran of the battle as a member of *Yorktown's* Torpedo 3, voiced the statement in Chapter 85 concerning the brutality of war. Mr. Childers was wounded in the attack but recovered and continued serving his country through Korea and Vietnam. Men and women like Mr. Childers and Mr. Hoff who bravely go in harm's way to protect our freedoms are heroes to us all.

Mr. Bill Vickrey is another veteran of World War II and an acknowledged expert on the battle and its participants. He helped me from the beginning with making contacts. He was there at the end to read over a review copy and give me welcome critique and fact correction. Most importantly, he placed my mind at ease with some of the decisions that I had made during my narrative. The accuracy of my words is a testament to his efforts, not mine. The remaining mistakes belong to me. I can not thank him enough.

The members of the B-26 Marauder Historical Society can be found at www.b-26mhs.org and are doing a great job of documenting and preserving the actions and contributions of the Marauders in World War 2. Their archives are filled with incredible first-person accounts from the men who flew this fine aircraft. I particularly appreciate the "Diary of Charles Lowe" which I referenced in relating Frank Melo's experiences during the B-26 attack on the Japanese fleet.

The Yahoo group Shattered Sword at: http://groups.yahoo.com/group/shatteredsword/?yguid=159792947, is a great place to find thousands of pictures about both the attack on Dutch Harbor and Midway. The content is updated weekly and it proved very valuable in my research.

Likewise, the Steeljaw Scribe at www.steeljawscribe.com is an incredible resource for all things pertaining to the American military both current and historical. The insightful editorial content alone is worth checking out.

I appreciate the efforts of Daniel Yu at www.handproofs.com in editing the manuscript and for all of his suggestions that improved this book. He did a great job and was a pleasure to work with. Daniel went beyond what I expected of him. I made a few changes after he had finished so any mistakes found are mine.

The greatest thing that came out of this experience for me was meeting and growing to know some of the veterans, their friends, and families, but also communicating with many of the people who seek to remember and honor our history. This has been an incredible time in my life and I thank each one for the memories shared.

Finally and importantly, thanks go to my beautiful wife and family for their patience and encouragement in helping me see this project through.

For justice guides the warrior's steel

And vengeance strikes the blow.

J. R. Drake to the Defenders of New Orleans

PREFACE

This novel concerns the Battle of Midway as experienced by several of the men involved. Each chapter is devoted to a single participant's point of view. The reader will witness and experience events as he does. For him, the outcome is undecided and his knowledge extends to the given moment in time. These lead characters represent both the American and Japanese sides of the battle. Some are well-known figures while others, though not as famous, played important roles at Midway. All of them deserve to have their stories told. It is my intention to go beyond the history and to add insight into the individual characters. I have known none of them, yet have endeavored to the utmost of my ability to render justice to their memories and contributions.

I researched both the older and latest information concerning the battle, judiciously changing a few of the facts. I condensed some of the action, endless meetings, and minor characters to provide a more concise, fluid narrative. I stayed as true to the facts as possible while still keeping the novel moving and of a reasonable size. Anyone who has studied or read about the battle understands the wealth of material available as well as the tremendous amount of time and effort that went into planning the operation on both sides. There is a Further Reading section in the back for those wishing to delve deeper into the subject. I encourage my readers to take advantage of these fine books and websites to learn more about the battle, its participants, and its consequences.

The reader should take note of the time stamp listed in each chapter heading. While the novel is written chronologically, there are some difficulties in this arrangement. As in all battles viewed from different perspectives, a good deal of the action occurs either simultaneously or closely together. The same is true for some of the chapters. When the scenes overlap, I have arranged the narrative to provide the greatest dramatic effect.

In as many cases as possible, I drew the dialogue from direct quotes or written documentation. The majority of it is fictional and based on my interpretation of the individual's personality under the given circumstances. All characterizations are my own. I

1

sincerely hope that I did justice to capturing the participants' unique personalities. Any mistakes made are solely my own and do not reflect my research materials. I ask that the participants' families forgive any indiscretion of mine made in ignorance of the facts. My motivation for writing this novel is to provide tangible evidence of my respect and admiration for every participant in this historic battle, both American and Japanese. May their memory live on in the hearts of those in their debt.

Where I felt comfortable using them, some of the minor characters are also real. Most of the subplots are fictitious. I did this for two reasons. The first is that the subplots are secondary to the main story of the battle. Their primary purpose is to add characterization and dramatic tension. The second and most important reason occurred very early in the writing of this novel. I was fortunate enough to contact one of the veterans of the battle and ask him a few research questions. In return, he asked why I wanted the information. I did a poor job of explaining myself and he became upset. He feared that I was about to rewrite history and possibly harm the legacy of the brave men who fought and died at Midway. At that moment, I realized how precious the memories are to those elderly and, in many cases, forgotten warriors who survive. I vowed to him that I would do nothing to spoil that. I believe the novel bears proof that I have kept my promise.

This story concerns human beings at war. War is killing. War is undeniably the most barbaric practice that mankind engages in. I do not seek to glorify such actions; I seek to illuminate the thoughts and emotions of the individual caught up in such a crucible. I am not ashamed to say one thing, and I hope this is one undeniable fact that the reader takes from my words: all of these men, American and Japanese, are my heroes.

Miracle at Midway is the title of a fine book written by the late Gordon W. Prange. During the writing of these pages, I often consulted it among others. While there is merit in his title statement, my research has led me to a different conclusion. This novel reveals my explanation for the battle's outcome.

Before Midway, there was much doubt among the Japanese leadership about the American will to fight. Its belief was that the Americans were not capable of sustaining substantial punishment and casualties. The heroic conduct of the American forces involved and the result of the battle proved the fallacy of this idea.

It is to these brave men, both those who gave their all and those who survived, that this book is humbly dedicated.

INTRODUCTION
Disaster in the Pacific

A simple lie can change the course of history.

Beginning with the surprise attack at Pearl Harbor on December 7, 1941, the next four months witness a continuous string of victories by Japanese armed forces throughout the Pacific Theater. Wake Island falls before year's end. The last bastion of Corregidor is poised on the brink of surrender, spelling an imminent end to the American presence in the Philippines. Australia, Hawaii, and the West Coast of the United States lie vulnerable to attack. By the early spring of 1942, the United States appears close to a catastrophic defeat to the Empire of Japan.

Yet, all is not what it seems. Japan makes a grievous error at Pearl Harbor. By striking while the American aircraft carriers are absent, the United States has sufficient resources for retaliation. The Japanese soon realize this. There is a sense of urgency among some members of the Imperial Combined Fleet to end hostilities before the American industrial might exerts itself. It is Yamamoto's belief that the total destruction of the American battle fleet will force the United States to the peace negotiation table. He seeks another surprise attack opportunity like Pearl Harbor, but dismisses an invasion of Hawaii or the West Coast as too dangerous due to patrols and available defensive air power. He decides to focus his enormous naval strike forces on an intermediate target. This target has to be beyond the range of air support from Hawaii but important enough that the United States will fight to retain its possession. Midway meets both of these requirements and offers the Japanese a presence in the central Pacific near the Hawaiian Islands. From there, a large invasion force could be assembled and supported for an attack on Hawaii. The Japanese are convinced that an air attack upon Midway will force the United States to respond in kind. In an attempt to lure the American aircraft carrier fleet into a final battle of annihilation, Yamamoto and his staff develop the Midway Plan in early 1942.

In the spring of that year, concern grows among American intelligence sources about Japanese communications and movements in the Pacific. A belief develops, especially among

5

Commander Joseph Rochefort's small code-breaking unit operating at Pearl Harbor called the Pacific Fleet Combat Intelligence Unit, designated HYPO, that another major Japanese offensive operation against a target code-named *AF* is imminent. Through long hours of hard study and due diligence breaking the Japanese cyphers, it is determined that Midway Atoll is the chosen target. Admiral Nimitz, Commander in Chief of the Pacific Fleet, has faith in HYPO's conclusions. Admiral Ernest King, Chief of Naval Operations back in Washington, wants more proof before agreeing with Nimitz's plan to defend Midway. HYPO comes up with an idea to have Midway transmit a false message advising Pearl Harbor that its fresh water condenser has broken down. This small lie is intercepted by a Japanese listening post and then broadcast to Tokyo as, "AF is low on fresh water." The transmission confirms the matter for King and sets in motion the battle to follow. Admiral Nimitz commences preparations to spring his own surprise on the unsuspecting Japanese fleet.

Despite opposition at every level, Yamamoto forces the Japanese Naval General Staff to adopt his plans by threatening to resign if he is refused; this is the same tactic he used to win approval for the Pearl Harbor attack. The prestige gained by him since then adds to the influence he commands. In April, the Doolittle Raid on Tokyo and the fears that ensue serve to end most of the arguments against the operation. Yamamoto's one concession to the General Staff is to include a simultaneous attack and occupation of the Aleutian Islands to protect Japan's eastern flank from American forces.

The plans as drawn up by Yamamoto's Senior Operations Officer Captain Kameto Kuroshima involve four separate attack groups. The Northern (Aleutians) Force under the command of Vice Admiral Moshiro Hosogaya is composed of a few cruisers, destroyers, the light carrier *Ryujo* and carrier *Junyo*. Its mission is an invasion and occupation of the Aleutian Islands. The First Carrier Striking Force led by Vice Admiral Chuichi Nagumo from his flagship the aircraft carrier *Akagi* includes the large carriers *Kaga*, *Hiryu*, and *Soryu*. Its objective is to neutralize American air power based on Midway and soften it up for invasion. The Main Force under the direct command of Admiral Yamamoto contains the bulk of the Combined Fleet's battleships including his flagship, *Yamato*, the largest such vessel currently afloat. The Main Force's job is to follow behind Nagumo's carrier force in preparation to pounce on the American fleet when it rushes in to defend Midway. Vice Admiral Nobutake Kondo commands the fourth element, the Midway Invasion Force, composed of a battleship, cruisers, destroyers, seaplane carriers, a light carrier, and the troop transports. Each group has a separate departure time and route to the battle area.

About a month before Operation AF is to begin, Japanese naval forces under the command of Vice Admiral Shigeyoshi Inoue intent on occupying Port Moresby clash with an American fleet led by Rear Admiral Frank J. Fletcher in the Coral Sea. A tactical victory by the Japanese in terms of ships lost by each side, the clash is nonetheless a strategic victory for the United States. The obvious American success is the withdrawal of Japanese invasion forces and removal of the threat between the Australian and American supply line. Not readily apparent at the time is that damage sustained by *Shokaku* and the air group losses suffered by *Zuikaku,* the newest and largest Japanese aircraft carriers, prevents them from participating in the upcoming Midway operation.

The Japanese believe they have sunk both the *Yorktown* and another carrier mistakenly identified as the *Saratoga* but is actually the *Lexington. Lexington* is in fact lying on the bottom of the Coral Sea. Though seriously damaged, *Yorktown* is enroute to Pearl Harbor for major repairs.

Yamamoto's staff presents the plans to the various commanding officers involved, and war game simulations conclude. Despite Doolittle's raid, there is still some dissension and opposition to the Midway operation. The various elements of the Combined Fleet hold final meetings in preparation to sail if they reach an agreement.

In Pearl Harbor, Admiral Nimitz rushes all available manpower and equipment to aid in repelling the invasion. Short on resources, he sends a conglomeration of aircraft to throw into the breach. He also waits for the arrival of the two men tasked with stopping the Japanese.

What happens next will determine the course of the war in the Pacific.

THE COMBATANTS

The Americans:

Rear Admiral Raymond A. Spruance currently serves as cruiser commander of Admiral William Halsey's Task Force 16. He is a slender man, fifty-six years of age, with a firm face and thinning hair. The total antithesis to the swashbuckling Halsey, he believes in calm, logical thinking preceding any action. He desires neither to promote himself nor to provide colorful comments for the war correspondents. He carries this attitude to the extreme of banning reporters from his flagship. They respond by popularizing the image of Spruance as cold and hard. His inexperience with aircraft carrier command could lead to indecision and disaster. The shadow of Halsey accompanies him to Midway.

Rear Admiral Frank J. Fletcher leads Task Force 17 comprised of the aircraft carrier *Yorktown* and her supporting vessels. He is of medium height, fifty-seven years of age, physically fit, with a weathered face. A nephew of the past Commander in Chief of the Atlantic Fleet, Admiral Frank Friday Fletcher, he bears the taint of benefiting from friends in high places. In late December of 1941, he is picked to lead Task Force 14 in reinforcing a beleaguered Wake Island. He shares the blame along with his superior, Admiral William S. Pye, when the attempt is called off shortly before they are close enough to launch an air strike. Wake Island falls to the Japanese that same day. In May of 1942, he commands Task Force 17 during the Battle of Coral Sea. When the aircraft carrier *Lexington* is sunk during this action, he comes under further criticism and scrutiny. The accusations fly afterwards that his lack of aggression allowed the Japanese and certain victory to escape. Defending Midway offers the chance for vindication. Or another opportunity at failure.

Lieutenant Commander John C. Waldron leads the carrier *Hornet's* Torpedo Squadron 8. He is a lean, dark-skinned man whose hawk-like profile bears evidence of a proud one-eighth Sioux bloodline and heritage. At forty-one years of age, he is the consummate professional officer who leads his boys with an equal mixture of tough taskmaster and playful older brother. His men are unblooded, most having never dropped a torpedo in any manner from their obsolete Douglas Devastator TBD torpedo-bomber aircraft. The core group has trained and lived together

8

long enough to become family. They affectionately call Waldron either *Skipper* or *Captain*. All are vocal in their dedication and willingness to follow him into hell. The hostile waters northwest of Midway Atoll might offer them the chance.

Lieutenant Commander John S. Thach commands *Yorktown*'s Fighter Squadron 3 flying Grumman F4F Wildcat fighter planes. A tall, quiet-spoken Southerner, he is recognized as an exceptional leader and teacher. Thirty-six years old, he has lived an interesting life that includes performing as stand-in pilot for Clark Gable in the motion picture *Hell Divers*. His brilliance at developing air tactics has resulted in a maneuver that he calls the "beam defense position." He believes this tactic will result in a greater chance of surviving an aerial encounter with the faster climbing, more nimble Japanese Zero fighter aircraft. He seeks an opportunity to test the tactic in actual combat to prove its effectiveness. His opportunity should soon arrive.

Lieutenant Commander William H. Brockman Jr. is captain of the submarine *USS Nautilus*. Thirty-six years of age, he is a burly man of average height with an open, sincere face. In his first command of a submarine, he and his crew are in the midst of evaluating the newly refurbished boat after its initial shakedown cruise. Like other officers forced into command by the war, he is youthful, and there are some doubts about his abilities. The same holds true for the inexperienced crew. He is determined to prove the doubters wrong. Proof waits in the deep, killing waters of the South Pacific.

Corporal Frank L. Melo Jr. is a radioman/gunner in a Mitchell B-26 Marauder medium-bomber attached to the Army Air Force's 22nd Bomb Group. He is in his mid-twenties, a short, dashing young man with a gleam in his eyes. His and another aircrew from the 22nd are left behind in Hawaii to finish preparing their B-26s for service while the remainder of the group proceeds on to the Southwest Pacific. Bored with days spent learning to launch torpedoes from the B-26, he envies those who go on ahead to the active combat zone. He wishes to join the real fighting. Unfortunately, the real fighting is about to reach out to him and his companions.

Major Lofton R. Henderson commands Marine Air Group VMSB-241 and is a graduate of the U. S. Naval Academy. He is thirty-nine years old and cuts a handsome, striking figure as an officer. A veteran of carrier air operations, he looks and acts the part of a Marine's Marine in his attitude and comportment. In late May of 1942, he is handed both a promotion and a new assignment on Midway Atoll. The assignment seems impossible to those familiar with it. Not to Henderson.

Commander Logan C. Ramsey is chief of staff for Hawaiian patrol planes. He is forty-four years old, a physically imposing figure with a visage seemingly forged from battleship steel. While unorthodox in his methods, he is a mental genius capable of figuring out complex mathematical problems while playing cards. Nimitz considers him the right man for the tough task of defending Midway from the air. Ramsey views the assignment as another job that needs doing. He forgets that life has a way of showing a man the error in his thinking.

Lieutenant Richard H. Best serves as squadron leader of *Enterprise's* Bombing 6 flying Douglas Dauntless SBD dive bombers. At forty-two years of age, he maintains his boyish good looks and a slender physical frame that belies his mature leadership skills. A graduate of the Naval Academy, he is an excellent pilot who served a stint training flight instructors at the Pensacola Naval Air Station. With a wife and child living in Honolulu, he has much more than a passing interest in the security of the Hawaiian Islands. His concerns lead to distraction that could prove fatal.

The Japanese:

Rear Admiral Ryunosuke Kusaka is Admiral Chuichi Nagumo's chief of staff. He is forty-eight years old and rather corpulent, with a broad, placid face. Though not a flier, he is a veteran of two separate commands of aircraft carriers. A Zen Buddhist, he often engages in philosophical discourses and holds a reflective outlook on life. Others view him as a talented negotiator and counselor, and his relaxed personality seems to make him unsuited for initiating bold action in time of crisis. He must overcome this perception if he is to become the military leader that Japan desperately needs.

Lieutenant Joichi Tomonaga is a recent addition to the aircraft carrier *Hiryu's* air group flying Nakajima Ninety-seven torpedo-bomber aircraft. A young, handsome man with high cheekbones and intense eyes, he is a veteran of the air war in China. A personality mix of serious and aloof combined with a reputation as a hard drinker makes him somewhat of a loner among his new squadron mates. He secretly seeks a challenge equal to his repressed samurai upbringing. That challenge awaits him over the horizon at a place called Midway Atoll.

THE AIRCRAFT

American:

Douglas Dauntless SBD is a single-engine dive bomber used by both Navy and Marine aviators. It has a crew of two consisting of a pilot and a rear-seat radioman/gunner. With a top speed of 255 mph, a range of 770 miles, and a load capacity of 2,250 lbs. of bombs, it has carried the brunt of Navy dive bombing attacks so far in the young war. Rugged and armed with two fixed .50-caliber forward machine guns and a flex-mounted rear .30-caliber machine gun, it is capable of putting up good defensive fire against Japanese fighters. Its signature large perforated dive flaps aid in stabilizing the SBD while dive bombing.

Douglas Devastator TBD is a single-engine torpedo-bomber bearing the distinction of being the Navy's first carrier-based monoplane. Unfortunately, by the time the war begins, the TBD is already obsolete. When armed with bombs, it has a crew of three, but it usually carries two men when mounted with a torpedo. A top speed of only 200 mph must be further reduced to 115 mph before the bomber can release a torpedo. Though TBDs enjoy some success at the Battle of Coral Sea, their vulnerabilities also become evident. Slow and clumsy, with light defensive weaponry and poor armor, the TBDs benefit at Coral Sea from the Japanese fighters concentrating at higher altitudes on the attacking SBDs. The belief among TBD crews is that their chances of survival are slim should the enemy decide to go after them.

Grumman F4F Wildcat is the Navy's primary fighter aircraft at the beginning of the war. With a top speed of about 315 mph, it is neither as fast nor as maneuverable as the Japanese Zero fighter plane. Its range is also much smaller. The F4F's rugged construction, self-sealing fuel tanks, and six wing-mounted .50-caliber machine guns compensate for some of these design weaknesses. All of these things considered, it is still at a great disadvantage when matched against the Japanese fighter. The common admonition preached to all American fighter pilots during early 1942 is to *never dogfight a Zero.* The men who choose to ignore this warning are quickly shown the error of doing so. For many it becomes a fatal error.

Martin B-26 Marauder is a medium bomber used in the Pacific Theater by the Army Air Force. When unloaded, the B-26 can obtain a top speed of nearly 300 mph from its twin engines, allowing for a fast exit out of harm's way. The seven-man crew consists of pilot, copilot, bombardier, navigator, radioman/gunner, top turret gunner, and tail gunner. With a wing size and design optimized for high-speed performance, the B-26 can be unstable at lower speeds during take-off and landing. Or when making a torpedo-launching run.

Japanese:

Mitsubishi A6M Zero is the premier fighter aircraft in the Pacific Theater during the early stages of the war. It is the best carrier-based fighter in the world combining speed, maneuverability, and extreme long range. This emphasis on performance, however, comes with a lack of armor and self-sealing fuel tanks. During late 1941 and early 1942, the Zero has amassed a kill ratio of better than 10 to 1 against its adversaries. It has a top speed of about 330-mph and is armed with two 7.7-mm machine guns located in front of the cockpit and two wing-mounted 20-mm cannons. At the time of the Battle of Midway, Zero pilots are combat tested graduates of one of the toughest flight training courses in the world. They are, quite simply, the best of the best.

Nakajima B5N2 Type Ninety-seven is the standard single-engine torpedo-bomber of the Imperial Japanese Navy. It has a crew of three comprised of a pilot, observer/navigator, and rear-seat gunner/radio man. The workhorse of the IJN, it can drop bombs or launch torpedoes with deadly accuracy. A top speed of 235 mph and lack of forward firing machine guns make it vulnerable to attack from American fighters. The pilots are willing to do whatever is necessary to complete their mission. Most ominous to the American commanders is that the Japanese ability to perform aerial torpedo attacks has no equal.

1. KUSAKA
May 25 – 20:00 Hours

Life is suffering.

Admiral Ryunosuke Kusaka meditated on that statement for a few moments. Today bears proof of that, but tomorrow is another day. His vision focused on the source of his suffering, Admiral Matome Ugaki, standing in front of the flag meeting room aboard the Imperial Japanese Navy battleship *Yamato*.

"The Americans are paper tigers lacking the will to fight," Ugaki was saying. "They abandon their weapons, flee before our armed forces, and when cornered, meekly creep out with hands raised in defeat expecting honorable treatment."

Ugaki's insolent, drooping eyes marched across the officers gathered around the tables. They settled briefly on Kusaka and Vice Admiral Chuichi Nagumo, seated side by side, blinked and moved on. To bear so much majesty for a mere mortal must be difficult, Kusaka thought. It must be a challenge for Ugaki to look into the mirror without bowing to his own reflection.

"Honorable treatment?" Ugaki continued, his voice rising and falling to emphasize the words. "This enemy demanding such honorable treatment is the same one who makes war on our women and children by bombing Tokyo! They did not seek out military targets like honorable men. They ignored our example set in the attack on Pearl Harbor. They used their weapons against hospitals and schools!"

Ugaki paused again, wiping his mouth, and he seemed to struggle with his emotions. Kusaka released a sigh and shuffled in his chair. It's a shame to waste such a performance on an educated, skeptical audience, Kusaka thought. We're not geishas or schoolboys easily impressed by grand gestures and flowery speech. Maybe Ugaki just tries his best to preserve the dignity of his revered superior. Seated near Ugaki, an impassive Admiral Isoroku Yamamoto stared straight ahead, his manner revealing nothing of the guilt Kusaka knew he bore for the American attack on the Japanese Homeland.

"The Americans and their incestuous British brethren make a great show of putting up a fight until things get tough. When the blood starts to flow in rivers, they quickly give up. They lack the desire and tenacity of the Japanese warrior. They do not understand the Code of Bushido. Yet, I don't totally fault the American soldiers on the front lines. Their leaders are chiefly to blame for setting a poor example. Did not MacArthur run for his life and abandon his men to their fate when faced with the hopeless situation at Corregidor? An honorable man, disgraced by such failure, would commit seppuku to atone for his actions."

Kusaka glanced at Yamamoto and wondered if committing seppuku had entered Yamamoto's thoughts when American bombs fell on Tokyo. He had vowed to protect the safety of the Emperor, so the attack must have placed a terrible burden on Yamamoto's shoulders. Yet, he should be given his due. It takes more courage to persevere in the face of such humiliation. It demands greater intestinal fortitude to continue fighting and atone for one's failure.

"As things now stand, we are ahead of our projected timetable for taking the Americans out of the war. The British must concentrate on the threat closer to their home shores, Germany. They offer little in the way of resistance to our operations. America stands alone as an obstacle. We shall overcome this obstacle and move forward down destiny's path. With the American presence eliminated and our territories secure, we will liberate the remainder of East Asia from Western imperialism. The Greater East Asia Co-Prosperity Sphere will become a reality under Japanese leadership."

Kusaka reached up and rubbed his eyes. Mixing political rhetoric with combat operations made him uneasy. Certainly, there are better reasons to die than the possession of a piece of earth or the souls of those that work it. He still agreed with the primary motivation for going to war. The Allied Powers, particularly the Americans, had pushed Japan into a corner; they had initiated this conflict by their high-handed, hypocritical policies designed to deny Japan an equal place in the world community. Now, after listening to a continuous inferno of inflammatory speeches praising aggressive imperialism, Kusaka began to feel a creeping doubt as to the true purpose of the war.

"We must take the next step . . . move our lines closer to the Hawaiian Islands. With these in our possession, our threat to the American West Coast is undeniable. Our advance will fall as the final blow against an enemy lacking true fighting spirit and cause panic among them. They will come running to us, begging to make peace. To achieve this, we must first occupy Midway and lure the American carriers out to battle."

He paused and wiped his brow as though exhausted from his speech.

"Admiral Yamamoto will lead the final briefing of our plans," he concluded.

Ugaki sat down. Yamamoto stood and waited for a few moments, undoubtedly to whet his audience's appetite, Kusaka decided. The smell of salt air and the sound of sea gulls filtered in through the open portholes.

"Let me begin by reminding everyone that this operation involves a large number of forces and extends over vast areas." Yamamoto's great voice battered against the walls as if in order to gain more space. "We must assume the unexpected can happen at any time. I stress the need to maintain coordination among all fleet elements, to not hesitate to send out critical messages when necessary, and to be quick to join other forces if needed. Regarding our aircraft carriers, fleet doctrine will be followed whereby half of your aircraft and best pilots are to remain in reserve, prepared to meet the Americans should they show up to offer battle.

"Radio interceptions suggest that over twenty enemy submarines have been deployed. The damage from their attacks is increasing. We must remain alert and take immediate action to this threat. One enemy submarine that spots our strike forces and is allowed to transmit the information will destroy the secrecy this operation depends on. The message will alert the enemy and prevent his fleet from coming out to meet us in battle. This must not happen."

Yamamoto's eyes wandered around the room. "Who wishes to speak?"

"I do." Kusaka rose from his chair.

Yamamoto's eyes narrowed as if viewing an unpleasant sight. Kusaka understood that Yamamoto had expected questions from Nagumo's staff. Kusaka also knew that Nagumo's air operations officer, Commander Minoru Genda, would not be the one to raise them. Genda owes much to Yamamoto and shuns any opportunity to openly disagree with him, Kusaka thought. He's young and destined to accomplish great things if he keeps his hands unsoiled.

15

I'm older and my path was decided long ago. I shall dig in the earth for all who share my concerns.

"This need to transmit and receive critical messages you speak of is indeed crucial to the success of the operation. Yet, there's also the need for the entire fleet to observe strict radio silence ensuring the secrecy of our attacks. At the time of crisis, one need must be weighed heavily against the other with regards to the consequences."

Yamamoto remained silent, lips pursed tightly together. Kusaka thought, he's waiting to see where I'm leading with my comments. He's judging me . . . prepared to pounce like a fat cat on a canary. Yamamoto lives for such moments as these. I mustn't disappoint him.

"The radio communications equipment carried by Admiral Nagumo's flagship, the aircraft carrier *Akagi,* is inadequate, as are the other carriers' radio equipment in our group. I'm concerned that our Task Force might fail to intercept enemy radio messages. Such messages could contain vital information for determining enemy movements and intentions."

Yamamoto nodded. "Continue."

"I would suggest that your flagship, *Yamato,* operate independently and relay all important radio messages to Admiral Nagumo's force. By not leading the main battleship group, *Yamato* would not have to observe radio silence."

"Any deployment of *Yamato* will necessitate screening vessels and air coverage," Yamamoto answered. "Our forces are spread thin as it is. This is impossible."

"Then *Yamato* should join our carrier force, *Kido Butai,* with you assuming direct command," Kusaka said.

"No."

"No disrespect, but might we know the reason why?"

Yamamoto squinted and then locked his vision onto Kusaka. Yamamoto studies me much as a crane consumes a fish first with his sight before using his beak, Kusaka thought. He wastes the effort. He should know that I am not easily intimidated.

"Fleet dispositions have been made, times and locations for fueling arrangements finalized," Yamamoto stated. "The countless weeks of planning and making tough decisions are not easily undone. Certainly you can understand this."

"I do understand this. Yet, had we been allowed access to these plans at an earlier time, perhaps before they were finalized, we could have offered valuable input to aid in making the tough decisions. There is a great host of combat knowledge and experience gathered in this room. I respectfully suggest that you avail yourself of it."

Yamamoto bowed up to rigid attention, his barrel chest fully flexed.

"Need I remind you that Admiral Nagumo's carrier force has been involved in almost continuous sea operations since December? The bowels of an aircraft carrier involved in battle are hardly the place to draw up plans for fleet operations. The prosecution of this war against the Americans will not wait for the convenience of a few."

"I'm well aware of that." Kusaka fought to keep a placid but firm manner. "I've been with him the entire time, engaged in waging war against our enemies."

A thin smile spread across Yamamoto's thick lips. "Yes, you have, doing your duty to the Emperor just like I do mine when planning fleet operations. I have full confidence in the fruits of my labor. Would that you had as much confidence in your abilities as I have in mine."

Yamamoto disappeared behind a crimson veil as anger threatened to seize Kusaka. Remember the breathing, Kusaka thought. Channel my mental discipline and maintain the mind in a state of equilibrium. I won't allow Yamamoto to engage me in a contest aimed at humiliating me.

"I appreciate Admiral Kusaka's concern." Yamamoto took advantage of Kusaka's silence to address the group. "I know his feelings are motivated by the success of our forces."

A slight bow toward Yamamoto and Kusaka seated himself. Yamamoto returned the gesture and also sat down. Ugaki stood, reclaiming the floor.

"As stated, one of the goals of these operations is to force the American fleet to come out and meet us in a great, decisive battle," Ugaki picked up. "Luck was with them at Pearl Harbor because their aircraft carriers were out to sea. Because of this, they maintain a serious air strike capability that needs to be eliminated. The recent battle at Coral Sea and the bombing of our homeland provide proof of their threat to us.

"Admiral Yamamoto has spent much time in America and understands its people. They proceed with caution when confronted with an unexpected foe, and do not blindly charge out to the slaughter. When we launch our attack and they discover Admiral Nagumo's carrier fleet, we'll force them to make a decision. I believe that given the risks and consequences of not acting, they will choose to engage us in combat."

His eyesight slowly swept over the room before settling on Kusaka.

"When they do, their weak resolve will again manifest itself, and the Main Force under Admiral Yamamoto will close in to finish the job we started at Pearl Harbor."

Admiral Yamaguchi raised a hand that Ugaki acknowledged.

"I welcome this opportunity," Yamaguchi said. "I've served time as Naval Attaché in Washington and agree with Admiral Yamamoto's assessment of the situation. We must challenge the American fleet and decisively defeat it if we wish to drive them to the negotiating table. Between our strikes on Midway and the Aleutians, they must respond."

Kusaka lowered his head and rolled his eyes. Leave it to a fire-eater like Yamaguchi to bravely walk Yamamoto's line and bark at shadows, he thought. This meeting should have taken place inside a temple. Would no one else blow out his candle and demand to stand in the true light?

"Is there no concern for our lack of shore-based air support that the enemy will have?" Admiral Kondo broke the temporary lull, addressing Yamamoto directly. "Even without their carriers, the enemy will be able to attack our forces with airplanes from Midway. Given this disadvantage, I believe an invasion of New Caledonia would be the wiser choice. By invading there we can cut the supply line between Australia and the Americans. This could be followed up by the invasion and occupation of Australia."

Kusaka smiled in agreement, glad to have a kindred soul. More dissenting voices could swing the discussion in my favor.

"The Midway plan has been agreed upon by the Combined Fleet and the Naval General Staff and cannot be changed," Yamamoto's voice rumbled, clanging against the ship's steel walls. "That time has passed. There are risks involved in all such operations, but there is no reason to fear defeat if we achieve surprise in our attack."

Kondo grunted and turned his attention toward Ugaki.

"Fleet Headquarters has raised no concerns about keeping Midway supplied once it's captured? It lies within distance of large land-based bombers from Hawaii. Unless this can be done, the occupation will be useless and a waste of time and materials."

Kusaka noticed Ugaki giving a fleeting glance at Yamamoto. Eyes closed, Yamamoto laid his head back against the wall as if the question bore no importance to him. Ugaki sighed, appeared to be resigned to the fact that he must offer a reply.

"When the American fleet comes out to fight, it will be crushed without mercy. With a lack of carriers and support vessels, their defensive lines must tighten around Hawaii and their West Coast. They will be anxious to negotiate peace and not concerned with attacking Midway by air."

Ugaki smiled, obviously proud with his answer.

"And if they choose not to fight they'll retain enough forces in and around Hawaii to threaten Midway and its supply line," Kondo fired back. "What then?"

Kusaka grinned as he enjoyed the sight of Ugaki wiggling around like a fish caught on Kondo's hook of intuitive logic.

Ugaki's smile collapsed and he shrugged. "We'll destroy all military installations and the airfield before evacuating our forces."

"*Hai.*" Kondo grimaced and made a wave of dismissal. Ugaki licked his lips and looked around the room as if seeking support. Kusaka saw dismay in his face when Ugaki noticed him motioning to speak. Ugaki's acknowledging nod to Kusaka's request appeared reluctant.

"Our success depends upon a surprise attack and the reaction of the American fleet primarily located in Hawaii," Kusaka said. "It's imperative that we know the composition of those forces as well as the location of the American aircraft carriers. If those carriers should suddenly and unexpectedly appear, the entire operation would be in dire jeopardy."

"I don't know if that would prove a disaster," Ugaki responded. "The battle reports from Coral Sea indicate the carriers *Saratoga* and *Yorktown* were sunk. We have another recent sighting of the *Enterprise* and *Hornet* near the Solomons. It's doubtful the enemy has a carrier near Hawaii."

"And if they do?" Nagumo spoke up for the first time.

Kusaka was surprised and pleased that the old warrior had finally stirred and joined the heated discussion. I'm but an annoying fly with my comments, Kusaka thought. Nagumo possesses enough of a martial reputation and the respect of many in this room to sway opinion with his words.

"I would think you'd welcome the chance to match your group against the enemy's," Yamamoto spoke up. "The Americans lost at Coral Sea against the least experienced pilots Japan has. They should be easy prey for your expert, battle-hardened veterans."

Kusaka bristled, knowing Yamamoto struck Nagumo in a place he could not defend—his pride. To argue the point would be conceding Nagumo's doubts about his ability to command and the men under him. Kusaka noted Nagumo's obvious anger, but understood why he held his tongue.

"Admiral Kusaka brings up an excellent point," Ugaki stepped in, defusing the tense situation. "It is important that we obtain the latest intelligence about enemy dispositions to aid in planning and reacting. Combined Fleet has authorized a similar plan as the one used before the attack on Pearl Harbor. It is designated Operation K. Before the invasion date, two flying boats will launch from Wotje. They will land at French Frigate Shoals for refueling by submarine before proceeding on to Hawaii to reconnoiter Pearl Harbor."

"What of Midway's air defenses?" Kondo asked. "There are certainly aircraft stationed on it capable of attacking ships. What do you propose to do if the Americans attack the carrier force while our fighters are escorting our attack on Midway?"

"Suppose something worse happens," Yamamoto broke in, taking command of the conversation. "Admiral Nagumo, what will your response be if an enemy carrier force suddenly appears within striking distance of your carriers while you are attacking Midway?"

Kusaka sat stunned that Yamamoto would pose such a question in light of the negative reception his Midway operation was receiving. He thought, why would Yamamoto add fuel to the fire burning away at his plans? Perhaps he seeks to demonstrate Nagumo's absence of enthusiasm for the opportunity of battle. Is Yamamoto building a case for Nagumo's lack of aggression, rendering him unfit to continue in his command role? Trying to trap Nagumo into voicing such doubts? If he is, he's wasting his time. Nagumo will allow Genda to answer the question. Kusaka knew that all eyes were now focused on Genda, an acknowledged expert on carrier operations and tactics. The fact that Nagumo normally deferred all such questions to Genda is no secret among the men assembled here. Yamamoto should know this, too.

"Commander Genda, can the carrier fleet be expected to deal with such an eventuality?" Ugaki asked.

Kusaka realized Genda was self-confident almost to the level of cockiness but was still surprised when the young officer said, "If the enemy carriers appear, one touch of an armored glove. They'll be destroyed."

Kusaka now understood the reason behind Yamamoto's question. A seasoned poker player, Yamamoto gambled that his protégé Genda would respond in such a fashion. The burden of carrying out Yamamoto's plans now fell squarely on Nagumo's shoulders. Should disaster strike and the attack fail for any reason, the suspicion would not be directed at the plans but at Nagumo's failure to execute them. Kusaka released a soft, humorless chuckle at the thought of Yamamoto's manipulation of the situation. I am awed with Yamamoto's remorseless genius in handling people and getting them to do his bidding without them realizing it. I can only hope that his Midway Operation displays evidence of the same keen intelligence.

2. SPRUANCE
May 27 – 13:00 Hours

Admiral Raymond Spruance sat in one of Rear Admiral Chester Nimitz's split-bamboo chairs patiently waiting for him to finish some correspondence. His gaze traveled around the bright, breezy office and took note that the seat cushions matched the flowery drapes. The fact that this space, with the exception of a few maps stuck to the walls with thumbtacks, gave no impression that its occupant was charged with waging war over most of the Pacific Ocean region struck Spruance as almost comical.

"I'm sorry, Ray, but I needed to finish this and get it in the afternoon post," Nimitz spoke while he folded and placed the page in an envelope. "Give me just a second, will you?"

He got up, carried the letter to the door, and stepped outside. Spruance thought, why does a man with a dozen aides hand deliver a piece of mail?

Nimitz returned, pulled the door closed. He sat and stretched his clasped hands out on top of the desk.

"I've been sitting here taking root since early this morning and I just had to stretch my legs for a moment. It keeps the blood circulating."

Spruance looked at him and thought, can the man read minds? Or, perhaps he's good at reading the expressions on people's faces. Was I that obvious?

"That's one of the bad things about this job," Nimitz continued. "There's so much to do that I have to grab my exercise whenever I can."

Spruance nodded. "I try to take a daily walk at sea, up and down the stairs and ladders. Kind of like an obstacle course."

"I've sent Bill Halsey on over to the hospital," Nimitz said, abruptly changing the subject. "He's in no condition to lead a fleet. It was quite a struggle getting him in the place. I threatened to place a guard on his door to keep him from leaving."

Spruance smiled. He could easily picture the fiery Halsey stalking out of the hospital wearing his admiral's cap and a hospital gown. "I can well imagine."

Nimitz leaned back in the chair and withdrew his arms. The noisy sounds from Battleship Row across the main harbor filtered in through the office windows. The smell of salt, smoke, and burnt oil painted memory on the breeze, a tangible reminder of the horror visited on the place in December of last year. Nimitz seems oblivious to everything, Spruance decided. He's preoccupied with his thoughts. Something's bothering him . . . something much more than Halsey's condition.

"I had a discussion with Bill before he left," Nimitz said. "There's an upcoming operation that won't wait and I've got to have a commander for his Task Force 16. Someone that I can trust to do whatever needs doing, make tough decisions, and have the personal conviction to stick to them."

He paused for a second and then said, "He recommended you."

Spruance fought to maintain his stoic mask and thought, this was unexpected. Why me? I'm not an aviator and there are available aviators senior to me. What was Halsey thinking? I'm honored . . . but me? I have to hand it to him, though. Halsey certainly holds influence in higher circles to pull this off.

"I just want you to know that I fully agree with his suggestion."

Nimitz is reading minds again, Spruance thought, but he said, "I'll do my best to live up to that recommendation."

What else can I say? Thanks, but no thanks? Isn't there someone senior with more experience? An aviator perhaps? Neither Nimitz nor Halsey would understand. Nor would I. A career naval officer never turns down an assignment.

"I know you will," Nimitz replied.

Nimitz sighed and looked off into the distance. "The Japanese are planning to attack and occupy Midway, with further attacks on the Aleutians. I intend to oppose these attacks with every available force we can muster."

He locked eyes with Spruance. "I believe that a climactic battle in the Pacific is at hand that we must not lose. There's just too much at stake. Since this war started, we've steadily retreated before the Japanese. They've shoved us off Wake Island and out of the Philippines. We must turn this ship around and head it in the right direction."

"I agree."

"Good. Here's what we've drawn up. Your group containing *Enterprise* and *Hornet* will be the first to sail and will rendezvous with Frank Jack's Task Force 17 containing the *Yorktown*. He's senior, so he'll have overall command of the operation."

Spruance remained silent. He watched Nimitz closely, trying to read his mannerisms. One second he was staring intently at Spruance. Then his gaze shifted to some object on the wall or floor as if he was trying to avoid eye contact. He's distracted as if he has something else to tell me, Spruance decided. Something he knows I'm not going to enjoy.

"When the battle's over, I want you to return to Pearl and assume the position of my chief of staff."

There it is as I'd predicted. Spruance wrestled hard with his emotions, determined not to show his reaction. He gripped himself mentally, resolved not to fall after having Nimitz build him up and then snatch the carpet out from under him. A tour of shore duty in the early stages of a large naval war is the last thing I want. I can think of several reasons why I can better serve at sea. Certainly, Nimitz would understand . . .

He resigned himself to the situation. A career naval officer never refuses an assignment, particularly one originating from the Commander in Chief Pacific. I will serve where needed.

"I know you're disappointed," Nimitz said, "but I need you here with me. Your knowledge, experience, and intelligence make you uniquely qualified for the job. Work with me awhile and I'll find another sea command for you later."

Spruance tilted his chin upward and looked directly into Nimitz's eyes. "I'll serve where needed."

"Good."

Nimitz stood and walked over to a small table covered with a chart of the Pacific. Spruance joined him in looking down at the map.

"It's a lot of ocean to cover and I'm committing the bulk of our forces to defending one tiny atoll," Nimitz said. "If I'm wrong and they attack elsewhere in force, it could be another disaster."

Spruance detected a note of uncertainty in his words.

"You've doubts?" he asked.

"Admiral King and some of the politicians in Washington have fears about the West Coast. General Emmons is concerned that Hawaii could be attacked again. They can be very persuasive with their arguments."

"What do you believe?"

"Like I said, it's Midway without a doubt, and we're going to be ready to surprise them."

Spruance smiled in relief. The doubt was gone, replaced with a firm resolve. If Nimitz didn't believe in his mission, how could he expect anyone else to believe? A leader must be fully committed if he expects his followers to carry out his orders . . . especially when the dying starts.

Nimitz picked up a long wooden pointer, setting the tip on the map. "Here's what we're looking at. The Japanese Main Body will be composed of between four and five carriers and will launch aircraft from the northwest of Midway. The Invasion Force composed of troop transports and warships will come in from the west. There's another separate group headed for the Aleutians."

"That's a sizable armada," Spruance observed.

"I'd say it's the largest enemy fleet assembled to date. Yamamoto really means business."

"There are a lot of targets to choose from."

"I want those carriers. The rest can wait for another day."

"I thought as much."

"Understand, I can't afford to hazard losing any more of our carriers unless you can inflict greater damage on the enemy."

That comment seems odd, Spruance thought. Are we going out there to protect Midway or not?

"Are you saying that Midway . . ."

"Is not your first priority," Nimitz coolly answered the unfinished question. "Sinking those Japanese carriers without excessive loss of ours is."

Spruance did not respond but returned his gaze to the map. He briefly thought about Wake Island and the refusal to risk forces to prevent it from falling into enemy hands. At the last possible moment before reinforcements came into range, an order flashed out to return to Hawaii. The outrage and criticism following the aborted attempt had yet to cease. Was Nimitz about to drag us into a similar minefield of angry public and official opinion?

"Understand," Nimitz explained, "I'm no happier about possibly losing Midway than you are. I'm still aware of the outcry and blow to morale we suffered when Wake fell. I realize that the press will crucify me if Midway is also captured, but it can't be helped."

The man *is* a mind reader, Spruance decided.

"But if we can pull off our attack and sink those carriers, we'll severely impact the enemy's ability to wage war in the Pacific," Nimitz pressed on. "We'll buy ourselves some needed time to build our forces back up. A large enough victory could place them on the defensive and allow us to take the initiative. That is all that matters to me."

He paused again and laid the pointer down. The soft *clack* seemed to echo throughout the warm room like a gun shot.

"There is a risk that they discover us first and sink what's left of our fleet. We can't allow that to happen."

"I understand."

"I trust you and Frank Jack to do whatever you believe is warranted given the circumstances and consequences of your actions. If you do or don't sink some or all of those enemy carriers, I don't want you risking a surface action in an effort to protect Midway against a superior enemy force. You get out of there fast and live to fight another day. I can't stress that point too strongly."

"Understood," Spruance repeated.

Nimitz pointed a finger at the chart. "Where would you suggest launching your attack from?"

Spruance placed both hands on top of the table, leaned over, and silently studied the map. He could not help but feel Nimitz's presence, realizing that the man was evaluating him. He's testing my grasp of tactics, Spruance thought. Perhaps I'm not Halsey, but I've learned some things from him. What would Halsey do?

"I'd wait for them right here," Spruance said, pointing to a spot northeast of Midway. "We'd be on their flank and in a perfect position to catch them off guard. They'd not expect an attack from that direction."

"Why not head straight for them? Attack from the north or northwest?"

"I'd run the risk of possibly bypassing them if they do intend to move on toward Hawaii or the West Coast."

Nimitz arched his eyebrows. "You have your own doubts about Midway being the target?"

Spruance allowed a brief smile as he cocked his head slightly. "I'm just playing the odds. I'll be in perfect position to attack from the northeast or cut them off. If they show up like you believe, we'll ambush them!"

3. FLETCHER
May 27 – 14:00 Hours

Admiral Frank Jack Fletcher shook hands with Nimitz, noticing the annoyed look that flashed across Nimitz's tanned face. I guess Chet smells the evidence of my stopping for a drink before rushing here, Fletcher thought. He was probably wondering what was taking me so long to report. Now he knows. Hell, I've earned the right to a little relaxation. My task force has been through a lot these past five months. *Lexington* is lying on the bottom of the Coral Sea. *Yorktown* limped into Pearl trailing an oil slick a couple of miles long and bearing severe damage from Jap bombs. I've lived this war for too long.

"How do you feel?" Nimitz asked.

Fletcher removed his cap. "Pretty tired . . . hell, we're all tired, Chet. It seems like we've been at sea since this war started. My legs wobbled when I stepped off *Yorktown*. They've forgotten what solid ground feels like."

Nimitz took his seat at the desk, intertwined his fingers, and rolled his thumbs. He chewed his bottom lip for a few seconds and then seemed to remember that Fletcher was in the room.

"I know *Yorktown* has earned a good rest, and under normal circumstances, you'd get one," Nimitz spoke. "Unfortunately, things are not normal."

I don't like the sound of this, Fletcher thought. Instead of waiting on the other shoe to drop, it feels like a hob-nailed boot is about to stomp down on me.

"There's no way for me to sugar-coat this and I respect you too much to try. There's an important operation brewing and I've got to have your task force participate."

"Participate?" Fletcher heard the disappointment in his own voice.

"When this is over, I promise you'll get some time at home," Nimitz offered. "It's the best that I can do given the circumstances."

Fletcher shrugged. "I'm ready to go wherever you send me. You know that."

Nimitz reached out and rearranged a few of the souvenir ashtrays lying on the desktop. Fletcher watched him curiously,

27

wondered what disturbed him so. Chet's one of the calmest people I know. Nothing much bothers him. Then again, I'm not sure if I *want* to know what's upset him.

"We have to get *Yorktown* fixed up immediately and get you back out to Midway."

Fletcher jerked his head backward several inches. This is about Midway? I've not seen anything in the past several weeks' worth of intelligence reports to indicate that something was brewing there. It must be serious to have Chet in such an uproar.

"How soon?"

"Three days. I've got to have *Yorktown* back at sea in three days."

Fletcher felt an itch, scratched an ear. Three days? Repair *Yorktown* in only three days? The first estimate I heard was three months . . . and that was optimistic.

"I'm sure you're surprised." Nimitz seemed to read his thoughts. "However, Midway is the target of a Japanese invasion force. As we speak, it's on the way and there are a lot of vessels involved."

Nimitz's busy fingers froze then grasped a pencil. He picked it up, examined its smooth length, and snapped it in two.

"The Japanese are so confident of victory that they've already appointed the officer who's to take command there in August. Can you believe that? How arrogant can they be? Perhaps we should just pack up and leave quietly while we have the chance. Save all of us a lot of trouble and bloodshed."

Fletcher remained silent, allowing him to vent. Lord knows Chet's earned it. He's caught hell for everything that happened before he took command as well as everything since. He's had to listen as politicians and desk-warming officers questioned his every move or non-move. *Why can't we strike back? Doolittle attacked Tokyo and he's Army Air Force. When's the Navy going to do something?* Chet hears it all and still manages to press onward in good spirits. I don't believe I could be so diplomatic.

"Bill Halsey's in the hospital," Nimitz said.

Does this misery ever end? Fletcher thought. First, the Midway attack and now Bill is out of action. It's no wonder Chet wants *Yorktown* ready to sail so quickly.

"He's got some type of severe skin rash that's preventing him from resting. He's lost a lot of weight and is exhausted. The doctors say his life's at risk. There's no way he can lead a task force."

"And he's fit to be tied," Fletcher added.

Nimitz grinned. "That's putting it mildly. I thought I'd need handcuffs and leg irons to get him into a hospital bed."

"What'd you do to keep him there, hide his trousers?"

"I gave that some careful thought, but his condition's bad enough that he's heeding the doctor's advice. Bill told me that a dead man couldn't keep sending Japs to hell. He has unfinished business waiting on him."

Fletcher chuckled. "Good for him and good for whoever that doctor is to explain things so well."

Fletcher heard a rustling noise coming from under Nimitz's desk and saw him bend down. His shoulder moved like he was stroking something, and Fletcher recalled him owning a dog; he had heard stories about the animal making its presence known whenever someone moved too near to Nimitz. Maybe I should get myself a dog to discourage a few of my closest critics.

"I'm giving Ray Spruance Halsey's command," Nimitz spoke without looking up.

"Spruance?" Fletcher asked. That seems like an odd choice, he thought. There are senior officers available . . . some with aviator experience. Certainly one of those is more qualified.

"Spruance is a cruiser commander," Fletcher said. "He's never captained a carrier, nor is he a pilot." He immediately regretted the last statement and knew Nimitz's reply before he said it.

"You're not a pilot, either." Nimitz sat up straight.

"I had that coming."

Nimitz smiled to take off some of the sting. "Regardless of what others might think, I'm not sure having a pilot's qualification is mandatory for commanding a carrier force. In some cases, it might be an advantage, but it also has its disadvantages. A man could get more involved with the smaller matter of flight operations and ignore the bigger matter of managing the overall mission."

"True."

"I also have Bill's glowing recommendation of Ray, and that carries weight with me. He's convinced that Ray has learned carrier tactics while serving under him. I'm impressed with Ray's intelligence. The fact is I'm moving him back here to Pearl after the upcoming Midway operation. He's my next chief of staff. All

29

those things considered, he's the best candidate for the command."

"You're the boss."

"And making the tough decisions."

Touché, Fletcher conceded. Chet is definitely not afraid to make the tough decisions, and he has the strength of will and the integrity to see them through and accept total responsibility for the outcome.

"What are we up against?" Fletcher changed the subject.

Nimitz stood and led him over to his map table. He retrieved the wooden pointer and stabbed at the ocean northwest of Midway Atoll.

"It's a large operation for them involving three separate groups. The Invasion Force will come in from the west and bring the troops and supplies needed for the occupation. Their Northern Force intends to make a landing in the Aleutians. The key to the whole thing, however, is the First Carrier Strike Force led by Admiral Nagumo. He has the job of destroying Midway's air defenses and any of our naval forces that try to intervene. His group will arrive from the northwest."

Fletcher digested the information but knew better than to ask where it originated. He believed the enemy's code had been broken and understood that it was definitely a topic not open for discussion. It was enough that Chet had the Japanese plans and intended to act upon them.

"Do we know the composition of the enemy forces?"

"Nagumo's bringing four or five large fleet carriers. There may be a smaller escort carrier with the invasion group. Possibly another escort with the Aleutians group."

Fletcher allowed a low whistle to escape from his lips. "That's a large part of their Combined Fleet."

"Now you know why I need *Yorktown* ready to sail in three days."

"I can understand the emergency, but the estimates I received said it'd take ninety days to repair her."

Nimitz shook his head. "Three days is all we can spare. I just need her made battle worthy, not completely rebuilt. She still has propulsion and operating elevators, and her flight deck is already repaired."

"You know that much?"

A sly grin brightened Nimitz's intelligent face. "I personally inspected her a short time ago."

And probably wondered where I was while doing it, Fletcher thought. Maybe I didn't need that drink.

"It's that important?" Fletcher asked.

"The advantage of surprise coupled with *Yorktown* being able to perform flight operations should even the odds and give us an excellent chance to do major damage to the enemy. It's too good of an opportunity to pass up."

"Let's go for it. I'll get my people to assist with the repair gangs and gather provisions and munitions."

Nimitz turned and leaned back against the table. His head tilted downward and his chin ducked into his chest. Fletcher noticed the attitude change, sensed the mood shifting. The disturbed man of a short time ago had vanished, replaced by a reflective, hesitant man. Something else is on his mind . . . something he doesn't want to discuss. Well, I'm not going to ask what it is. He'll tell me whenever he's ready.

Nimitz crossed his arms over his chest and glanced up. "There's one more thing."

"Yes?"

"What happened at Coral Sea?"

Fletcher had to struggle to hide his surprise. "Coral Sea?"

"There's some question as to your lack of aggressiveness."

The bright room dropped into shadow as the air grew thick. Fletcher swallowed, licked dry lips, thought, no wonder Chet was so hesitant in broaching the subject. He's just finished telling me how crucial the Midway operation is and how much depends on *Yorktown*. Now he's questioning my command ability. Or is he? It's more likely someone else is behind this. King and that Washington group?

"I'm not really prepared to deliver a full report at this time," Fletcher carefully answered. "I'd need to consult my log and ship's documents. Might I be able to review them?"

Fletcher felt Nimitz's embarrassment ease at his unemotional response to the awkward question. Chet is voicing another man's doubts about me, not his own. I believe that, but I also know that he won't hesitate to replace me if I can't adequately explain my actions. Such a move at this moment of crisis could cause a major disruption in fleet operations. I won't let that happen.

"I'll go through my documentation tonight and prepare to discuss this tomorrow," Fletcher offered.

"That's a reasonable suggestion, but I want you to put everything down in writing. That way, I can share it with all interested parties. Come back here in the morning and we'll go over it."

Fletcher took Nimitz's offered hand.

"To make the hard decisions, I must ask difficult questions," Nimitz said.

The burden of command, Fletcher thought. "I understand, and you'll have your answers."

4. KUSAKA
May 27 – 18:00 Hours

Kusaka inhaled the tangy ocean air while taking a quick glance around the bustling aircraft carrier *Akagi*. His sea legs gently rocked with the large vessel's motion as he enjoyed the ocean's gentle heartbeat. He exhaled deeply before stepping into the control post for the flight desk. Commanders Fuchida and Genda, seated on folding chairs, rose to attention.

"Please, gentlemen." He returned their sharp salutes and waved them down. "Might I join you?"

"Of course, sir." Fuchida offered his chair and bent to retrieve another for himself. Kusaka heard him grunt with the effort and grab his stomach with his free hand.

"I heard you were ill back at Kagoshima," Genda said. "Are you all right now?"

Fuchida shrugged. "I've been having occasional stomach aches."

Kusaka felt a stab of concern. "What's the problem?"

"The Army doctors at the hospital examined me and said it was ulcers. I was told to stop drinking for a while."

Genda gave Kusaka a knowing glance. "That explains why he was so well behaved back at the base."

"The secret is revealed," Kusaka agreed, and then grew serious. "Will this affect your leading the upcoming operation?"

Fuchida vigorously shook his head. "No, sir, I will be at my post when duty calls."

The roar of a departing Mitsubishi Zero fighter plane taking off for combat air patrol halted the conversation. A group of men exercising on the flight deck scrambled out of the way and cheered as the machine swept by. Pride surged through Kusaka as the beautiful aircraft gracefully lifted off the wooden surface and winged its way skyward. The large ship trembled while turning back onto base course.

"I never tire of seeing this," Kusaka remarked.

The other two nodded in agreement and Genda echoed, "Nor I." He coughed, tossed away the remains of a cigarette. The coughing turned into a spell lasting several seconds that left him teary-eyed with the strain.

"Black market cigarettes?" Fuchida needled him.

Kusaka scrutinized Genda, noticing the sweaty brow and pale skin. Hours spent inside studying charts and directing air operations allowed little time for enjoying the sunlight, but Genda's chalky appearance was disturbing to see.

"You are also ill?" Kusaka asked.

Genda waved a hand in dismissal. "Just a cold that I've had for a short while. It's nothing to worry about. I should be fine after a few days of breathing ocean air."

Kusaka rubbed his nose. "On the eve of battle both the air operations officer and flight group commander are fighting illness. One would think thunderclouds gather over us and our endeavors."

"I'm sure Commander Genda and I will be at full strength when the need arises," Fuchida said. "We've both prepared ourselves for this moment."

"And your fliers," Kusaka said, "are they prepared?"

A hard glint came into Fuchida's eyes. "There was little time for training, but my fliers are ready. I've never seen their confidence so high. Their morale is another matter."

"The posthumous promotions of the midget submarine crews at Pearl Harbor?" Kusaka asked.

"Yes, sir."

"While in harbor, I spent the majority of my time working to secure the same for our fliers lost in the attack. I'm sorry, but I was told there were too many to recognize."

Fuchida winced and rubbed his side. "It's not that we seek to discredit the midget submarine crews, but airplane torpedoes and bombs did the damage to the enemy. We lost 55 brave fliers that day and have nothing to honor their memory. The men are disgusted with the situation. Some believe the top echelon is trying to discourage us. I don't know what to tell them."

"Their concerns are my own. Yet, they must not let this distract their minds from the crucial operation ahead. If we're to succeed, every man must do his duty. I give my word to continue pursuing this for them."

Genda lit another cigarette, took a deep puff, and coughed. He stood up and walked over to the railing. The strong odor of rusted metal and oil weighed heavy upon them.

Kusaka detected uneasiness in Genda's mood. "Is something wrong?"

A coughing fit gripped Genda for a few seconds. He flicked the smoking cigarette away and turned to face Kusaka.

"May I speak freely, sir?"

Kusaka noted a formal change in Genda's tone and pulled himself upright. "Of course."

Genda glanced down. "I want you to know the men appreciate your efforts on their behalf. You seem to be the only one standing up for us."

There's more, Kusaka thought. "Continue."

A brief pause and Genda looked up. "I'm concerned that you've not devoted the time necessary to studying this operation."

Kusaka forced himself to remain silent, thinking, Genda and Fuchida voiced the loudest objection to the injustice rendered to the dead fliers at Pearl Harbor. I've spent countless hours on shore trying to remedy the situation and have angered many powerful men by my efforts. In spite of this, Genda voices doubt about manner in which I perform my duties?

A sudden burst of activity below drew their attention. The steady vibration beneath their feet changed as *Akagi* turned into the wind. The deck crew scurried about preparing to land a circling Zero. The three of them focused on the task, knowing that landing an airplane on the deck of a pitching aircraft carrier was one of the most hazardous things a man could do.

Kusaka felt his hands clamp down upon his knees and tightly grip them. The Zero made its approach carefully following the directions given by the landing lights. Wheels extended, it fluttered past the edge of the deck moving in precise synchronization with the carrier. The skilled pilot handled his machine like a calligrapher wielding his brush . . . gliding smoothly across the wooden expanse, tires almost kissing the surface. At the proper moment, Kusaka heard the power cut off. The engine roar ceased. The airplane dropped heavily to the deck. Propelled by momentum, it thundered toward the far end. A quick hop upward caused it to miss the first arresting cable stretched across the deck. With the squeal of rubber on wood, it smacked solidly down and snagged the second wire, bringing it to a sudden stop.

A feeling of relief washed over Kusaka until he noticed Genda watching him. Genda's remark from a few moments before immediately dampened his mood. He fought to subdue rising anger and forced a smile. Kusaka thought, no one takes his job responsibilities more seriously than I do. I won't dwell on such questions raised by a junior officer. However, I will remind him of his place.

"I appreciate both your concern and honesty," Kusaka began. "Perhaps I have been trying to push a rope for too long, but I thought it was what the men and you wanted. It seems that I wrongly assumed too much. For that I am at fault."

Genda blanched. "I did not mean—"

Kusaka flashed a harsh look to silence him.

"As I was saying, I did what I thought was expected and desired of me." His eyesight swept over both men. "Be assured that I am spending the majority of my time studying the Midway operation and am prepared to perform my duties. I trust that every man involved may say the same."

He rose from his seat. Fuchida scrambled up, knocking his chair over.

"You must excuse me, I've things to do," Kusaka finished.

He returned their salutes, spun on his heels, and held himself erect as he walked away.

* * *

The incessant knocking on his cabin door brought Kusaka awake. His mind numb for a brief few seconds, the rolling motion of the ship reminded him of the time and place. Swinging his legs over the side of the bed, he sat up and switched the light on.

"Yes?"

The door opened, revealing the pale, worried face of Genda.

"Might I have a word, sir?"

Blinking and rubbing the back of his neck, he waved Genda to enter.

"I've just come from sick bay," Genda said.

Those words brought him instantly alert. His head snapped up and eyesight locked on Genda.

"Yes?"

Genda cleared his throat. "Commander Fuchida is having an emergency appendectomy performed."

"Appendectomy?" The fog lifted. *This* was the cause of Fuchida's stomach pain.

"He wanted to wait until after the battle," Genda continued speaking, "but the surgeon insisted. I had to add my voice to his in

36

order to convince Fuchida to have the operation." He coughed then wiped his sweaty brow with the back of a sleeve.

Kusaka slowly shook his head. "I don't like this. It bodes ill for the upcoming operation. Has Admiral Nagumo been told?"

"I'm on my way to his cabin with the news. Should Admiral Yamamoto be alerted?"

"No. You know we're under strict orders to observe radio silence."

"I thought this might warrant a brief message. We've lost our air strike leader."

Kusaka scratched a stubbly chin. "Certainly, between four aircraft carriers we have another experienced officer who can lead the strike group?"

Genda seemed to think for a moment before replying. "Fuchida is our best . . . he'll be difficult to replace. There's also Admiral Yamamoto's admonition to follow fleet doctrine and keep our better pilots in reserve to deal with enemy carriers. We must consider that. That rules out Egusa and Kobayashi."

"I feared this would happen," Kusaka thought aloud. "Radio blackouts, decisions that must be made, and illogical restrictions that hamper the ability to make a correct one. This is a poor manner in which to conduct operations."

Genda chose not to respond.

"Maintain radio silence. Advise Admiral Nagumo that the situation is in hand."

Genda saluted, bowed, and turned to leave.

"Genda?"

Genda stopped and glanced back over a shoulder.

"Find us a strike leader."

5. FLETCHER
May 27 – 23:00 Hours

Fletcher rubbed burning eyes and stole a glance at his wristwatch. A long day became longer, dissolving into a short night. Alone in his small office aboard *Yorktown*, the events of the past five months flooded over him, pulling him under. He considered slipping into his nearby bedroom for some needed rest but decided against it. Chet expects this report in the morning, and he's the last man on the face of the earth I want or need to disappoint. He picked up his pen, returned to writing.

The stated concern centers on my conduct during the Coral Sea operation, he thought. Perhaps Chet raised the issue, but I know the true voice behind it. Admiral Ernest King spends every spare moment criticizing my leadership of Task Force 17. Perhaps this time King will succeed in having me removed from command.

He jotted down a few more lines and paused. Of all the times to engage in such petty efforts, why must King do it on the eve of perhaps the largest battle of the war? Facing off against four or five enemy carriers and their veteran pilots with a mixed command of *Enterprise*, *Hornet*, and a damaged *Yorktown* places me squarely behind the eight ball. I can do without this added aggravation of defending my actions for the past six months.

Numb fingers groped through a stack of Coral Sea reports and located the ones concerning the night of May 8. He read them once more, felt his temper rising with each paragraph. Notified on *Yorktown* of possible enemy carrier or carriers about 30 miles from his task force bearing 090 at 1930 hours, he refused to launch a night torpedo attack of either destroyers or TBD aircraft. I can well imagine the reaction of both Chet and King after reading those lines.

He returned to writing, specifically about the fact that *Lexington*, through radar tracking, determined the possible appearance of enemy carriers and delayed sending the report to him on *Yorktown* until almost 2200 hours. The only radar contact *Yorktown* tracked around 1930 was a lost Grumman F4F Wildcat fighter aircraft. Why it took almost two and one-half hours to forward me the enemy carrier information I can't say, nor did it seem important at the time. When I finally received the message, the enemy could have moved 30 or 40 nautical miles in any direction. Even so, I did consider sending cruisers or destroyers toward the location of the earlier contact and rejected the idea. The attack group would need to separate in order to make maximum use of its radar in scouting for the enemy. Finding the Japanese and then trying to regroup and mount a coordinated attack was difficult enough in daylight . . . at night, near impossible. The rational thing to do was to keep my force together and seek out the enemy carriers the next morning. Given the circumstances, I did the proper thing. How wonderful the world would be if hindsight were granted in the midst of the noise and confusion of battle.

A soft rap on the door disturbed his train of thought. Head still buried in his task, he said, "Come!"

A weak shaft of light fell across the floor as the familiar voice of his yeoman, Frank Boo, said, "Pardon the interruption sir, but will there be anything else?"

He grunted, waved the young man to leave. The door clicked shut and he heard the smack of shoes upon the deck.

"Boo!"

The noise paused then grew louder. A few seconds later, Boo opened the door.

"I apologize, sir," he said. "I'd never disturb you without first being called but—"

Fletcher raised a hand to silence him. "At ease, Boo. I'm just a little busy right now."

"Aye, sir, may I get you something? Perhaps some iced coffee?"

A drink and twenty-four hours of sleep if you can arrange it, Fletcher thought, but he said, "No, thanks."

"Did you need something else?"

"I'm afraid so. I'm going to need this report typed up before morning."

Boo smiled. "Is that all? How many copies?"

Fletcher lit up his corncob pipe, took a puff, and exhaled. "Working late doesn't bother you?"

"You're working late."

"True, but I'm an admiral." He removed the pipe stem and grinned. "I get paid for working late."

"Ship operations go on around the clock, and I'm no different from any other sailor." A firm look came over Boo's face. "We've a job to do and I intend to do my share."

Fletcher's teeth clamped down on the pipe as he sat surrounded by a thin haze of blue. The color blue had meaning not only for him, but also for all the sailors serving these days in death's shadow, he thought. The color they wear, of the oceans sailed, and the skies the fliers braved. Blue defines our world. He looked down at the writing, thought about *Lexington* buried at Coral Sea. His mind drifted outside to the twisted, burnt remains of the battleship *Arizona*, her sad, scarred superstructure a constant reminder steeling America's resolve. How many young men lie entombed within her? How many hopeful lives snuffed out in a cowardly surprise attack? December 7th, 1941 scarred an entire nation. The world blurred as realization came; the chance to fight was all that really mattered.

"Sir, did you hear me?"

He blinked and realized Boo had said something. "I'm almost finished. I'll call you in a short while."

"Aye, sir."

He listened to Boo leaving and picked up his pen with clear focus. No one will steal my chance to fight.

6. WALDRON
May 28 – 05:00 Hours

"Reveille, Torpedo 8, reveille! This is no drill! This is no drill! MOVE!"

The booming crack of a .45 caliber Browning automatic pistol split the early morning air of the Marine Corps Air Station at Ewa, Hawaii. Lieutenant Commander John Waldron stood inside the Quonset hut, firing out of the open door. His squadron of men, most clad in shorts and nursing hangovers, tumbled out of their bunks and piled into chaos on the floor. Some grabbed pants, one a bucket to clamp onto his head as he made for the exit. Pistol emptied, Waldron holstered it and caught the arm of the bucketed man as he rushed by.

"I said reveille not air raid." He pulled the bucket off the frightened man's head. "Enough grooving the sack. Get your clothes on and all of you fall outside in five minutes."

He stepped through the door and confronted an armed guard rushing up.

"Beg your pardon, sir," the guard spoke as he saluted, fighting for breath, "but I thought I heard gunfire coming from here."

Waldron carefully assumed an apologetic look. "I'm to blame, son. Merely an exercise to test my boys' combat readiness. An officer has to do that every now and again. It lets him know where things stand. I'm sad to say they failed."

"Uh huh." The guard tilted his helmet back on his head. "Let's try not to have any more such exercises, sir. Many of these fellows around the base have nervous trigger-fingers and it wouldn't take much to get them started. Once started, they're hard to stop."

Rifle slung over his shoulder, he turned, and headed back to his post.

Several minutes later, the members of *Hornet*'s Torpedo Squadron 8 staggered and stumbled out into the growing sunlight. Several shaded their eyes; others grabbed their heads. Moaning came from most of them. Waldron stood silently watching and smiling.

"A little too much Barber's Point cocktail last night?" Waldron remarked.

A chorus of groans answered the question, and one of the men fell to his knees puking. Waldron calmly strode over to stand in front of him.

"Are you bucking for Sick Call, Whitey? Trying to shirk your duty?"

Whitey Moore wiped his chin and looked up. "No sir, Skipper. Just let me at them Japanese and I'll show you a thing or two."

Waldron clucked and shook his head. "You might begin by showing me you can stand up."

Waldron returned to his spot in front of the group and waited for Whitey to struggle upright. The sorry spectacle both amused and worried him. *The boys need their recreation, but the unforgiving enemy waits just over the horizon. I'm holding their lives in the palms of my hands, and my decisions affect all. It's tough knowing when to stop acting as morale officer and revert to being the commanding officer.*

"Listen up," Waldron began. "I'm sorry the powers that be decided to confine us here instead of allowing us liberty, but that's the way things are. I can do nothing about it. I'm also pleased you seem to be making the most of the situation."

He paused to look at Whitey. "Some of you more so than others."

A sheepish grin lit up the young pilot's cherubic face and Waldron fought off a smile. *The idea that anyone so innocent looking could constantly wind up as the ringleader of the squadron's bad behavior never ceased to amaze him. Perhaps it was more incredible that the men could so easily return to the fun so quickly after leaving the war zone.*

"Let me remind all of you that we're here for one purpose and one purpose only." He allowed his vision to sweep over them. "And what's that?"

In unison, the group joined him in raising a clenched fist and shouting, "*Attack!*" A low-flying B-17 bomber added the deafening thunder of its four engines to the din. He waited until the noise subsided before continuing.

"I know we've gone over this many times before, but it's important you learn to do things automatically. In the midst of a battle's confusion, it's easy to become distracted and to forget things. If you follow my instructions, you're sure to get hits."

He pointed to a nearby man. "Tex, what's the most important thing to remember while landing a U.S. government Douglas Devastator torpedo-bomber airplane onto an aircraft carrier?"

Tex Gay scratched his head before saying, "The damn thing's severely underpowered, so be sure it's over the deck before cutting the throttle."

"The damn thing's severely underpowered, so be sure it's over the deck before cutting the throttle what?" Waldron asked.

Gay frowned for several moments. "The damn thing's severely underpowered, so be sure the damn thing's over the deck before cutting the throttle, sir." He smiled with pride.

Waldron nodded. "Aye to the double damn thing concerning those old crates that we fly. Save the sirs until we're back on *Hornet* in front of the admiral."

The sound of engines overhead drew Waldron's attention skyward. His head tilted up and focused on a small group of PBY Catalina flying boats winging out over the ocean. There go the only flyboys with a worse job than we have, he thought. At least we have a chance to strike at the Japs. All they do is locate them and hope they're not spotted at the same time. A Zero will fly circles around one of those slow, clumsy birds and flame it. Bless them. We can't do our jobs without them doing theirs first. Keep a sharp eye out, guys.

"Any chance we'll get some practice taking off with a torpedo strapped to the airplane?" Abbie Abercrombie pulled him back to earth. "Most of us have never had the opportunity and I think it's something we need to do as part of our training. I admit, though, that it could be just a waste of time. I've heard tell those Mark 13 torpedoes are more likely to go off when they're dropped into the drink than they are when hitting the side of a ship."

Waldron shook his head. "When it comes to time and equipment, we've the same amount of both and that's little. I don't see us mounting a pickle until the chance comes to use it."

A loud groan greeted his statement, and Abercrombie flushed. "What in the hell does CINCPAC expect from us? Ordering us to take off for the first time carrying a torpedo from the deck of an aircraft carrier in the midst of battle is nuts! If that's not bad enough, the chances are that even if we somehow make it off the ship, locate the enemy, and release the things, they're not going to detonate. This is a *Coffin Squadron* and I'm going to find a way out of it."

"Wait a minute." Waldron held up a silencing hand. "I understand your feelings and extend my condolences. What can I say? Life is a bitch. It's a hell of a mess, but we've a job to do and we're damn well going to do it. As for taking off, I seem to remember Doolittle's boys did just fine getting airborne off the *Hornet*. They were flying two-engine medium bombers for Christ's sake. Just do the same thing they all did. Aim the nose toward the far end of the flight deck and give her the gun. Or are you telling me you boys don't measure up to them U.S. Army Air Corps fliers?"

He paused, waiting for a reply he knew would not come. As a rule, Navy pilots had total confidence in their abilities and didn't suffer lightly the fools that questioned it. For the moment, this subject was closed.

Waldron pointed at the man standing to the right of Gay. "Ellie, tell us all what an anvil attack is."

Ellie Ellison took a sharp step forward as the edge of his hand snapped up in a salute. "An anvil attack is performed by three men. Two of them hold the Jap down while the third smashes his balls with a large sledge hammer, sir." The arm dropped and he smartly moved back into line.

Waldron briskly rubbed his mouth and stifled a laugh. Leave it to Ellie to lighten the mood that Abercrombie darkened, he thought. He cleared his throat and eyed the smiling pilot. It's a shame, but I have to refocus them on the job ahead.

"Would you care to try again or do you prefer a brisk five mile run this morning?"

Ellison paled. "When you put it that way, I believe I'll try again."

Waldron bowed slightly, extended an arm. "By all means, whenever you're ready."

"An anvil attack is performed by the attacking planes dividing up into two groups and coming in on both sides of the target vessel's bow at the same time. By doing this, the group prevents the vessel from safely maneuvering away, thus increasing the group's chances of hitting the target."

"Not bad for a second try, but I'd like to hear what our Yale man thinks about it." Waldron looked at another man. "Squire, as our most educated member, I'd like your thoughts on the matter."

Squire Evans licked his lips. "I am honored that you value my insight so highly and find myself in general agreement with Ensign Ellison's description of the maneuver in question."

Waldron paced backward a few steps. "That's good. You're learning. Sounds simple enough, but remember that the Japs like to make hard, continuous turns when under torpedo attack. You have to keep bearing in and dicing around until you get close enough and low enough to release. Those Devastators are slow so you must be sure and true on your first approach. You probably won't get a second."

He felt a slight chill fall over the group and paused. *I went too far with the last comment and stirred up their fear. I need them alert . . . not afraid. I can't do anything about the fear. That will come. However, I must help them control it.*

"But you boys won't need a second approach," he added. "You're the best there are and will get hits on the first pass. I've no doubt."

"Skipper?"

He recognized Kenyon's Bronx accent and motioned to him.

"Do you suppose we're going back out anytime soon?"

"I smell something brewing. Something on the wind is blowing our way. The fact we're cooling our heels here instead of on liberty in Honolulu makes me even more certain."

Waldron clasped his hands behind him. Kenyon's question didn't help improve the mood. He started to pace back and forth, carefully gauging what to say. *I can almost smell the nervous anxiety gripping them. That's fine, but I can't have them panicked. A panicked man can't perform his duty when the moment comes. I must prepare frightened men to remain calm and do their jobs while facing death.*

"No matter what happens, you're ready." He stopped and looked at them. "You've done all that I've asked of you and more. You've applied yourselves well, and I'm proud of every last one of you."

He took another few steps and paused again. "Fear's nothing to be ashamed of in a man facing battle. It's inevitable but controllable. What you choose to do with that fear is up to you. I

45

remind you of what the enemy did to this place in December of last year. The Japs have run roughshod over the Pacific for the past six months. They've killed thousands and helped themselves to whatever they wanted. I'm fed up with it. It's time we taught Tojo a lesson. Don't piss off America."

He turned, raised a clenched fist and was gratified to see all of them following his lead. "You use that fear as motivation to release those pickles and get a hit. Attack!"

7. TOMONAGA
May 28 – 08:00 Hours

Lieutenant Joichi Tomonaga stepped through the door of his shared cabin aboard the IJN aircraft carrier *Hiryu* to find Lieutenant Rokure Kikuchi seated on his bunk reading a battered copy of *Hagakure: Book of the Samurai*. Kikuchi glanced up as he entered and smiled.

"Have you read this?" Kikuchi extended the book.

Tomonaga shook his head and took a seat in the single chair. He removed his shoes and socks and wiggled his toes. Heavy sweating and the damp atmosphere below deck provided fertile soil for fungus to sprout.

"Words of wisdom to guide one's footsteps," Kikuchi continued. "I've read it through many times and have learned something new with each reading."

I'm happy for you, Tomonaga thought. Finding inspiration in the dead words of a dead man bears proof of a mind seeking knowledge anywhere it can find it.

"You may borrow it when I've finished. I know you'll enjoy it."

"I'm not interested in such things," Tomonaga said, leaning his head back against the warm, slick bulkhead. He closed his eyes.

"You dislike the samurai? We should be grateful to them for the lessons they've handed down, especially to us warriors. They've taught us how to fight and how to die. By studying their teachings, I know what to do in the midst of battle. I live by the Code of Bushido."

"One's time is better spent improving his flying skills and studying the enemy rather than the faded writing in a dusty book."

"Samurai is the ideal of the Japanese warrior and worthy of emulation." Kikuchi's voice grew louder. "My fondest desire is to join their ranks. It should be the desire of every Japanese military man. We can learn much from their example about how to act."

"The samurai have been gone for over half of a century," Tomonaga replied. "It's a New World, with new challenges and ways to meet them. To dwell in the past is to deny the moment and ignore the future. If you prepare for what is to come, your actions will flow naturally."

The small room fell quiet, and Tomonaga knew that Kikuchi was studying him. I've said too much, he thought. Instead of leading Kikuchi back into the reality of our situation, I've sown more questions into his mind.

"You speak like a samurai," Kikuchi said, breaking the silence. "Those words echo this book. You've read it."

"No I haven't."

"You do yourself dishonor by lying."

Tomonaga's eyes flicked open and fixed on Kikuchi. He held his tongue, enjoying the sight of Kikuchi sweating and involuntarily squirming under his gaze. Should I strike or allow his racing heart to surrender to his fear of my intentions?

"You do yourself a greater dishonor by accusing a man whose heart you've not glimpsed," Tomonaga softly said.

Kikuchi bowed his head. "I was wrong to speak without judging your feelings. I ask your forgiveness."

Kikuchi would cower before me, yet he seeks to call himself samurai? He studies a book and considers himself knowledgeable, but knows nothing of the Way. He should concern himself with piloting a Nakajima Ninety-seven.

"Do you spend as much time practicing your flying as you do learning to be a samurai?"

Kikuchi closed the book and stood. "I'm the equal to anyone in the cockpit of my aircraft."

Tomonaga pulled his mouth into a tight line. "Now you speak like a samurai."

"Lieutenant Joichi Tomonaga, report to Admiral Yamaguchi on the bridge!"

The echo of the intercom vibrated off the metal walls and deck. Tomonaga retrieved his socks and tugged them on. Kikuchi dropped back onto the bunk and returned to his reading.

* * *

Tomonaga entered the bridge and paused. His eyesight swept over the small, cramped space, and he wondered at how difficult it must be to work there. The odor of perspiration and ocean air formed a salty mixture that he could taste. A solemn row of pedestal-mounted spotting binoculars gazed out the windows waiting a summons to action. Six men stood around a small chart table, bumping into each other and studying the map lying on it. As he entered, one of the men glanced up and smiled. His friendly

48

face bore a smirk that seemed to radiate a confident attitude. Admiral Yamaguchi made his way over to him.

"Lieutenant Tomonaga reporting as ordered, sir."

"Tomonaga, it's good to see you," Yamaguchi responded.

"It has been a while, sir."

"Kaku!" Yamaguchi called over his shoulder to a large officer wearing a small mustache. "This is Tomonaga."

Captain Kaku looked up to acknowledge Tomonaga's salute. "Admiral Yamaguchi advises me that we are fortunate to have a pilot with your skills and leadership ability."

"*Hai!* Tomonaga was one of my best fliers in China," Yamaguchi said. "No one is better at threading the eye of a needle with a bomb."

Tomonaga felt Yamaguchi's hand on his shoulder and tried not to flinch. I did not realize Yamaguchi was aware of my service in China, although he certainly has access to my records, and we have met before. Is that all he knows about me?

Tomonaga bowed and felt relief as Yamaguchi released him. "I'm honored, sir."

"Your first time fighting the Americans?" Yamaguchi asked.

"Yes, there were some mercenary American pilots flying for the Chinese, but, as far as I know, I never encountered one."

"If you're expecting hard combat, you'll be disappointed. They're not warriors at heart. They'll fight as long as they have the advantage, but easily succumb when things go against them. It's been the pattern since the first day of the war. Our victory is all but assured."

Tomonaga remained silent, unsure how to respond. He thought, certainly Yamaguchi has called me up here to do more than reminisce about experiences we haven't shared. He's much too busy to waste time speaking with me.

"I went to college in the United States and learned much," Yamaguchi continued. "They're an arrogant people who question a neighbor owning a cat while stroking their pet tiger. This war would never have happened without them backing us into a corner with their economic sanctions and disproportionate armament treaty. They take possession of the Philippines thousands of miles from their shores, claim it for their own, and then denounce Japan for attacking our aggressive neighbor China. What honor is there in such actions and attitudes?"

Tomonaga kept his peace and wondered at the nature of the conversation. Why would a superior officer voice such opinions to a subordinate? Why is he telling me these things? I'm a combat pilot, not a politician; the two jobs aren't compatible. Let the fat, soft men back in Tokyo decide official policy. I'm content in fighting the war.

Yamaguchi's face fell at Tomonaga's lack of response, and he stepped to the window. Hands clasped behind his back, he rocked backward and forward on his toes.

"Enough of this talk," Yamaguchi said. "I wanted to inform you of the great honor bestowed upon you."

Interest piqued, Tomonaga's gaze locked onto Yamaguchi. "Honor?"

"We've received a signal from Admiral Nagumo informing us that Commander Fuchida is medically unable to lead our attack against Midway."

Fuchida ill when his service is most needed? Tomonaga thought. What type of disabling illness could keep a warrior of Fuchida's great reputation from fulfilling his duty? Could Admiral Nagumo's supposed lack of aggressiveness extend to the officers under his command?

"This honor you spoke of?"

Yamaguchi turned around to face him and smiled. "Commander Genda has recommended you to assume the position of strike leader for the Midway attack. My one request is that you remain here as part of *Hiryu's* flight group. I need your experience and expertise to guide my young pilots."

Refusing to display his pleasure, Tomonaga maintained a straight face. His grandfather had taught him that a warrior allows none but his beloved access to his heart and emotions. Confidence and humility find strength in each other. The Emperor needs a warrior to lead the attack against the enemy. Now he has one.

Banzai.

8. THACH
May 28 – 09:00 Hours

The lone F4F-4 Wildcat fighter plane made a lazy circle around the Kaneohe airfield and dropped down to a perfect landing. It taxied up to a spot near the open hangar door and braked to a halt. At the sound of the Pratt and Whitney engine dying, a waiting mechanic known as Smitty ducked under the wings and installed wheel chocks. Standing with arms folded across his chest, he watched the pilot release the belts and scramble out of the cockpit.

"What's about this one, sir?" Smitty asked.

Lieutenant Commander John Thach made some quick notes on his plot board and then glanced up at the hulking mechanic. He pulled off his flying hood and smoothed down his damp hair.

"The same as the others," he answered. "Not enough power for the added weight of two more machine guns."

"I reckon the Burrow of Anuts figures you flyboys needed to bring more guns to the fight if you're going to shoot down any of those Jap Zeroes." Smitty removed the stub of a large cigar from a grimy shirt pocket and clamped it between his teeth.

Thach chuckled at the sarcastic reference to the Bureau of Aeronautics but understood the reason for it. Having the final say on all airplanes purchased for service, the Bureau provided a convenient target with their unpopular decisions. The pilots' grumbling about the latest version of the Grumman Wildcat was no louder than the mechanics'. The extra guns made for more maintenance and repair for the overworked flight crews.

"I'd rather have more speed and maneuverability to keep up with the Japs than two more gun barrels," Thach answered. "Not to mention we've gone from having over thirty seconds of firing time to less than twenty. I'll be out of ammunition before I've cranked up the wheels."

Smitty shuffled the unlit cigar around to the corner of his mouth. "And I'm tired of repairing wings damaged by people folding them up wrong."

The two of them fell into step together and walked toward the operations' hut. The explosive roar of large engines snarling to life combined with the smell of gasoline and grease tainted the bright

51

atmosphere with heavy shades of calming gray. Warming air lifted off the paved surface in transparent waves. Thach inhaled a huge breath and shook his head, thinking, why do I love this so?

The mechanic stopped at the edge of the hangar door and glanced at the organized chaos inside. The cigar migrated to the other side of his mouth, and he spat.

"Any orders, sir?"

Thach motioned a thumb over his shoulder. "I'm supposed to be meeting with my new XO, and the two of us are going to greet the replacement pilots from Fighting 42. We'll bring them back here and let them get familiar with the new Cats. I'd like them to do some field carrier landings, too."

The mouth dropped open and the cigar dangled to the point of falling. A large, callused hand reached up and rubbed a bronzed jaw. "Forty-two is the Lexington's old bunch. You fixing to split them up and put some of them with you? I don't think they'll care for the idea."

Thach shrugged, glanced off into the distance. "It's not my doing, but it's necessary. I understand there's a major battle brewing and not enough time to please everyone."

"You've got a point. Talk is that Admiral Nimitz is jumping up and down trying to get *Yorktown* patched up and sent back to sea. He took every spare man I had and put him on repairing that carrier."

"It can't be helped."

Smitty removed the cigar and thumped off some imaginary ashes. "Perhaps not, but try telling that to aircraft mechanics who're crawling around inside a ship."

Thach stared at the mechanic. "Would they rather be standing inside a Japanese prisoner of war camp?"

* * *

Thach sat next to the window of the small office and looked out at the busy airfield. A procession of aircraft came and went, headed for places unknown or relieving the active Combat Air Patrol. A knock on the door barely drew his attention; his thoughts remained fixed on the world outside.

"The door's open."

He felt rather than heard someone enter the room, and a throat cleared.

"Executive Officer reporting for duty, Mr. Jack Thach, sir!"

The voice sparked something inside him. He thought, it couldn't be. No one called him Jack except his family and . . .

Thach turned and leapt to his feet. "Don! What are you doing here?"

The two men warmly clasped hands. Happiness flooded through Thach as he shook his head in disbelief. One of his closest friends and former XO of Thach's Fighting 3, Don Lovelace was an excellent pilot and officer. Assigned to return stateside over a month ago to command his own squadron, he had somehow found his way back to Thach's side just when he was needed most.

Thach composed himself and repeated, "What are you doing back here?"

A sly smile crept across Lovelace's handsome face. "You didn't think that you could get rid of me that easily did you?"

Thach snorted and twisted his head. "Can't blame me for trying."

He motioned toward a chair and they both sat. The room fell silent for a few moments.

"I missed connecting with my new group in California," Lovelace finally explained, "and wound up here all by myself. It's going to be several weeks before I can get them all assembled and rebuild Fighting 2."

Thach perked up at the mention of Fighting 2. "A fighter squadron? I thought you'd been assigned to flying SBD dive bombers."

Lovelace's eyebrows arched up and down. "You underestimate the power of my golden tongue. I managed to persuade the right people that my flying talents would be wasted if I gave up fighters."

"I can believe that, but how did you come to be XO of Fighting 3 in the meantime?"

"That's the best part. When I arrived here and discovered the delay, I heard the talk about an upcoming operation. I knew you still needed a replacement XO and volunteered. Admiral Noyes discussed the matter with Admiral Nimitz, and both approved the temporary assignment. There's something big about to happen."

Thach released a sigh. "I'm certainly glad to have you back, but you're stepping right into a big mess. I don't think you bargained for that."

"I guess you're talking about the air group reorganization."

53

"You've heard?"

"Some of it."

Thach removed a small notebook from his back pocket and opened it. He scanned the pages for a few seconds and glanced up at Lovelace.

"The bombing and torpedo groups are being moved around, but Fighting 42 is the most affected. Sixteen of its pilots are being detailed for temporary duty with my Fighting 3."

"They're losing both their own leaders and squadron identity? That's a lot to swallow in one mouthful. I don't envy you."

"Thanks, but it gets better. They've assigned me a group of green ensigns to fill out the squadron. They've dribbled in here for the past month or so and I've been sizing them up. There's a lot to do and little time to do it."

"We were all green once," Lovelace reminded.

Thach snapped the notebook shut and stuck it back in his pocket. Glancing out the window for a few seconds, he then turned his attention back to Lovelace.

"True. I just hope these young men have the chance to become veterans. I intend for us to do our best to help them."

"Your 'beam defense position'?"

"Butch O'Hare and I proved the theory is sound by doing some mock dogfights. He's as good a fighter pilot as there is, and he couldn't penetrate my two-plane sections' defense. It's not a perfect answer, but I believe it does give a Cat a fighting chance against the Zeroes. I just haven't had the opportunity to try it out against those nimble, fast bastards."

"And my part in all of this?"

"I need you to help with these new pilots as much as possible to get them trained. We don't have much time and I'm afraid I'll be busy with other details during the transit."

A sudden thought made Thach glance at his watch and stand. "We need to go meet the flying boat bringing the 42 fliers over."

Lovelace rose to join him.

"I'm glad to see you, Don. I sure can use your help."

Lovelace smiled. "Wild horses couldn't have kept me away."

9. FLETCHER
May 28 – 09:00 Hours

Fletcher sat watching Nimitz read over his report. Boo had finished typing it early that morning while Fletcher tried to grab a short nap. Tried was all that he did. Sleep proved elusive with this ax poised over his neck. After a few restless hours, he finally surrendered to the frustration and got up. A brisk shower followed by a cup of black coffee revived him and would hopefully sustain him for a while. At least until this nonsense is over, he thought.

Nimitz looked up from the papers and placed them on the desk. "I'm satisfied with this and I'll forward it to Washington with a letter stating so."

Forward it to King, Fletcher knew. Maybe this will keep him off my back. Let me focus on fighting this war. He relaxed, crossed his legs, and grabbed one kneecap with both hands. Keep King off my back? Who am I kidding?

"Task Force 17 is yours," Nimitz continued. "I take it you're doing everything you can to expedite sailing?"

Fletcher thought, it's nice to be discussing the Midway operation again. "I've every available man either helping with repairs or loading out. We'll be ready when *Yorktown* is released from dry dock."

"Good. Anything you need?"

"No."

The two of them left their chairs and moved over to the chart table. Both looked down and focused on the small shapes labeled *Midway Atoll*.

"Ray will lead Task Force 16 containing *Enterprise* and *Hornet* out of Pearl this afternoon," Nimitz said. "You'll follow with *Yorktown* and your task force two days from now. You'll rendezvous with Ray at a spot to be determined and await the Japanese fleet. As senior officer, you'll be in overall command."

"Where are you thinking about positioning us to wait on Nagumo?"

Nimitz placed a finger on a point to the northeast of Midway. "Ray suggests here. That will place you on Nagumo's flank."

And in position to block him off from Hawaii in case he decides to attack here instead, Fletcher told himself. Nice thinking, Ray. Maybe Halsey was right in recommending you for command.

"Ray will join us here shortly," Nimitz said. "I'll have Milo Draemel and Ed Layton on hand to bring us up to date on any last minute intelligence information. We'll have a chance to discuss the operation one more time and answer any questions."

"Sounds good."

"Let's hit them hard and make them howl."

Spoken like a true Texan, Fletcher thought. "My feelings exactly."

* * *

Chief of Staff Draemel finished the briefing and closed his notes. All eyes turned from Draemel to focus on Nimitz. Draemel might be leading the meeting, but there was no doubt about who would have the final word, Fletcher thought. Everything up until now was appetizer. Here comes the main course.

"Thank you, Milo," Nimitz said. "Well, that's everything we have about the enemy's plans. Now you know what I know. I believe we have better information on them than they have on us. When the entire enemy fleet gathers, we'll be outnumbered. It's critical that we achieve surprise, make the first strike, and catch their carriers in a vulnerable position."

He placed the pointer tip on a spot northwest of Midway. "It's assumed the enemy will begin launching their airplanes at dawn. Their attack will head southward toward Midway and they'll probably search to the south, east, and north of their position. Your forces will maintain a southwest course through the night and should be at a spot about two hundred miles north of Midway by morning. When you receive the first report locating the enemy, you must be ready to launch your strike. If we can time things right, we might catch the Japanese carriers with at least half of their aircraft absent attacking Midway. That should be the crucial advantage we're looking for."

Spruance raised a finger to catch Nimitz's attention.

"Go ahead, Ray."

"As far as scouting aircraft, what are the plans?"

"Good question. Midway will provide the search airplanes and cover most every area where the Japanese could arrive. If they do come in from the northwest, Midway will be in the best position to make first contact. I'll have them relay by cable phone everything they receive to me here in Hawaii. We'll transmit the information out to you but you are not to acknowledge receipt. Under no circumstances are you to break radio silence unless there's no doubt the enemy has spotted your carriers. The element of surprise is critical to the success of your mission."

Fletcher thought, considering the importance of establishing first contact, it seems risky having Midway handle all of the scouting chores. I'd feel better with some eyes and ears out there myself.

"May I make a suggestion?"

Nimitz looked at Fletcher.

"I'm thinking that we should launch some scouts of our own and search our immediate vicinity. It's possible that the enemy might pull a fast one and approach from another direction."

"That's a good idea," Nimitz answered. "If that turns out to be the case, I'll expect you two to improvise and do whatever you think is best. I'll leave the details of the scouting to your staffs. The only condition I'd place on them is that you keep the bulk of your aircraft waiting to launch a preemptive first strike on the Jap carriers."

"Anything else? Milo? Ed?"

Both Draemel and Layton shook their heads. Nimitz walked over to his desk and sat down. The others followed his lead, pulling their chairs up into a semi-circle surrounding him. A cooling breeze, struggling to survive against the strengthening Hawaiian sunshine, crept through an open window.

"I'm not going to give you a pep talk or insult you with bad clichés," Nimitz said. "We all know what's at stake if Midway falls. The Japanese will have a perfect launching point to attack either Hawaii or the West Coast. They've had their way in this hemisphere since December of last year, and we seem unable to do anything to stop them. Frank Jack's efforts in the Coral Sea might have caused them a slight pause, but they're far from discouraged. This Midway operation bears proof of that.

"I can't stress too strongly that we can't afford to engage them in a straight-up slugfest. Their numbers alone will overwhelm us. The principle of calculated risk must govern everything you do. This means you shall avoid exposing your force to attack by superior enemy forces without the prospect of inflicting, as a result of such exposure, greater damage to the enemy."

Nimitz paused for a moment, and Fletcher had a feeling that he was mentally running back over his notes, making sure he had not missed anything. Fletcher's eyesight roamed over the other men, assessing each one. Spruance's stone face never varied in its expression, but Fletcher sensed his mind cataloging each piece of information, storing it away for further study. Draemel was poised to render assistance to Nimitz as always, yet Fletcher felt an invisible barrier between the two. Maybe the news of Spruance replacing Draemel had made the rounds. Layton, the youngest, sat on the edge of his chair and appeared anxious to offer more from his vast store of intelligence information.

"Understand that we risk more than Midway," Nimitz picked up. "Admiral King and I both believe the enemy intends to trap a large part of our fleet. The size of their strike force seems to bear this out. They're thinking that we'll come racing out of Hawaii to assist Midway without thought to the numbers we're up against. Lambs to the slaughter. We can't let that happen."

Spruance cleared his throat. "One thought I've had is that the Japanese hit Pearl Harbor from the north. Perhaps they might decide to follow the same plan at Midway? We could sail right into their midst while waiting for a scouting report."

"Sir, if I may respond to Admiral Spruance?" Layton spoke up.

"Go ahead," Nimitz said.

"Intelligence has never been more convinced of the authenticity of any enemy information that we've uncovered. The puzzle pieces fit together perfectly. I'll say unequivocally that I anticipate first contact will be made with the enemy at 0600 Midway time, the fourth of June, 325 degrees northwest at a distance of 175 miles."

Fletcher thought, hasn't Layton heard about pride going before a fall? That also applies to too much confidence.

"You can't be more specific in your estimation?" Fletcher asked.

Slight, anxious laughter flowed between them, lightening the mood.

"You seem mighty certain of yourself," Fletcher followed up.

"I'm certain of the men that I work with. There're none better, sir."

Nimitz smiled. "They've convinced me, but Ray's point is well taken. Frank Jack's idea about the extra scouts checking the northern sector is a good one. Other than that, you both must exercise flexibility as well as secrecy. Don't hesitate to improvise in response to whatever the situation warrants. I've confidence in your abilities to make the tough decisions and then act upon them. You must observe, however, the principle of calculated risk. Those three carriers in the harbor outside are all that's standing between Yamamoto and the American mainland."

"What kind of preparation is Midway making?" Spruance asked.

"I've sent them everything we can spare as far as equipment and men. I've also packed their airfield with every type of spare aircraft that I could lay my hands on. It's a varied selection but I'm hoping they'll take some of the heat off you."

"Are they aware of your plans?" Fletcher spoke up.

"No. I thought long and hard about it but decided the less they know the better off they'll be."

Especially if the Japs do occupy the atoll and take prisoners, Fletcher knew. You can't torture out of a man information that he doesn't know.

"I'm sending Logan Ramsey out there to take command of air operations and free up Captain Simard and Colonel Shannon to deal with other matters pertaining to Midway's defense."

Fletcher chuckled. "You're sending Logan Ramsey to Midway? Have they been warned?"

Nimitz grinned and raised a hand. "I know Logan has his ways and operates a bit differently from most, but he's intelligent and excellent at his job. He's also an outsider and won't hesitate to stir things up if it needs doing."

"You've got that right."

Fletcher's remark drew another brief round of laughter from the others who knew Ramsey by reputation. To say he's unorthodox doesn't begin to describe his manner of getting things done, Fletcher thought. Ramsey's large frame added to a physical presence that could easily intimidate others, even superior officers. Chet was covering all the bases on this one.

"Okay." Nimitz reclaimed their attention. "Anything else?"

"You seem to be taking a tremendous gamble," Spruance said.

Nimitz shook his head. "No, I'm not. We have superior intelligence, fighting men just itching for a chance at the enemy and, most important of all, the element of surprise. Don't underestimate all of these factors. Above all, surprise must be secured if we're to be successful."

"Gentlemen," he said, looking at each one in turn, "this can be our finest hour of the entire war or a crushing defeat and a prelude to an invasion of the American mainland. We must not fail."

10. THACH
May 28 – 11:00 Hours

The pilots of Fighting 42 came to rigid attention at Thach's command. Lean and tan from weeks spent at sea flying combat patrol, they immediately brought to mind a pack of wild dogs ready to pounce. He spent a few minutes calling names against the muster sheet and checking off each one. Finished, he lowered the clipboard and told them to relax.

He pointed toward Lovelace standing nearby. "This is Commander Donald Lovelace who will be acting XO for the immediate future. Unlike the rest of us, he volunteered to be here so you might want to question the sanity of any decision he makes."

A ripple of laughter coursed through the ranks, but Thach sensed that the tension remained high. The events of the past few days were not easily forgotten, and Thach knew his job would not be easy. Taking a core group of unhappy veterans desiring their former identity and mixing in green replacements to create a new fighting group was an action primed to fail. I can't allow that to happen. These men needed to think and react as one cohesive unit.

"I realize you're not happy with the current situation, but things are what they are. I can't help that."

"Sir?" A voice called out.

His gaze sought and landed upon the speaker. Like all the others, he looked too youthful to be flying fighter aircraft, and his dark eyes burned with intensity. The erect posture, even while at ease, and slight tilt of the head spoke of a man keenly aware of his own skills and confident in them. The uninitiated in the life of a fighter pilot often called such a display a superior or cocky attitude. Thach knew better. Flying fast, powerful machines capable of dealing death or receiving a mortal blow in the blink of an eye called for a special type of individual. There was no room for doubt in a combat cockpit.

Thach pointed to him. "Mister?"

"Lieutenant jg William Leonard, sir."

"Bill?"

A pleased grin crossed Leonard's face. "Aye, sir."

"Bill it is. Go ahead and speak freely. We're all friends here and we're all in this together."

"Thank you, sir. Please understand we're all team players and want nothing more than a chance to fight. We're not asking for special treatment."

Leonard paused to look around at his silent comrades. A flying boat taxied by behind them prepared to take off. He waited until the craft and noise receded into the sky.

"We've fought together and have lost good friends as Fighting 42. We're proud of our combat record. And now . . ." Leonard's voice trailed off as his head lowered.

"I said you may speak freely," Thach reminded. "Go on."

Leonard's head snapped up, the fire back in his eyes. "They've ordered our skipper and XO to stay here in Hawaii. They've stripped us of our squadron number and thrown us into a new air group. We're being punished for Admiral Fletcher's conduct at Coral Sea."

Thach felt a weight settle on top of him and shook his head. "I've heard the same scuttlebutt but know better. Admiral Noyes is shuffling people as he deems fit to fill out air groups and provide for future operations. He needs experienced officers to return stateside to train new pilots and form new squadrons. Those left behind must still fight the war."

"We don't have a problem with fighting," Leonard replied. "We just want to do it as the 42 and with our own officers. We believe we earned that right at Coral Sea. No disrespect, sir."

"Commander," Lovelace broke in, "if I may?"

Thach moved aside and allowed Lovelace to take his place. He watched as Lovelace's gaze swept over the group and settled on Leonard.

"I understand your feelings." Lovelace said, pointing to Thach, "but not as well as him."

Leonard's brow wrinkled in apparent confusion and he licked his lips. The other pilots leaned in to listen.

"Lieutenant Commander Thach led us in Fighting 3 off *Lexington* during the early part of this year. We saw action around New Guinea and the Solomons. I'm proud to say that he's the finest pilot and officer I've had the pleasure to serve with. I can assure you that all of the men who flew under him feel the same way.

"When *Lexington* returned to Hawaii for rest and refitting, I was ordered stateside to assume a squadron command. Lieutenant Commander Thach remained here to form up a new fighter squadron with replacement pilots. As things turned out, *Lexington* was called back out to the Coral Sea to join your *Yorktown*. *Lexington* needed experienced pilots and Fighting 3 had the only ones available. Those men shipped out on *Lexington* as Fighting 2 while Lieutenant Commander Thach stayed here."

Lovelace paused and flashed a smile. "Sound familiar?"

A murmur of agreement drifted through the men, and Leonard nodded as if in understanding.

"I'm lucky. My assignment is on hold for a few weeks and I have a chance to go back into battle with Lieutenant Commander Thach. When this is over, there's no doubt in my mind you'll feel the same way."

"Aye, sir," Leonard replied. "I apologize if I was out of line or disrespectful. The men and I just wanted you to hear our side of things."

Thach nodded. "Like I said, we're all in this together and have a job to do." He directed his attention to the entire group. "Understood?"

"Aye, sir!"

"Good. Now I'd like to get your opinions on something. You faced them at Coral Sea. What are your thoughts on the Mitsubishi Zero fighter aircraft?"

The men exchanged glances and allowed Leonard to take the lead again.

"They climb too fast and turn too tightly for our F4Fs to deal with them, sir. You don't have a chance trying to dogfight one of them. The Jap pilots are skilled. I guess they received a good deal of practice fighting in China against Chennault's men."

Chennault, Thach thought. It's odd that Leonard mentioned Chennault. Those reports Chennault posted from China early last year provided some of the first crucial information he saw about the Japanese's deadly new fighter plane. Believing in Chennault and his pilots' stories about the Zero's performance provided the spark for Thach to develop his beam defense tactic.

"Anything else?" Thach asked.

"It seemed to me that, if you were lucky enough to put a burst into one, they flamed easily," another man spoke out. "The F4F can take much more damage and keep flying."

"I agree," a third echoed. "I saw several of our planes that made it back to *Lexington* riddled with bullet and cannon shot holes. It gave me a little more confidence in the Wildcat bringing me back home after a mission."

Thach thought, that's fine as far as defense goes, but we have to find a way to offer more of an offensive fight. We can't just keep on trying to survive an attack while our bombers and torpedo-planes are shot down around us. I need to put the beam defense position through a combat test and see if I'm on the right track.

"I appreciate the information," Thach said. "I'm going to turn you over to the XO. He'll get you squared away, and then I want all of you to spend some time getting familiar with the newer model F4F. It's a good deal different in speed and handling characteristics, but I'll let you find that out for yourselves."

He lit a cigarette, watched Lovelace lead them away. A deep drag and exhalation produced a puff of smoke that seemed to follow. Thach thought about life's little irony. How many of them will go down trailing smoke? He looked up at the sky and noticed remnant exhaust trails from the continuous air traffic over the island. Scars against the heavens. Or lines . . . a line in the sand. He considered the lurking enemy, felt his presence. The Japanese have crossed the line. It's our job to throw them back. Perhaps the upcoming battle will provide the chance.

11. BROCKMAN
May 28 – 14:00 Hours

A knock on the doorframe of his quarters aboard the U. S. submarine *Nautilus* drew Lieutenant Commander William Brockman's attention away from the packet of sailing orders. Sitting in his chair at the tiny desk that served as his office, he glanced up.

"Come," he said.

Lieutenant Commander Roy Benson, the XO, opened the curtain and stuck his head inside, nearly bumping into Brockman.

"You wanted to be alerted when we reached our station."

"Report."

"We're at periscope depth. The sky and horizon are both clear," Benson answered.

"Sound?"

"Clear."

"Let me finish this and we'll take her up for awhile and get some air," Brockman said, returning to his reading.

"We'll be standing by—"

"Wait, Roy, don't leave." He motioned toward his empty bunk. "Have a seat. I want to speak with you."

Benson found a spot inside the small cabin. He sat drumming his fingers on the bed frame and humming softly to himself. Brockman glanced at him from the corner of his eye, fighting the urge to ask Benson to stop. I guess we all have good reason to feel some nervous energy, Brockman thought.

He rose up, extended the orders to Benson. The XO read for several minutes before breathing out a long whistle. Brockman waited until Benson finished and looked over at him.

"The talk about Midway appears to be true," Brockman said. "Admiral English is sending almost every boat in the Pacific to form a picket line from the west around to the north of there. We'll need to maintain good discipline to stay within our patrol boundary and not wander into someone else's."

Benson shook the paper. "I didn't hear any mention in the scuttlebutt about the *entire* Combined Fleet being involved. Looks like Yamamoto's not taking any chances."

Brockman took the orders and secured them in the small desk safe. They sat in silence for a few awkward moments.

"Are we really prepared for this?" Benson spoke up.

"Meaning?"

"I've some concern, not so much about the men's ability but about their mental preparedness. It's a feeling I get when I'm around a group of them. I'm not sure they're all comfortable with the boat."

"Not comfortable with the boat?"

"You have to admit, *Nautilus* is one of just a handful of larger submarines. The men look at her and wonder if she'll have a difficult time slipping past enemy escort vessels when the shooting starts. It's easier to gig a whale than a sailfish."

Brockman understood what he meant, and said, "I'll grant you she's an older class boat of a poor design for submersible combat, but we have 6-inch deck guns and external torpedo tubes. Those give us a good deal more firepower for battle surface. It's a trade-off."

Benson placed a leg on top of the other and jiggled a foot. "I'm just wondering how often the opportunity to fight a surface battle is going to come along. We'd be fools to try to match up with an enemy combat vessel that way. We're trading maneuverability and speed for guns and extra torpedo tubes that we may never have a chance to use. Our response speed is slower than that of a *Gato* boat. A slow submarine is a vulnerable submarine."

Brockman admitted that Benson made a good point. But the situation's not going to change, he thought. There's no need to waste time wishing that it will. *Nautilus* is our boat. She's going to fight to the best of our ability. On that, I won't compromise.

"Response speed can be increased with practice," Brockman answered. "That's the reason for all of the drills we've been having."

Benson pulled an empty pipe from a shirt pocket and clamped down on its stem. "True, but only up to a certain point. The physics and mechanics involved have a large influence on the amount of time required."

"Meaning?"

He removed the pipe and grinned. "No matter how much you practice, the opening in the bag and size of the shovel determines how quickly the manure fills it."

Brockman extended a hand. "I surrender to your logic and experience in the matter."

They both chuckled and then grew quiet. The noise of the boat operating normally and the hum from the large electric propulsion motors offered a comforting background. Brockman caught himself about to doze off, but snapped up as Benson spoke again.

"It's funny," he said around the pipe stem, "I've overheard some of the boys calling her a pigboat. I could sure enough tell them what a pigboat is. I believe that I served on most of them at one point or another. The boys at Annapolis never let me forget it. The entire time I taught navigation there my nickname was *Pigboat Benny.*"

He offered Brockman a wink. "Of course I wasn't supposed to know that."

Brockman smiled as he recalled hearing Benson's nickname and envied his familiarity with the crew. Due to Benson's interaction with them, the XO held a closer relationship with the men than the skipper did. He hears things I don't, Brockman thought. The men are more likely to confide in him. It's his job to listen. The crew might have a point about the boat's limitations. But that's how things are.

"I can understand the crew's feelings, but that doesn't change things. We've been charged with sinking enemy shipping and that's exactly what I intend to do. Damn the risk."

"This is a green boat and crew going into combat for the first time," Benson said. "We've all got a bunch of learning to do and it appears most of it will be on the job."

"No one said things would be easy. Few things in life are."

"I hear what you're saying, but don't forget that we're all new at fighting a war. It's not just the enlisted men. The Japs have several years' head start on us from China."

"We'll learn and adapt or go down fighting."

Benson removed the pipe and seemed to study it. "Aye, that we will."

"Do you really smoke that thing?" Brockman tried to change the subject.

Benson smirked and stowed it safely away inside his shirt pocket. "No, I started posing with the thing while teaching. I thought that it made me look distinguished and intelligent. After a while, it became a habit to chew on it, kind of like an adult security blanket."

"Did it work to improve your image?"

"Didn't you just hear me say that my nickname at the Academy was *Pigboat Benny?* Does that sound distinguished and intelligent to you?"

They both chuckled and the room fell silent again. Brockman sensed that Benson had more to say.

"Something else?" Brockman prompted.

"A little self-doubt, I suppose. These men will be watching us closely to see how we handle things. Our response is critical to how they act."

"That's why it's called *command*. We lead by example and expect the men to follow suit and do their duty. This seems to be a good group. I believe that they'll rise to the occasion no matter what gets thrown at us."

"Agreed." Benson said.

Brockman could tell that Benson still held doubts. We all have our doubts and fears before going into battle, he thought. It doesn't matter if it's the first time or the one-hundredth time, one never grows accustomed to it. Any man who says different, is a fool . . . or a liar.

"Roy, for what it's worth, I intend to allow the principle of risk versus reward guide my actions. If the potential reward warrants it, we're duty-bound to accept the risk. None of us asked for this war, but we sure as hell have got to fight it."

"That we do," Benson agreed. "That we do."

Enough said, Brockman thought. It's time to let our actions do the talking for us.

12. SPRUANCE
May 28 – 14:00 Hours

"Admiral on the bridge!"

Spruance stepped through the open portal and found his new staff waiting on him. His flag lieutenant Robert Oliver, the single officer Nimitz had allowed to accompany him to the *Enterprise*, was the only man who did not look nervous. Spruance's gaze drifted over each one and settled on the lean figure standing in front to study it for a few moments. That officer's eyesight darted between Spruance and Oliver as nicotine-stained fingers drummed against his trouser legs. Hopefully, Miles Browning would not prove to be as difficult a character to deal with as advertised, Spruance thought.

"Good to see you, Commander Browning," Spruance said, offering his hand. "I'm depending upon you as my chief of staff just as Admiral Halsey does."

"It's unfortunate about Admiral Halsey, but I believe Admiral Nimitz has made a wise choice for his replacement," Browning said.

Spruance shifted his attention to the man standing at Browning's right shoulder. Commander William Buracker was another unknown, but he was Halsey's choice of operations officer. The same held true for Captain George Murray, *Enterprise's* skipper, who stood at Browning's left. Spruance knew all of these men enjoyed Halsey's confidence.

"Gentlemen, I want you to know I have no concerns about any of you," Spruance said as he addressed them. "If you were not the best, Admiral Halsey would not have had you with him. I've faith and trust that your abilities and the abilities of all the men serving on this operation will see us through."

A chorus of thanks greeted his words. Murray excused himself and returned to running the ship. The others relaxed visibly, waiting for Spruance to continue.

"I expect each man to do his job, but I don't stand on unnecessary formalities while at sea. I'm not concerned with whether or not a man wears a cap, but he'd better have a helmet on at battle stations. I'll not overlook that. Wearing a tie is a man's personal choice, and you can see that I like to roll up my sleeves. This time of the year it gets hot in this part of the world."

He noticed Browning's face register relief at this last statement and felt certain the tie Browning wore would soon disappear.

"Is there anything you require from me at this time?" Browning's head lifted, and he looked directly at Spruance.

"I'd like a roster of all your flight crews and pilots," he answered. "I'm also interested in reviewing any action reports from the past two months."

"I'm not sure that I understand the request for reports," Browning said. "You were present with the task force at that time."

"True, but my concern at that time were the cruisers. I'd like to familiarize myself with *Enterprise* operations."

"I'd be happy to brief you on anything in particular, sir."

Spruance caught himself about to snap, but then realized he depended on Browning's expertise. No need in getting off to a bad start, he thought. I'm sure all of these men are concerned about how I'm going to measure up to Halsey. They're accustomed to doing things a certain way. I'm out of my element and only the student here. It's better to exercise some restraint and patience.

"Very well, I'll send for you in a little while and we'll go over things," Spruance replied, noting the look of satisfaction on Browning's face.

"Commander Buracker," Spruance said, turning to Buracker, "I'd like to get the fliers together and have a brief word with them."

"They're not all due in from Ford until later this afternoon, sir," Buracker replied.

"That'll be fine. I'm going to my cabin for a while. Let me know when the fliers are all aboard and assembled."

He glanced at Oliver. "Do you have time to accompany me?"

"Of course, Admiral."

The two of them left the bridge to make their way below into the depths of the large vessel.

* * *

"What's your impression of Browning?" Spruance asked. He and Oliver were away from prying ears, safely behind the closed door of Spruance's stateroom. He seated himself on the bed while Oliver sat in a chair next to it.

"Given all of the bad things we've heard about him, probably the same as yours. I noticed him sweating and fidgeting when you arrived on the bridge but his attitude changed as you spoke, sir."

"I noticed the same thing. His demeanor shifted after I explained my feelings on proper attire."

Oliver chuckled. "I know why. He'd asked me before you arrived what your policy was on ties. When I told him the same thing you eventually said, he seemed relieved, but I'm also thinking that he didn't trust me enough to believe it."

"When he began questioning my request for the action reports, I thought I was talking to a different person. He's protective of his duties, isn't he?"

"You certainly were tolerant and patient with him. I'm surprised you didn't explain the chain of command to him."

Spruance disregarded the comment with a wave of a hand. "I need him and all of these people. I'm stepping into an entirely new world, and there's no time for pride to interfere in things. This mission is too important for petty actions. Admiral Nimitz has placed his faith and gambled his reputation on all of us. I'll be damned if I let him down."

"I agree, sir."

Spruance got up and stretched. "I think I'll unwind and take a stroll around the flight deck before meeting with the pilots."

"Would you like some company, sir? Perhaps one of your new staff officers?"

Spruance briefly considered the idea, thought particularly about inviting Browning. Asking someone to share his daily walk was a habit he developed some time ago to allow for some informal interaction. He noted the invited individual became more open and less inhibited as the sweat proceeded to flow. On the other hand, I don't want them to become too familiar with me too soon. It's better to maintain some objective distance for a day or two. Allow me to size them all up.

He shook his head. "Just my thoughts. I doubt I'll have much time alone with them for the next week or so."

13. TOMONAGA
May 28 – 16:00 Hours

Tomonaga entered the cabin to find Kikuchi still lying on his bunk reading.

"You've not been here the entire time," Tomonaga said.

"We had physical training on the flight deck and, yes, the weather's still terrible. Where have you been?"

"Mission briefings. I'm taking Fuchida's place as strike leader."

The book lowered. "You're taking Fuchida's place?"

Tomonaga sat down on the single chair. "Fuchida's ill and Genda recommended me. We knew each other in China."

Kikuchi leapt to his feet and rummaged among his things. He located something and turned to face Tomonaga with a bottle of sake clasped tightly in his hands.

"You'll not begrudge me?" he asked.

"That's against regulations."

Kikuchi grinned and shrugged. "So is dying, and we're bound to do that before this is over. Shut the door."

Tomonaga pushed the door closed while Kikuchi filled a small drinking bowl, handed it over and then repeated the process. They both took a drink and Tomonaga felt the dry-tasting liquid make its way down into his empty stomach. He braced himself, immediately noticing the alcohol calming his brain. Sweet refuge, he thought. It's too long since I've visited.

Kikuchi noticed his empty bowl and refilled it. Without hesitation, Tomonaga drained the vessel in one continuous effort. Kikuchi watched and smiled in admiration.

"You drink like a man," Kikuchi said.

The numbness slowly started wrapping itself around Tomonaga's body like a dragon, its hot breath warming his face. He welcomed its scaly embrace, desired to flee the war for a few minutes and live like an ordinary man. How nice it would be to inhale cherry blossoms and stroll amidst a garden, he thought. To watch goldfish in a pond and see the face of my beloved reflected in the water. He released a deep sigh. But the dead and dying keep calling me back. Reminding me of my duty.

"You do understand the way of samurai, don't you?" Kikuchi's voice disturbed his quiet moment. "I can tell by your speech and manner. Will you share what you know with me?"

Tomonaga blew out a deep breath as he recalled his grandfather's admonition to be selective in choosing friends. I know little about Kikuchi, he thought. Warriors do not associate on a casual basis or to make idle conversation, his grandfather had taught. His revered grandfather had said many such things. Had there ever been a time when his grandfather wasn't teaching his favorite grandson, Tomosan, the way of the warrior? Living life by the Code of Bushido? When his grandfather had been just . . . a grandfather?

I seek no companions on this path. One can't lose a friend that he hasn't made to a flaming death. Yet, Kikuchi has shared his sake with me. Allowed me to forget about this time and place for a few treasured moments. A kindness freely given is a kindness earned. I should return his kindness. Grandfather would not begrudge me that.

"Not from books," Tomonaga answered.

"How?"

"My grandfather was samurai, as was his father, and his father's father . . . back through the generations. In my mother's house, he was the last of his class. His status was reduced to dust when the nationalists ended samurai stipends and created the new Japan."

A sour look drew up Kikuchi's face as if he had bit into a green persimmon. "I see no reason why we can't have the new Japan and maintain the samurai class. Saigo was right and died in glory fighting for those beliefs."

"No one knows why Saigo died," Tomonaga corrected. "He never voiced the reason behind his rebellion."

"He and his followers died fighting to maintain local control of their government—"

"Perhaps," Tomonaga cut him off, "but he never said as much. Only the Myth of Saigo tells these things."

He watched with remorse as Kikuchi capped the sake bottle and stored it back away.

"What's your purpose in saying that?" Kikuchi asked, picking up his drinking bowl.

"To speak the truth. Saigo was a brave samurai and should be remembered as such. His legacy, however, is less about him and more about the men who created it."

"Saigo represents that which is pure and noble in the Japanese spirit. The Code of Bushido is reborn and important once again to our people. There is a need for a warrior class, and it's our duty to create it. You can't dispute this."

"My father taught me that Japan had to become modern and industrialized in order to survive as a nation. Saigo and his followers stood in the path of progress. Old traditions and ways, such as the samurai's beliefs that they are the only men capable of being warriors or government officials, had to be changed. Where would our nation stand today against the western world if Japan had continued to live in the past? We would be bravely charging against machine guns and tanks, waving our samurai swords and bravely dying by the thousands. Japan could not survive."

Kikuchi squeezed his eyelids closed as if denying Tomonaga's reason. "And your grandfather?"

"Disagreed."

Tomonaga allowed the hint of a smile to show as Kikuchi's eyes blinked open and searched his face. The sake was now warming Tomonaga, loosening his tongue.

"There are many sides to a story," Tomonaga said.

"Whose side do you believe?"

"Tradition belongs to the past. The future belongs to those who seize it and claim it for their own. A man should be judged on how he conducts himself, not on whether he follows behavior expected of his class. We're all Japanese and should share a common martial spirit and destiny. There are many paths that a warrior may take to fulfill his duty to his master."

"What would your grandfather say to that?"

"He would disagree. He taught that a warrior can only be called one if he meets his enemy in hand to hand combat. A man must prove his worth in individual battle. He must look his foe in the eyes as he kills him. The infantry was the only true place for a samurai to serve his master."

"And what do you believe?"

"I disagree," Tomonaga said, adding, "I wanted to fly. It was a dream of mine since childhood when first I saw an airplane circling the sky. To soar on wings and fight like a dragon."

74

"And here you are."

"Yes, I've brought honor upon myself and my family by doing so."

Kikuchi's face reflected confusion. "How so?"

"Like I said, it's my first sortie with *Kido Butai* and I'm named strike leader for the entire task force."

Kikuchi's face split into a large grin. "This is the great honor bestowed upon you?"

The abrupt shift in Kikuchi's demeanor caught him by surprise. "You think otherwise?"

"You don't expect Genda and Nagumo to risk their best pilots against Midway, do you?" Kikuchi's tone seemed to mock him. "They're saving them in case the enemy carriers show up."

"What do you mean?"

Kikuchi drained his bowl and wiped his mouth with the back of a hand. "I thought you knew. It is fleet doctrine to keep half of the available aircraft in reserve armed with armor-piercing bombs and torpedoes just in case an enemy task force appears. The admiral and his staff also hold back the best, most experienced pilots to deal with the enemy carriers. At least, that's what they'd like to believe. "

The briefings did call for only half of the planes to make the Midway attack but said nothing about the skill level of the pilots in either group, Tomonaga thought. It didn't seem important at the time. I was too busy studying the attack plan. Could it be true? How does Kikuchi know these things?

"Come now, use your head," Kikuchi continued as if reading his thoughts. "Egusa and Kobayashi are part of this carrier force. They're the acknowledged masters of dive bombing attacks, and neither one is participating in the Midway strike. Does that not seem odd to you? Do you really think you'd be leading if either one of them was allowed to go?"

So that was it, Tomonaga thought. I'm more expendable than Egusa or Kobayashi. My skills are not considered equal to theirs. This honor rings hollow.

"Cheer up," Kikuchi added. "I'm assigned to the Midway strike group, too. While Egusa and Kobayashi are waiting their turns, we'll be taking the fight to the enemy. That's a warrior's aim in life."

"We'll prove to be their equals?"

75

"No, we'll prove ourselves their superiors."

"Just like samurai?"

Kikuchi smiled and raised his empty bowl. "Just like samurai."

14. MELO
May 28 – 17:00 Hours

"Beautiful."

Corporal Frank Melo Jr. pulled back the bolt of the .30-caliber Browning machine gun, released it, and watched it slap home. He carefully wiped the receiver and barrel with an oily rag and briefly thought about a Japanese Zero caught in the crosshairs of its iron sight.

"Flame one Zeke," he softly said. Will I ever get the chance to prove my skill in actual combat?

A hand slapped against the fuselage, and he heard his pilot, Lieutenant Pren Moore call, "Are you in there, Melo?"

He gave the right-side machine gun one last wipe and made his way back up front, exiting the plane.

"Let me guess," Pren said as Melo emerged from beneath, "you were saying sweet nothings to those Brownings again?"

"Just want them to be ready when the time comes."

Pren snorted. "You mean *if* the time comes."

Melo looked away. "It'll come. It has to. And I'm going to be ready."

"Look at that." Pren pointed to the B-26 Marauder parked next to theirs. "I don't know who's worse, you and those guns or Muri and that ship of his. He had *Susie-Q* painted on it like it's a real flesh-and-blood female. I hope you don't think I'm going to do something like that to this bird."

"Lieutenant, I go where my guns and radio go. I don't care who I hitch a ride with or what's painted on the side of the aircraft. I just want the chance to fight."

Pren grinned. "Such undying loyalty from one so young. I'm touched . . . truly touched."

"I say, old chaps, what are you two on about?" Lieutenant Muri asked as he approached with the bombardier, Johnson, at his side. Ashley followed close behind.

Pren pointed at Ashley. "I see you're bringing up the rear as usual."

Ashley's boyish face lit up. "Where else should a tail gunner be? Besides, I know my place in the pecking order. Always walk at least three steps behind any officer."

"Did you forget the one about how lowly privates should be seen and not heard?" Muri remarked.

"Remember that the next time you're up in the wild blue yonder with Jap Zeroes buzzing around trying to flame your ass, sir," Ashley countered. "Some lowly private banging away on a .50-caliber machine gun might just come in handy."

They joined Melo and Pren in front of the aircraft, and Johnson reached up to touch the Plexiglas nose. Pren elbowed Melo, saying, "Now you've got him doing it."

"Would you like to be alone with your loved one?" Pren asked Johnson.

Johnson snorted at the comment, ducked underneath and moved toward the access hatch. He shoved his bag through the opening and hoisted himself up behind it.

Muri pointed at the torpedo rack hanging from the fuselage's bottom. "To think, I joined the Army Air Force to learn how to become a Navy flier. Not that I have any regrets about this turn of events. I've always wanted to fly a torpedo plane. No Devastator, Aggravator, or Vibrator for me. No siree. I've got a Martin B-26 Marauder torpedo–bomber!"

"If only your mom could see you now," Pren said.

Melo smiled at Pren's patented response. By now, he was accustomed to any awkward statement or embarrassing act witnessed by Pren garnering the same comment. He thought of his being sick after having too much to drink at a squadron party, bent over vomiting and joined by an equally ill Pren who managed to mumble it for the both of them. Good old Pren, his irreverent outlook on life had helped them make it through the past few weeks of mounting anxiety mixed with utter boredom. We waste away in Hawaii while the rest of the 22nd Bomb Group fights the real war from Australia.

"Just be sure you do a proper job of it." Pren's voice took on an unctuous tone. "We don't need you muddling things up for the rest of the chaps. You have one torpedo and one chance. Make the most of it."

Muri hopped his legs up one at a time as he snapped to strict attention. "Yes, sir!"

Melo grinned and moved closer to watch the officer's interchange. He had seen their act before. Muri and Pren were a natural pair of comedians feeding off each other.

"That's better, old chap." Pren fell into character. "Tell me the proper procedure for launching the Mark X-I-I-I naval ordnance torpedo."

Muri scrunched his face up as if he was thinking and then rattled off, "Forty-five degrees of down angle, eight-hundred yards of distance to target from release point, and one-hundred and fifty miles per hour of speed."

"Bloody well done," Pren said while offering a weak handclap.

"Sir?"

"Yes, you've something else to say?"

"There's a slight problem, sir."

Pren cocked one eyebrow upward. "Problem? What kind of problem, my good fellow?"

"The B-26 Marauder aircraft cannot fly at one-hundred and fifty miles per hour of speed. She will stall, followed by a fall, ending in a sudden cataclysmic stop."

"Cataclysmic stop?"

"One hell of a crash, sir."

"The dickens, you say. Are you certain of this?"

"As certain as the fact there will always be an England, sir!" Muri fought to keep a straight face.

Pren walked several steps away and turned back to look at Muri. "Oh well, just do the best that you can. I'll be in the operations hut having crumpets and tea."

The group broke up with laughter as the officers moved off. Melo reached down and picked up a stone. Tossing it side-armed, he watched it skip across the runway. He looked over at Ashley.

"Do you think we'll ever get into the real shooting war?"

Ashley shrugged. "I suppose. The rest of the group has gone on and we're supposed to join them, but you never know what the Army is thinking. Maybe they're going to make permanent B-26 torpedo aerial instructors out of us."

"I can't believe the Army trained me for this. I'm a qualified radioman as well as an aerial gunner. My place is in combat, not taking root here in Hawaii."

"You were a green kid from New Jersey just a few months ago," Ashley reminded.

"That's New *York*, buddy. Guys from Jersey just wish they were from New York."

"Yeah, yeah, so you say."

A jeep came up squealing and bearing their squadron mate Lieutenant Mayes. He beeped the horn and waved them over.

"Get in," he said to Muri and Pren, "Captain Collins is looking for you."

"What's the scoop, Lieutenant?" Melo asked.

"We'll be back in a few minutes to start loading up," Mayes replied. "We've got our orders to head out and join in the fighting. We're taking off first thing in the morning."

"All of us?" Muri asked. "We've got two and a half crews and only two airplanes."

Mayes ground the jeep into gear. "That's what the captain wants to fill you in on. You and Pren are taking your ship and joining the guys to form one crew. He'll give you the details."

"Did he say where we were going?" Melo asked as Mayes popped the clutch and started away.

Mayes tilted his head back and shouted over his shoulder, "Ever hear of a place called Midway?"

15. HENDERSON
May 29 – 13:00 Hours

And I wanted to be a Marine officer, Major Lofton Henderson thought. What was I thinking? I never figured on situations like this. He glanced out of a window at the dismal atoll called Midway, watching two gooney birds performing a drunken waltz of a mating ritual. Would that my life were concerned with such simple matters. Instead, I have two types of aircraft with different flight characteristics. A mixed bag of veteran and green pilots to man them. To top things off, the scuttlebutt says the Japs are headed our way in force to kick us off this place. I wanted a challenge and I got one.

"You can add an SBD to your scratch list," said Major Benjamin Norris, the XO, as he entered the hut.

"What now?"

"One of the men got a little antsy while waiting to take off."

"Antsy?"

Norris shrugged both shoulders. "Maybe he fell asleep and had a bad nightmare, who knows?"

I don't think I want to hear the rest, Henderson thought. "And?"

"He raised the landing gear and bellied down. It won't be flying any time soon."

Henderson pinched up his face, cracked one eye open to stare at Norris. "It didn't occur to him that the SBD needed those wheels on the ground to taxi the aircraft, achieve sufficient speed, and lift off?"

"Don't forget what we're dealing with here. If it wasn't for the war and the need for all of the combat pilots we can get, most of these boys wouldn't be allowed to sit in a cockpit, let alone fly a plane. Be patient. They're learning. It's a slow process."

"Learning? Airplane up before landing gear up was one of the first things they taught me in flight training."

"Maybe flight training's changed since you and I went through it."

"Maybe."

Henderson opened a small notebook lying on the table. After thumbing through several pages, he paused and made a mark. He snapped it shut and glanced at Norris.

"That's two Vindicators we're short due to ground-loops, and one Dauntless. At this rate, if the Japs don't get here soon, we're going to run out of airplanes to throw at them."

"Maybe we can talk the Japs into allowing some of our boys to fly their planes. That should even the odds some."

"Maybe."

"Things could be worse. We have more Vibrators to replace the damaged ones. We should still be able to mount a full complement of attack aircraft."

"True, but I'd rather have spare SBDs. I'm thinking the men would, too. That is, the small handful who can tell the difference. The majority of them have enough on their minds just taking off and landing."

Norris moved over to the wall and pulled down his Mae West life jacket. Hoisting it over his head, he turned back toward Henderson.

"Speaking of Vibrators and Dauntlesses, have you decided how to organize the squadron?"

"Yes, but it wasn't easy. The difference in handling and performance between the SB2Us and SBDs is too great to expect even experienced pilots to stay together."

"And, for the most part, we don't have experienced pilots," Norris said. "We don't have a prayer of maintaining combat formation with our mixture of men."

"Right. I'm going to have to divide the squadron into an SBD and an SB2U group. I'll take the more experienced pilots with me in the SBDs. I'll need you to lead the rest of the men in the SB2Us. I hate to do this to you, but it's important that we make the hardest strike possible."

"Isn't that what XO stands for, Expendable Officer?" Norris smiled. "You do whatever you must. We're all Marines. We'll do our duty."

"I've no doubt."

Henderson got to his feet and followed Norris outside. Hustling men darted around the airfield, setting up weapons and digging. Others strung out rolls of barbed wire along the beach and hammered steel picket posts in the surf to impede landing craft.

The smell of birds, salt, and aviation fuel reminded him of how far he was from home.

"Do you think they're coming?"

Norris's question jerked him back to Midway.

"If they don't, Harold and Cyril are going through a lot of trouble for nothing. It'll take a week or more to clear the beaches of all the mines that have been sown. I hope you're not a sleepwalker, or you could lose a leg one night."

A jeep squealed up, jerking to an abrupt stop and trailing a chalky dust cloud. A haggard-looking Lieutenant Colonel Ira Kimes, Commanding Officer of Marine Air Group 22, unloaded and brushed himself off. He glared at the smiling young man sitting at the steering wheel.

"I think you missed one or two of the bigger potholes, Diego."

A pained expression fell across Diego's tanned face. "I tried to miss them all, sir. A couple of them must have jumped out in front of me, sir."

"Uh, huh. You almost make that sound believable."

"Ira, I didn't think you came out in the daylight," Henderson broke in.

Kimes turned his attention toward Henderson and Norris.

"I needed some air and decided to see how things are going," Kimes explained.

"We're trying to give the new men all of the seat time we can with the small amount of gas we have," Norris said. "They've got the classroom stuff down. Everything else will only come through practice and experience."

Kimes looked at Henderson. "Joe?"

"They're green, no doubt about it, but they're eager to learn," Henderson replied. "I just wish we had more time and fuel to practice dive bombing. Most all of them need it."

"You know that we're short on both of those things and there's nothing I can do about it. Do the best you can. Both of you."

"Any news?" Norris asked.

"Admiral Nimitz is sending out a flight operations' officer sometime today. He's supposed to free up Cyril to concentrate on other matters."

"Things are heating up," Henderson remarked.

Kimes looked around, seeming to study the bustling activity. "I don't know how much hotter things can get. All of us are nearly to

83

the point of exhaustion now. I can't remember the last time I slept for more than two hours or had a hot meal. If the Japs don't show up soon, I'm seriously thinking about us going to find them and dragging them here."

Norris and Henderson chuckled. The rumble of engines overhead caused them to glance up. A group of four twin-engine aircraft heaved into view, circling the airfield to land.

"What do we have here?" Norris asked.

"Those are B-26 Marauders come to give us a hand," Kimes answered. "The Navy boys back in Pearl taught them how to launch torpedoes. Cyril's going to send them out against the Jap fleet. Admiral Nimitz is pulling out all the stops."

"I don't suppose there's a zeppelin cruising around somewhere," Henderson remarked. "If there is, it'll show up here. Just give it some time."

Norris looked at him and grinned. "Do you suppose someone could drop a torpedo from one?"

"Why hell yes. A sailor can drop a torpedo from anything they can get off the ground. I noticed two of them holding down a gooney bird trying to fit a rack to it."

"Ben, did Joe explain the squadron organization to you?" Kimes spoke up. "What I helped him decide?"

Norris flashed Henderson a questioning look. "Only that he would be taking the more experienced pilots with him in the Dauntlesses. I'll bring up the rear with the others in the Vindicators."

"I insisted on that, not him. Joe wanted to discuss the assignments with you and reach an agreement. I vetoed that idea. Joe's our most experienced pilot. From my understanding of what we're up against, we have to hit the Japs with our best shot the first time out. I'm sorry."

Norris smiled. "I'll tell you the same thing that I told him. I'm a Marine. I'll follow my orders to the best of my ability."

Henderson took note of a B-26 loudly taxiing by. "Looks like the Army intends to do their part to protect this place. And the Navy's flown in some of the new Avenger TBFs to help out."

"Are we going to be able to do our part, Joe?" Kimes asked. "We've got obsolete Vindicators and green pilots to fly them. As for the SBDs, the men are inexperienced with them, too. I don't envy you. This assignment is damn near impossible to perform."

Henderson turned to and focused on Kimes.

"You know us, Ira. That's the kind of assignment we thrive on. The Marines will do their part. I guarantee it."

16. RAMSEY
May 29 – 14:00 Hours

Commander Logan Ramsey exited from the PBY flying boat and stretched. So this is Midway Island, he thought. Blink and I'd have missed it. Pausing, he allowed his eyesight to make a complete circuit of the native surroundings. Palm trees, sand, shrubs, and where in the hell did all of these birds come from? He popped his neck and turned to see a captain striding up to greet him.

"Captain Simard?" Ramsey asked.

Simard nodded and extended a hand. "How was the flight, Commander?"

"Call me Logan."

"Cyril."

Ramsey returned the shake. "Rough on both ends and bumpy in the middle."

"Rough?"

Ramsey pointed back toward the ungainly PBY sprouting a torpedo under one wing. "Is that the latest model TBF coming from the states?"

"Hardly," Simard answered. "We're just trying to be prepared in case a PBY happens across a stray Jap carrier. It's also a good way to ferry more torpedoes to Midway."

"Maybe so, but I had serious doubts that the pilot was going to get the thing airborne and dropped to my knees in prayer as he made his landing approach."

Simard chuckled. "You're a naval officer, aren't you? You should know that a torpedo's propeller has to turn a number of revolutions before the thing arms. It can't explode without arming itself first."

"It wasn't an explosion that I was worried about. It was the lopsided load throwing us into a ground-loop."

The two of them walked over to a waiting jeep and climbed in. Simard sat next to the driver while Ramsey perched on the back.

"Take us to the Castle," Simard instructed the driver.

"The Castle?" Ramsey asked.

Simard glanced back at him. "That's what Shannon calls the house he commandeered to be his headquarters. I believe it's his idea of a private joke. "

Ramsey found himself holding on for dear life as the vehicle dodged Marines and sailors hurrying about their tasks. Everywhere he looked, men feverishly prepared for battle. Shovels and picks tossed beach sand or chipped away coral and rock, hewing out gun pits. A long line of sweating, shirtless bodies strained to fill sandbags with the excavated material for use in lining the numerous dugouts dotting the island. At another location, an anti-aircraft gun crew appeared to be making final adjustments before test firing their weapon. Barbed wire in seemingly endless loops encircled everything, an endless roll of spiked pain poised to scourge anyone unfortunate enough to entangle himself in it. The thought brought a wince to Ramsey's face.

"I never knew there was this much barbed wire in the entire South Pacific," Ramsey shouted over the noise of jeep and construction.

"Shannon's a veteran of the Great War and a hell of a combat officer. He believes barbed wire will stop anything. He's got his men preparing a nasty reception for the Japs."

"From what I see, it looks like you're all set to put up one hell of a fight."

"I think the men are doing a great job. We're working them just as hard over on Eastern Island, digging out bunkers for the planes and storage pits. I'm proud of the response from all of them."

With a squeal of brakes, the jeep pulled up in front of a nondescript house. Ramsey stiffly climbed out and stretched his cramped muscles. Simard passed by, walking up to the open door, where a burly figure stepped outside and stood.

"Colonel Harold Shannon," Simard said in greeting, "this is Commander Logan Ramsey. Admiral Nimitz sent him out here to be the air operations officer."

Harsh eyes stabbed out from Shannon's craggy face as he studied Ramsey. The image of a bulldog sniffing a steak flashed through Ramsey's mind. I hope he's had his lunch. Obviously satisfied with his visual analysis, Shannon shook Ramsey's extended hand. "Call me Harold."

"Logan." He took note of Shannon's powerful grip and returned it.

"Care to come inside and have a seat?" Shannon asked.

Ramsey rubbed his sore backside. "If it's all the same to you, I'd like to stand. I've been sitting for a long time today."

Shannon snorted and joined them in the small yard.

"You've been briefed on the situation?" Simard asked Ramsey.

Ramsey nodded. "Admirals Nimitz and Draemel were very thorough. It appears we're charged with stopping a Japanese invasion of this place . . . airstrikes followed by troop landings."

Shannon led them around back and motioned at the bustling activity surrounding them. "Let the sons-of-bitches come. The United States Marine Corps is here in force. The only Japs that are going to be found on Midway will be dead ones."

"That's good to hear, but Admiral Nimitz is hoping to stop their task force before it has a chance to unload troops," Ramsey answered.

A figure appeared from around the corner of the house and walked over to join them. Flaming red hair and freckles to match framed a pleasant face.

"Major Parks," Simard said, "this is Commander Ramsey. He's the new air operations officer."

Ramsey offered his hand. "Call me Logan, and I'll take a wild guess you're called Red."

Parks grinned. "You've got it. I'm the squadron commander of VMF 221. I'm in charge of defending Midway from air attack."

"How many fighters do you have operational?"

Parks frowned. "I've got seven F4F Wildcats and sixteen Brewster Buffaloes."

"Buffaloes? I thought the Navy was getting rid of those outdated crates."

"They are and they're giving them to the Marines." He reached up and rubbed his carrot-hued hair. "We're red-haired stepchildren you know. Not that it matters. My boys can fly and fight in anything."

Ramsey shot a glance at Shannon and noticed him smiling at Parks's comment. One thing a Marine never lacks is confidence, Ramsey thought.

"I certainly hope so," Ramsey answered. "It looks like they'll get a chance at the Japs soon."

"You've got the latest intelligence?" Simard broke in.

"Yes, I'd like to share it with everyone. Give them a good idea of what we're up against."

"I'll call an assembly tonight. Anything else?"

Ramsey thought for just a moment. "I'd like an updated roster of fliers and available aircraft. We'll need to start making some plans to greet our uninvited guests."

Ramsey looked at Shannon. "From the looks of things, you're doing your part."

"Damn right." He pointed out to the waves breaking on the beach. "First the Japs will have to make it through our mines and steel obstacles. Then there are several layers of barbed wire to hold them up while our mortars and howitzers rain hell down on them. If they somehow get through all of that, every inch of sandy ground on this place is crisscrossed with enfilading machine gun fire."

Shannon dropped his arm. "We're doing our job, yes indeed."

Ramsey's sight shifted to Simard and Parks. "Now it's up to us to do ours."

* * *

Ramsey rubbed his burning eyes. Seated at a battered desk inside Simard's bunker headquarters, he briefly considered the nearby hot plate coffeepot. I'd better not, he decided. No need to compound the effect of this heat. Besides, I have enough worries to keep me awake. I don't need caffeine kicking me in the ass, too.

He glanced down at the aircraft roster and shook his head. What is Nimitz thinking? Midway seems to have at least one of every type of flying machine currently utilized by our armed forces. The only thing I haven't seen is a Flying Jenny biplane. I'm sure there's one of those somewhere hereabouts. Yet, there's not enough modern aircraft of a single design, and the pilots are combat inexperienced. I've a lot of thinking ahead to form this motley group into a cohesive strike plan. I only hope that I get the time to do it.

He picked up the paper and turned it toward the dangling light bulb, hoping the light could transform the writing on the page. This is worse than I anticipated. Brewster Buffaloes for fighter planes? The Navy stopped taking shipments of those inferior relics almost a year ago. I guess Parks was right . . . Navy castoffs turned into Marine mainstays. I sure hope that he's right in his assessment of his men's ability to fight inside them.

The Marine dive bomber pilots fare little better. Vought SB2U Vindicators make up over a third of the squadron's strength.

Those crates are so shaky in flight that some wag named them *Vibrators*. The name stuck and spread. He recalled hearing stories of how the fabric tore loose from the wings during diving tests. Those planes are liable to be more dangerous to the men flying them than the enemy will be.

Another item caught his attention and made him scowl. Douglas Devastator torpedo-bombers? They were obsolete before coming off the assembly line. A maximum speed of 200 miles per hour and a cruising speed of 125 while armed? In view of the enemy fighters, that's like bringing an elephant to compete in a horse race. You'd just as well leave them parked on the runway and let the Japs strafe them as attempt an airstrike flying them. The results would be the same.

There are a few newer model aircraft: some Wildcats, Dauntlesses, and Avengers. Midway expects a group of the large, four-engine B-17 Flying Fortress heavy bombers to arrive from Hawaii. I also noticed a handful of B-26 Marauders. Still, what is Nimitz thinking? If an artist desired to paint a picture and call it *Desperation,* he could certainly find his model in Midway's defense situation.

He surrendered to his craving and got up for a cup of coffee. Sipping the wicked brew, his eyesight fell onto the papers littering the desktop. What in the world have I gotten myself into? This place needs divine assistance, not me. Easy, Logan, remember what Admiral Nimitz promised. *Take care of this job for me and I'll bring you back from Midway.* Stay focused on the light at the end of the tunnel . . . hope that it's not an approaching freight train.

That's all this is. Another job that needs doing.

* * *

"So that's what we're facing," Ramsey said, finishing the briefing. "A carrier attack followed by an invasion and occupation. Admiral Nimitz has made it very clear what he expects from us. He needs information and he needs it fast. In response, I'm making the following changes effective immediately. There will be no more one-day patrol flights with two days off. Every patrol plane will fly a seven-hundred mile route daily. I'm sorry. I know that you're already tired, but it can't be helped. We must locate the enemy as soon as possible if we're to strike first."

He paused, expecting to hear a groan of complaint from the large group of men gathered inside the mess hall. His audience remained silent, offering no response. He felt a strong sense of purpose radiating from them, and he smiled. Things had certainly changed in the armed services over the past several months, he thought. Pearl Harbor had seen to that.

"When the enemy is located and within range, we'll be throwing everything we have at them. I've been told to take the fight to them and that's exactly what we're going to do. We're going to strike and continue to strike for as long as we have aircraft available. We'll utilize every resource possible to accomplish this. If it means launching a night torpedo attack to gain an edge, we'll do it."

"You won't have any problem getting volunteers!"

A loud chorus of cheers echoed the anonymous shout. He stopped to acknowledge the sentiment and waited for the noise to subside.

"I'm glad to hear it," he said.

"Commander Ramsey?"

A hand raised in the front row. Ramsey acknowledged it and waved for the man to stand.

"Major Lofton Henderson," he said without being asked. "Are we making this fight alone or will we have help from our aircraft carriers?"

"I'm not aware of any naval forces available to assist, nor did Admiral Nimitz advise me of any. As far as I know, this is our battle to win or lose."

An ominous stillness fell over the building like the eye of a hurricane passing through. The men glanced at each other. Just wait, Ramsey thought. So far, this storm has only been a drizzle. There is a lot more rain and wind coming within the next few days.

Henderson glanced around the assembly and back at Ramsey. "Good. That means more Japs for us."

Ramsey covered his ears against the deafening roar of agreement.

17. THACH
May 30 – 08:00 Hours

Thach glanced up as Lovelace entered the office. The throaty, rumbling roar of an entire squadron of idling Wildcat fighter planes, music to Thach's ears, accompanied him. Lovelace closed the door, lowering the clamor to a tolerable level that allowed for normal speech. A wide grin lit up his friend's face as he turned a chair around and seated himself backward. His hands clasped the posts as he rocked back and forth on two legs.

"The squadron's assembling and preparing to mount up," Lovelace said. "*Yorktown's* waiting."

Thach signed off on the bottom of the clipboard and slid it to the edge of the desk. "I had to finish these reports. Every round of ammunition and gallon of gas has to be accounted for. If it's not, it'll be taken out of my pay."

"Pushing a pencil doesn't suit you."

Thach smiled. "Now you know what's waiting for you back stateside with your own group. The life of a fighter squadron leader isn't all girls and glamour."

For a brief moment, Thach thought he saw a misty glint come into Lovelace's eyes. If so, Lovelace quickly masked it with his usual mischievous look.

"You're not worried that I'll teach my guys to use your beam defense position and that we'll shoot down more Japs than yours will, are you?"

Thach lit a cigarette, took a long draw, and blew out a mouthful of smoke. "That," he said as he pointed toward the blue-tinted puff, "is what I think about your guys ever outdoing mine."

"We shall see. We shall see."

A sudden thought hit Thach, and he grew serious. "I know we've not had much time, but what kind of progress do you think we've made forming our separate groups into a team?"

"They're slowly coming along, but trying to mix veteran and green pilots makes for a dicey situation. It's funny, do you remember Leonard, the vocal one from VF 42?"

Thach nodded.

"I think he's probably the unhappiest one, and it's a shame because he's also showing the most promise at leadership. He's senior, but I don't think that's all there is to it."

"Then what?"

"The other men constantly look to him and how he responds to a given situation and follow suit."

"I'm not surprised. It's often the guys who aren't afraid to speak out who make the best leaders. It's more a matter of whether or not they'll shut up and do their jobs when they've been overruled that separates the team players from the whiners."

"Perhaps so. I definitely think Leonard has the makings of a good leader."

"I need you to do one more thing when we get on board *Yorktown*," Thach said, shifting his thoughts.

"Name it."

"Gather up the experienced pilots and spend some time going over the beam defense. They've been through combat at Coral Sea, so that part won't be new to them. I want to familiarize them with using the tactic against Zeroes. The green pilots will have their hands full just trying not to be shot down."

The chair's feet thudded against the floor. "You've got it."

"Speaking of green pilots, are you sure about using one of them for your wingman? You can have your choice of any of the experienced ones."

"Well, we're trying to mold this group of mismatched parts into a fighting whole, and a good leader always leads by example. I'll do my part by looking out for a greenie."

"Don, are you sure? I mean we can—"

"No." Lovelace's firm voice silenced him. "Everything will come out fine and we'll gain an experienced fighter pilot instead of losing a young man to some hotshot Jap pilot."

Thach stood. "Whatever you say. It's your choice."

He picked up his flying helmet and goggles, pausing to look at Lovelace. "You know that I really appreciate everything you've done. I couldn't have pulled this off without you."

Lovelace's bright smile flashed again. "Don't think I won't remind you of that when we're old, gray and sitting in our rockers at the Old Pilots' Home."

* * *

Thach climbed out of the cockpit of his Wildcat in time to see *Yorktown*'s deck crew tear the flaps trying to fold the wings. He jumped down, quickly confronting the plane's captain to stop the job for a moment.

"I'm sorry, but we're in a hurry, sir," the man replied. "We've got to get these birds stowed away so the other pilots can land."

"Have any of you ever so much as seen one of these F4F-4s?" Thach asked.

"Just from a distance back on the flight line at Kaneohe," was the answer. "Chief Wester has one copy of the maintenance manual, but it wasn't detailed enough for us to figure out how to do stuff without looking at the plane."

"Let's not damage any more planes. Gather your group around me and I'll show you how to fold the wings."

Thach spent the next few minutes demonstrating the proper way to perform the job. Satisfied they could do it, he instructed them to help the other crews as needed. Hungry, he walked toward the carrier island to find some lunch. As he neared the open portal, a sudden memory of the squadron's green pilots caused him to turn around. He stood watching a few more of the Wildcats land, easily picking out the inexperienced fliers. A pilot's first combat was a bad time for on-the-job training, he thought. His sharp eyes perceived that the next plane down would be Lovelace's F4F. He smiled. There's no reason to be concerned with Don's performance.

Lovelace showed the entire ship the correct way to make a carrier landing. His Wildcat smoothly touched down with nary a bump, caught an arresting wire that brought him to an abrupt halt, and taxied over the lowered safety barrier. He patiently waited in the cockpit while his crew conducted him forward to a parking spot and the barrier rose for the next landing.

Thach decided to have Lovelace join him for lunch and walked back toward the parking area, careful not to stray onto the busy, dangerous landing zone. A sudden motion out of the corner of his eyesight drew his attention. Lovelace's wingman was demonstrating his inexperience by sharply dropping his aircraft's nose as he cut power. Increasing speed, the plane roared across the deck missing the arresting wires. The pilot tried to correct by roughly snatching it down onto the wooden surface. Rubber tires briefly squealed and then leapt upward. The berserk aircraft hopped over the safety barrier. The spinning propeller churned into Lovelace's cockpit, tossing hunks of metal and Plexiglas into the wind.

Stunned, Thach felt his feet plod forward a step or two before sprinting toward the accident scene. Deck crewmen scrambled over both Wildcats spraying fire-extinguishing foam and skillfully trying to extract the pilots. A muscular, tattooed arm snared Thach, lifting both of his feet clear of the deck. Thach's head pivoted; he found himself restrained by Smitty.

"I'm sorry, sir," he said, his loud but gentle voice seeming false compared to his large presence, "but regulations say to stay clear and let the rescue crews do their jobs. It's safer back here."

Thach felt Smitty's firm resolve and realized it was foolish to argue. He relaxed and the powerful grip eased. The two of them stood silently together, watching Lovelace's blood-splattered body tenderly lowered to a waiting stretcher.

* * *

Thach strode into the ready room to find his squadron silently waiting. His gaze briefly dropped onto Lovelace's grief-stricken wingman before moving on to survey the entire group. He thought, where do I find the words? If this war wasn't terrible enough, now I'm dealing with a casualty that wasn't a direct result of combat.

"I've called you here to clear the air and get on with this thing," he began. "We've lost an excellent pilot and commander and I've lost a close friend, but life and this damn war will go on."

Thach stared at the young wingman. "What happened was an accident that won't be dwelled upon. We've neither the time nor the right to dishonor Commander Lovelace's memory by losing focus on the difficult task ahead."

He looked up at the others. "I realize that most of us have not flown together before in any fashion, let alone as a combat group. That's unimportant and there's nothing I or anyone else can do about that. It is what it is.

"Having said that, there is one thing we can do something about. We have the vital, critical task of protecting this aircraft carrier and striking at the enemy. The only way we're going to succeed at this is by working together as a team."

95

He paused, slowly looking at each man in turn . . . faces so young and full of promise and the future so dark and uncertain. Damn the ones responsible for this blasphemy against mankind.

"It's as simple as that. A team we shall be, and I expect every one of you to make this happen. I don't care if we're called VF 42, VF 3, or the Homeless Bastards of *Yorktown*, we're American servicemen charged by our country to defend it. We can all learn a valuable lesson from those men entombed in the *Arizona*."

Thach halted again to clear his throat, thinking, it's hard to believe that a pilot ready room could be so quiet. The normal noise and bustle of a functioning carrier filtered in but seemed to die in the solemn silence.

"Those men and Don Lovelace gave their all," he continued. "Can we do any less?"

The men exchanged looks among themselves before Leonard spoke up. "Sir, may I say something?"

"Go ahead."

"We're with you all the way. Just point us in the right direction and stand back."

A murmur of agreement echoed his words. Thach glanced at the ceiling. Perhaps the sun was breaking through the dark clouds. No silver lining yet, but there's hope. He held up a hand for silence.

"I'm glad to hear it," he said. "Now let's talk a few details. I understand you're new to flying the F4F-4s, but that can't be helped. This is the hand we've been dealt and these are the cards we have to play. My biggest concern is the reduced ammunition supply of the newer model. Your firing time is now about half of what it was before. It's more important to make each burst count.

"Be that as it may, I'll say it again, we absolutely must protect this carrier at any cost. *Yorktown's* been through a lot the past few weeks, and she's still hurting. The biggest threat to her will be enemy torpedo planes. It's critical we stop them before their release points, even if it means ramming them."

He paused to allow this last point to sink in. His eyesight flicked back and forth, waiting for a question or comment that never came.

"To perform a ram," he continued, holding up his hands and mimicking the motion of two airplanes, "you must move in from below and pull up to allow your prop to cut through the enemy's fragile tail section. Do it correctly and you'll send him spinning down while you fly on."

He spent the next hour discussing various subjects involving attacks and the importance of staying together. He called upon the veterans to share their experiences in combat and helped to dissect the movements of each pilot and his opponent. Gratified, he noted that the conversation flowed freely between the men, and a sense of camaraderie was slowly spreading throughout the group. As the meeting dissolved, he waved to Leonard and told him to stay.

"Yes, sir?" Leonard asked when the room had cleared.

"Due to circumstances, I'm reorganizing the squadron. You're senior, but that's not the reason I'm naming you the new executive officer."

Leonard's brow wrinkled in confusion. "I don't understand."

"I don't know exactly what we're about to get into, but the fact that a damaged *Yorktown* is being shipped right back into battle is enough to make me believe it's important. From what I gather, Admiral Nimitz is committing almost everything he has on the upcoming operation. That tells me this thing is very serious. At times like this, I'm not about to stand on Navy tradition if I believe there's another man more qualified to perform a critical job."

Thach paused to allow Leonard to consider his words and then continued.

"One of the last things that Commander Lovelace and I talked about this morning was the need for teamwork and leadership in this squadron. To be blunt, we're not there yet and we've little time to pull this thing together."

Leonard swallowed but remained silent.

"Don told me you have the makings of a fine leader. It's time you live up to your promise. This is the reason you're taking his place as XO."

Leonard swallowed hard once more, and Thach noticed his eyes taking on a crimson lining. "I'm honored and certainly realize the large shoes I'm trying to fill. I just hope I'm equal to the task."

Thach smiled. "Don and I both believe you are. Now go out and prove it to this squadron."

18. HENDERSON
May 30 – 10:00 Hours

"Major Henderson."

Henderson looked up from his report and saw Ramsey enter the office. He laid his pencil down.

"Call me Joe," Henderson said, extending a hand.

"Logan." Ramsey returned the shake and sat down.

"What can I do for you?"

"I came over here for a meeting and noticed your men practicing. As the air operations officer, I decided that I needed to have a word with you."

Henderson waited, knowing what was coming. Yes, he thought, we're doing what it looks like.

"Glide-bombing?" Ramsey asked.

"Well, it's not my first choice for making an attack, but it's my only option."

Ramsey exhaled deeply. "Go on, please."

"I'm facing some severe limitations here. I've a group of green pilots and an assortment of aircraft that most of them have no experience flying. We're short of spare parts and other materials."

"Yes, I know you're low on resources," Ramsey replied.

"Low? That's a nice way to put it. I suppose you heard about the snafu involving the fuel dump?"

"Cyril mentioned something about crossing some wires while rigging it to explode in case the Japs landed."

Henderson smirked. "Hell of a way to test a wiring job . . . blow up the fuel dump doing it."

Ramsey smiled. "We're all learning on the job about how to fight this war. There are going to be a few setbacks from time to time."

"I suppose, but the reduction in fuel supplies meant that I was allocated two hours of practice flight time for the SB2Us and one hour for the SBDs. Given all of those limitations, I believe that glide-bombing is our only chance of making a serious strike against the Japs."

Ramsey got up and walked over to the open door. He stood there looking outside while Henderson studied his broad figure. There's a man who commands respect with his attitude and presence, Henderson thought. No wonder Nimitz sent him out here to take charge of this diverse group. I wouldn't want to be standing in his shoes.

"Glide-bombing exposes the pilot to as much danger as a torpedo attack," Ramsey said without turning around. "Maybe more. I was hoping that dive bombers would take some of the heat off the torpedo planes. Make the enemy fighter pilots choose between defending at high or low altitude."

He glanced back at Henderson. "It's a shame."

"Logan, I've been in the Corps for fifteen years and have served all over the world. I've done my duty as ordered just like all of these men have and will. I want to go home when this war ends. I don't like the idea of glide-bombing any more than you do, but I figure it's the best way–the *only* way to hit the Japs hard enough to take the fight out of them. The quicker we do that, the sooner we all get to go home."

Ramsey's eyelids narrowed as though studying Henderson. "And that comment you made last night that drew all of the cheers? You're not hunting for medals or seeking revenge the wrong way?"

Henderson felt a flush of anger that he quickly subdued. Calm down. The man means no harm. He's trying to fulfill his duty as air operations officer. He's asking questions that deserve answers.

"No, I wasn't trying to make light of the situation or of your concern." Henderson measured his words. "Most of the men in my squadron had never flown an SBD until a few days ago. The others are fresh out of flight school. I don't know how they can be more inexperienced than they are. Fear of combat and of the unknown can cause a man to lose concentration and make a fatal mistake. I have to keep their thoughts focused on doing their jobs no matter what might happen. They must believe we're equal to anything the Japs throw at us. My show of bravado was for their benefit, not for yours or anyone else's."

Ramsey removed a cigarette from a crushed pack. He placed one between his teeth and snapped open a Zippo. A flicker of flame, a deep inhalation, and a perfect smoke ring floated out of his mouth.

"The things that a man can learn when he has too much spare time on his hands," Ramsey remarked as he watched the vaporous circle drift away. "Things that have absolutely no value whatsoever."

Henderson smiled, wondering where the conversation was headed.

"Given the circumstances, do you consider attacking Nagumo's fleet a suicide mission?"

Ramsey's question caught him unawares. Exactly the way he planned it, Henderson thought. He's clever, no doubt about it.

"What circumstances are you talking about?"

"What you just told me. We have a cast-off group of aircraft, many of which are obsolete. The majority of the pilots are inexperienced. Nagumo's bringing better aircraft and veteran pilots to the dance. Now your group must attempt a glide-bombing attack against enemy carriers protected by the best fighter plane in the Pacific. You must admit that this could look suicidal to many people."

Henderson slowly shook his head. "No. I don't accept that, and neither do my men. There are no such things as suicide missions, just quitters."

"Quitters?"

"I want you to understand something about you and me. We're both graduates of the Naval Academy, but that's as far as it goes. I'm a Marine. That has a special meaning for me and my men."

"I've heard all of that and I'm not questioning–"

Henderson held up an open palm to silence him.

"Allow me to finish. Every Marine here believes he's the fighting equal to any other man. I don't care if he's baking bread or flying a Grumman F4F, each one of them considers himself a warrior at heart. When the time comes, they'll each pick up a rifle and join the firing line. You can call us cocky or arrogant. Hell, we don't care.

"For a man to consider a given assignment suicide means that he's already defeated. That he's quit. We're fighters, not quitters. I intend to lead my group out to the enemy and attack. To do anything possible to inflict the most amount of damage. Then we're going to return here, load back out, and hit them again. We'll keep doing that as long as possible, or until Nagumo gets the hell out of here.

"I'm not saying your sailors or the Army men will do any less. I expect they'll all do their duty. As for my men, I *know* they'll do theirs. We don't consider this a suicide mission. Marines don't think that way."

Ramsey remained silent for a few moments before nodding in agreement. "I believe you."

"Good."

"And I'll tell you something else. I'm aware of how Marines fight. I studied Belleau Wood, too. I wouldn't want to be aboard one of Nagumo's ships."

Henderson smiled. "Semper fi."

19. FLETCHER
May 30 – 11:00 Hours

Fletcher stood watching Captain Buckmaster pick up the microphone. He felt the tremor of *Yorktown* beneath his feet and reveled in being back at sea. The smell of salty air, petroleum and paint drifted on the breeze, an old friend extending a welcome. The Coral Sea faded behind him with each turn of the carrier's screws. It's good to be home, he thought. Back where I belong. Fate pulls us onward. Redemption lies ahead at Midway.

"This is the captain," Buckmaster said. "I know that *Yorktown* went through a hell of a fight recently and the three days we spent at Pearl weren't enough to make total repairs. There's no choice in the matter. We're needed once again. Admiral Nimitz is convinced the Japanese are about to invade Midway Island. We can't let them have it. If Midway falls to the enemy, Hawaii and the American Mainland could be next.

"Admiral Nimitz has arranged a little surprise for the Japanese. The *Yorktown* along with *Enterprise* and *Hornet* will be there to greet them. While they're busy launching and landing air strikes against Midway, we're going to ambush them from the flank.

"To make this succeed, they mustn't know we're coming. For this reason, we'll be observing strict radio silence until further notice. No one, absolutely no one, will broadcast without my prior approval. I can't stress how critical this point is. We must secure the advantage of total surprise for Admiral Nimitz's plan to have a chance. This means that any pilot getting lost or straying from the carriers won't have radio direction to guide him back. He'll be on his own. I'm sorry, but we've no choice in the matter.

"Now for the good news. Admiral Nimitz has directed me to assure you that we're all going to the West Coast for rest and recreation just as soon as this little scrap is over."

Loud cheers rocked the vessel as Buckmaster finished. He glanced over at Fletcher and smiled.

"That was a boost for morale."

"Giving the Japs a good ass kicking will also do wonders for their disposition," Fletcher responded. "If Admiral Nimitz's plans work, we should be able to accomplish that."

"Let's hope they do succeed," Fletcher's chief of staff, Admiral Spencer Lewis, said. "I'd hate to think we sailed all the way out here for nothing."

"I don't know, we could always get in a little fishing," Fletcher replied. "I hear they pull up some big ones way out here in this deep water."

Lewis looked out over the ocean and then back at Fletcher. "We're a long ways above the water up here and my line's too short. I believe I'll stick with doing my part to win this battle."

Fletcher glanced up at Oscar Pederson, *Yorktown's* Air Group Commander. "*Yorktown's* ready to do her part?"

Pederson grinned. "*Yorktown's* ready to lead the way, sir."

"Good, glad to hear it. You'll be working with Leonard Dow on *Enterprise*. Admiral Spruance and I decided to place him in charge of the combined carrier fighter operations. If it becomes necessary for our Task Force 17 to operate alone, you'll be directing *Yorktown's* fighters like you normally do."

"Aye, aye, sir."

"As you were men, as you were, don't mind me." The familiar voice brought attention to the bridge doorway. A short, barrel-chested officer came sweeping in, flashing salutes all around. Perched solidly on his head, a combat helmet proudly proclaimed *Dixie* in large, stenciled letters. He marched over to Fletcher and snapped out another crisp salute.

"Commander Kiefer reporting without being ordered, sir."

"Without being ordered?"

"Aye, sir," Dixie Kiefer replied. "It was lonely downstairs in the officers' mess, and I finished sweeping the place up. I heard all the Big Brass was up here, so I thought I'd join you . . . with your permission, of course."

"The more the merrier."

"Breaking out the combat gear a little early aren't you?" Buckmaster asked.

"I don't trust those Japanese," Kiefer replied. "They're sneaky bastards. You never can tell where they might pop up. When they find out *Yorktown* wasn't sunk at Coral Sea, I figure they'll be mighty angry and want to rectify the situation, sir."

Fletcher knew better than to ask but took the bait anyway. "If you're so concerned about an attack, why aren't you wearing a life jacket?"

Kiefer smiled, apparently pleased with Fletcher playing along. "Admiral Halsey borrowed mine and never brought it back. From what I hear about his skin condition, I'm not sure I want it back, sir."

Fletcher chuckled and heard a general round of laughter echo through the bridge. The comforting sound, though genuine, seemed out of place. It's strange how men facing death can find humor in their situation, he thought. Chalk it up to the resiliency of the human spirit, I guess. It gives me hope that this war will end someday, and when it does, life can return to normal.

Fletcher walked over to the window and looked down at the flight deck. The damaged aircraft from the earlier fatal accident had been carried below. On top, four fighter planes warmed up. Following the signal officer's directions, the first in line taxied forward. A pause, the engine rose to full throttle, and then the plane roared down the wooden surface before it slowly rose.

His attention shifted to a single aircraft at the far end of the deck. It was positioned in line with the long axis, and a crew of ordnance men scrambled all around it. Several lifted the tail up and placed it on a stand while others adjusted the machine guns. One man stood apart from the group, intensely watching the process. Fletcher thought, we're headed out to confront the Japanese Combined Fleet and *still* doing maintenance on Grummans? I don't like this.

He motioned to Buckmaster and pointed at the activity. "What's going on?"

"Dixie?" Buckmaster called Kiefer to join them.

Kiefer, hovering nearby, hurried over.

"Oh that; the mechanics didn't have time to correctly sight the guns on the new F4Fs, so they're doing it now. They'll bore sight 'em, clamp 'em down, and McCuskey will fire 'em over the side. He'll be able to tell if the aim's correct by watching the tracers through the gun sights. That is, I think McCuskey will fire 'em. As protective and nervous as some of the pilots are about their airplanes, they'll probably want to do that themselves. I see one of them down there right now. Looks like an expectant father, doesn't he? Can't say that I blame them. I was always mighty particular about my own bird, sir."

"This couldn't have been done before sailing?" Fletcher asked.

"No, sir, Jimmy Thach didn't have the manpower to get it done. He spent the majority of his time test flying the new version and checking out his patchwork squadron."

"How long before they're finished?"

"Those ordnance boys are working overtime to get done. They know how important it is. I've faith the birds will be ready to fly and fight when needed."

"Stay on them. I don't want to confront the Jap fleet with part of my air cover unavailable."

"Aye, sir."

"They're going to fire those guns over the side?" Buckmaster asked.

"It's a lot less dangerous than firing them straight down the deck just like she's headed, sir."

Fletcher fought to hide his grin as Buckmaster briskly rubbed his mouth. Only Dixie could get away with remarks like that, Fletcher thought. I know I can't encourage it, but I'm not going to discourage it, either. When the situation allows, the men need the levity.

"You tell them I want all of that fired brass gathered up for salvage," Buckmaster said.

"Aye, aye, sir." Kiefer offered a grand salute and swept toward the door. He paused in the portal and looked back. "Remember men, above all, don't get excited!"

20. BEST
May 30 – 17:00 Hours

Lieutenant Richard Best joined the small group of officers entering Admiral Spruance's stateroom. He glanced around at the room's large size and nice furniture and tried to contain his awed surprise. So this is how an Admiral roughs it with the men at sea, he thought. Rank does have its privileges. He found a folding chair among some others gathered in a half-circle around Spruance and took a seat. The Admiral smiled and acknowledged each man as he settled down.

"I'm sorry that I don't know all of you personally," Spruance began, "but your fine reputations have preceded you. Would you mind helping me match the names to your faces and assignments?"

"Clarence Wade McClusky," the officer seated to Spruance's right said. "I'm *Enterprise* Air Group Commander."

"Mister McClusky, I certainly remember you." Spruance's voice held real warmth. "Your fighters guarded my cruisers on several occasions. Glad to have you as CEAG."

"Thank you, sir."

Spruance looked at the next man in line.

"James S. Gray, Fighting Squadron 6."

"Richard H. Best, Bombing Squadron 6," Best heard himself say.

"Wilmer E. Gallaher, Scouting 6." Earl Gallaher's voice had a nervous tone to it.

"Arthur V. Ely, Torpedo Squadron 6," the last man said. "I'm the executive officer in temporary command while Lieutenant Commander Lindsey recovers."

Spruance addressed Ely. "I heard his plane went over the side while he was attempting to land, but that he wasn't badly injured. I understand he's already demanding to be released and to be returned to duty."

"Aye, sir. He's a fighter, no doubt about it."

"Good, and thank you all. Admiral Halsey speaks highly of each one of you. That's certainly all I need to hear to know that my air groups are in good hands."

Spruance crossed his right leg on top of his left and cupped the knee with both hands. "I wanted to give you men a little more information on what Admiral Nimitz believes is about to happen. I also hope to make you understand how critical it is that we stop the Japanese here."

Best leaned forward, anxious to hear what Spruance had to say. He found himself warming up to the admiral's casual, laid-back style. Though Best had heard the talk of Spruance being a cold fish, the man seated before him seemed genuinely concerned that they fully accept the duty facing them. Most commanders issued orders and expected them to be obeyed without question; one that took the available time to explain the necessity of such orders was rare indeed.

"Like I said earlier, there's a large Japanese operation targeting Midway. Intelligence is certain that Admiral Nagumo is leading a strike force composed of between four and five aircraft carriers along with their supporting vessels. It will make the initial attacks to pave the way for another task force bringing the invasion troops."

Best sat back in his chair and felt the others doing the same. He thought, four or five enemy aircraft carriers? Supporting vessels that will surely include some large cruisers if not battleships? I doubt the task force that attacked Pearl Harbor was much larger than that. This is one hell of a major operation for the Japs. His palms suddenly felt sweaty. Dropping them to his legs, he started brushing up and down to dry them.

"Intelligence believes that Nagumo will arrive at his point of attack within the next four or five days. Once there, Admiral Nimitz says that an early morning strike based on the model of Pearl Harbor is their most likely plan of attack. While they're busy with Midway, we plan a surprise air strike on Nagumo's forces. The hope is that we'll catch them lightly defended and vulnerable."

Spruance rose out of his chair and walked over to a large chart attached to one wall. Midway Island occupied the position directly in the center of it. A finger touched a spot in the ocean to the northwest of the atoll.

"Here's where Intelligence has pinpointed Nagumo's position will be when he launches his aircraft. He seems to have caught some luck in transit. Our meteorologist advises there's currently a large cold front blanketing this area bringing wind, rain, and fog. He's convinced visibility is limited to non-existent within that

107

frontal zone. It's doubtful that our submarine picket line will catch sight of the enemy. Midway has PBYs flying patrol routes out to seven hundred miles but the thinking is the Japanese are going to be hard to spot. They might not be located until the morning of the attack."

Spruance turned back toward his audience. Best wondered if the others felt the nervous tension that he did. *Is my face betraying my emotions? McClusky appears perfectly at ease. Gray and Gallaher both look the way I feel. I can't read Ely.*

"What this means is a PBY might not discover Nagumo's group until it's well within striking range of Midway, and possibly after the Japanese planes are airborne. Each one of us must be prepared to instantly react when we receive a confirmed spotting report. There will be no time to waste."

Spruance sat back down, looked at each man. "You can bet Nagumo will have his own planes up as soon as possible searching for an unexpected threat like us. I don't have to tell you that whoever strikes the quickest and hardest stands the best chance of winning this battle. We're facing odds of nearly two to one. We can't allow our response to be slow or ineffectual."

"Sir, may I ask what the proposed plan of action is?" McClusky said.

Spruance exhaled. "Admiral Fletcher and I are preparing for what Admiral Nimitz is convinced is going to happen by his timetable. Admiral Fletcher and the *Yorktown* group are supposed to rendezvous with us in about two days at a spot in the ocean labeled 'Point Luck.'"

"*Yorktown*?" Gray asked. "No wonder it's called Point Luck."

A chuckle spread through the group, and Spruance joined in before saying, "That's not the only reason for the name. Admiral Nimitz is hoping it also brings us good luck and delivers Nagumo right where he's expected and when he's expected."

"The last I heard, *Yorktown* was out of action for at least three months," McClusky said.

"That was before Admiral Nimitz held a private conference with the dry dock crew," Gray remarked. "I'm beginning to believe that man can part the Red Sea."

"He does have an admirable, persuasive manner," Spruance agreed. "I didn't think anyone could pull Admiral Halsey out of a command headed into battle, but Admiral Nimitz did it. What's more, Admiral Halsey actually thanked him for it!"

Thoughts of the feisty, determined officer normally in command of *Enterprise's* task force agreeably relinquishing his post for any reason caused another round of subdued laughter. Best tuned out the casual conversation and focused on the chart. Thoughts of his wife and child back in Honolulu and the guilt he felt for leaving them came to him. I'm an officer stationed on a ship at war, but it was still hard to sail away from Hawaii. Now this. It seems like a lot is being gambled on the fact that Admiral Nimitz's intelligence reports are correct and can be trusted. What if those reports turn out to be wrong? In the days leading up to the attack on Pearl Harbor, the Japanese transmitted false information. Could this be the same situation? Are the Japanese setting a trap that we're blindly sailing into?

"Admiral Spruance, what would happen if the Japs bypass Midway and come straight to Hawaii?" Best's question brought a sudden halt to the conversation.

An uncomfortable silence descended upon the group and Best found himself the object of Spruance's scrutiny. Perhaps I'm out of line asking, but I must know. Is this a large gamble on Admiral Nimitz's part? Is Hawaii being left to fend for itself? Spruance gazed at him as the seconds slowly ticked past.

"Well." Spruance's soft voice cracked against Best's ears. "We just hope that they will not."

Hope? We *hope* that they will not? What kind of an answer is that? Innocent lives are at stake in Hawaii, not at the military installations on Midway. There are women and children living in harm's way. Shouldn't that be our first concern? Best started to reply but then thought it wiser to hold his tongue. I've said too much already. My role is not to question but to follow orders. He silently prayed Spruance knew something he would not or could not share.

The meeting broke up soon after, and Best returned to his small cabin. He drifted into an uneasy sleep that night and jolted awake from a nightmare of enemy bombs falling and his wife screaming his name.

21. KUSAKA
May 31 – 09:00 Hours

Kusaka roamed among the groups of fliers gathered on the flight deck, watching them exercise. Pulling his collar up against the nasty weather, he paused occasionally to offer a small word of encouragement or a gentle jibe at someone struggling to keep up. A husky voice calling his name drew his attention to Genda standing near the forward elevator.

"You're feeling better today?" Kusaka asked.

Genda's pale face and hoarse cough answered his question. Dark circles beneath the officer's watery eyes bore testament to a night devoid of sleep. Kusaka sighed, thinking, how long can even a fit young man like Genda continue holding up under such physical and mental strain?

"My illness shall pass with time and duty won't wait, but I must admit this rain and cool air aren't helping things."

Another fierce bout of coughing doubled him over and Kusaka looked away. He hummed along with the martial song the fliers were singing, patiently waited for Genda to recover.

"Have you word of Fuchida?"

Genda's face brightened at the mention of his friend. "He's much better but still very weak. He'll be confined to sick bay for a few more days at least."

Kusaka shook his head. "If I were a believer in omens, this would cause me great concern. Our largest air operation since Pearl Harbor facing us and we're without the services of our best flight leader."

"I've located another serving on the *Hiryu*. Lieutenant Tomonaga is an experienced pilot and a fine leader. I served with him in China."

"One of Yamaguchi's pilots? Is Admiral Nagumo aware of this?"

"Yes. He's not happy with it, but he understands that we must use the best qualified man for the job. Duty comes before his personal feelings on the matter."

"And Tomonaga is the best qualified?"

Genda cleared his throat and spat. "All things considered, yes sir."

"All things considered?"

110

"As I reminded you when this need first came up, we must follow Fleet Doctrine as ordered by Admiral Yamamoto," Genda explained. "Half of our striking force must remain in reserve on the chance that an American task force appears."

"*Hai,*" Kusaka quietly cursed. "You did say that, and I recall something was mentioned about it at the final meeting, but I thought Admiral Nagumo would assume the authority to fight the battle as conditions dictate. Surely he sees the danger in strictly adhering to rules set forth in planning discussions?"

Genda gave him a knowing look. "Admiral Nagumo had the fire inside him doused long ago. Admiral Yamamoto looks harshly on anyone who does not follow his plan. You should know that, sir."

Kusaka chose to ignore the gentle reproach, understanding that Genda meant nothing disrespectful.

"So half of our pilots will be cooling their heels onboard the ship while an insufficient number of planes attempts to destroy the Midway defenses. What logic is this?"

"Not just half of our pilots, but the less experienced half will be making the Midway strike."

"Yamamoto again?"

"Yes, sir. Egusa and Kobayashi, our finest air commanders, will be held in reserve. They are to deal with the American fleet if it arrives. That's why I chose Tomonaga to replace Fuchida. He was the next best qualified and experienced."

"He has flown against the Americans?"

"Not to the best of my knowledge. I would doubt that it matters, sir."

"And will one air strike remove Midway as a threat to our invasion forces?"

"I don't think so. We're ordered not to cause extensive damage to the airfields so that we can put them into immediate service for ourselves. That alone could prove to be a large obstacle in totally eliminating Midway's ability to strike back."

"How does Admiral Nagumo feel about this?"

Genda glanced toward the sweating pilots. "He will follow orders, just like the rest of us."

Follow orders, Kusaka thought. How simple a description for such a dangerous idea. Is this what we're reduced to doing? Following orders? We no longer fight a battle as circumstances dictate. We follow orders. One can only hope that the enemy does the same. That he questions not. That he refuses to adapt to developing circumstances. That he follows orders.

Kusaka looked up at the bridge and felt Nagumo watching them. How such a man, once so dashing and full of promise, fell into nothing more than a puppet for Yamamoto and the Combined Fleet I will never understand. Is it a weakness of character? Might I have the same weakness?

"He's changed, hasn't he?"

It took a few seconds before he realized Genda had asked a question.

"He?"

"Admiral Nagumo. I'd heard great stories about him as a young officer and eagerly looked forward to serving under him." Genda seemed to struggle for a second as though trying to find the right words. "It has not been as I expected." A coughing fit punctuated his last statement.

Kusaka walked several steps away from the ship's island. Genda obediently followed. A group of jogging pilots passed by, singing a bawdy tune and laughing. Kusaka and Genda paused to watch them circle around at the far end of the deck and start back.

"The eternal vivacity and optimism of youth," Genda said, at Kusaka's shoulder. "I'm not yet forty, but those ideas abandoned me long ago."

"I can only feel sadness at the thought that many of them will never see our home shores again." Kusaka sighed and spat. "I hate this war."

They lapsed into silence. *Akagi*'s noise and bustle dissolved into a subdued roar as they stood facing the breeze. Wet, salty air stung Kusaka's eyes, leaving a sticky film on exposed flesh.

"You asked about Admiral Nagumo?" Kusaka finally said.

"You've known him much longer than I. Were the stories I heard about him untrue?"

"No. Admiral Nagumo was an excellent officer and one of the most knowledgeable men on torpedo attacks in the entire Combined Fleet. He was considered a rival to Admiral Yamamoto himself, and his ascendance seemed assured. I often watched as people grew quiet and listened whenever he spoke. He was a sage and his word was revered."

"And now?"

"I don't know, and I ask myself the same question. It almost seemed like he was uncomfortable with all of the increased attention directed at him. With greater attention comes greater scrutiny and criticism. The prospect of becoming a staff officer never appealed to him. I believe that he truly despises military politics and the men involved in them. Look at him now. He's a sailor at heart. Only when he's standing on the bridge of a ship at sea does he seem to be happy."

"The antithesis of Admiral Yamamoto," Genda observed. "Admiral Yamamoto thrives in such surroundings. He bends people to his will with ease. And thinks nothing of it."

"Exactly, and that's the reason for much of the discord between the two of them. I believe Admiral Yamamoto sees a threat in Admiral Nagumo. A threat that doesn't exist. "

"It seems like such a sad struggle that neither one can win."

Kusaka looked at Genda. "Life is a struggle and war even more so. We must strive to do the best we can no matter the circumstances."

He turned to leave and felt Genda's hand on his arm.

"Sir?"

"Yes."

"I wanted to apologize for my harsh words directed at your attempt to honor our Pearl Harbor casualties. I did not mean to offend you or question your actions. I realize you're truly concerned about the fliers, and they know it, too. I thank you for your efforts on their behalf."

Kusaka smiled. "I do not dwell on the past and neither should you. The present is more than enough to occupy our attention. The future is a story yet to be written. Let us strive to remain in the moment with our thoughts and deeds."

Genda bowed. "You are most understanding, sir."

Kusaka returned the gesture. "And you are a fine officer whose skills will be needed in the coming days. You should get some rest."

Another fit of coughing as reply, Genda waved and walked away.

"A message, sir." A runner appeared and handed Kusaka a slip of paper. He remained discretely nearby, prepared to deliver a reply.

Kusaka opened the page and read: *Operation K canceled. Enemy ships present at French Frigate Shoals prevent refueling of scout plane.* His eyes closed and then flipped back open. He thought, to most people, this would appear to be another ill omen. I'm not like most people. Breathe . . . reflect. Things are not as they appear. Nor are they otherwise. Remain in the present. The future is but a promise . . . as hollow as bamboo. Things happen as a result of causes and effects . . . not due to luck or fate.

"Has Admiral Nagumo seen this?" Kusaka asked the messenger.

"Yes, sir."

"You are excused."

The young man bowed and hurried away. Kusaka held up the paper and released it, watching it float away on the breeze.

22. RAMSEY
May 31 – 09:00 Hours

Ramsey took one last look at the weather report before making a few more notes on his search plan. Over the next several days, rain and heavy fog were due to move in from the northwest. It will be hard to locate the enemy arriving from that direction, Ramsey thought. He glanced up when one of the large gooney birds that Midway was famous for wandered through the open door. It made a clumsy circle of the Quonset hut flapping its wings and staring at him.

"You don't know how to knock?" seemed like the proper thing to ask.

It reached the door, halted and glanced back at him. A long, low mooing sound broke from its beak as it lumbered out into the sunshine, almost knocking Simard down. He nimbly dodged, stepped through the opening, and watched the bird wobble off.

He pointed a thumb out of the door. "Friend of yours?"

"That happens once or twice a day. I'm wondering if it's a female looking for something. She seems rather irate. You didn't happen to put this hut on top of her nest did you?"

Simard smiled, pointed to the chart spread out in front of him. "Have you figured it out?"

"I'm thinking with the inclement weather moving in we can expect an early morning attack in a few days. Nagumo's bunch is probably sailing in the midst of it, trying to stay concealed. That is, if Admiral Nimitz's is correct in his assumptions."

"You think he could be wrong?"

"We've got to be prepared whatever the case." Ramsey pointed at the chart. "Admiral Nimitz wants to include the B-17s in the search patterns. He needs them at the expected Japanese rendezvous point around 1500 hours every day. It should give us a heads up that the strike will come the next morning."

Simard studied the flight plans. "Sounds like you've got everything covered. We're expecting another flight of nine B-17s today."

"And General Neal. Was he advised of this?"

"I talked to him this morning. He's under orders to put them at your disposal."

"Admiral Nimitz has long arms," Ramsey remarked.

"He certainly jumped on the list of things that Shannon and I sent him. He provided us everything he could, as quickly as possible."

"Yes, just not enough of any single commodity."

Simard offered Ramsey an amused look. "Speaking of General Neal, you seem to have made quite the impression on him during his short stay here. He and I spent some time this morning in deep conversation with you as the subject matter."

"Trying to conceive a way to get me that next promotion I so desperately deserve?"

"More like hand-picking a firing squad."

Ramsey shrugged. "What can I say? My pleasant personality and manners allow me to quickly make friends and influence people. Normally, it only takes a month or so after I report to a new post before the tar and feathers are issued. I gave up trying to understand the reason a long time ago. Some ignorant people just do not understand me and my ways."

"I don't suppose that you ever considered the confusion could be your fault?"

Ramsey pasted a reflective look upon his face and stroked his chin before shaking his head and answering, "No, it never crossed my mind."

Simard chuckled and walked over to the coffee pot. He reached to pick it up and glanced back at Ramsey. "Fresh?"

"I'm not sure that the word 'fresh' pertains to *anything* on Midway."

"I'll take my chances."

Ramsey raised his mug containing cold coffee, considered it for a second, and set it back down. "Speaking of the equipment that Admiral Nimitz rushed out here, I just hope it's enough. The thought of five or six enemy fleet carriers bearing down on us makes for long nights of waiting."

"I know what you mean. You almost wish they'd hurry up and show and then feel guilty about such thoughts. When it happens, many good men are going to die. That's nothing to wish for."

Ramsey locked eyes with Simard. "Just keep telling yourself that we need to give them more casualties than they give us. We can't afford to remain on the losing end of things. The Japs are rapidly forcing us into a corner from which there is no escape. It's the only way to look at it. The only way to keep your sanity."

"That's the key?"

"Yes, and remember one more thing."

"That is?"

"While you're clinging to your sanity in all of this madness, try not to lose grasp of your humanity. I truly believe it's the one thing that separates us from the enemy."

* * *

"We're glad to have your men," Ramsey said to Lieutenant Colonel Walter Sweeney Jr., whose hand he shook. "We've got one nasty battle brewing and we can certainly use all the help we can get."

Sweeney's youthful, handsome face broke into an easy grin. "Are you kidding? My guys are aching for a chance to get at the Japs. We've been twiddling our thumbs too long. This is a golden opportunity for us."

Ramsey cocked his head to study Sweeney. "I hope they still feel that way when they see how primitive the conditions are around here."

"My men can deal with anything these sailors and marines can deal with. The Army Air Force will do its part."

"Amen," Ramsey said.

Sweeney flashed him an odd look but remained silent. The two of them fell in together and walked toward the operations hut. Ramsey eyed Sweeney scrutinizing the runway lined with aircraft. Brewster Buffaloes shared the immediate area with a small group of relatively new Dauntless SBD dive bombers. Men were everywhere, working on machines or moving material and equipment. A tangible sense of urgency lined each weary, dirty face.

Sweeney pointed at an obsolete Vindicator. "I don't know about the conditions, but you certainly have some primitive aircraft. This place would make a fine museum."

"It'll fly and carry bombs or torpedoes," Ramsey replied. "We intend to throw everything we've got at the Japs."

Sweeney halted and stared. "Why are those men fueling that F4F by hand out of a drum?"

Ramsey had to sigh. "Those are some of the primitive conditions. About a week ago, demolition charges were placed around some of the facilities to blow them in case the Japs succeed in landing."

"And?"

"Someone decided to test the wiring of the charges and found a problem."

"A problem?"

"Some wires were crossed and the test concluded when the fuel supply accidentally blew up. The good news was the demolition stuff works. The bad news was it played hell with our refueling operations. Right now, the only way we can get fuel inside aircraft is to do it by hand. It's slow and hard but it gets the job done."

Sweeney licked his lips and tilted his head. "A casualty of war I suppose."

"That's what I keep reminding myself. It makes the time pass a little easier."

"I'll have my men lend a hand."

"We'd appreciate it. I'd like to get your bunch back into the air as soon as possible. Admiral Nimitz wants to add your group to the search parties. We'll need to modify your B-17s with a bomb bay fuel tank and give them a half load of bombs."

"No rest for the weary?"

"I'm sorry. We'll all be exhausted by the time this thing is over. Exhausted or . . ." Ramsey's voice drifted off to hang heavy in the hot, salty air, his meaning clear.

"I understand, and we'll get right on it," Sweeney said. "Is there some place where I can toss my bag?"

Ramsey forced a smile as his eyesight darted to a row of tents nestled on the far edge of the field. "Now we're back to the primitive conditions I was telling you about."

23. WALDRON
May 31 – 14:00 Hours

Waldron strode into the full conference room and found a chair with the other officers. He nodded at Commander Ring, the Carrier *Hornet's* Air Group Commander and waited until Admiral Mitscher and Captain Mason walked up to the front. Mason took a seat, leaving Mitscher standing alone.

"I wanted to take this opportunity to discuss our upcoming air strike," Mitscher said, "and allow for discussion and comments. To assure the best chance of success, we'll use group attack procedure. I want those SBDs and TBDs making their drop runs at the same time, giving the enemy too many targets to concentrate on and forcing them to divide their defenses. It'll take coordination and concentration from all of you."

Not to mention more than a little luck, Waldron knew. The key to the operation is for all of the various flight groups to arrive simultaneously at the target. I don't like the odds of that happening.

"We'll follow standard procedure and launch the fighter escorts first, followed by dive bombers, and bring the torpedo planes up to an empty deck last," Mitscher continued. "Any questions?"

"Admiral." Waldron raised his hand, "wouldn't it be better to launch my slower TBDs first? It'd give us a head start in making the trip. The faster SBDs and F4Fs will have no trouble running us down and joining formation."

"No, your planes will require maximum deck length to take off and will fly much lower than the fighters and bombers. They can use the time it takes to launch your torpedo planes for climbing to altitude."

Waldron focused on Mitscher and rubbed his chin. Both of the other groups will climb to altitude? Could that mean?

"Sir, do I understand you to say the fighters and dive bombers will form up together and make transit?" he asked. "I'd like to request at least some of the fighters stay with my slower, more vulnerable planes."

"I'm forced to split my fighter resources very thin as it is," Mitscher replied. "I learned from Coral Sea that the Grummans need an altitude advantage to dive down and attack the Zero.

Without it, they are a very vulnerable target themselves. They'll remain upstairs with the SBDs."

"I must agree with Johnny," Ring spoke up, "that at least some of the escort remain with the TBDs. His group will be an easy target for the enemy Zeroes. If the number of our fighters currently delegated to the mission isn't sufficient, add some more and use them to cover our TBDs."

Focusing on Ring, Mitscher rubbed his jaw. "Need I remind you the primary duty of our fighter aircraft is to protect *Hornet*? Without her flight deck to conduct operations from, nothing is possible or accomplished in regards to attacking the enemy. We must keep a large group here to provide CAP. The number of fighters assigned to escort duty is too small to split between the SBDs and TBDs. All things considered, I have made my decision."

A concluding silence dropped over the room like a theater curtain closing at the end of a show. Waldron reached up, scratched the back of his itchy head. He glanced at Ring and offered a slight shoulder shrug and smile. The king has spoken, Waldron thought. Long live the king.

* * *

"Gentlemen." Waldron's calm voice cut through the idle chatter in the ready room. He stood up front bathed in the severe, yellow lighting and wreathed in cigarette smoke. The noise died as each man focused attention on him.

"I guess you've all figured out by now that we're headed for battle. Let me tell you it's going to be a big one. About as big as the one held at Little Big Horn when Colonel George Custer found himself on the losing end of a disagreement with some of my ancestors. In fact, this entire affair is shaping up to be similar to what happened to Old George and his boys back in seventy-six."

He paused as his eyesight swept the room. The intercom squawked, ordering the executive officer to the bridge. The deep-throated rumble of an airplane engine briefly coming to life amidst the background noise of a carrier at war barged through the open outer door.

"The difference is this time we're playing the part of my illustrious ancestors, and the Japs are the Seventh Calvary. We're going to make sure the results are the same.

"Some people think this battle might be the biggest of the entire war . . . maybe even the turning point. If so, it will be a historical and glorious event that we'll all look back on one day and feel proud we participated in it. You'll be telling your grandkids about your service in the war."

He sensed anxious distraction among the men, backed up to the blackboard, and lifted a piece of chalk. Skating it across the board produced a loud, irritating screech. The sound, very reminiscent of an owl in extreme pain, drew an angry murmur from the men. He glanced over his shoulder and grinned.

"I just wanted to make sure you're all awake and paying attention," he said.

"Skipper, you couldn't have just asked us if we were all awake?" Ellison asked.

Waldron tilted his head and assumed a puzzled expression on his face. "Did I just hear you say that you wanted to go run the flight deck for the next hour, or would you rather shut up and listen up?"

Ellison swallowed and flashed a sheepish grin. "I do believe if it's all the same with you, I'll shut up and listen up, sir."

Waldron scanned the room. "Anyone else want to volunteer for something instead of shutting up and listening up? Don't be bashful. I'm sure there're decks to swab somewhere on this ship."

Waldron cast a quick glance over at his executive officer. "They do still swab decks in this man's navy, don't they?"

The XO squinted, thought for just a moment. "If they don't, I'm sure there's something that needs scraping or painting."

Waldron grinned. "That'll do. Does anyone want a scraper or paint brush? Come on. Speak right up."

Silence answered the question. The intercom boomed once more to herald the watch change. The vibration on the soles of their feet increased, signaling that the large ship was picking up speed.

"As I was saying," Waldron said, turning back to the board and drawing a large circle near the top, "the Japs are expected to arrive within the next day or two somewhere from the west or northwest. There'll be many enemy vessels, including between four and six carriers, so there'll be plenty of targets to go around. Everyone should find something to get a hit on."

The chalk dropped to the lower right of the board where he sketched three rectangles. "Within the next day or so, we'll be meeting up with *Yorktown*'s group a little northeast of Midway. Admiral Nimitz named the rendezvous spot 'Point Luck.'"

"Did you say *Yorktown*?" a voice called from the back of the room.

"She's patched up, but ready to go. The fellows at Pearl are miracle workers."

"And her air groups?" someone else asked.

Waldron tilted his head down as he raised his right hand. "That's all been taken care of. She's loaded with a full complement of aircraft and itching for a fight. Any more questions?"

He stepped back from the board and stood for a moment in silence. His vision fixed upon the large circle as he considered what it represented. *We've yearned for a chance to meet the Japs. To use their own tactics to engage and defeat them. Give them their due; the Japs are excellent at airborne torpedo attack. It's time my boys demonstrate that the U.S. Navy can release hell from the skies, too.*

"The plan is to launch the first attack before daylight. We'll hit them from the east, right out of the rising sun. What's it called . . . poetic justice?"

"Naw, it's called a Texas-sized ass whipping!" Gay twanged out.

A round of hoots and laughter swept the room. A horde of brown shoes rattled against the steel deck like a summer hailstorm on a tin roof. Waldron grinned and waited for the metallic symphony to cease.

"We'll go in low and angry, just like we've discussed. Bellies flat against the water so the Zeroes can't get to them. We'll wait until we can count the rivets in the side of one of those flat-topped sons-of-bitches before cutting those pickles loose and heading for the barn. We'll come back, reload, and go out again. We'll keep right on attacking throughout the day."

He cocked his head back. "Any questions?"

"What kind of fighter escort are we going to have?" Abercrombie asked.

Leave it to the squadron's resident doom and gloom predictor to ask the one question that I don't wish to answer, Waldron thought. *I'd rather them worry about making a good torpedo run and release. That's what we're here for. But . . . I owe them the truth.*

He shifted his voice to a serious tone. "Admiral Mitscher is keeping most of the F4Fs here to fly umbrella over *Hornet*. He believes protecting her is the priority. As for the strike, he wants the small fighter escort group to stay together with the SBDs at higher altitude."

He paused and looked around the room, noticing nervous-looking faces staring back. The snap of cigarette lighters and a few dry coughs filled the air with restless noise. Hell, even I didn't like the way *that* sounded. My boys deserve a better explanation.

"I don't necessarily agree with the admiral, but it's not my place to judge. He's faced with making decisions affecting every man on this ship and determining the course of action. His decisions could decide the battle's outcome. Command can be one hell of a lonely spot. He deserves our support. He certainly has mine."

He looked down and then back up. "I'm sure he has yours, too."

Heads nodded in silent agreement. The intercom buzzed in the background calling someone to the forward hangar. He welcomed the interruption, which gave him a chance to finish up.

"The SBDs are faster, and should arrive over the target first. There's a chance they'll draw off some of the Zeroes and allow us to sneak in underneath, but don't count on that. Let's be prepared to shoot it out with the damn Japs."

"Any more questions?" he asked, but heard none. "Training time's over. For the next few days, I want all of you to get some rest and prepare your minds for combat. We need to tidy up our personal business. Make sure you write those letters to your loved ones. There's a chance some of us won't come back."

He pursed his lips and walked toward the door. Pausing, he turned back to face them.

"Let's be prepared for all of those damn Zeroes to jump on us, and glory in the combat."

24. RAMSEY
June 01 – 21:00 Hours

Ramsey choked back another mouthful of cold coffee and made a notation on the chart. He briefly thought about the tropical night falling outside chasing the daylight away and tried to remember what day of the week it was. *Does it matter? I'm still on Midway. The Japanese are still headed this way.*

He had to lean sideways to keep from casting a shadow on his workspace under the weak lighting. Completing the day's communications, Captain Simard sat across the room next to the radio operator.

"I'd like to have word with you, Mister Ramsey."

The voice rolled into the dugout like thundering surf, and Ramsey instantly pictured the sour visage of Brigadier General Neal, Army Air Force, before he entered. The inspection by Neal over the past few days was an ordeal he definitely did not want to endure again. Ramsey's head ducked between his shoulders as he heard the ominous footsteps stomp closer. *I wonder if I can sneak out and swim over to Eastern Island. I could watch the airplanes taking off and landing. Make an evening of it.*

"I'm talking to you, mister."

Better to hear the man out and get this over with as painlessly as possible, Ramsey decided.

"I asked you to call me Logan, sir." He continued marking for a second and then steeled himself and glanced up. He flashed a smile. "The mister is not necessary. After all we've been through, must we still be so formal?"

Neal's weak chin jutted out as his hands clamped down on his thick waist. "And I'm still not amused at your attempts at humor. Nor do I appreciate your dismissal of military protocol. You happen to be talking to a general officer who severely outranks you."

Dismissal of military protocol? Ramsey thought, before he said, "General, I'm certainly aware of that fact and I mean no disrespect. I'm also terribly busy. Sometime in the next few days, this place is facing a major enemy attack leading up to an invasion. I have patrol routes to issue and aircraft sorties to plan. I don't have time for chitchat." He threw a loose salute and returned to his navigation computations.

"Chitchat?" Neal gasped and seemed to sputter.

A barbed pause followed as Ramsey heard Neal sucking in deep breaths. Perhaps he'll take my subtle hint and leave, Ramsey thought. Neal cleared his throat. Perhaps not.

"The upcoming Japanese operation is what I want to discuss with you." Neal's voice sounded strained and clipped off. "My B-17 crews are flying too many hours and not getting sufficient rest. They'll be in no shape for flying combat missions if the enemy shows up. This is no way to prepare for a suspected attack of such magnitude."

Ramsey looked over at Captain Simard and noticed him conveniently occupied with writing out a message. That's right, leave me to deal with this all by myself, he thought. I don't have enough problems as it is. Make me the bad guy.

It's just another job, Logan, a nasty one, but one that needs doing. Keep on telling myself that. This, too, shall pass. He sighed, placed the pencil down, and turned to face Neal.

"Might I respectfully ask if they told you that, sir?"

"What?" Ramsey's sudden change of tone seemed to catch Neal by surprise.

"Colonel Sweeney's bunch. Did they complain to you? I mean, in those exact words . . . flying too many hours and not getting enough rest?"

Neal snatched himself fully erect and glared down at Ramsey. "That is privileged information between my officers and me. I'll not discuss it with you. The only concern of yours is correcting the situation."

Ramsey dropped his head and slowly rubbed his bristled jaw. Now what? Nimitz had stressed interservice cooperation. *We are all in this fight together and must remain united.* Hallelujah and pass the ammunition. That was easy enough for him to say back at Pearl Harbor. I have to deal with the real world of a front line combat zone and the martinets who inhabit it. He looked up at Neal.

"General, all I can say is that I'm demanding no more of your B-17 crews than I am of the PBYs and all the other men stationed here. We're all working long hours and getting too little sleep. We're not eating enough or allowing ourselves to wind down after a stressful day. We just don't have the time for such things. We snatch a quick nap and get right back to work. The enemy is coming to invade this place whether we're prepared or not. I'm doing the best that I can to see that we are prepared, as is every man currently stationed here. Agreed, these are not the ideal circumstances leading up to a major battle, but we have no choice in the matter. The war won't wait."

Neal's head leaned to the side. "Are you saying that you intend to do nothing about this?"

Ramsey's arms rose slightly and then he slapped his palms down onto the tabletop. A twinge of satisfaction coursed through him as he noticed Neal flinch visibly and take a step backward.

"To put it in a nutshell, yes sir, that's exactly what I'm saying. I don't know who said what to you or what the context might have been. To be honest, I don't really care. Perhaps the concern is purely your own. I can respect that. I've heard no complaints from Colonel Sweeney or his men. They're diligently performing their duty and I appreciate it. The daily routine shall remain unchanged until the enemy carrier force is sighted. Then it will get a lot worse."

"And I maintain that my crews must have sufficient rest in order to carry out attacks should the enemy show up. In my opinion, *that* assumption is a matter for debate. Hawaii could very well be the Japanese's target, not this place. General Emmons back at Pearl Harbor certainly seems to think so. Rest assured that I will personally report this situation and my other inspection results to General Tinker in Hawaii for prompt review. Perhaps you'll sing a different tune afterwards."

Neal turned to leave.

Ramsey bit his lip, felt blood trickle down. Let him go, Logan, let it go. You have a job to do. Do it. This too shall pass. It's not worth getting angry and saying the wrong thing.

Or is it?

"Well." Ramsey carefully chose each word. "I'm not much of a singer and this is certainly not a Broadway show. Admiral Nimitz is convinced that the enemy will show up here and that's good enough for me. I'm proceeding as if that's a fact . . . not an assumption. I'm following his direct orders and will continue doing so until he changes those orders. He made his point very clear to me before I left Hawaii. No disrespect, sir." Ramsey offered a tight smile.

"Humph," Neal replied as he took a step toward the entrance.

"General, what time are you planning on taking off tomorrow?"

The unexpected question brought Neal to an abrupt stop.

"Why do you ask?" he said without turning around.

"I'm enforcing a military quarantine first thing in the morning. There will be no flights out of here without my express authorization. Such authorization could take a while. If I have to get my combat aircraft up quickly, I don't want the airspace and landing strip tied up. If I were you, I'd plan to leave right at dawn otherwise you could be stranded here for a while. We should be able to squeeze you in after the morning patrol takes off."

"That's a threat and I don't believe you'll follow through with it," Neal replied as he glanced back at Ramsey. "I shall leave whenever I'm ready tomorrow."

"He will follow through," Simard said as he spoke up for the first time. He rose from his seat and walked over to stand next to Ramsey. "I'm in command of Midway and in complete agreement with Logan. He's doing exactly as Admiral Nimitz directed. If he believes that the airfield shouldn't be tied up, I will enforce those orders."

Neal snatched his jacket tail down and barreled out of the dugout. Fighting a smile, Ramsey felt relief at Simard's support. This is a change, he thought. It's about time the cavalry came riding to my rescue instead of trampling on me.

"You were a little rough on him," Simard remarked.

"Was I?"

"Yes, you were."

"The Japs will be a lot rougher."

"I didn't say he didn't deserve it, but you could have tossed him a bone. Promised to look into the matter."

"I don't make promises that I don't intend to keep. Besides, I might've gotten fleas."

Simard returned to the communications desk, stopped, and glanced over at Ramsey. A smile crossed his creased face that Ramsey mirrored.

"I must admit, *Mister Ramsey*, there's never a dull moment with you around. I didn't believe half the stories I'd heard about you. Now I have some of my own."

Ramsey shrugged. "Just doing my job. Sometimes you have to step on a few toes to get a fellow to pull his feet in."

"Uh, huh," Simard said and sat down. He picked up a communication and glanced over the top of it back at Ramsey.

"Would you really quarantine his aircraft?"

"What do you think?"

25. KUSAKA
June 02 – 10:00 Hours

Fighting to maintain his calm facade, Kusaka stood between the two beds in *Akagi*'s sick bay looking down at their occupants.

"So, Fuchida, you felt lonely here and asked Genda to join you?"

Weak smiles upon two pale faces greeted his jest. Genda coughed, tried to answer but could not.

"I should be up very soon," Fuchida said. "I grow stronger each day."

Kusaka took note of the officer's frail condition and doubted his brave words. Appendicitis aggravated by the stress from his duties had wrought havoc on Fuchida's body. Rest and time were critical for his recovery. Such things could not be hurried. Kusaka motioned toward Genda.

"And our friend's condition grew worse? I feared that would happen."

"Some type of respiratory infection," Fuchida answered. "He's not to exert himself. You can see that talking often brings on the coughing fits."

"Ah, the perfect junior officer . . . one who cannot talk back," Kusaka joked. He felt joy at the smile on both men's damp faces.

The cloying smell of alcohol hung heavy in the hot, damp atmosphere, and sweat soaked through Kusaka's stiff uniform. As a refuge for the sick and injured, an aircraft carrier's sick bay buried within the bowels of the large ship seemed an unhealthy place to be. He reached up, crooked a finger inside his collar and pried the sticky clothing free.

"I'll not linger," he said. "I just wanted to check up on the two of you."

"It was most kind of you, but please don't leave so soon. I'm anxious to hear of the latest developments and I'm certain Genda would be, too."

Kusaka saw the pleading expression in Genda's eyes, fought down his urge to flee. He paused for a second to center his breath and focus. In times of extreme stress, the line separating physical from mental illness is easily crossed, he thought. Taking a small step away from the beds, he forced a smile.

"We're proceeding on course toward Midway, and for the present time, the rain seems to have stopped. It's still dark and foggy, which is keeping us screened from enemy submarines and aircraft."

"Poor visibility?" Fuchida asked.

"Yes, it's difficult to maneuver the ships safely. Tomorrow we're scheduled to rendezvous with tankers and refuel. That could be postponed a day or two."

"This was to be expected," Fuchida reminded. "The weather is still forecast to clear?"

"Yes."

Kusaka cast a glance around at the constricted surroundings and tried to come up with a convincing reason to leave. Life is suffering. This place focuses it. Pain and dying inhabits this place. I feel unwelcome. I must go. Two sets of eyes bore into him; the thoughts that he sensed behind them clamped his feet to the spot.

"Sir, you seem disturbed," Genda finally croaked in a hoarse voice.

"This entire operation depends so much on surprise and secrecy," Kusaka said to explain his behavior.

"And?"

"I question the secrecy of our endeavors."

"You have reason to feel this way?"

"Intelligence tells us that enemy radio traffic out of Hawaii has increased and many of the messages are marked *urgent*. It would seem their suspicions are raised. I'm concerned they've caught the scent of our operation."

Fuchida's mustache twitched. "Considering our ship movements, that would seem oddly coincidental. Could some of our forces have been observed?"

"Perhaps. There's also a report that some of our patrol planes out of Wotje encountered American PBYs and fired on them. Unfortunately, they didn't shoot them down."

"Anything else?"

"Wake Island reports an increase in enemy submarine activity to the northeast of there. The coincidences continue to multiply."

Fuchida slid an arm behind his pillow and stared at the ceiling. "The PBY encounter leads me to believe the enemy has extended his air patrols from Midway out to seven hundred miles. It makes me wonder if their suspicions are indeed raised."

"I agree," Kusaka echoed, "and I also believe the Americans have established a submarine patrol line to the southwest of Midway if not further. The weather situation is good in that area, with plenty of visibility."

Fuchida's eyes and thoughts met his. "Given our delays in departure and the poor weather surrounding *Kido Butai*, it's very likely that Admiral Kondo's Invasion Force is a good ways ahead of us in reaching its staging point. It could be discovered a day or two before our scheduled air strike. That could indeed complicate matters for us."

Kusaka felt relieved to discover his concerns had merit. Fuchida was a cool, logical thinker whose opinion Kusaka valued. It seems I'm not barking at shadows. Perhaps something is indeed hiding out of the light.

"What does Admiral Nagumo say about this?" Fuchida asked.

A nasty taste soured Kusaka's mouth. "What can he say? We've heard nothing on enemy fleet movements from our own submarine scouts. There's no definite information that the Americans are aware of our plans. We can't break radio silence to ascertain whether we've missed any messages transmitting intelligence updates. Admiral Yamamoto made it clear that his orders are final and not to be broken. He's certainly tied Admiral Nagumo's hands and feet together. We sail blindly onward, hoping for the best."

A sound from Genda drew their attention. He coughed, cleared his throat and inhaled deeply.

"We are prepared and our fliers are the best there are," he croaked. "Admiral Yamamoto knows this and so do I."

Kusaka stared at him thinking, leave it to Yamamoto's handpicked air officer to defend the man. The sound of Japanese bombs falling uncontested on Pearl Harbor still echoed in the ears of both men credited with the planning. Yet, it's foolish to believe all such surprise attacks will go off so smoothly and uncontested.

"So my concerns are nonsense?"

Genda shook his head, coughed, and extended a hand until the spell passed. "I didn't say that, sir. I'm just pointing out that we've seen no reason to believe the enemy is capable of stopping us. They have neither the equipment nor the skilled pilots to match our best aircraft and fliers."

Kusaka dropped his mouth open. "Did you learn nothing from Coral Sea? Those unskilled American pilots sunk *Shoho* and damaged *Shokaku*. The Port Moresby Invasion Force was turned back. Perhaps they lack true fighting heart, but they can still be dangerous under the proper circumstances. You must not forget this."

Genda strained and his face turned beet-red. "Admiral Inoue had nothing but junior pilots, and they still sank both the *Yorktown* and *Saratoga*. He had victory within his grasp when he broke off and—"

The loud clatter of a tray falling onto the deck sent a metallic clang vibrating against the walls. Kusaka felt relief when the clamor choked off Genda's fervent reply. The presence of sick or wounded men had always disturbed Kusaka. The open spaces of the flight deck called out to him. He made to leave.

"I must return to my station," he said.

Genda and Fuchida fought to rise and he quickly waved them back down. "You must both rest. We'll soon have great need for your services."

They bowed their heads and he returned the gesture. Spinning on his heels, he quickly strode away. He worked his mouth fiercely as he walked and thought. If blind belief in one's ability were a weapon, we would soon win this war.

* * *

"Admiral Nagumo, it's imperative that we maintain the sailing schedule if we're to attack Midway as ordered tomorrow," Kusaka said. "We must notify this task force that the change of course will go through as planned."

A scowl came over Nagumo's face as an open palm rose up toward the bridge window. A cold, heavy fog blanketed the glass, obscuring vision. *Akagi* might have been alone in the vast Pacific for all of the evidence their eyesight could gather.

"And how would you have me do this? Visibility is zero, signal flags and blinking searchlights useless."

Kusaka was surprised at the fire in Nagumo's voice; he looked at him with approval. Perhaps the approaching battle was stirring the warrior within the old sailor's soul.

"You know the answer to that question. We must break radio silence and notify the fleet of the course change."

"*Hai.*" Nagumo's hand flew up to his neck and slowly stroked it. "It would appear that I'm caught between the proverbial rock and a hard place. I must send out orders to make a course change but am denied the means of doing so."

Kusaka sympathized with his plight, but recognized the immediate need. He pressed his point. "If we do not destroy the Midway-based air forces and prevent them from defending the atoll, our landing operations will be strongly opposed. The invasion and operation schedule will be upset. We must focus on this now."

"But where is the enemy fleet?"

"We don't know. If it's at Pearl Harbor, our forces will have plenty of time to take position to meet it provided we follow the plan schedule."

"And if all of the recent urgent enemy communications are evidence that the Americans have already sailed, what then?"

"Those are questions I can't answer, but we must stay the course set out for us. I'd recommend we use the short-range interfleet radio to relay the course change."

Nagumo turned away from him and stared out the bridge window. Hands clasped behind his back and shoulders stooped, he stood in silence. Kusaka watched him, felt the great burden weighing the man down, and silently cursed Yamamoto for placing Nagumo in such a difficult situation. He caught himself, recognized the discord of his thoughts. Those who are free of resentful thoughts surely find peace. To find peace he must free himself of these resentful feelings.

"Admiral Nagumo?"

"Send the message," Nagumo said, "and make it as short and as quick as possible. If I am to perish by my deeds, let me die with a sword in my hand."

26. SPRUANCE
June 02 – 10:30 Hours

Spruance buttoned his coat up against the drizzle and then continued his walk of the flight deck. The salty breeze carried a damp, claustrophobic feel to it. A vague feeling of unrest, not known before, pushed him like chaff against the wind. As time grew short and battle neared, his daily exercise period steadily dropped off. He paused to look out across the expanse of airy ocean at the faint but comforting sight of the cruiser *Northampton*. The familiar confines of her bridge beckoned to him, ready to welcome him back should he choose to give up this notion of commanding a carrier task force. He thought, but how can I do that? Too much depends on me to back out now. Nimitz has confidence in my ability to lead. To make the difficult decisions. Senior officers with air operations experience were available, but the critical command fell to me. Hard work and perseverance does pay off if a man is willing to apply himself.

"Sir!"

He turned at Oliver's call and waited for him to catch up. Oliver appeared red in the face and gasping deeply from the effort. Bending over, he placed his hands on his knees, and fought to catch his breath. He spat on the deck before glancing up at Spruance.

"How in the world can anyone walk as fast as you do?"

"I get lots of practice while waiting for things to happen. If you've come to join me, I'd rather be alone today. Perhaps tomorrow."

"No, sir. As much as I'm sure I'd enjoy that, I've other duties. I just wanted to let you know that Browning has already released orders for the day's air operations to the entire task force."

"Good."

Surprise registered on Oliver's face. "Good? You always wanted to review the daily orders before issuing them to the rest of the force."

"I was commanding cruisers. That's something I understand and am experienced at doing."

Oliver slowly shook his head. "I'm not sure I understand."

"Planning air operations is an entirely different area for me. For now, I intend to leave that to the experts. Browning is an expert. I'm not."

Oliver saluted. "Aye, sir. I'll return to my duties."

Oliver turned to leave with Spruance watching him. There's something else on his mind, Spruance thought. I'll give him a few seconds. Oliver rewarded his patience by exhaling deeply and pivoting around.

"Something else?"

Oliver appeared to take courage from his friendly demeanor. "Permission to speak freely, sir?"

"Go ahead."

"I'm certainly not the one to question your methods, but with all due respect, is that a good idea? Allowing Browning to issue orders without your approval?"

He paused for a moment until Spruance replied, "Go on."

Oliver glanced around at the busy flight deck before stepping closer.

"I understand your reasons for doing this but there's more involved here. The men, especially the officers, are watching to see how you handle yourself. Given your lack of air operations experience, I'm thinking they're questioning your ability to command this task force. If you continue to allow Browning the freedom to make decisions without your consent, they're never going to develop confidence in you."

Spruance slowly rubbed his jaw, considering Oliver's words. Oliver seemed to grow concerned by the silence. He shuffled his feet and cleared his throat.

"All due respect, sir," Oliver blurted, "I didn't mean to suggest—"

"I understand your feelings and appreciate your candor, but there's something larger and more important here," Spruance said as he cut him off.

"Sir?"

"We're about to engage a superior enemy force in a crucial battle. Admiral Nimitz believes it could be pivotal in determining our future strategy in the Pacific. I don't have time to concern myself with making a favorable impression on anyone. I must do whatever it takes to secure a victory. If that means giving

Browning extra leeway in conducting air operations, so be it. He's experienced in these matters. I trust Admiral Halsey's opinion."

"Aye, sir." Oliver moved backward.

Spruance thought, I shouldn't take my frustration out on him. It's not his fault that I'm learning on the job. Browning could be assuming more than he should, but I'll give him the benefit of the doubt. So far, he seems to be conducting operations correctly. I'll remain patient. At least until he does otherwise. In the meantime, it wouldn't hurt to speak to Browning . . . make sure he keeps me informed of his actions. I mustn't be too lenient.

"I'll talk to Browning. Have him meet me in my quarters in an hour."

* * *

"Miles." Spruance glanced up at the large man towering over his desk, "I wanted to discuss with you the issuance of orders without my approval."

He deliberately did not offer Browning a seat, wanted to maintain the cold formality of the meeting. The trickle of sweat coursing down Browning's neck and collecting in his collar drew Spruance's attention. It is indeed warm inside my cabin, but not that warm, he thought. Browning is nervous. Good.

"Sir, you're referring to?" Browning appeared puzzled.

"I'm referring to the air operations orders you issued to the task force this morning. You've been sharing them with me for approval. Why not today?"

Browning shrugged. "You were busy taking your walk and I didn't want to disturb you."

"I can appreciate that, but performing my duties does not disturb me. It's my job. I will not be left out of the command loop again. Is that understood?"

"I thought you had confidence in my abilities."

"Admiral Halsey has confidence in your abilities, and I have faith in his opinion of you. I'm doing my best to remain in the background and allow all of my officers to do their jobs, not just you. It's how I run my command. That does not mean that I'm totally uninvolved or to be left out of command decisions."

Browning's florid face darkened and he came to rigid attention. "I understand, sir. I'll remember my place from now on, sir."

Spruance felt his pulse quicken, thinking, why does he provoke me so? As if he's trying me. It's almost as if he feeds on discord.

I'm sure Halsey doesn't put up with it. I'll be damned if . . . no. Losing my temper is not an option. I will not stoop to that, nor is there time for doing so. Over the next few days, I'll need Browning's knowledge. The outcome of the battle could depend upon it.

"Attention Admiral Spruance," the buzzing intercom broke in. "Your presence is immediately required on the bridge."

Spruance stood and opened the door to find a flushed Oliver poised to knock on it.

"You heard the summons?" Oliver asked. Without waiting for an answer he said, "We just received a message dropped from an SBD. Admiral Fletcher is waiting for us at Point Luck."

27. RAMSEY
June 3 – 08:30 Hours

Ramsey stood outside of the command post bunker and looked up at the awakening sky. Abundant sunlight and patchy clouds precluded a beautiful day in the South Pacific. Pounding surf against sugar-white sand beckoned him to indulge his hidden child with a barefoot romp in the water. *If only I could,* he thought. *Relieve some of this tension. Forget some of the worry. Enjoy my life . . . if only for a short time. But not today. Today those emerald Pacific waves bear a threat. The threat of something much more devastating than a typhoon. The Japanese sailed on such a peaceful tide. Does the enemy lurk just beyond the hazy horizon?*

"Waiting's always the hardest part." Simard appeared at his shoulder and offered a cup of coffee.

"Thanks." He took a long drink, enjoyed the strong liquid burning its way down. "It is indeed."

Simard glanced at his watch. "The B-17s should be returning soon. Do you want to refuel and get them back up as soon as possible?"

Ramsey considered the intelligence reports on the Japanese's possible arrival time. *Today or tomorrow seemed most likely,* he thought. *We still have a large force of PBYs out making their scouting runs. Everyone's exhausted. Perhaps I should give Sweeney's group some down time.*

"Let's service them and let the crews catch a little rest. Give the PBYs time to locate something."

Falling silent, they enjoyed the last few wisps of the early morning sea breeze. The sounds of birds combined with the roaring of aircraft engines offered a discordant symphony of nature and man. A rust-eaten truck lumbered by bearing cursing marines amidst more rolls of barbed wire. The temperature rose, a sure forecast of the hot day to follow.

"Talking about the waiting," Ramsey said as he raised a pair of binoculars to his eyes, "reminds me of the first few weeks at Pearl Harbor following the Japanese attack. We waited for them to come back and finish the job . . . sure it was just a matter of time. Every door slam, horn blow or car backfire was another bomb landing. I went to bed every night with a helmet and loaded pistol close to hand. I woke up bathed in sweat."

"But this isn't the same," Simard replied.

Ramsey lowered the glasses. "No, it's not. I don't believe it's just a false alarm this time. The enemy is really coming."

A yeoman stuck his head out of the bunker. "Captain, we just received a message from Admiral Nimitz. Dutch Harbor is being attacked." He ducked back inside, leaving the two officers standing alone.

"Looks like Nimitz was correct on the first part of Yamamoto's plans," Simard said.

"I'm betting that he called the second part correctly, too," Ramsey answered. The binoculars rose, sighted on several large airplanes approaching. He focused to make out the familiar shapes of B-17s shadowed by a combat air patrol Wildcat.

"There's the first of Sweeney's bunch coming back."

They watched and counted as the heavy bombers slowly appeared, circled the field on Eastern Island, and made dusty landings. Each taxied to its designated service spot and cut the engines.

"I counted all of them," Simard said.

"Captain." The same yeoman reappeared and said, "I think you want to see this."

They followed him through the sandbagged doorway and into the dark interior. Gathered around the radio, a small group of men watched the operator fingering the touch key. One hand pressed the headphones tight to his ear as he quickly wrote down the incoming message on a large pad. Finished, he tore it off and handed it to Simard.

"Two Japanese cargo vessels sighted bearing 247 degrees, distance 470 miles," he read aloud. "Fired upon by AA."

Ramsey strode over to a table with a large chart and located the stated position. "Just two ships and they're coming from the southwest. That's not where Admiral Nimitz puts Nagumo's group. I'd also expect a carrier-based task force to have destroyers and escorts screening out in front."

"I agree."

Simard turned to the yeoman seated next to the phone. "Raise Pearl on the cable and send the message. Tell them we're holding tight until more information comes in."

Ramsey walked over to the coffeepot and poured himself another cup. He raised it to his lips while thinking about the men flying those clumsy-looking PBYs and the danger their flights entailed. They're too slow and vulnerable to put up much of a defense. A Jap pilot armed with a .45 Colt could shoot one down. However, the outcome of the impending battle hinges upon them performing their duty. He offered a silent toast in salute to their courage.

He glanced over as Colonel Shannon ambled into the dugout. Wearing a helmet and sidearm, he looked the picture of what he was, a grizzled, experienced veteran aching for a chance to meet the enemy.

"What do you make of the sighting?" Shannon asked Simard.

Simard motioned toward Ramsey. "We agree that it's not the one we're waiting for. Intelligence insists the primary attack will come from the northwest."

Shannon turned to Ramsey, his craggy face souring at the mention of the intelligence group. "Could they be wrong?"

Ramsey glanced into his cup and then over at Shannon. "I guess anything's possible. Admiral Nimitz has faith in their information. The Japs are attacking the Aleutians as Layton predicted. Layton's people also said there'd be a separate Occupation Force involved with Nagumo's operation. This sighting report could be that enemy group."

He took another sip and thought for a moment. "I don't believe the intelligence information is wrong. The fact there's no mention of destroyers or other screening vessels leading the way convinces me. Carriers would have a screen well in front of them."

Movement from the radio operator drew their attention. The young sailor picked up his pencil, jotted something, and handed it to Simard.

"Main body," he read. The two words popped like a flashbulb in the room.

Simard frowned and glanced at the operator. "That's all? No course, speed, type?"

"No, sir. It's also a different scout. JP Lyle sent the first message. This one came from Jack Reid."

"Tell them to amplify." Ramsey moved closer.

Skilled fingers worked the transmitter key, demanding more information. A few moments later, the pencil moved again and another note passed to Simard.

"Bearing 262 degrees, distance 700," he said. "That puts the PBY at the far end of its travel leg."

"That PBY has more than enough fuel to remain airborne for a long while," Ramsey said. "Repeat the directions to amplify. Ascertain ship type and numbers."

"Perhaps Intelligence was wrong. The Main Body is coming from the west." Shannon's voice contained just a trace of satisfaction.

Ramsey kept his eyes glued to the radio. "Perhaps, but it's too soon to tell."

The room fell quiet as the minutes trudged by. Ramsey forced himself to remain patient, ignoring the small jolts of electricity running throughout his body. I can do without the waiting, he thought.

Time continued to accumulate and the small group of men around the radio drifted away to their duties. Shannon returned to his own command post, leaving Ramsey and Simard to maintain close vigilance. Ramsey lit and took a few puffs of several cigarettes before tossing each away as different concerns struck him. He considered stepping outside the damp, musty concrete bunker for a breath of fresh air and changed his mind. Some inner desire forced him to stay and be present should anything develop. He would witness this battle just like the attack on Pearl Harbor.

"I'm going to get another set of eyes up in the air and headed for that last contact position," Simard said. "We still don't know enough to commit our forces."

Simard picked up the phone and made the call over to the air base on Eastern Island. An animated conversation ensued, drawing Ramsey's attention away from the radio. He flashed Simard a questioning gaze as he replaced the receiver.

"Sweeney wants to take off right away and bomb the contact," Simard explained. "I tried to tell him that we need a detailed report before blindly jumping into things. I had to remind him that Admiral Nimitz's top priority target is the Jap carriers before he agreed to wait."

Ramsey smiled in spite of the situation. I can understand Sweeney wanting to initiate an attack, he thought. It's a helpless feeling this waiting. Almost as bad as the combat. Almost. Simard's correct, though, in refusing to act blindly. Not without some idea of what we're facing. What was the old saying? Fools rush in where wise men fear to tread. Those words bear greater relevance and truth when the entire Japanese navy is bearing down on a tiny atoll that I happen to be standing on.

His eyesight fell upon the radio. He found himself wishing it were possible to reach inside and extract the needed information. He thought, what could possibly be taking Reid so long to amplify his report? He recalled his earlier thoughts about the danger of flying one of the plodding PBYs in close proximity to an enemy guarded by speedy Zero fighters, and understood. The pilot must carefully work his way closer to get a better look at the contact. Dash between the clouds and spend as much time watching the sky around you as the ocean below. It's the only chance to survive.

A sudden motion from the radio operator sent him hurrying over. He stood next to Simard and felt cold sweat slide down his back as the sailor took longer this time to decode the message. Wide eyes glanced up at both of them as he handed the sheet to Simard.

"Eleven ships, course 090, speed 19, including one small carrier, one seaplane carrier, two battleships, several cruisers, and several destroyers," he read as he gave the paper to Ramsey.

Ramsey confirmed the wording and waited while Simard instructed the phone operator to send the communication on to Pearl. Rubbing his hands together, Simard turned back to Ramsey.

"I don't know what it is, but it is a definite target," he said. "I'm going to get Sweeney mounted up and headed out that way. There's plenty of time for him to make an attack today and still be ready to make another tomorrow."

"Let's do it."

And so it begins, Ramsey thought. God help us all.

28. FLETCHER
June 03 – 1300 Hours

"I don't care what that says, I don't believe this is the Main Body."

Fletcher, Lewis, and Buckmaster sat in the flag mess, nursing cups of coffee. Fletcher held the floor, pointing to a sheet of paper lying on the table in front of them that Pederson had brought in.

"The position given is a lot farther south than Chet figured. The types of ships sighted don't add up to a carrier strike force either."

"And the Dutch Harbor attack?" Lewis stirred up a whirlpool inside his mug. "This thing appears to be starting exactly the way Admiral Nimitz predicted. Midway could be next . . . and soon."

"Not yet."

"You sound mighty sure of that," Buckmaster replied. "Is there something you're not sharing with me?"

Fletcher smiled. "You've been around long enough to know not to ask those kinds of questions, Buck."

"I suppose so, but you can't blame a fellow for trying."

"No, I guess not." Fletcher picked up the paper. "I'm more concerned with why we haven't spotted Nagumo's force. This group must be way out in front of the carriers."

"Weather report says there's still an area of stormy weather to the northwest," Lewis suggested. "If Nagumo is coming from that direction, it could be slowing him up."

Pederson took a seat and cleared his throat.

"Go ahead, Oscar, say what's on your mind," Fletcher said. "Everyone's opinion is valued."

"Suppose the enemy carriers *are* part of this group . . . that the PBY spotted some flanking vessels and Nagumo *is* coming from that direction. I mean, that's certainly a possibility. The Japs have thrown curve balls at us before. What then?"

Fletcher clasped his hands and watched his own fingers moving up and down like wings flapping against a swift breeze. He thought, could Pederson be right? Are we depending too much on intelligence analysis? Layton's group seemed very sure of itself. Too sure? Could the Japanese be aware that we have broken their codes and be pulling an enormous ruse on us? Are they keeping us waiting here out of position while they attack Midway and then turn on us when we come rushing in tomorrow? If this is Nagumo, we're too far away to launch a strike today. Are we the hunted instead of the hunter?

"There is that chance," Buckmaster echoed. "If Admiral Nimitz is wrong and this is Nagumo's group, we'll be caught on the wrong end of things. Nagumo will level Midway and be waiting for us to come charging to the rescue."

Fletcher's vision dropped to the coffee in his cup and noticed the level slope as *Yorktown* maneuvered against the choppy seas. Buck has a point. We stand to lose everything if we're caught out of position. We'd have to steam at full speed all night to close the distance by tomorrow morning. We'd be traveling blind, vulnerable to enemy patrol planes hunting a possible threat like us. We could lose the element of surprise . . . surrender the most crucial advantage we have. We'd toss all of CINCPAC's planning and deployments to the wind. Or we could do what Chet directed. Run and fight another day. Let Yamamoto take Midway. But what would be the consequences? Can we afford them?

If this *is* the Main Body.

He looked up and found his companions watching him, waiting for a decision. A sudden clatter as a mess steward dropped a serving tray visibly jolted the other officers. Fletcher remained calm and took a sip of coffee. He thought, and if it's not the Main Body? If we pursue and then attack the wrong enemy force? It could be the same disastrous result but for no gain. We'd be the ones flanked and vulnerable should Nagumo appear from the northwest, as Chet believes. Lined up like lambs to a slaughter as Japanese bombs and torpedoes rain down on us.

If this is *not* the Main Body.

A quick glance at his watch revealed the afternoon racing along. Time is mocking me. It could care less about my problem. It offers no respite while I struggle to decide. It pitches and flows like that ocean outside. Tossing me up and down. I'm just along for the ride.

They questioned my lack of aggression at Coral Sea. Made me write a report defending my actions. Chet agreed with my explanation. Yet, could he have harbored doubts? Halsey was out of the picture. Spruance lacks experience in commanding a carrier task force. Chet needed *Yorktown* and me. Could that fact have overridden his concerns? Perhaps I should have done things differently at Coral Sea. If I choose to remain here, am I repeating my mistake? Giving them more ammunition to use against me? Not taking advantage of the opportunity?

If this *is* indeed the Main Body.

His fingers splayed out and gripped the table edge. No, I didn't make a mistake at Coral Sea. Given the circumstances, I took the correct action and I'd do it again. Occasionally, a man has to follow his gut instinct . . . do what he believes is right. Damn what others think of me.

"This is not the Main Body," Fletcher said. "There's not enough proof to convince me otherwise. Chet was convinced by all of the intelligence reports. So am I. We're going to follow the operational plan laid out at Pearl Harbor."

A whistling Kiefer walked in with a message in his hands, helmet still perched jauntily on his head. He offered an exaggerated salute then motioned toward the coffeepot.

"How many stars does a working man need to get a cup?"

Buckmaster took the paper. "At least three, that's Admiral Fletcher's personal blend."

"Well, if I see a working man, I'll let him know." Kiefer helped himself and took a seat.

Buckmaster scanned the page, looked over at Fletcher. "Admiral Nimitz seems to agree with you. He says this is not the Main Body but the Occupation Force."

Fletcher relaxed, pleased that Chet's evaluation of the situation matched his own. The question plaguing him remained, though. If this isn't the Main Body, where is it?

"The SBDs are all out on patrol?" He directed this to Kiefer.

Kiefer lowered his cup and loudly smacked his lips. "Aye, sir. We're covering a southwest to northeast arc like you ordered. If anything should happen to pop up out there, we should hear about it."

"Anything on radar?

"Nothing showing up but our own CAP, sir. There's also a group of SBDs on anti-submarine patrol. If there's a Jap within fifty miles of here, he's lying on the bottom of the ocean, sir."

Fletcher ignored the joke, choosing to remain focused on the sighting report. "Admiral Spruance is aware of this latest message?"

"I'd think he received it just like us," Kiefer answered. "There's no reason to think otherwise."

Memories of problems caused by poor communications at Coral Sea returned and Fletcher decided to take no chances. "We're in a combat zone and that's reason enough to think otherwise. I want it relayed to him. Lack of proper communication is not going to be a problem this time."

"As you wish, sir." Kiefer finished his coffee and stood up. "I'll see this is taken care of immediately."

Fletcher watched him walk to the hatchway before calling out. "Dixie!"

Kiefer stopped to look back.

"No matter what happens, don't get excited."

A broad grin split Kiefer's face. "Words of wisdom that I strive to live by."

29. KUSAKA
June 03 – 17:00 Hours

"The Invasion Force has been discovered and attacked?" Nagumo asked. He and Kusaka stood on the starboard side of the bridge studying the latest radio intercept from Tokyo.

Ono, the staff intelligence officer, answered, "By land-based large bombers, most likely B-17s. Aircraft of that size could have only come from Midway."

"Damage?" Kusaka asked.

Ono smiled. "None. Accurate anti-aircraft fire forced the enemy to drop their bombs from high altitude. Admiral Kondo's ships easily dodged them. They continue onward without pause."

Nagumo sighed. "That is good, but the fact remains that Kondo's location is known to the enemy. They will be more vigilant in their scouting and prepared for an attack."

"But this might also lure the enemy fleet from Pearl Harbor to rush to Midway's defense," Ono countered. "We should be pleased. That is an important objective of this operation."

"I'm familiar with the objectives of this operation."

Kusaka sensed the mounting tension and stepped forward to intervene. "Were there any changes in orders radioed from Tokyo?"

Ono glanced at him with relief evident on his face. "None, sir. We should proceed as planned."

Message delivered and time you disappeared, Kusaka thought. Nagumo's ill turn of mind grows darker with each passing day. The farther one remains away from him the better.

"You may return to your duties," Kusaka said. "Keep us apprised of any important messages."

Ono saluted, bowed, and stole away. Nagumo grunted and turned back to the window. Kusaka joined him staring out at the clearing skies. The smell of gasoline and boiler smoke reminded him of the time and place.

"Am I wrong to be uneasy?"

Nagumo's question caught him by surprise.

"I'm not sure I understand what you mean," Kusaka said.

"Ono sees nothing but good news in all that happens. I see more reasons to worry."

Kusaka considered his statement for a few moments. It's easy to see why Nagumo feels that way, he thought. Yamamoto and his staff are breathing down his neck, waiting on him to fail. He's appointed to be in control of things that he can't possibly control . . . things no one could control. He's lost the services of both his air operations officer and strike leader. He must follow unrealistic fleet doctrine that's not compatible with an evolving battle. Life is suffering. One need only examine Nagumo's situation for proof.

"You're the commander and you need to prepare for whatever might happen," Kusaka replied. "You don't enjoy the luxury of focusing on a small part of the matter. Your eyes must view everything and question everything. You have reason to be vigilant, but not worried."

Both reached out and braced themselves as *Akagi* veered into the wind. The sudden change blew a heavy odor of salt water through the bridge that washed away the stink of gasoline. A Zero rumbled to life on the aft flight deck and sat growling like a contented tiger after a meal.

"Genda and Fuchida are both in sick bay," Nagumo said over the noise. "Operation K is canceled, denying us important intelligence information. Now the Invasion Force is located and attacked. These ill omens are warnings. Fate mocks us."

The Zero swept by the island, drowned out the conversation, and offered Kusaka a brief respite before replying. How do I respond to such beliefs? To believe in omens of any kind is to deny the rationality of life. There is no refuge in an enlightened mind for omens or superstitions.

"If you'd prove these omens false," Kusaka carefully proceeded, "you must do everything within your means to make the correct decisions at the critical times. We must prepare ourselves so there's no delay in doing what's necessary. Timing is everything."

Nagumo sighed, lifted his binoculars, and stared out at the ocean. "You've a gift for philosophy, Kusaka. The bridge of a ship at war is a strange place to find such a gift."

"We must embrace life wherever we are, whatever we do, and question not the tide that carries us."

Nagumo lowered the glasses and looked at him. "And what must I do to share in these feelings?"

"The secret of health for both mind and body is to not mourn for the past, worry about the future, or anticipate troubles, but to live wisely and earnestly in the present moment. We are promised nothing."

"*Hai*, you make it sound so simple. Show me the way."

Kusaka shrugged. "Open your eyes. Were you not worried about breaking the radio blackout yesterday to order the course change?"

"I could have given our position away to the enemy."

"Yet, Kondo was attacked and not us. We remain cloaked in secrecy. Would you call that fate or luck?"

"What do you call it?"

"The laws of nature not denied." Kusaka smiled, anticipating Nagumo's challenge. "Our transmission was low band, designed for traveling short distances. It was also very brief. Kondo's position is in advance of ours, within the enemy's search radius, making it much more likely for him to be spotted. Given these facts, is it not logical to assume these things? To understand neither fate nor luck determined the course of events?"

"And Genda and Fuchida?"

"Illness can strike a man at any time, just as it has struck Fuchida. Genda pushes himself relentlessly trying to fulfill his duties, not allowing proper time for rest. A tired body is an open invitation for a physical breakdown. Every human being is the source of his own good health or the diseases that afflict him."

Nagumo snorted. "You've all the answers."

"Only my answers to your specific questions. You're free to believe as you will."

Nagumo raised his hands and then dropped them. "I'd feel more at ease if we'd heard some word on the American carriers."

Kusaka understood his concern, but didn't know the words to say. Their submarine cordon line should sight any enemy ships making way from Hawaii, he thought. We'll have scouting aircraft of our own in the air by first light tomorrow. If the enemy does show up ready to fight, *Kido Butai* is more than equal to the challenge. We should welcome the opportunity for battle, not fear it.

"We must trust in our planning, our resources, and our men to do what must be done. These have carried us to victory since this war started. There's no reason to believe things will change."

"To hear Ugaki tell it, the American's lack of resolve has more to do with our victories than anything else. We're fighting a

149

defeated enemy, he says. The Americans just don't realize it yet. We need only push them a little longer before they concede. Raise their casualty rate so high that they plead for concessions. Ugaki has most of the Combined Fleet parroting his words."

"I'm no disciple of Ugaki, but his point has some merit," Kusaka said. "They've offered little in the way of resistance to our forces. They've constantly retreated as we've marched forward. I was expecting more fight from an enemy who roars like a lion."

"Are you forgetting Wake Island? For two weeks it was bravely and tenaciously defended before our forces managed to overwhelm the Americans. If I remember correctly, losses were much heavier on our side."

He remembers fine, Kusaka thought, but his point is ill made. Wake Island is the exception to the rule. The demon of indecision and worry threatens to steal Nagumo's fighting spirit again.

"Life is full of exceptions," Kusaka countered. "The Americans in the Philippines retreated from and surrendered to forces much smaller than theirs."

Nagumo rubbed his neck. "Then we should wish that the Midway defenders are like the one in the Philippines and not like the ones at Wake Island."

30. RAMSEY
June 03 – 20:00 Hours

Ramsey and Simard stepped off the PT boat shuttle from Sand Island and climbed into a waiting jeep. Raising a choking cloud of chalk-white dust, the vehicle spun around, heading for one of the large hangars. It banged along, one minute sliding through the sandy ground and the next sailing above it, only to crash down and hop up again like a drunken kangaroo. Ramsey clamped on for dear life but contemplated releasing one hand and choking the bare-chested driver until he slowed down.

Ramsey leaned forward and remarked to Simard in the front seat, "This isn't the way I want to win a Purple Heart."

"Diego," Simard barked at the driver, "ease up a little."

Blinding-white teeth defined the young man's face as he said, "Aye, sir."

The jeep slowed and eventually stopped in front of a corrugated metal building serving as the flight shack. Ramsey climbed out, took a few seconds fixing Diego's face in his mind, thinking, here's a guy who has a bright future driving ambulances.

"Something wrong?" Simard asked.

"Not in the least. I just wanted to remember what he looks like in case I see some of these boys hauling explosives."

Simard chuckled as an exhausted-looking Kimes stepped out of the building. His almost emaciated appearance provided ample evidence of a lack of sleep and proper nutrition for the past few hectic days.

"Ira, you look as bad as I feel," Simard remarked.

"We're getting ready," the man replied. "Lots to do and not enough time to do it."

Ramsey wandered over to four PBYs parked nearby. They brought to mind pregnant, metal gooney birds, their awkward shapes made more lopsided by the torpedo strapped beneath one wing. Carbon copies of Diego—perhaps it was the filthy, bare torsos slick from exertion giving that impression—climbed into each one, preparing it to fly.

"The crews are in here," Simard called out.

Ramsey followed them into the poorly-lit structure. A group of about a dozen men seated on a rummage sale's worth of mixed furniture stood as they entered. Simard waved them down and pointed a thumb toward Ramsey.

"Commander Ramsey wants to speak with you."

"We intend to launch a night torpedo attack on the enemy fleet sighted earlier today," Ramsey said, going right into it. "I realize this has never been done before, but we must throw everything we can at them. I want you to understand this mission is on a volunteer basis. If you have doubts and think you can't do it, you're not ordered to go. I know this is a risky operation and it will not be held against you if you decide to opt out. Turning this down might even demonstrate a high degree of intelligence. You must decide."

He paused to study their faces in the annoying yellow light. Give me a sign, he thought, any sign you question your ability to do this. If this is not a suicide mission, it's the next thing to it. I'll not knowingly send any man up who harbors doubts about his return . . . not on a risky, almost foolhardy stunt as this. I don't want to send them out, but I've no choice in the matter. I'm damn sure giving them a choice about going.

The room remained silent; their faces betrayed no emotion or clue into their thoughts. Ramsey proceeded to fill them in on the mission's details. He answered the few questions offered and stressed the desire to locate and attack a suspected carrier. Briefing completed, he turned to Simard.

"Anything else?"

"This is Lieutenant Richards." Simard motioned at one of them. "He's XO of VP-44 and flight officer for tonight's mission. He's one of my best radar technicians."

"I'm still learning, sir," Richards remarked.

"We all are," Ramsey replied, "but it's time to demonstrate what you know. The enemy is out there and I aim to extend a warm welcome to him. Understood?"

"Understood, sir," Richards said and the others echoed.

"Have any of you ever made a torpedo attack from a PBY?" Ramsey asked.

The four exchanged glances but none answered.

"Have any of you ever made a torpedo attack from anything?"

More silence, this time accompanied by nervous shuffling, greeted the question.

Ramsey blew out his cheeks, pursed his lips, and tried once more. "Have any of you ever *seen* a torpedo attack?"

"I have, sir," an ensign said, "at Pearl Harbor. The only thing is it was the Japs launching them at us."

Ramsey focused on the young man. "Are you taking this flight for a chance at revenge?"

The ensign shook his head. "No, sir. I'm not as angry now as I am worried . . . I mean after Wake and the Philippines."

"Worried?"

"Are we ever going to stop those bastards?"

Good question, Ramsey thought. Let's make sure that everyone understands how important this fight is. Desperation is a more potent motivation than revenge. The most dangerous animal is one backed into a corner.

"We're capable of getting the job done, sir," Richards said. "All we need is a chance."

"Good," Simard broke in. "How soon before you take off?"

* * *

Ramsey and Simard bent forward against a heavy cloud of dust and propeller-driven wind, carefully approaching the taxiing B-17. Deft hands on the controls brought the tail end swinging around into its parking spot. A few moments later, the roar from the four powerful Pratt and Whitney engines slowly died as each powered down, the huge propellers coasting to a halt. The hatch opened to reveal a jubilant Sweeney. He dropped onto the ground and strode over to them.

"Those Japs certainly found out what a B-17 is capable of!" he exulted. "It's too bad there was no air cover. My gunners wanted a chance to mix it up with a Zero."

They turned and watched the dark shapes and exhaust trails from more of Sweeney's flight group circling the field and landing. Through the glow of the hooded landing lights, Ramsey studied each aircraft rumbling by, curious to find no damage. Was the Japanese antiaircraft fire that ineffective?

"What was the flak like?" he asked Sweeney.

"Well, they threw a lot of it our way but it all exploded behind us. I don't believe they understand the concept of deflection shooting. Their aim's terrible."

"How high were you when you released?"

"We used a three-tiered attack, dropping from eight thousand, ten thousand, and twelve thousand feet."

"What could you see—"

Sweeney held up a hand to cut him off. "Give me some time to huddle up with all of my men and debrief them. I'll fill out a complete report and answer the rest of your questions."

"Okay," Ramsey agreed. "We'll be waiting in Captain Simard's headquarters."

The dazzling smile flashed again. "I'm sure I'll find you."

Ramsey watched Sweeney throw his arms around the shoulders of two surprised crewmen and walk off. Simard seemed to take note of the same thing and chuckled.

"I guess the term "brothers in arms" refers to guys in the same branch of military service," he remarked. "I shouldn't say anything. The Marines hate to acknowledge their kinship with the Navy."

"Maybe," Ramsey said without taking his eyes off the retreating figure of Sweeney, "but you'd think what happened at Pearl Harbor changed all that. We're all in this thing together."

He glanced at Simard. "Aren't we?"

* * *

"Have you read this report?" Ramsey held up a packet of papers to Simard. "Sweeney's fliers are claiming hits on just about every type of ship Yamamoto has. I've definite hits and probables on two battleships, a cruiser, and several troop transports. Another one says he saw a battleship and a transport burning. At this rate, I can let the rest of the flight groups stand down. Sweeney's bunch has the battle as good as won. They should finish things up tomorrow."

Simard pulled a chair up next to the table. "What did Sweeney say about this?"

The document smacked against the tabletop. "That's the best part. No fighter protection or air cover, but he decides not to press his luck. He heads back here without verifying the damage. I don't know what to make of it."

"No mention of sighting any carriers?" Simard changed the subject.

"No and that's the only welcome news I've heard. I shouldn't complain. If we can get Sweeney's bunch just one shot at Nagumo's force, I can pack up and head back to Hawaii."

"That's a little harsh, don't you think? Certainly all of those large bombers must have done some damage."

Ramsey considered the speed of an alerted warship and the amount of time it would take for a bomb to fall from eight thousand feet or higher. Unless it was a very slow ship or the captain was a complete imbecile and did nothing, it was hard to believe anything other than a lucky hit struck home.

"Maybe, but I've my doubts."

"What's your official version going to say?"

Ramsey pointed at the report. "Certainly not those wild claims. I don't think Admiral Nimitz would be inclined to believe them."

"Perhaps not, but he does believe in interservice cooperation and friendly relations among the troops. If you question everything in Sweeney's report, you'll stir up some hard feelings."

Ramsey lifted the sheet once more and scanned the lines. Simard was right. Now wasn't the time for petty squabbles among the men. The enemy threat was real and deadly enough without him compounding it with unimportant things that could easily spiral out of control. He looked up at Simard.

"I'll give them the benefit of the doubt and claim a hit on a battleship and another one on a transport."

Simard stood up to get a better view of the large chart spread across the table. He pointed at the pencil marks signifying the sightings and B-17 attack.

"You're convinced now this isn't Nagumo's force we're dealing with?" he asked Ramsey.

"Aren't you?"

"I agree the position is way off from where it's expected to pop up."

Ramsey felt tired muscles cramping and carefully stretched out his body in the chair. "The fact that there are no carriers with this group convinces me. As high as Sweeney flew, they should have spotted any carriers in the vicinity."

"They could've been farther back beyond the horizon," Simard offered.

"Then why no combat air patrol over the entire fleet? You heard what Sweeney said. I can't believe that a carrier strike force would blindly sail along without a CAP circling around it. It just doesn't make sense. I feel certain this is the Occupation Force."

Simard pointed to the northwest corner of the chart. "So we're back to the cold front still hanging over that area. You said that's where Admiral Nimitz believes they're coming from. According to our scouts, visibility is severely limited, which would explain why there's been no sighting. If Admiral Nimitz is correct, tomorrow morning should bring Nagumo calling."

Simard sighed and sat down. "It's a long wait until then."

For both sides, Ramsey thought. For both sides.

31. THACH
June 03 – 20:00 Hours

"Come on in, Jimmy." Lieutenant Commander Lem Massey sat in a chair next to his small desk waving Thach into his cabin.

Thach entered to find Lieutenant Commander Max Leslie seated on Massey's bed. Both of them held a handful of playing cards.

"Poker?" Thach asked as he sat down next to Leslie.

Leslie snorted, glancing at Massey. "I learned a long time ago back on *Enterprise* to never beard Lem in his den using his deck of cards. I'm better off just handing him his winnings. It saves a lot of time. We're playing gin rummy for cigarettes neither one of us has."

Massey ignored the remark and picked up the remainder of the deck. "Deal you in?"

Thach shook his head. "No, thanks. I just wanted to speak to you two for a few minutes."

Leslie sorted his cards and then looked over at Massey. "It's your throw."

"Go ahead, Jimmy," Massey said, tossing an eight of hearts on top of the pile.

"Just what I was looking for." Leslie scooped it up and tucked it away.

"I was wondering who you think the escort fighters need to accompany on the attack," Thach said. "Admiral Fletcher has only given me a few. With the SBDs flying at high altitude and the TBDs lower, I'll have to distribute my F4Fs."

The play halted as both men looked at him.

"There's no question those fighters need to be with Max's dive bombers," Massey answered. "I figure the Zeroes will be at a higher altitude searching for incoming attackers. They're sure to spot his group first and jump him. They won't pay much attention to my boys down below. We'll sneak in before the Japs know we're there."

"Nonsense," Leslie argued, "your slower torpedo planes will be sitting ducks for Nagumo's Zeroes. Without fighter escort, they'll flame your entire bunch before you get within release distance. A

157

coordinated attack means that both of our groups need to be around to disperse the enemy."

"You're forgetting the reports from Fletcher's SBDs at Coral Sea. The Japs tore into them and left the torpedo planes alone. Ask Jimmy, he'll tell you. I know he read them even if you didn't."

"I don't have to ask Jimmy anything. My SBDs are faster and armed well enough to defend themselves against attack. Not like those antique TBDs you're mounted in. Once we get into our dives, the Zeroes won't be able to keep up anyway."

Thach sat slightly amused and listened to them go back and forth for several minutes. This sounds like an Alphonse and Gaston routine, he thought. After you, Alphonse. No, you first, my dear Gaston. Neither man wants to admit the necessity of an escort. Both are worried about the other's vulnerability to attack. Neither wants to concede the point, but the answer is obvious to me. Lem's TBDs are slow, awkward firetraps. They need the protection more than Max's SBDs.

"How about letting me decide?" Thach broke in as both paused to take a breath. "I agree with Max. The TBDs are in greater need of close escort support. The SBDs will be flying faster and a lot higher. I do recall the enemy's tactics at Coral Sea of keeping his fighters at higher altitudes to deal with dive bombers instead of flying lower and striking our torpedo planes. Because of those tactics, our TBDs placed at least a couple of torpedoes into the Jap carrier that sank. The enemy's not likely to make the same mistake twice. They'll be watching out for torpedo attacks this time. You can bet on it."

"The decision is made," Leslie echoed.

Massey shrugged. "Whatever you say. Now can I deal you in?"

* * *

"Are you afraid of dying?"

Leslie having left nearly an hour before, Massey and Thach sat alone. From a distance, the sound of a record player spinning scratchy disks added its weight to the hot, damp air. The Andrew Sisters gaily singing about "The Boogie Woogie Bugle Boy of Company C," seemed sadly ironic considering the impending battle. Massey reached into the bottom drawer of the desk and removed a full bottle of scotch. He broke the seal and then poured a small amount into a coffee cup. Looking over at Thach, he waved the bottle at him.

"Care for a small nightcap?"

Thach thought about the rapidly approaching morning and what it promised before shaking his head. "Save me one for tomorrow night."

Massey took a sip. A sharp grimace pinched his face as he loudly burped.

"I was never fond of the stuff straight but I figured I'm pressing my luck just by having it with me. I'll not mix a cocktail, too. Admiral Fletcher wouldn't be happy if he knew about this."

Thach smiled, remembering some of his past encounters with Fletcher at various watering holes. The admiral's fondness for enjoying a drink or two was no secret. Fletcher is probably more understanding than Lem thinks . . . so long as it doesn't affect his flying.

"You're probably right," Thach agreed. "I can see him confiscating the bottle just to make sure that it doesn't fall into enemy hands."

"You didn't answer my question." Massey ignored the joke.

"Question?"

"I asked if you were afraid of dying."

Thach lit another cigarette off the butt in his mouth and then stubbed the smoked one out in Massey's ashtray. He sat up straight and exhaled a large cloud of smoke.

"I guess I never really took the time to think much about it," he answered. "Lately I have had so many other things going on that required my attention. When I'm in the middle of combat . . . well, you've been there. You're too busy trying to do your job and stay alive to think about it."

He took another deep draw, held it and then slowly let it go. "I must admit Don's accident really—"

"I'm sorry about that," Massey cut in. "I know the two of you were good friends and hadn't thought about the impact on you."

"Thanks, I guess I should be ashamed of myself. We've both lost friends in this damn war. We're bound to lose more. Don's death should have no more meaning than any other."

Massey held up a hand, belched. He smiled and returned the bottle to the drawer.

"You know you're full of it," he said as he rose. "Don was a good friend who volunteered, I said volunteered, to give you a hand when you sorely needed one. He could've stayed in Hawaii and waited on his transport but decided his place was in combat. You've got a right . . . no, make that a responsibility, to feel his loss more deeply."

He fixed Thach with road-map eyes. "And I'll personally whup your ass if I ever hear you say anything different."

Thach felt a burden lifted. "Thanks, Lem."

Massey waved his thanks away. "Just speaking the truth. Hell, too many good men will die over the next few days. That's what war is all about . . . fighting and killing. We'll miss some of them more than others . . . the ones that we trained with and shared liberty with. Yet, each one will leave a void in someone's life with his passing. We can't ever be caught up in all the bloodshed and forget that every life matters. If we do, we stand to lose our souls."

Thach remained silent, considering Massey's words. *There's a good deal of truth in what Lem is saying. After a while, combat can make a man callous. It's a defense mechanism to keep him from losing his sanity. Casualties become nothing more than names on a list. Empty seats in the ready room are soon filled with replacement pilots. You learn the names . . . put them with the correct faces, but that's all that you want to know about them. You can't lose a friend that you never had.*

Massey's head dropped down onto his chest. Thach read his action as a cue to leave, placed his feet firmly on the deck, and leaned forward.

"The odds are mighty long against my squadron making it back," Massey said without looking up. "Them damn TBDs are so slow and Nagumo's fighter boys too fast. Even with your bunch escorting us, when we show up near their carriers they'll be like ants in a mound guarding the queen. Your F4Fs are going to have their hands full just trying to keep your own asses from being flamed without worrying about mine. They talk about Coral Sea and the fact that the Zeroes left the TBDs alone to jump the SBDs. But this isn't Coral Sea. You hit the mark earlier with your comment. The Japs aren't likely to use the same tactic twice. But, do you know what? It really doesn't matter in the end. Every mother's son of us has a job to do. We're sure as hell going to do it. You'd damn better know that."

His head tilted up, his expression clear and solemn. "I probably shouldn't be saying these things, but they're on my mind." He seemed to force a weak smile. "Besides, everyone appreciates a little gloom now and then."

Thach stood, reached down, and clapped him on the shoulder. "Don't forget the Japs won't be expecting us near Midway. That gives us the advantage of tactical surprise. That's a hell of a good advantage to have. You just remember all those evasion techniques that I shared with you and your pilots a few days ago. I'm telling you they'll work. I've seen the proof with my own eyes."

His hand dropped away and he pointed toward the bed. "Do yourself a favor and do what I'm going to do, hit that rack."

He moved toward the door as Massey brushed by rolling into his bunk.

"That Max is really something, isn't he?" Massey asked. "Imagine him trying to give up air cover so I could have it."

"Yes, he is," Thach agreed, switching off the light. Leslie is indeed really something. So is Lem Massey.

32. MELO
June 03 – 21:00 Hours

"What does a guy have to do to get a beer around this place?" Melo rapped on the makeshift bar set up inside a tool shed.

A massive, angry-looking individual wearing a torn undershirt stepped out from a rear storage room. Two gorilla-sized, hairy arms, the upper right one bearing a tattooed heart with the word *Mother* on it, leaned against the counter. He looked at the much smaller Melo and sadly shook his head.

"I ain't got any sody pop, young 'un."

"I'd like a beer," Melo repeated.

Melo noticed critical eyes appraising his attempt to grow a mustache and stood a little taller. Squinting, the giant pointed a bent finger. Melo registered scars all across his wide knuckles.

"Did you know there's a caterpillar crawling on your lip?"

Melo heard several loud snorts and chuckles and realized a group of marines and sailors had gathered near the door to watch. The sharks smell blood, he thought. He took a few deep breaths and decided to make one more attempt. Perhaps I was rude. It's been a long hot day. Everyone's in a bad mood.

"Can I get a beer?"

Muscular arms folded across a beer keg-sized chest and *Mother* winked at him.

"Does your mama know you drink?"

More laughter greeted this last stroke of brilliant wit. Melo felt flush, knew the ape could mangle him but wouldn't put up with guff out of anyone. He'd never backed down from a fight and wasn't about to start now. If I run from him, I'll be running from all of these jarheads. Long Island had a way of toughening kids up. I'm no exception.

Melo smiled. "Did your mother and father both quit the Freak Show when they got married?"

Blood-shot eyes grew wide as the giant's nostrils flared. A vicious gaze swept over the crowd outside daring anyone to utter a sound. The audience wisely remained silent, waiting to see what happened next.

"They didn't do that," he answered.

Sympathy reflected on Melo's face and he sadly shook his head. "They didn't get married? That explains things."

The expression remained puzzled, but wary. "Explains what?"

"The reason you're a bastard."

Complete silence, save for the sounds of aircraft engines floating through the night air, ensued. Melo waited, felt movement behind him, and heard the door banging shut. The rats are deserting the sinking ship, he thought. He did not turn around; he knew without looking that he faced the beast alone.

"You got a death wish, squirt?"

"The name's Frank."

"Fair enough. You got a death wish, Frank?"

"If I did, I'm sure the Japs will be glad to give me a hand in making it come true. That's what I came here for. To give them the chance. I'm damn sure not afraid of you."

The marine tilted his head and squinted, seemed to size Melo up. Melo raised himself higher and maintained eye contact. I don't know if the first man who blinks loses, but I do know I'll not show fear.

"I'd break you in half."

"You could try," Melo agreed, "but you'll feel it in the morning. I don't go down easy and I don't fight clean. Did you ever see a badger rip up a bear? The bear might win but he'll sure enough know he'd been in a fight."

The giant rubbed his bristled muzzle and appeared to be thinking or as close to thinking as he could come. "You mean that, don't you?"

"I'm here to fight Japs, not fellow Americans. They're the enemy and they started this war. Why should we beat up on each other?"

Standing there, the marine's mouth worked furiously back and forth. He's probably trying to choose which arm to tear off first, Melo thought. That's okay, I'm fast. I'll get in a few shots of my own. And he won't like where I deliver them. Melo balanced himself lightly on his feet, prepared to move.

"The name's Pauly and I owe you an apology." He extended a mitt.

Melo hesitated for a brief moment, suspecting a trap, and then returned a brutal handshake. Pauly doesn't strike me as the type who'd sucker punch a guy, Melo decided. With his size and build, he didn't need to. Pauly stepped into the back room and returned a few minutes later with two beers. Using an opener hanging from a neck chain, he popped the tops and handed a foaming bottle to Melo.

"It's hot but it's all we got," Pauly apologized.

Melo offered a toast and then joined him in chugging the brew. The warm, sour-tasting liquid slid down his throat, landing with a cannonball-sized splash in his stomach. Melo thought, was this *really* worth risking my neck for? He coughed, belched, and crooned, "*Smooth!*"

Pauly chuckled. They both glanced over at the door as another marine walked in.

"Hey, Steve," Pauly greeted him, "how about watching the beer locker for a while and letting me catch a little fresh air. Colonel says don't take nothing but chits for the stuff. Business has been steady."

Steve paused, glanced around at the empty building. "Looks like it."

"They'll be back," Pauly said as he joined Melo on the other side of the counter. "I think they got called away."

"Uh huh. Way I hear it you were about to murder some guy." His eyesight settled on Melo. "Sarge sent me over to remind you that's how you lost that stripe before."

"Ah, you know how scuttlebutt gets started. This is Frank, my new friend. Me and him are going to have a beer and talk about our hometown."

Steve offered Melo a strange look. "Are you from Chicago, too?"

Melo shrugged and smiled. "Sure, why not? I just love that windy city."

"Uh huh." Disbelief on his face, Steve disappeared into the back.

Melo and Pauly walked out into the night air. A low rumble rolled out of the western sky like continuous thunder heralding a storm. Melo glanced up and saw a blinking light that grew into the massive shape of a B-17 coming in for a landing. Looks like more of Sweeney's group has made it back, Melo thought. I wonder if they had any luck finding the Japs.

"You remind me of my younger brother, Daniel," Pauly said. "Your smart-ass attitude and sense of humor."

No wonder he warmed up to me, Melo thought. He's homesick for his family. It's nice to know that I can be a help to him.

"I wish I had a nickel for every time I wanted to choke the hell out of that little brat."

Uh oh, so much for that idea. I hope he doesn't want to use me as a substitute. We'll be back to the bear and badger thing. I might not be as convincing this time.

"My ma, bless her soul, wouldn't put up with that, so I took it out on any guy who crossed me. I lived quite a rowdy life up through high school. I guess I was more than she could handle by herself, what with having three more boys and two girls to feed."

Pauly took another pull on the beer and spat. "Hell, I was actually happy the day the judge gave me a choice between letting the Marines turn me into a man or letting a prison do it. He'd seen me all he wanted to and my ma needed relief. I was one less mouth to feed. Besides, I send most of my paycheck home to her to help out."

Melo remained silent and nursed the beer. I wonder if he's expecting a response. Probably not. Sometimes a guy just wants to talk. Doesn't really matter who's listening . . . as long as someone is. Maybe this is one of those times.

"I'm not boring you am I?" Pauly abruptly asked.

"No, of course not. I've seen a gooney bird, had a warm beer, and dodged a fight. My day's been full enough already. I've nothing else planned for tonight. Go on."

Pauly chuckled. "I like you, Frank. You make me laugh and forget about things."

"And your rotten brother?"

Melo detected a sudden shift in Pauly's mood.

"My ma had trouble with Daniel pretty much from the time I left. I don't know . . . it seems like he wanted to follow my lead. It got so bad that ma asked me to come home on leave and talk to him. So I did. I gave him one hell of a dressing down. Told him I was ashamed of him for doing all those stupid things I had done. I said he was being a burden to ma. I told him he needed to grow up and act like a man. I told him good."

"It sounds like you did."

"Yeah, it got pretty emotional . . . a few tears and such. I guess we both had things that needed saying to each other. I still had some growing up to do, too. I'm not ashamed to admit it."

Melo shrugged. "There's no need to be ashamed. A little heart to heart talk is good for the soul."

"Thanks, Frank."

Pauly looked up at the sky for a few moments. The sound of heavy engines again drew their attention. Melo joined him at stargazing and saw another B-17 circling the field preparing to land.

"There's another one," Pauly remarked.

"Did you manage to straighten your brother out?"

Pauly lowered his head. In the weak lighting from the beer shack, Melo could see a sad smile on the marine's worn face.

"Yeah, I straightened him out alright. He decided to join the service like I did. The Marines wouldn't have him because of his being a squirt like you. The Navy's not as picky so he wound up a sailor. It's a shame."

Pauly drained the last of the warm beer and tossed the bottle away. Melo remained silent, sensing the man had something else to say. The proof came a few seconds later.

"The last time we talked he was a different person. All growed up and acting like a man. Apologized to me for being a little brat and causing ma so much trouble. Hell, what could I say? I'd set a poor example for him with all the trouble I got into. We laughed for a while. Had a few beers. It was good. I was damn sure proud of him."

Melo thought, why do I have the feeling he's leading up to something bad? Maybe I should run now and avoid what's coming next.

"He was stationed on the *Arizona*," Pauly said, confirming his suspicions.

Melo did not have to ask. He knew Daniel was not one of the few survivors of the attack. Everything that had happened between him and Pauly had led to this moment and revelation. He also understood Pauly wanted to hear no words of sympathy from him. Sharing the story was more than enough. Hopefully, the effort brought him some peace.

"And here I am," Pauly continued, "wanting to be sent to where the fighting is. Kill me some slant-eyed sons-of-bitches. Instead I'm wasting time and handing out warm beer on Midway Atoll." He stressed the first syllable *a* in *atoll*.

"That's my biggest fear . . . that I'll spend the duration of the war here on this pile of sand and coral and never make it into combat. I figure the Japs owe me one scalp for every mother's son that went down on the *Arizona,* and ten for Daniel."

Melo pitched his own empty bottle away. "You might get your chance right here. There's supposed to be an invasion group accompanying that Jap task force out there."

Pauly looked at him; his face assumed a wolfish appearance from the shadows cast by the harsh incandescent lighting.

"Wouldn't that be something?"

"Yeah," Melo agreed, "a chance to finally get into combat. To do what I've been trained to do."

"I see you've got the itch for combat, too. Well I've told you my story. So what's up with you? How did you get to be . . . whatever it is you do? I know you're one of the Army flyboys. You're wearing a corporal's stripes, so I don't figure you're a pilot."

"I'm a radio operator/gunner for one of the B-26s. I wanted to fight the Japs and to do it somewhere I didn't feel overwhelmed. An infantryman or sailor is one among many that have little control over their situation. They're thrown right into the middle of total chaos and often have no say in what happens to them. We're a small crew, in one airplane, and all I worry about are my radio and firing my .30-cal Brownings. I can handle that."

"So what are you doing here?"

"We were headed out to join the rest of the 22nd Bomb Group but were detained in Pearl Harbor. Someone had a bright idea that a B-26 would make a good torpedo plane. All we've done is make practice drops and cool our heels. The real fighting goes on out here."

"Maybe me and you both are finally going to get a crack at those Jap bastards."

"I'm ready."

Pauly withdrew two cigars from a shirt pocket and offered one to Melo.

"No, thanks. I promised my mother I wouldn't smoke or drink. I'd like to keep at least *half* of my promises to her."

Pauly chuckled and lit up. A few seconds later, the pungent odor of burning tires wafted through the night air. Melo coughed, feeling his eyes smarting. No wonder there are so few mosquitoes here.

"You're a real puzzle to me," Pauly said between puffs.

"How's that?"

"You say that you want to get into the real war, but you're doing it from an airplane. Seems like you should have enlisted in the infantry."

"And wind up with you sitting on this rock?" Melo instantly regretted saying it.

Pauly shrugged the comment away. "You've got a point. You surely do."

"Yeah, nothing's guaranteed. I did what I thought was best for me. The AAF will have a say in this thing before the smoke clears."

"This war can't be won by small groups of guys in airplanes."

"Perhaps not, but it can be fought that way. We intend to prove it."

"I hope you do, Frank." Pauly flipped some ashes away and extended a hand. "I need to relieve Steve. Luck and keep things under control."

Melo returned the shake. "Good luck to you and I will. You do the same."

Melo walked away and then heard Pauly call.

"Frank!"

"Yeah?"

"While you're up there flying around, fighting your version of the war, see if you can bag a Zero for Daniel, eh?"

168

33. BROCKMAN
June 03 – 23:00 Hours

"Message intercept, Skippah," Ensign Yates called up through the open hatch in his thick Alabama drawl.

Brockman lowered his binoculars, cursed the rough seas and intermittent squalls that continued to douse the lookouts and him. He gazed upward at the dark, overcast sky and thought about the nearly full moon hidden up there. Its light would be most welcome in silhouetting the enemy.

"Skippah?"

He moved over to the hatch. "Any returns to it?"

"Aye, sir, one from Pearl. Bobby waited five minutes or so to make sure they were done. He ain't heard anything since."

Brockman felt a sudden rise of the boat, knowing a matching dip accompanied by another soaking wave would follow. He grasped the hatch ring, braced his legs, gritted his teeth, and tried not to shout as the cold water struck him a solid blow.

"Send Lieutenant Hogan up," he called down, "and tell him to wear every piece of rain gear he has. It's misting one moment and blowing the next."

A few minutes later Hogan, the diving officer, took Brockman's place on the bridge and he climbed below. He passed through the conning tower and down into the control room. Benson extended a cup of coffee to him and waited while he shed his wet coat and hat. The heaving ocean, so violent up top, was no more docile inside. Brockman's body instinctively rode the up and down motion, his legs and knees doing everything possible to compensate for the unstable deck. He quickly dismissed a brief thought of submerging below the rough waves. The boat must run on diesel as long as possible to save the battery charge.

"If I were prone to sea sickness, tonight would be a good excuse to have a case," Benson remarked. "A little medicinal alcohol might help. Why can't we adopt that old Royal Navy bit about each man receiving a daily allowance of grog? It steadies the nerves as well as the legs."

"I'll make a note of that in the next dispatch."

"Will you really?"

"You read the messages?" he asked Benson before taking a soothing drink of the warm liquid.

Benson nodded and held up the paper. "They're between Spike Hottel in *Cuttlefish* and COMSUBPAC concerning the earlier order he received."

"Did he find the damaged Jap battleship that Pearl sent him after?"

"Nope, but he did run across a tanker. He said his lookouts kept spotting aircraft. He decided to take his boat down and lost contact. A short while ago he came back up to recharge batteries. No sign of anything."

"And Pearl's response to the news?" He could already well imagine.

Benson's head tilted downward as his eyes rolled upward to look at him." A polite reminder from Admiral English of the importance of making and maintaining enemy contact. It's a shame. Spike struck out both on sinking the tanker and finding the battleship that Midway said was out there."

"*If* it was out there." Brockman said.

"Ours is not to reason why. Ours is but to . . . you know the rest."

"Yes, so does Spike."

Both of them moved over to the chart table and took note of the latest marked position for *Cuttlefish*. Brockman could not deny that it coincided with the location given by Midway for the Japanese strike force. He thought, how could contact be lost so easily? *Cuttlefish* was not in the area of rough seas like *Nautilus*. On a moonlit night like this, silhouette visibility should be excellent out to the horizon. Yet, somehow, Spike lost touch. He rubbed his nose, told himself to stop it. I shouldn't judge Spike's actions in the presence of the enemy. Until I face the same circumstances and act differently, I've no right to question another skipper. When the moment of decision arrives, I can only hope and pray for the courage and resolve to do my duty without hesitation or concern for my personal safety.

"Regardless of everything," Brockman said, "the fact remains there was a bomber attack on a group of Japanese ships this afternoon. They claimed that a battleship was damaged. Midway was very explicit about that as was Pearl when it rebroadcast the message."

170

He motioned toward the chart. "How much truth the report contains isn't important. What is important is that the enemy is definitely out there. Of that, there is no doubt. Perhaps just near *Cuttlefish* now, but we've every reason to believe we'll be making contact before long."

"This is a great big ocean," Benson remarked. "And we're a little old boat despite what the men say."

Brockman held his tongue, fell into thinking. Too many things are starting to multiply. The sudden deployment of the submarine fleet to picket positions near Midway. The B-17 bomber attack this afternoon. *Cuttlefish* spotting the tanker and its reports of enemy aircraft. Where could those enemy planes have come from way out here except a carrier? Wake Island? Not very likely. Something big is building . . . like a typhoon. A blow is coming. And it feels like *Nautilus* is catching the first warm breeze. The time has come to batten down the hatches.

Benson grabbed onto the table to counter a sudden heave of the boat and glanced upward. "It's going to be hard finding them in this mess. We'll be lucky if we don't collide with something before seeing it."

"It is nasty," Brockman agreed, "and we've a long day tomorrow . . . long days for the foreseeable future. Things are just going to get worse and we have to be prepared."

"Why do I feel like you're leading up to something?"

Brockman glanced around at the sailors at their stations and then motioned Benson toward the officers' mess. Entering the vacant room, Brockman poured another cup from the large urn and joined Benson at a table. The smell from the galley of bread baking fought to build an appetite in Brockman's queasy stomach.

"I want you or me on duty until this thing's over," Brockman said.

"You're thinking this Midway business is about to break loose? That this time it's for real?"

"You read our orders. Too many of the pieces are falling into place. I'm thinking tomorrow or the day after we'll be right in the middle of a battle . . . a big battle."

"And you or I need to be the one minding the store."

"We'll cover it in four hour shifts until we make contact with the enemy."

Benson wiped his eyes and sighed. "Just the two of us?"

"I'm sorry, but there are too many unknowns about this boat and crew. We've drilled and drilled. I believe the men are ready. But until I see how they respond to combat, I intend to be cautious."

"You're the skipper, but remember what you told me about command. We lead by example. We expect the men to follow suit and do their duty. I'm wondering what kind of example we'll be setting by not trusting them to do their jobs."

"It's not a question of whether or not the crew can do its job, it's a matter of making sure we're prepared."

"I hear what you're saying and can understand your thinking, but you need to consider how the men will react. I believe they'll see it as you doubting their ability to perform their duty. Is that wise? Are you being too cautious?"

Brockman started to reply but paused. *Am I being too cautious? Not trusting the men? Perhaps Roy has a point. We've drilled and trained. They should be ready. Perhaps I should rethink this idea. Maintain the regular officer schedule.*

He got up to top off his coffee. Warming the brew, he took a long sip, lowered the cup and set it down on the counter. *No. The crew's much too inexperienced. A first battle is the wrong time to gamble that the men will respond quickly and as expected.*

"You make a good point," Brockman admitted, "but let's play it safe this time. The men don't have to know what's up. One of us will just happen to be awake and instantly available at all times."

"Do you think that they won't figure things out? Certainly the other officers will."

"I'm sure they will but we won't make an obvious issue of it. I'm hoping they'll give us the benefit of the doubt for a day or two."

"If you're right, after that it won't matter. We'll be too busy fighting Japs."

Brockman drained the cup and set it down. The boat bucked again, nearly throwing him off his feet. He reached out to clamp onto the bulkhead.

"Now you've got it."

"And if you're wrong, the morale of this boat could take a serious blow right off the bat on this war patrol. A blow that could take a very long time to recover from. You're running the risk of losing the crew's support and belief in you."

Brockman forced a thin smile. "Don't sugarcoat it. Tell me exactly what you think."

Benson held up a palm. "Okay, I've said my piece. I'm just trying to help out."

"I appreciate your candor and expect it, but I've considered everything that you've mentioned. Trust works both ways. The crew has to believe that I'm willing to take whatever steps are necessary to get the job done. That goes for you and the rest of the officers, too. I won't sway from that."

A mock look of pain flashed across Benson's face. "That hurt, but you make a good point. Trust does work both ways. You've convinced me."

"Good," Brockman responded. "I have some reports to write, so I'll take first watch. Go ahead and get some sleep. We'll swap out in about four hours."

Benson stood and made to leave. "I'll tell the stewards to keep a fresh pot on. I've a feeling that we're both going to need it."

34. RAMSEY
June 04 – 04:00 Hours

Ramsey yawned and tried to focus his eyes on the PBY torpedo attack report from a short time earlier. Dawn having yet to break, he poured himself another cup of coffee and glanced at his watch. There was no doubt in his mind that four o'clock in the morning was the most unholy hour of the entire day. He held up the message and waved it at the nearby radio operator.

"Is this all they've sent?"

The young sailor, feet propped up, paperback novel in hand, and headphones securely clamped onto his head, looked over at him.

"Aye, sir. Would you like for me to request more information?"

Ramsey squinted. "Do you think Zane Grey can spare you for a few minutes?"

The radio operator caught Ramsey's meaning. His feet hit the deck. The book disappeared. Finger pounded the key, beat out a staccato rhythm that echoed against the concrete walls of the bunker. Captain Simard came walking in, followed by a tall, red-haired, broad-shouldered man. His manner of dress instantly made Ramsey suspicious. He wore a disheveled, mishmash uniform composed of a tropical Army shirt and khaki trousers. Dark glasses wrapped his rugged face in a veil of anonymity.

"Commander Logan Ramsey, this is Commander John Ford," Simard said.

"It's Jack," Ford corrected.

"Logan." Ramsey shook the offered hand, staring at the Army Lieutenant Colonel insignia dangling from one of Ford's collar tabs. He had heard stories about the Hollywood film director, but nothing had prepared him for this. *He looks more like a character in one of his movies than a naval officer. I hope he understands that the bullets and blood are real, not some makeup artist's handiwork. What was Nimitz thinking by sending this man into a combat zone?*

"I suppose you're wondering what I'm doing here?" Ford said, his voice filling the space.

Ramsey's eyesight darted to Simard and then back to Ford. "I know that it has something to do with Admiral Nimitz, but the question does beg asking."

"Damned if I know," Ford answered and chuckled. "Chet corralled me to Pearl Harbor, shoved me on board some rust-bucket boat bound for this spot in the Pacific, and waved goodbye. I didn't know there *was* a place named Midway Island . . . now here I am."

He jabbed a thumb at Simard. "Maybe Cy will fill me in."

"I do have a job for you," Simard said.

"Good, let's hear it."

"You've been to all the briefings and heard all of the talk about what we're expecting to happen tomorrow." Simard walked over to the coffeepot as he talked.

"I wouldn't be surprised if everyone between here and the West Coast knows what's supposed to happen tomorrow," Ford remarked. "I just hope Tojo hasn't heard the word."

Ford's face shifted toward Ramsey, who wondered if the man had winked behind the shades. Ramsey returned the suspected gesture by turning one corner of his mouth up. He furrowed his forehead as he silently studied Ford. How can you see at night wearing dark glasses? Why would someone do that? I wonder how he keeps from bumping into stuff as we walks.

"We've tried to keep this thing as our little secret," Ramsey replied. "I guess we failed."

"I'd like to position you on top of the powerhouse during the attack," Simard continued. "Do you mind?"

"Not in the least. It's a high vantage point and a good place to shoot film. I should get some great footage from up there."

Simard poured a cup and motioned to Ford with the pot. The director strode over, picked up an empty mug, and waited while Simard filled it.

"Forget the film," Simard said as he replaced the pot. "I want you to have a phone that's connected to me here in the command post. With your knowledge of detail, experience with large, complicated scenes, and photographic eye, you'd be a natural in reporting what's going on. I can think of few things more complex and chaotic than what is about to happen to this place."

"You don't have to flatter me to talk me into it."

Simard smiled. "It's not flattery, just the truth. You're the perfect man for the job."

Ford took a sip and replied, "Agreed. It sounds like a good idea to me."

"I won't lie to you," Simard said. "It could be dangerous standing up there on top of that building. You'll stick out like a sore thumb. The Japs could single you out for attack. There will be bombs exploding and flying shrapnel."

Ford glanced over at Ramsey and might have winked again. "Is Cy trying to talk me out of doing this or into doing this? I'm confused."

Why would you wear dark glasses and wink? Ramsey thought, but said, "He just wants to give you all of the facts."

"I owe it to you," Simard agreed. "Take a moment to think it over."

Ramsey watched as Ford considered Simard's request, trying to discern his thoughts. That the Japs could target Ford was an understatement. Not only *could* they target Ford standing exposed on top of the powerhouse, but they *would* target him. I saw too many examples of that on December 7 at Pearl Harbor. Zeros strafed anything that caught their notice. To do as Simard asked undoubtedly places Ford in mortal danger.

"I'll do it under one condition," Ford answered. "I want to give Jack Mackenzie, my assistant cameraman, the option to volunteer for this assignment. He's regular Navy like the rest of you and I don't want him ordered to stand up there with me. He wouldn't be placed in the position except for the fact he's working with me. I want him to have a choice in the matter."

"I'll see to it," Simard agreed. "Logan, do you have anything to add?"

Logan shook his head. "Other than that if it gets too hot, get down and seek shelter. A wise man knows when it's time to get out of the rain. The kind of rain that the Japs will be dumping is deadly."

Ford smiled and tilted his head. "I'll try to keep that in mind, but can't promise anything. That's the stubbornness of us Irishmen. We never know when we're licked and it's time to run."

They all chuckled, and Simard said, "Go ahead and get your phone line set up and anything else you need. Let me know if I can do anything to help."

Ford handed Simard the cup and left the bunker. Ramsey returned to studying the chart. Leaning over, Simard tapped his finger on the spot where the B-17s had attacked the day before.

"I'm thinking we send Sweeney's bunch back to hit that Jap transport force," Simard said. "Maybe they can run across whatever they damaged yesterday and finish sinking it. That'll put us one up on the Japs. It's certainly worth a try."

Ramsey spoke without glancing at Simard. "Pearl received a message from *Cuttlefish* about that. They failed to locate a damaged battleship at the stated position. All they found was a tanker. It appeared to have no damage."

"Perhaps it sank? Those B-17s might have worked it over good. Sent it right to the bottom."

"I guess there's a chance. It must have gone down in a hurry, with an even speedier rescue of survivors to leave no trace. You'd think something as large as a battleship would leave a field of debris several miles wide when it sinks. *Cuttlefish* reported none of that."

"Yeah, I agree. What about the tanker? Certainly, it wasn't alone. She should have had an escort vessel or two. We did receive a contact report to follow up on, right?"

"Enemy aircraft drove *Cuttlefish* under and kept it submerged."

Simard cursed softly, slapping the tabletop. The action drew the radioman and the other men working in the bunker to stiff, upright positions. Ramsey took silent notice and smiled. There was nothing like a display of temper to get everyone's undivided attention . . . even if the men were not the reason for the outburst.

"There is some good news," Ramsey offered. "The PBYs' radar located about ten ships not too far from that position. Three of them made their torpedo attack with two hits on what they believe to be large freighters. The fourth plane lost contact with the others and didn't release."

Simard seemed to digest the information as he walked over to the phone. "I'm going to send the B-17s out there and see what they find."

"Admiral Nimitz believes Nagumo's carrier force will come steaming out of that cold front northwest of here today," Ramsey reminded. "So far, he and the Intelligence boys have been on the money with their predictions. Are you sure you want to commit those bombers before our scouts get out there?"

Simard cupped his palm over the mouthpiece. "I'll tell Sweeney to monitor his radio in case a PBY makes a contact and his target changes."

Ramsey studied the chart and compared the known target with Nimitz's suspected location for Nagumo to appear. With the extended range of the B-17s, Sweeney could easily change if needed. Besides, if Nagumo did show up and launch an air strike, it would be imperative to get everything airborne including the B-17s. Having an airfield full of bomb-damaged aircraft would mean disaster and a failure to defend this place.

Simard returned to the table. "Combat air patrol's taking off first, followed by the search planes, and then Sweeney's B-17s. Everything else that can fly will warm up and remain readied to leave at a moment's notice. All they need is a definite location to attack."

Ramsey stood up straight and stretched. His sight locked onto the chart as he tried to visualize the wide expanse of ocean it represented. He could only hope that Nagumo appeared where expected; he could only pray their preparations and plans would prove adequate to defeat him. He glanced at his wristwatch one more time. Soon, he thought. Very soon.

35. KUSAKA
June 04 – 04:00 Hours

"*General Quarters!*"

The warning call rushed through Kusaka's sleep-dimmed mind, pushed by the incessant audible alarm. He crawled from bed, fumbled to dress, and made his way to the bridge. Entering into a bustle of frantic activity, he saw each officer standing with binoculars clamped to his eyes, scanning the dark skies off to starboard.

Captain Aoki lowered his glasses to glance around. His face pinched in evident frustration, he seemed to seek something to lash out at.

"And I tell you I see nothing," Aoki said. "Not now nor the first time. Bring the lookout to me and leave someone else in his place."

Kusaka stood back watching a scared young sailor ushered into the officers' midst. The taint of fear radiated from him like a blowfish's spines. He bowed deeply, keeping his eyes locked onto the deck. Hands clasped together, he patiently waited in trepidation. The servant before his master, Kusaka thought. Or a disobedient child confronted by an angry father.

"You twice reported seeing the lights of an enemy patrol plane in the same direction, yet nothing was found," Aoki said. "*Twice.* I warned you and everyone else to be careful and not mistake stars combined with the ship's motion for moving aircraft lights. Did you not hear my caution?"

Head lowered, the man answered, "Yes, sir. I heard."

"Is there some reason why you do not follow orders? A fault in your upbringing? A fault in your training? Was I not speaking clearly?"

Eyesight locked onto the deck, he replied, "No, sir."

Kusaka winced as Aoki reached out and cuffed him on the head.

"This ship depends on each man performing his job. The Emperor expects it. I expect it. Your shipmates expect it. You must do better in carrying out your duties."

The shaved head remained stationary.

"Confine yourself to quarters until I send for you. Think about this. Regret the fact that this lapse on your part has placed hardship on all. Reflect on the shame that you've brought upon yourself."

The sailor straightened, then bowed once more, and hurried off. Kusaka held his tongue, not wanting to question the captain's conduct in front of the crew. Aoki is new to a combat assignment, he thought. Such a large operation as this is a poor time to learn how to deal with men in battle. In such circumstances, the rules of conduct change. Kusaka allowed himself a moment of compassion for the disgraced young man and drew upon his own memories of being a midshipman prone to mistakes. His face seemed to betray his feelings to Aoki and allowed Aoki to read his thoughts.

"Make a harsh example of one and the rest fall into line," Aoki said in justification.

Kusaka responded, "Whatever words we utter should be chosen with care, for people will hear them and be influenced by them for good or ill. How do you believe that young man was influenced?"

Aoki pulled himself upright and stepped closer to Kusaka.

"I am captain of this vessel and will command as I see fit. I don't need your Buddhist proverbs to light my path. I hold my crew to a very high standard. Repeated mistakes will not be tolerated."

Kusaka held eye contact, thinking, you would test your will against mine? Prove yourself equal to the task with words rather than actions? That is not the way of good leadership.

Kusaka said, "And would you hold yourself to the same high standard? Combat has its own rules. At such times, these scared young men need understanding and a good example . . . not harsh discipline. It is a mistake to think otherwise. A mistake should not be repeated by one who would grow in wisdom."

A wicked-looking smile curled across Aoki's lips. "He repeated his mistake, so I took the opportunity to nurture him and help him grow smarter. He should feel grateful for my dedicated attention."

"Your disingenuous words knowingly stroke an ego lacking in the experience of proper conduct in battle. You have as much to learn of such matters as him."

Aoki's nostrils flared as his eyes squinted. "My inexperience in combat is offset by my knowledge of command. I care not for—"

"Gentlemen." Nagumo came through the door. "I'm interrupting something of importance?"

Both bowed and Aoki said, "Disciplining a sailor for poor performance of his duties. I'm sure it won't happen again."

Nagumo glanced at one and then the other.

"Kusaka?" he asked.

This discussion with Aoki should continue at another time, Kusaka thought. "Responding to the General Quarters alarm and preparing for today's operation. The men are ready and so am I. We should not keep the enemy waiting."

Nagumo studied both, seemed poised to respond, and then remained silent. *Akagi*'s loudspeakers cut in, ordering all aircrews to turn out and assemble for launch. Nagumo led the others over to the window and they looked out at the frenetic activity below on the flight deck. The deafening thunder of engines warming up grew into an almost tangible mass of roaring like that of a tsunami crashing against the shore. Relentless. Sweeping everything away in its path. A tsunami of death and destruction.

Kusaka felt a sudden presence at his left side, turned his head and found a pajama-clad Genda leaning against the window frame. He smiled, nudged Nagumo on his right, and pointed toward Genda.

"Genda!"

The joy in Nagumo's voice was undisguised and heartfelt. Nagumo moved over, throwing his arm around the young officer's thin shoulders.

"It's good to have you back. How do you feel?"

"Sir, I have neglected my duties too long and apologize for my absence. I have a slight temperature but am feeling much better."

Kusaka took note of his feverish eyes and suspected his condition to be worse than stated. He also saw the glint of Genda's fighting spirit gazing out, taking stock of the situation and what needed doing. Kusaka felt a sudden lifting of the heavy mood that had prevailed over the bridge the past few days. One man can indeed make a difference, no matter the size of the operation.

"You heard the sound of aircraft engines and couldn't bear to be left out," Kusaka said. "Your presence is most welcome."

The two of them left Nagumo at the window and moved over to the small chart table. Genda spent a few moments studying the marked positions of ships and suspected contacts. A pile of recent message transmissions lay nearby, and he scanned them before glancing at Kusaka.

"There was another attack on the Transport Force?"

"A few hours ago. Enemy aircraft torpedoed an oiler causing minimum damage. The ship was able to maintain speed with the rest of the task force. Our antiaircraft fire claimed at least two hits on the attacking planes, most probably Catalina flying boats."

"Catalinas making a torpedo attack?"

"The range to Midway was still too great for smaller aircraft. I doubt the Americans would risk their heavy B-17s on such a foolish idea."

Genda managed a feeble grin. "The Americans haven't acquired our skills at night engagements."

"Nor at torpedo attacks." Kusaka pointed at the message, "It says at least three torpedoes were released at pointblank range and only one hit the target."

"*Hai*, would that they grow no more proficient at such attacks. I enjoy the advantage we presently have."

"Indeed. Still, it is somewhat disturbing that the enemy is going to such lengths to attack us. They appear ready and planning to put up a stiff resistance. Admiral Nagumo questioned if we might be looking at another struggle such as the one Wake Island proved to be. He could be right."

"And if he is? We've brought more than enough air and land forces to annihilate Midway's defenses. Admiral Yamamoto has planned for such an eventuality."

"Perhaps."

"From the activity outside it's safe to say that things are progressing as planned?" Genda changed the subject.

"Yes, the air patrol will take off very soon followed by all of the strike aircraft. Admiral Nagumo wanted the search planes to leave after the attack is launched."

"After we launch our Midway attack?" Genda glanced over at Nagumo. "You wish to delay our reconnaissance planes?"

Nagumo stood at the window with hands clutched behind his back and spoke over his shoulder. "I don't wish to take the chance of having our scouting planes discovered before the carrier strike reaches Midway. I want to catch the enemy with most of his aircraft on the ground and destroy them. With no means of retaliation, they must surrender. Admiral Kondo's troops will be able to wade ashore in safety."

Kusaka walked over to the window and gazed up at the blossoming sky. An occasional star winked from behind rose-tinted clouds, offering the promise of a fine day and good flying weather. He looked down and saw the first of the patrol Zeroes roaring by, headed off into the air. As soon as it cleared the deck, the next one rumbled past in quick succession.

"What of the search plan?" Genda called over to him.

Kusaka rejoined him at the table, removed another chart from beneath it, and spread it out. It showed seven lines radiating outward from the task force like the spokes of a wheel. The lines began due south, followed the eastern axis, and ended approximately three-quarters of the way north of its center. Genda studied it for a few moments.

"It's basically the same pattern I drew up for Pearl Harbor and the Indian Ocean operations."

"It proved adequate before and should now," Kusaka said. "There was a small problem in numbers. There weren't enough search aircraft available from *Tone*, *Chikuma*, and *Haruna*. I've allocated one each from *Akagi* and *Kaga* to cover all of the routes."

"It sounds sufficient."

"I agree." Nagumo faced them. "We've no sightings of enemy activity from our submarine pickets. The reports from Admiral Tanaka indicate that the enemy patrol planes are focusing to the west and south of Midway. In spite of the poor weather that has forced a break in our communications blackout, the enemy remains unaware of our plans."

Kusaka felt relief as he saw the familiar spark once more in Nagumo's eyes. Their discussion yesterday afternoon had left Kusaka worried that Nagumo harbored serious doubts as to the outcome of the operation. Nagumo's face now seemed to glow from the heat of impending combat, a look not present at Pearl Harbor when he decided to withdraw. Some had said Nagumo left the job unfinished. If he does differently this time and destroys the enemy fleet, the questions will cease.

"The Americans seek to avoid a fight, but it's likely that our occupation of Midway will force them to launch a counterattack," Nagumo continued. "Our opportunity's at hand to destroy what little resolve they hold and force them to the negotiating table."

183

Kusaka turned away and looked out the window, thinking, a night's sleep and time for reflection seem to have improved Nagumo's attitude. Or . . . a nagging idea came to mind. He's finally saying what he knows he is expected to say. Playing the role of combat leader once more. Acting . . . not believing.

A strengthening glow tinted the horizon and preceded the rising sun. Kusaka drew strength from the sight, thinking, may it herald the dawn of Imperial domination over the entire Pacific Ocean.

36. TOMONAGA
June 04 – 04:00 Hours

Tomonaga sat off to one side of the wardroom eating breakfast. He was surprised at the rather sumptuous offering of rice, soup, and pickles, having expected a typical meal of cold combat rations. A dessert of chestnuts and sake, a traditional food combination eaten by warriors entering battle, served to remind each man of their deadly mission. He consciously licked his lips, savored the welcome taste of the sake, and wished for more.

"A fine meal for the condemned, *hai*?" Kawaguchi, *Hiryu*'s air officer, loomed over him. He pointed at Tomonaga's empty tray. "All of this symbolism has me rethinking how serious our Midway assault might be."

"Any battle is serious and should be treated as such," Tomonaga replied.

"Of course, I didn't mean . . ." Kawaguchi's voice trailed off as Tomonaga picked up a weather report and began reading.

"The call should come any time now," Kawaguchi said and walked away.

After days of poor visibility and low ceiling, the weather report boded well. Tomonaga noticed a message intercept sent by the submarine *I-168* to Tokyo. Stationed just two miles off shore of Midway, for the past few days it had maintained close watch of the atoll's activity. The mention of increased aircraft surveillance and reinforcements raised a slight concern that the enemy suspected something was impending. He brushed the feeling off, thinking, *and so they are alerted. As things now stand, it doesn't matter. There's no way the available enemy air power will stand a chance against the whirlwind poised to strike in just a few short hours. Dead men walk the sands of Midway.*

"I see that your mind is on the mission," Kikuchi said as he sat down next to him. "The weather report is excellent."

"And you?"

"I've cleansed myself and am ready to take the battle to my enemy. I know what I must do and have prepared myself to die should the moment come. I shall not die in vain. I will retaliate no matter what happens to me."

Tomonaga stared at him.

"You doubt me?" Kikuchi asked. He lifted his tunic, revealing a battle flag wrapped around his stomach. "I serve his Imperial Majesty and the Empire."

"An obi?"

"No, a shroud. A shroud of glory to cover me should I make the ultimate sacrifice for my master."

Tomonaga remained silent.

"The time is near, my friend. Who do you serve?"

Tomonaga gazed around at the noisy room, considering Kikuchi's words. Whom do I serve? Japan and the Emperor or my own ambition? Is it wrong to desire the recognition for being the finest flight leader in the Imperial Navy? To prove to Genda that I am the equal if not the superior of all? By doing so, do I not also fulfill my duties? I *can* serve both my master and myself. None but my heart shall know the truth. The heart is incapable of speech. Incapable of naming the false servant . . . the one who hides in shadows to conceal his true purpose. The heart performs many functions. It contains joy and love, bringing great happiness. When filled with compassion, it can alleviate the pain of others. Yet, the heart also holds the deepest pool of shame.

Whom do I serve?

"Attention pilots!" Kawaguchi stood at the front of the room, arms raised for silence. From the flight deck above, the sudden roar of aircraft engines coming to life and warming up filled the space with thunder. The incredible racket forced Kawaguchi to raise his voice to almost shouting level.

"The weather has cleared as predicted, and the forecast is for broken cloud cover and good flying all the way into Midway. Submarine reconnaissance informs us there's a large air group present at Midway. Thirty-six Zeroes will provide close escort. They'll sweep any enemy fighter opposition aside as they always do.

"After launching, the carrier force will maintain the present course for three and a half hours at a speed of twenty-four knots. As the time approaches for your return, the fleet will come to a heading into the wind to allow for recovery. If something happens to change these plans, a ship will be sent to the original recovery area to redirect you."

Kawaguchi then cast a glance over the crowd. "Any questions?"

Tomonaga saw tense faces looking back at Kawaguchi, but no hands rose.

"This operation is critical to the success of our forces in the Pacific," Kawaguchi picked up. "If we win today, the enemy must recognize the ultimate triumph of the Empire. Our hour of complete victory is at hand. I'm urging each one of you to put your nerve into making your attack. Do not sway from performing your duty, no matter the price. The Emperor and all of Japan are watching. Watching and depending on you. Do not bring dishonor upon yourself or your house."

Tomonaga ducked his head to hide his disgust, thinking, I can do without the patriotic speech. Why do the men furthest from the fighting speak the bravest words? They weave brilliant tapestries of rhetoric and venom as if such arguments are necessary to steel one's soul for combat. If a man needs such talk to do his best, he's already defeated. The presence of the enemy will simply confirm matters. Battle for the sake of battle and to prove one's mastery over his enemy is reason enough for a warrior to fight. It's the *only* reason that a man needs to fight. This war is not about political ideologies but rather one people's domination of another. Will we wear the boots or be the ones who lick them? Nothing else matters. Kawaguchi drones on like a politician exhorting the troops to great deeds while he remains safely behind.

"All hands to launching stations!"

The welcome blare from the ship's loudspeaker brought them to their feet and hustling for the door. Kawaguchi reached out, grabbed Tomonaga rushing by, and extended his hand.

"Good luck flies with you," he said.

Tomonaga bowed slightly and returned the shake. He paused in front of the small Shinto shrine to offer a prayer of appeasement to the kami for the lives he would take that day. A few minutes later, he ran across the deck with the other pilots. Mounting the wing of his Nakajima Type 97 torpedo-bomber, he proudly noted the distinctive yellow tail stripes indicating his status as strike leader and then scrambled into the cockpit. A crewman helped him buckle up and bowed before climbing down. Tomonaga glanced back and made certain Hashimoto, his observer, and Murai, his radioman, had belted in.

Not trusting the mechanics with such a crucial task, he stepped through the preflight checklist. His grandfather had warned that a warrior is only as effective as his weapons. He allows no one the responsibility to prepare them for battle. To do so is disrespectful to the craftsmen who made them and dishonorable to the Spirit of Bushido.

As he worked, his thoughts again drifted to his conversations with Kikuchi over the past few days. Kikuchi seemed at peace, prepared for anything. Kikuchi's speech and manner call to mind one who walks the path of thorns, but will his actions? Is it enough to call oneself samurai and use a flag as an obi to become samurai? Must one be born to such a calling or is it possible to obtain the title by the manner in which a man thinks and lives his life? Is samurai a right of birth or a rite of passage? What would grandfather say?

He focused his attention on the surrounding activity. The Zeroes composing his strike escort and the combat air patrol over the fleet howled down the wooden flight deck and lifted gracefully into the air. His plane, the first torpedo-bomber slated to depart, had the shortest amount of space to work with in getting airborne. He raised an arm to signal his readiness to the Air Operations Officer.

The takeoff light flashed on, prompting him into action. He jammed the throttle full open, popped the brakes, and wished good fortune to see him clear. The heavy aircraft lumbered forward, fighting a seemingly losing battle to gain speed. He saw the flight deck end approaching too quickly and thought, I'm not moving fast enough to launch. I wonder how it will feel to roll over the end and into the waiting water below. Who will lead the strike then? Who is the next expendable pilot?

At the final second, the wheels lifted free as the plane nosed upward. He circled to port and formed up a holding pattern to wait while the rest of his squadron took off. He led his group as they climbed to altitude and gathered together with the forces from the other carriers. Pointing the mass toward Midway, he settled in for the flight. A look around at the armada of deadly aircraft brought a smile to his face. Damn the words and hollow promises of the politicians. Death rides the wind. The warrior works his trade.

37. HENDERSON
June 04 – 04:30 Hours

Henderson looked out at the assembled men while waiting on Norris to finish scribbling the latest weather information on the blackboard. He deeply inhaled the salty dampness of the new day trickling through the open door. The cool breeze tickling his cheek held the promise of nice flying weather. The gods of war must crave watching a memorable battle, he thought. They've prepared the perfect stage for it.

His vision took in the group, and he noted the youth evident in every face. It is always the same in every war. Young men poised at the brink of making their mark on the world . . . martyred for God and country. Just because someone would shackle his mind and actions. Deny him the freedom won by the blood of those who went before. We owe the legacy of those brave souls to prevent this from happening to our generation.

"Alright, this is what we've been training for and what we've been waiting for," he began. "Our recon planes should be taking off in search of Nagumo's force. Yesterday, the B-17s located what's now thought to be the Invasion Group headed this way. The chances are good that the Japs are going to appear to the northwest of here early this morning. They're long overdue. We need to be ready."

He got up, walked away from the desk, and stood in front of the room.

"When the order comes, we'll take off and head out twenty miles on magnetic course ninety degrees and rendezvous at coordinate *Point Affirm*. At that time, we'll proceed as two separate units. The SBDs will go with me. The SB2Us are with Major Norris."

He waited for a few moments while the pilots made quick notes on their plotting boards. He felt—*saw* tension coursing through them as they quietly worked. A nervous cough here and a throat cleared there. He'd witnessed this before. There's nothing like facing combat for the first time to force a man into confronting his fear. For that matter, there's no lonelier feeling, either. It's a shame that it doesn't get any easier or less stressful with repetition. The term "fearless" should never be used to describe a man entering battle unless he's also a fool.

"I know we've been over and over this the past few days, but let's do it once more. I don't want anyone thinking about making the attack. When the ack-ack starts and the Jap fighters show up, confusion will try to destroy your concentration. I want everything to be automatic. It's critical that we hit this bunch and hit them hard. If we don't, they're bringing enough explosives to level this place. Let's get our punch in first and make it count.

"We'll fly out to them at about 9,000 feet and start a fast power glide when the enemy's sighted. At that time, we'll level off around 4,000 feet to make our final approach. I'll find us a good position to attack from, preferably with the sun at our tails. Then it's up to each one of us to glide in and dump our bomb on something flying a red meatball flag. Admiral Nimitz prefers that we target carriers. That's fine if you believe that you can get close enough to nail one. I'm more concerned with making our bombs count. That is our primary purpose for mounting this attack. I want us to leave the Japs circling around, fishing up swimming survivors, and trying to put out fires. That will keep them busy while we swing back, rearm, and hit them again. We do that enough times and Nagumo will search for easier prey."

He paused to glance around the room and saw apprehensive faces staring back at him. I've known these men for such a short amount of time. Some of their faces I can't yet put names to. I wonder how much longer we have to be acquainted. How empty will this room be this evening?

"We need to get down before dropping the bombs. I'm talking 500 feet or lower. You'll still be moving at a good clip. You won't have to pull straight out of a dive, so you shouldn't have any problem with being caught up in the explosion. I want you to stay low . . . hug that water like it's your best girl. When you get clear of the immediate killing zone, hunt a nice cloud for cover. Don't let a Zeke have room to get under you. It's also harder for enemy ack-ack to reach you while you're weaving between their ships."

A hand rose in the back of the room that Henderson acknowledged.

"Sir, if we drop at low altitude, will the bomb have time to arm?"

"Good question. After loading the bombs, the ground crews turned the fuses seventy turns by hand. Another twenty turns while falling should finish arming them. They shouldn't drop far before those twenty turns spin off."

He glanced over the room. "Any other questions?"

"What's the rendezvous plan after we drop?" a different voice called out.

"First of all, everyone stay low on top of that water like I told you, and don't spare the horsepower. Kick that mule in the ass and stay on her. Gunners, keep alert even when you think you've cleared the area. Maintain a sharp eye out because those Zekes will be pissed after we torch their carriers. They're going to be as mad and as thick as hornets. They'll want to take their anger out on the cause of their not having a place to land. That means us. Absent opposition, we'll assemble twenty miles away from the nearest enemy surface craft on the course leading back here. If it's complete chaos, do the best you can by yourself."

He paused again to allow for questions. *The fear is still here, but so is the thrill of facing the unknown,* he thought. *Almost a relief that the wait is nearly over and the fighting about to begin. Give me an airplane and a target. I'll do the rest. Each one of us must believe that.*

"I'm not much at giving speeches, and now's not the time to learn. We all still remember December 7 of last year. We recall with pride the fight that our guys put up at Wake Island. It took half the Imperial Fleet, a couple of thousand troops, and two weeks to whip four hundred marines and capture the place. Hell, our guys ran out of ammunition before they ran out of fight. You'd better believe the Japs suffered tremendous casualties before the last shot was fired."

He tilted his head up and forced a smile. "Now it's our turn to show Tojo and his monkeys how Marines fight. I expect no less from you."

He lowered his chin for a few seconds to collect his thoughts and then rose up. He raised his right hand and pointed out toward the east where he knew the rising sun brought the uncertainty of a new day.

"Our home is in that direction and Yamamoto knows it. He wants to carry this war right to our doorsteps . . . to bring suffering upon our loved ones and families. Doolittle's raid embarrassed

Japan and they're itching to return the gesture. They intend to take Midway and then use this place as a staging area for invading Hawaii. Once their ships berth at Pearl Harbor, our West Coast is next. I've a feeling that we have a chance at significantly influencing the course of this war. To halt the barbarians in their tracks. It begins here today."

His arm dropped as he studied each face one last time.

"I don't intend to return home to a country laid waste to by the enemy. Nor am I going to kneel while Hirohito places his foot on my neck. I'm doing my damnedest to stop them here."

He paused once more, waiting for the tension to peak.

"Who's with me?"

38. SPRUANCE
June 04 – 05:30 Hours

Spruance rose early and made his way to the flag shelter. He stepped through the door and saw Browning and Oliver already seated near the overhead radio loudspeaker. Glancing at him as he entered, they started to rise.

He waved them down and asked, "Anything?"

Browning shook his head. "Our radio doesn't have Midway's base frequency, so I had them tune it to the Midway search plane frequency. Other than a few weather reports, nothing."

Spruance took his chair and sat back with legs crossed. He felt the changing noises and vibrations of the great ship as crews and pilots prepared for the upcoming day. On the flight deck below, the sound of Wildcats warming up and preparing to take off on the morning air patrol grew louder. The sticky sea air crackled with static electricity. Boiler smoke and igniting aviation fuel trumpeted the foolish notion that man held power over the elements. I've witnessed a few typhoons and hurricanes, Spruance thought. I know different.

A sudden blast from the loudspeaker cut cleanly through the ambient noise. "Enemy carrier," followed by a few garbled words tilted all heads to look up.

"That's Nagumo," Spruance said. After the long wait for the massive carrier force to appear, the fact that the smaller American fleet must defeat it tempered his feelings of relief. Admiral Nimitz was right in his assumptions, he thought. The moment for combat nears . . . the situation is placed in our hands. We must not fail.

He stared intently at the loudspeaker, trying to wish it back to life to provide further information on the contact. I can't launch a strike on those few words. I can't radio back asking to amplify. I understand the need for communication silence, but it's still not easy to sit by and helplessly wait for more information. Details . . . I need details.

"Where in the hell is that carrier?" Browning spoke up. "Why wasn't the report repeated and more thorough? Those scouts know better than that. Damn them for not performing their duty correctly. "

Spruance looked at him. "I've seen what those PBY boys go through making a report. That aircraft is slow and clumsy and makes an excellent target for an enemy fighter of any type. Those pilots are maneuvering around, trying to stay out of sight and reach. If they're shot down, we certainly won't receive any more information. Give them a chance. I'm sure it won't be much longer before we hear something else."

Browning's jaw muscle tightened and he blew out his cheeks. "I know. It's tough sitting here waiting."

"Many planes headed Midway bearing 320 degrees, distance 150," the loudspeaker suddenly squawked.

Spruance slid to the chair's edge. Steady, he thought. Remain calm. This is it and from the direction Nimitz had said the attack would come. The details remained unclear, too unclear for any response just yet, but he felt the noose tightening. Tension peaked throughout the room; he noticed Browning's legs vibrating up and down on his toe tips.

Commander Buracker hurried in and halted as the loudspeaker broadcast, "Two carriers and main body of ships, carriers in front, course 135, speed 25."

The message detonated an explosion of action. Browning and Oliver leapt from their chairs and joined Buracker in racing over to the navigation chart. They all grabbed for and briefly fought over the measuring dividers. Browning won and spent a few minutes plotting the contact report. Finished, he wiped a sweaty brow and turned to Spruance standing next to his chair.

"No doubt they're coming from the northwest and we've got a good line on them." Browning clacked the dividers together. "They're sailing right into Admiral Nimitz's trap."

Spruance motioned Oliver over to the phone. "I want someone in the radio shack to repeat and authenticate that report."

Oliver rang up the radio operator and voiced Spruance's command. He listened for a few seconds and then hung up.

"Repeated word for word and authenticated, sir."

"Have a message sent to Admiral Fletcher about this report and verify that he received it, too. If not, send it to him and request further orders."

Spruance stepped over to the plotting table and looked down at Browning's plot. He felt their eyes latching on to him awaiting the next move. He thought, I mustn't hurry or commit too soon. Now is not the time for rash action. *The principle of calculated risk must govern all that we do,* Nimitz had stressed. Do not expose our forces unless there's the prospect of inflicting greater damage on the enemy. Those are words to live by . . . or die by.

Spruance retrieved a rolled document from his seat, carried it back to the table, and unrolled it. He spent several minutes bent over the small maneuvering board drawing lines and making notations. Browning coughed and shuffled about. I know that you're there Miles, he thought. Nothing personal. It's just the way that I like to work. I prefer making my own plots, especially for something as critical as this.

Satisfied, he glanced up. "They're coming exactly as Layton predicted."

"Message from Admiral Fetcher," Oliver called out. "Proceed southwesterly and attack enemy carriers as soon as definitely located. He will join us when *Yorktown's* scouting aircraft are recovered."

Spruance glanced at his watch and then back at the chart. By the reports, the Japanese are not yet within the limits of my TBDs' range. If I launch now, the TBDs and Wildcats won't have enough fuel to return. The attack would be wasted. *Calculated risk must govern all that we do.* The first strike is critical . . . but only if it accomplishes something. Otherwise, I will have alerted the enemy to our presence for no reason.

"Sir?" Browning prompted.

"Let's keep closing the gap," Spruance answered, rolling up his board. "I calculate at 0900 we'll be about 100 miles away from them. If we wait until then to launch, our planes should have enough cushion to find Nagumo, execute the attack, and make their way back here without a problem."

The pained look on Browning's face signaled his reaction to Spruance's plan. I expected as much, Spruance thought. He and I have knocked heads over everything concerning air operations since I assumed command. I'm growing tired of his constant disagreement with me. Still, this is his area of expertise. Halsey would have allowed him to speak his mind. I should listen to what he has to say.

"Go ahead, Miles. I expect my officers to voice their opinions, not blindly follow my lead."

"Sir, we must attack Nagumo at our earliest opportunity. You can be sure he's launched scouting aircraft to locate any threat like us. The longer we wait, the greater the possibility the Japs will discover us. We'll lose the advantage of surprise. We can't give that up. This entire operation hinges on our surprising them."

"What do you suggest?"

"Launching at 0700. By then, we'll be around 155 miles away from them. I realize that puts us at the edge of our attack range, but it can't be helped. We must hit Nagumo before he discovers us. Success depends on it, sir."

It's risky, Spruance thought. There won't be much room for error. If the Japanese aren't where we expect them to be, we could lose most of an entire strike group. Time spent hunting Nagumo will exhaust their strained fuel tanks. Many of the planes are sure to make ocean landings. With luck, our destroyers can fish out the crews . . . but their aircraft will be lost. It's a gamble.

One that we must take.

Spruance nodded. "I agree."

Relief revealed itself on Browning's face as he said, "About the composition of the striking force."

"I'm thinking on that," Spruance replied.

"Sir, if I may–" Spruance's raised hand silenced Browning.

Nimitz said there would be four or five enemy carriers in Nagumo's force, Spruance thought. They'll be bunched together, surrounded by screening vessels. The contact reports only list two. Where are the others? Poised somewhere else ready to strike? Do I send just part of my air groups to attack this contact? Keep something in reserve in case the other carriers appear? Another gamble.

I can't operate under the restriction of what *might* be out there. I have a definite location on two Japanese mainline carriers. That is a given. I must hit them and hit them hard. That is also a given. Send all of my strike force or only part of it? Either way is a risk.

I can't waffle or show indecision. I have two large, dangerous targets that will be searching for a threat like us. Those two carriers alone are capable of wiping out my entire task force. I have to send enough aircraft to get the job done on the first attack. There may not be a second.

"I want everything we can spare set to take off at 0700," Spruance said. "Hold back a sufficient CAP and some scouts for anti-submarine work. The rest we're sending after Nagumo."

"Aye, sir," Browning replied, moving off to set the operation into motion.

Spruance regained his seat, stretched out, and closed his eyes. The decision is made, he thought. Only time and circumstances will tell if it was the correct one.

39. FLETCHER
June 04 – 06:00 Hours

Fletcher looked up from the map at the assembled officers. "Those two carriers are undoubtedly Nagumo's task force headed for Midway. Chet certainly called this one."

"That's two of them," Buckmaster agreed, "but Admiral Nimitz said there'd be four or five carriers in Nagumo's force. Where are the others?"

"Perhaps the Intelligence people are wrong," Lewis offered. "Yamamoto might have decided that two aircraft carriers were enough to do the job. Either that or he's holding them back for a different place. Hawaii? Strike there while we're engaged here?"

Fletcher shook his head. "I don't think so. Yamamoto would send more than enough to do the job. He proved that at Pearl Harbor. Whichever target he's aiming for, he'll go all out. I believe we can scratch Hawaii for now."

Fletcher glanced over at Pederson. "Oscar?"

"I agree with you, sir. Due to the inclement weather of the past few days, I'd say they dispersed somewhat. The fact that things are playing out exactly as Admiral Nimitz predicted makes me believe they're either bringing up the rear or further off to one side. At this point, nothing else makes sense."

Fletcher studied the plot, considered the situation. There are two Japanese carriers identified and spotted. Launching all of Ray's and my aircraft against those targets virtually assures us of seriously damaging if not sinking them. Taking two of Yamamoto's large fleet carriers off the board is no small feat. That could have quite an impact . . . swing the battle in our favor from the outset.

Memories of Coral Sea and the report of sighting two carriers flashed through his mind. I sent a full strike from both *Yorktown* and *Lexington* only to discover the contact plane's message encoder was misaligned. There were no enemy carriers at the given location, only cruisers and destroyers. I was on the brink of wasting two carriers' full complement of aircraft because someone made a simple mistake. Good fortune sailed with me that day as another report came in locating a carrier not far from the dispatched attack group. Thank goodness we successfully diverted them to the new target . . . gained *something* out of that dire situation. We did sink a small carrier. Much better than nothing. If the enemy had spotted my force and launched a strike from an unknown location, a crushing defeat could have ensued. Am I setting myself up for the same scenario here?

"Newsome," he said to his combat talker, "contact Admiral Spruance on TBS and ask if he's received the intercept concerning the two enemy carriers."

The young man spoke into the microphone dangling from his neck, paused, and held his headphone tightly against his right ear. He nodded once or twice and then talked for a few more seconds before addressing Fletcher.

"Aye, sir," he said. "*Enterprise* was in the process of sending us the same dispatch. Admiral Spruance advises that he's waiting for your orders."

Here it is—the first critical decision of the battle, he thought. The sighting report question of yesterday pales compared to this. Should I take the apparently safer alternative to keep my forces together and attack the two sighted carriers en masse? We'd have the advantages of surprise and numbers. We could draw first blood by sinking both carriers with the opening blow. At that point, the numbers would be even if not in our favor.

And if the other two or three Jap carriers suddenly appeared after our air groups dropped their ordnance? What if they come sailing over the horizon with flight decks full of aircraft and bones in their teeth? We'd have nothing left to attack with. No time to rearm and refuel. We'd be sitting ducks.

The other option means dividing my carriers and launching an attack with Ray's group. I could hold on to mine in case more carriers appear. Perhaps not as aggressive a move, but less risky. Less risk means less reward. I've a large number of inexperienced pilots and crewmen scattered throughout the fleet facing their first combat. How will they respond? We might not sink or critically damage both enemy carriers without *Yorktown's* aircraft making the strike, too. The Japs could launch an attack of their own while Ray was retrieving his planes.

But *Yorktown* would be in reserve.

We'd still have a chance.

The principle of calculated risk, Chet had stressed.

After Coral Sea, the accusations flew. Was it only a week ago that I officially defended my actions with a written report? My

199

future and career uncertain? The threat of losing my command poised over my head like an axe ready to drop and plenty of willing executioners. *Not aggressive enough,* Chet said. This situation is setting up the same way. Will it be a repeat? Will I be defending myself a month from now? Perhaps in front of an Official Court of Inquiry?

He looked up and found everyone in the room watching him, understanding they would follow his lead in their own actions. Everything trickles down from the top. I can't afford to show hesitation in anything that I do. This crucial moment requires firm determination from all involved. *The principle of calculated risk.* Chet meant those words. I hope that my calculations prove correct.

"Instruct Admiral Spruance to proceed southwest and attack those carriers as soon as they're definitively located and plotted," he said to Newsome. "Advise him that I'm going to recover my scout aircraft and then follow behind."

"Aye, sir," Newsome answered before cuing his microphone.

We have two definite targets. Logic dictates that we must deal with them. In the time that I'm landing those scouts, the situation could change. More enemy carriers could show up. Perhaps not. I'll wait to make a final decision about my launch at that time. That's the smart– the *only* way to play this. If I'm wrong, my detractors will rise up even louder. If I'm right, they'll never admit it. Harsh words will still batter my reputation. Damn what they say. I have a battle to fight and win.

"Hang on, boys!" Kiefer had appeared from out of nowhere. "This cruise is about to get rough."

40. BROCKMAN
June 4 – 06:00 Hours

"Here we go, Bill." Benson extended a message to Brockman.

Brockman sat on his bunk, rubbing his head, trying to wake up. The battle hasn't started and I'm already exhausted, he thought. He glanced at the chronometer mounted inside the bulkhead. I've been asleep for two hours? It feels more like two minutes.

"You nailed it by having us monitor the Midway search plane frequency," Benson continued. "We intercepted this a few minutes ago. It looks like the Japs have shown up."

Brockman took the offered note. *Many planes headed Midway. Bearing 320, Distance 150.* An electric shock jolted him fully awake as he looked up at Benson.

"Authenticated?"

Benson smiled.

Brockman felt the boat gently rising and falling with the waves. He heard the rumble of diesels, smelled the familiar odor of burning fuel oil, and briefly considered submerging. Not yet, he decided. No one woke me, so the lookouts have seen nothing. We'll make better time and save the batteries on the surface.

"Come on." Brockman got to his feet and led Benson into the control room. Bending over the large chart table, Benson pointed to a marked spot northwest of Midway.

"Right here's the location given," he said. He picked up the dividers, did a few fast calculations, and drew a line extending farther to the northwest and then down onto Midway. "The Jap carriers figure to be somewhere along this area."

A nervous thrill went through Brockman. That's on the northern edge of our patrol station, he thought. He glanced up and found Benson watching him.

"You're thinking the same thing that I am," Benson said.

"That's within the boundary of our patrol zone."

"Great minds do indeed think alike."

For the first time, Brockman became aware of the silence in the control room. Every station was adequately manned and the officers on watch were standing by, but no one spoke. He felt the tense expectation, knew the men waited for orders. They're curious to see how I'm going to respond. I mustn't disappoint them.

He stepped over to the wall intercom and switched it on.

"This is the captain speaking." The strange sound of his voice echoed through the boat. "We've received a radio transmission reporting Japanese planes headed for Midway. There was also a location given. It is my intention to intercept the enemy and attack. *Nautilus* shall lead the way, not follow. We're going to do things just like we've drilled, except now it's for real. I have faith in each of you to do your duty. I've no doubt as to our success."

"Plot us an intersecting course," he said to Benson. "Bring us up as close as you can."

"Helm, all ahead full," Benson said. "Stand by for course change."

"All ahead full. Standing by for course change."

Brockman glanced around, sensing the tautness enveloping the boat's crew. The normal joking and banter forgotten, everyone seemed locked into performing his job, as if nothing mattered but the present task. For the first time, he considered each man and what he was thinking. *It's too soon for the fear. It's all nervous energy and expectation for now. How will they handle the realization of combat?*

He spotted the Chief of the Boat standing next to the helmsman and motioned him over.

"Let's make preparations, COB. I want a detail to comb each space and secure everything. Check and double-check your procedures. Have both torpedo rooms test their equipment and run through their drills. Anticipation's the key. Let's anticipate the problems and plan for them. Let's leave nothing to chance or luck."

"Aye, sir," the COB answered, quickly shuffling out to follow his orders.

Brockman thought for a moment and looked at Benson. "I'm going up topside to check on the lookouts. I need you to make sure that we're ready down here."

Brockman climbed to the conning tower to find LT (jg) Mitchell on periscope watch.

"Full power and extension, Mister Mitchell. I want a continuous sweep until further notice. That Jap fleet will be making plenty of stack smoke. We should be able to spot them."

He retrieved his binoculars and mounted the ladder to the bridge.

"Permission to come on to the bridge?" He called through the open hatch.

"Permission granted, sir," Lynch answered.

Brockman emerged into a bright, breezy morning. The sweet smell of ocean and engine exhaust welcomed him. He paused, slowly swept the horizon with his glasses, and then joined Lynch leaning against the fairing.

"Report, Mister Lynch."

"All clear and routine, sir. The weather has finally improved."

"Eyes sharp, Mister Lynch, the Japanese are out there. Let's be prepared to take immediate action."

"Aye, sir. I'm ready."

Are you? Brockman thought. Is anyone ever ready for combat? To try to kill someone who's doing his best to kill you? It's doubtful. All we can do is follow orders and allow our training to guide our actions. The enemy lies within probable striking distance. How will *Nautilus* respond?

41. WALDRON
June 04 – 06:30 Hours

"With all due respect, sir, I don't believe those Jap carriers will be where they were spotted." Waldron's words to Mitscher cut through the chatter of *Hornet*'s bridge, where the squadron commanders and Ring, the CHAG, had gathered for a final meeting.

"Perhaps not," Ring broke in, "but that report only involved two enemy carriers. The latest intelligence says there're at least two more in the strike force. If we search in that direction, we should be able to locate some part of Nagumo's fleet. If we don't, then I'll turn south and search."

"That's seems like a gamble to me," Waldron countered. "Given their current location in relation to ours, we'll be short on fuel. We're better off developing the first contact instead of hoping to stumble across something that might not be there."

"Something will be there. Admiral Nimitz has been right on the mark with everything he's said. He practically called exactly where and when first contact would happen. There're at least two more carriers headed in. We're bound to locate something to attack."

"And what if Admiral Nimitz is wrong, or if those other two carriers were just out of sight of that patrol plane? They could be closer than you think."

"Wait a minute." Mitscher held up a hand to silence Ring's reply. "What are you basing your comments on, Johnny?"

Waldron took a breath to compose himself, thinking, this is too important to allow emotions to control me. My boys waiting in the ready room below are depending on me. We've trained too hard. Waited too long for this opportunity. I must make Mitscher understand.

"From the position given, Nagumo launched his strike a good distance away from Midway. He's trying to make sure he gets in the first blow. To hit Midway before it can retaliate. His staff must expect some losses in the attack. He's going to want to close up some of that distance to recover his damaged, shot-up planes when they return. He'll not sit still and hope that they'll all be able to make the return leg home."

Stroking his chin, Mitscher studied the chart. "You believe he'll keep heading for Midway instead of standing off?"

"Aye, sir."

"And if his scouts locate us in the meantime, what then?" Ring asked. "He'll scramble to put distance between himself and Midway. Possibly recall some of his attack groups. He'll need the time to assemble a strike against us. Either way, we should spot some evidence of him by my plot."

"If we're spotted, he'll turn in this direction and head this way," Waldron answered. "Close the distance to us. That still puts him more to the south of your estimated plot."

"He's mistaken," Ring said directly to Mitscher. "Following Johnny's track, we'll miss out on finding any parts of Nagumo's force. We could be out there flying blind and wasting gas while the enemy launches strikes against us."

Waldron twisted his head to focus on Ring. "You're in favor of attacking a position report that'll be over two hours old by the time—"

"Gentlemen, that's enough!"

Mitscher's rough voice brought instant silence to the bridge. He stalked over to the forward window, turned around, and stood with both hands on his hips. His eyesight swept over his squadron commanders and staff officers.

"I appreciate everyone's concerns and suggestions, but the decision is mine and mine alone."

He addressed Ring. "Stan, your thinking goes along with Admiral Spruance's order for a search-attack procedure. Let's use your initial heading while being prepared to make a deviation if we transmit new information to you."

Mitscher's gaze locked onto Waldron as he addressed the group. "Any questions or further discussion?"

"No, sir." Waldron bit his tongue and heard his answer echoed by the others.

"Let's get to it then."

* * *

Waldron sat at the desk in front of the ready room, knowing he was being watched. Occasionally, the Teletype blinkered into illuminated life, chattering away the latest communication from the bridge. The XO tore off the page, carried it to the blackboard, and chalked in the enemy data and flying conditions. Heads bent, hands made notations on plotting boards, and then faces lifted back to Waldron. The tension, heightened by two earlier orders to man planes followed by instructions to stand down, rippled throughout the room. If I stomped on the floor, they'd scatter like scalded dogs, he thought.

Waldron glanced down at his own plotting board and thought about the discussion with Ring and Mitscher. Why can't they see the illogic in the Japs maintaining a stationary position after sending off their air strike? We're going to fly around in circles over that damn ocean, wind up ditching when we run out of gas. For what? So that Ring can stroke his ego by being in command? Why won't he listen?

His tongue licked his dry lips as he reached a decision. Ring is wrong. I'm right. I'll lead my boys to Nagumo's fleet. I owe it to them. They'll do their duty and damn anyone standing in the way.

"Skippah?"

Gay's voice broke through his thoughts and he looked up.

"Did anything new come out of your meeting with the admiral?"

Waldron's hands landed flat on the desktop as he pushed himself to his feet. He moved around to the center of the room and paused to study each face. The youthful exuberance and trust reflected by each man moved him. No matter what might come, he wanted—no needed—to remember this moment for the rest of his life.

"Nothing's changed, but that doesn't matter. You're ready to get the job done and I've no doubt that's what we're going to do. I think these reports are wrong about where Nagumo's headed, but we shall find him. I don't care if we run out of gas hunting, we will indeed find him."

"What happens if we run out of gas out there in the middle of the Pacific Ocean?" Whitey Moore asked in mock seriousness. "It's a long swim back to Pearl."

"Then I suppose we'll park in the water and have a nice little picnic waiting for the PBYs. You can bring dessert."

Brief laughter filled the space, placing him at ease. There's no doubt that my boys will rise to the challenge. That's what sons do for their father.

"I figure we'll be back here by noon to compare notes," Waldron said. "I'm not concerned about you. I actually believe under these conditions, we're the best in the world. My greatest hope is that we encounter a favorable tactical situation. If the worst does happen, I expect each one of us to do his utmost to destroy the enemy. If just one plane gets through to make a run-in, I want that man to get a hit."

"*Pilots, man your planes!*" the loudspeaker trumpeted again.

"This is it," Waldron summed up. "May God be with us all. Good luck and give 'em hell!"

Feet clattered to the deck as the men surged toward the door. Waldron stood back, allowing them to pass. He caught Gay rushing by and pulled him aside until the others left the room.

"Tex, you're Navigation Officer and I'm sure you've made a good plot from Ring's information, but he's wrong about this thing. I want you and the boys to follow me. Don't think that I'm lost. Just follow me and I'll take you to them."

42. TOMONAGA
June 4 – 06:30 Hours

"Wildcats!"

The shrill voice breaking over Tomonaga's static-popping headphones brought his head swiveling around to scan the sky behind. A flash to his right followed by an explosion confirmed the attack by enemy fighters.

Where did they come from? he thought. I should have been more observant. Made certain the men remained vigilant against such an attack. To fly so blindly begs the enemy to take advantage of us. Our carelessness has allowed the enemy a kill. Such mistakes must not be repeated.

"Murai," he said, speaking into the voice tube, "you must do your duty. Open your eyes and keep them open. My successfully doing my job depends on your doing yours."

"Yes, sir. I apologize for my negligence."

"Don't offer apologies, just–"

The steely pings of bullets striking his left wing bit off his reply. Tomonaga instinctively banked away. Slivers of flame briefly licked at the damaged wing before the slipstream snuffed them out.

The sound of Murai firing punctuated by the smell of burnt gunpowder alerted him to danger on his tail. He fought the urge to break away and maneuver, knowing it was critical for the formation to remain together. He gritted his teeth; his hands gripped the controls tighter as more lead pebbles rattled against the Nakajima's sides. The enemy is determined to shoot us down, he thought. Where are our escort fighters?

Searching ahead, he latched onto the sight of Midway Atoll looming in the distance. How strangely peaceful and serene it looks, he thought. Fate enjoys her joke. Death rides the air. Destruction accompanies him.

Tracer fire streaked through the sky over his open canopy as an aircraft roared past in a shallow dive. Scant seconds later a Zero streaked by in deadly pursuit of the attacker. He watched in silent satisfaction as 20-mm cannon rounds from the Zero's wings thundered large holes in the enemy's airplane. In a puff of smoke followed by a roaring blaze, the enemy plane spiraled down, crashing into the ocean.

His eyesight shifted around, registering the unfolding events. The once composed sky now transformed into chaos as aircraft twisted and turned in a wicked dance of death. Kill or be killed, Tomonaga knew. That is the warrior's way.

The cool breeze fanned his face, offering a false contrast to the heat and flames soon to be visited upon the swiftly approaching Midway Island. His sight focused on the western atoll, Sand, as he sized it up for the attack.

"Murai," he said into the speaker tube again, "send this message. Assault Method Number Two . . . wind 90 degrees, 9 meters, approach course 270 degrees."

He led a gentle turn, bringing the formations into attack position from the east. The rising sun at our backs will hamper anti-aircraft spotters, he thought. It will give us that extra edge. Any advantage gained in combat is a large one.

His head wheeled around, noted hordes of Zeroes blasting the enemy opposition out of the skies. The air space over Midway promised to be clear of American aircraft for their assault. I need concentrate only on making my bombing run.

Formation lined out, he said, "Murai, send this message. All aircraft assume attack positions."

His eyesight settled on the oil storage tanks located on the northeast tip of the atoll. Those shall be my target, he decided. Deny the enemy fuel and he loses the ability to escape. The Invasion Force will capture the entire installation and its occupants.

"Hashimoto, we'll strike the oil storage facility," he advised the observer.

Beneath him, his wounded Nakajima leveled off. The enemy flak now rose up furiously to greet them, a lucky round or two inflicting further damage to his aircraft. Surprise at the intensity if not the accuracy of the enemy anti-aircraft fire struck him. He thought, these Americans have not crawled into a hole to hide . . . they fight like demons. No air support, yet they continue exposing themselves to strike back at us. The metal-torn sky battered his Nakajima, threatening to slap it down. He struggled with the controls to maintain a true, level approach.

"Lieutenant," his observer, Hashimoto, said over the interphone, "target coming up on your right."

"I see them."

Another flashing explosion nearby briefly distracted him. He looked sideways, saw fire consuming a familiar-looking Nakajima. *Kikuchi!* Tomonaga turned his head to watch Kikuchi open his canopy and wave goodbye. The doomed man leaned into the controls, aiming his aircraft. Die as a samurai, Tomonaga silently instructed Kikuchi. The crippled machine arched downward like a flaming spear, disintegrating into the hostile sands of the American outpost.

"Steady, steady." Hashimoto's voice brought him back into the present.

Tomonaga's attention returned to the task, focusing on making the bombing run. More puffs of smoke with their bursts of deadly shrapnel shattered the air like metallic thunder, buffeted the aircraft, and banged him from side to side in the cockpit. He rode the bucking ship, pounded by waves of raw turbulence. His ears rang with a sound like that of a sledgehammer striking a bell. An unexpected taste wormed into his consciousness. Salt? A wipe of his chin revealed blood smeared on the back of his hand. Now came the pain and the knowledge. I've bit my tongue, he thought.

"Target dead ahead," Hashimoto advised.

Eye pressed against the bombsight, Tomonaga's right hand gripped the bomb release handle. Raw energy coursed through him, raising a chill across his body. He held his breath. Poised to strike. Steady. Steady.

Now.

"Bomb released!" Tomonaga yelled for Kikuchi as his hand yanked the handle.

An immediate upsurge of the lightened aircraft echoed his call. The Nakajima gently curved away to the right, allowing him to view his efforts. Storage tanks ruptured in violent flumes of yellow and orange as choking clouds of burning fuel oil dimmed the morning sunlight. A killing spray of jagged metal ripped through the air like gigantic razor blades, indiscriminately slicing through everything in their path. More bombs exploded in a random display of hell-born blossoms that gradually reached outward toward the center of the atoll.

He continued winging around, admiring the storm of havoc cascading down upon the enemy installations below. Eruptions of sand, coral, and building materials curved upward and outward, small volcanoes knocking down everything near them and dealing death without remorse. A morbid landscape of blackened vegetation and smoking craters shimmered through the jaundiced haze. Anti-aircraft fire, an almost solid blanket of red-hot metal, seemed to provide a paved means of reaching the other atoll named Eastern.

Tomonaga circled the runways of Eastern and cursed the lack of similar destruction by the air groups assigned to bomb it. The almost total lack of aircraft on the ground provided ample evidence of the enemy's having received advance warning of the attack in time to clear their airfield. The damage to the landing areas and surfaces was so minor he knew it would only take a short while to return them to operation. It's foolish to leave the enemy the means of mounting air strikes against us, he thought. We need to demolish this place, not try to preserve it for our use.

The Nakajima continued away from the smoking islands, heading for the rendezvous point. He considered the airfield's condition and figured the enemy still had airborne craft to use it. The decision was simple and most logical, he thought. Midway remains a threat to *Kido Butai*. Admiral Nagumo must send another air strike to finish the job.

43. RAMSEY
June 04 – 06:30 Hours

"They've blown right through Red Parks's fighters and are heading in," Simard called over to Ramsey. "Our fighter communications' circuit has gone silent. I don't believe that they ever had a chance."

"I know," Ramsey replied. "The only planes I've seen falling in flames are ours. Those Zeros have no equal in the air."

Ramsey stood in the doorway of the command bunker watching in awe as one of the first Japanese bombers received a fatal blow from a gun battery. It slid downward through the flak-speckled air and then slammed to earth not far away. A sudden, inexplicable impulse grabbed him. He scrambled after a mess steward out to the wreck. The two men reached it simultaneously. Ignoring the heat and flames, they tugged the pilot's body free of the demolished cockpit and carried him a short distance away. Ramsey knelt and furiously dug through the dead man's pockets seeking anything of interest for the Intelligence boys. His search in vain, he glanced back toward the burning aircraft and considered checking it out. The radioman might have a codebook, he thought. Perhaps some notes that he used, or a map.

"What in the hell are you doing out here?" Simard grabbed him by the arm and shoved him toward the bunker. Screaming at the steward, Simard pointed him in the same direction.

Ramsey and Simard bounded through the doorway a step or two behind the steward and leapt inside. A split second later, an enormous explosion rocked the small atoll. Debris showered down upon the bunker, landing with ominous thuds. Gazing out, they saw geysers of flame shooting up from the fuel storage tanks.

Ramsey ducked as the horrendous noise and oily stink washed over him in a tidal wave of destruction. Each blast hammered against his skull and seemed to grow closer as if pursuing him. He retreated further inside the structure . . . away from the angry beast denied its prey moments before and now seeking another. Glancing over at Simard, he watched him lurch toward the bunker's entrance and wondered if his face wore the same shocked expression as Simard's.

"Damn." He could see Simard mouth the word.

"Captain!"

Ramsey moved closer, had to shout louder. "Captain, don't you think you should come inside!"

Simard stood framed by the opening and watched enemy bombs pounding down like thunderbolts, igniting sand and corral with pillars of fire. Ramsey felt his pain and understood the helpless agony Simard endured witnessing his command reduced to rubble. Each casualty will haunt the man for years to come. He'll wake up from nightmares. Bathed in cold sweat. Wishing that the darkness would chase the memory away. After surviving Pearl Harbor, I thought this time it would be easier. I thought wrong.

"Captain, you need to come inside!"

A thunderous roar jarred the building again, the smoke temporarily blotting out the sunlight. Loose sand from the dugout's roof showered down upon them. A choking cloud of gritty dust billowed through the air, making Ramsey cough and stinging his eyes. Seeing enough to convince him of the eminent danger, he lunged forward, latching onto Simard's shoulder. Simard started and turned angry eyes upon him.

"Captain, this isn't the place to be standing! I think these Japs mean business!"

Simard nodded and then followed him back inside the bunker. As they reached the center of the room, one of the radiomen extended the phone to Simard.

"It's Commander Ford, sir."

Simard grabbed the receiver. "Jack, it's not getting too hot up there for you is it?"

Simard listened and glanced over at Ramsey. "The seaplane hangar went up first thing, and the Japs are swarming around the buildings."

"What about yourself?" Simard said into the phone. "You come on down if you need to. I don't want to explain to Admiral Nimitz why I got his Hollywood movie director shot."

He paused again and his face fell. "Jack? Jack, you there?"

Lowering the phone, he looked at Ramsey. "I heard an explosion and the line went dead."

Ramsey shrugged. "I wouldn't worry. He seemed like a tough character to me. He could've ducked the blast and dropped the phone."

Simard sighed and hung up. Ramsey clapped him on the shoulder and walked over to the radioman.

"Any reports from the strike we launched?"

"I haven't heard a thing, sir."

"Well." He looked around the shelter and found nervous, tense faces looking back. "Keep listening. It shouldn't be too long now until our guys return some of this to Nagumo's bunch."

A large grin broke across the sailor's face. "Aye, sir. That we will."

Ramsey turned toward the bunker entrance, noticed the explosions dying down. He thought, did Yamamoto actually think this small air strike could cripple Midway? The idea seemed almost insulting. It was hard to believe that after coming all the way from Japan, they had not brought more bombs to drop on them. In spite of the situation, he smiled at the thought and lightly shook his head. I'm questioning the number of bombs that the Japs dropped as if I am disappointed in their effort. A man thinks the damnedest things in the midst of battle.

The ringing phone sounded like a ship's bell clanging in the building. Simard snatched it up and barked, "Hello."

He listened for a few seconds, then glanced over at Ramsey and lifted a thumb up. Ramsey returned the gesture, thinking, Ford's on the other end of the line.

"A bomb hit nearby and knocked him goofy for a few seconds," Simard explained at a pause. "Says he's okay and still taking pictures."

"I'm glad to hear it, but tell him not to do anything foolish. Hunt some shelter if he needs to. Damned if I want to recommend him up for a posthumous medal."

Simard remained on the phone for a few more moments and hung up. Wiping his brow with the back of a hand, he offered Ramsey a strange look.

"Jack says it looks to be over. There're a few Zeroes making strafing runs but the Marines and the PT boats are giving them hell and driving them off. It should be safe to have a look. I want to see something."

Simard led the way outside and the two of them stood for a moment surveying the damage. Demolished buildings, some like the seaplane hangar just a burning framework of steel, stood out in stark relief against the white sand and coral like a skeleton awaiting muscles and skin. A few damaged and several destroyed vehicles lay tossed about where bombs and 20-mm cannon rounds had hurled them. Dead gooney birds lay strewn around. An evil breeze drifted past bearing smoke, sand, and feathers.

Ramsey noticed several Marines leaving their gun pits to inspect the downed Japanese planes. He thought about the dead enemy pilot stretched out near the command post and strode over that way. Looking down at the mangled body, he noticed something white sticking out below the flying jacket. What is that? He bent, lifted the coat, and found a Rising Sun flag wrapped around the pilot's waist.

Someone's standing next to me? Simard . . . is staring at the dead man and his sash.

"I guess this says a lot about the way those men feel about their country," Ramsey remarked. "As much as I hate them as a people for what they've done to us, I have to respect them as combat pilots."

"Perhaps," Simard said, pointing, "but look over there."

Ramsey stood and his eyesight fell upon the Stars and Stripes flying from the flagpole.

"That's what I came out here to see," Simard said. "In all of the confusion this morning, someone realized that we had forgotten to raise the flag. Jack told me our boys had corrected the oversight in the midst of the attack. He captured it on film."

"I guess now we know what was going through Francis Scott Key's mind as he watched the bombardment of Fort McHenry," Ramsey replied. "I'll never look at that flag the same way again."

44. MELO
June 04 – 06:45 Hours

"What's the plan, sirs?" Melo stuck his head up into the cockpit between the pilots' seats. He caught a glimpse out of the front windshield and noticed the other B-26s flying in a diamond formation. From his vantage point, they appeared to be in the slot position.

"We're following those TBF Avengers that took off ahead of us," Pren Moore, flying as copilot, answered.

"Any idea of the target?"

"Nobody's said," Muri replied. "I'm thinking a merchant ship. The word is that's all those P-boats stumbled across last night."

"Those enemy planes coming in means there're carriers out there somewhere," Melo said. "I don't believe they could make the trip this far from Wake."

Pren looked at him. "You need to be ready then. You might want to go check on those weapons of yours."

Melo nodded and made his way through the radio room and into the aft area of the aircraft. He entered the tunnel compartment, moved under the top turret gun, and glanced out the left gun port.

"Hey, Sarge." He reached up and jerked Gogoj's pant leg. "Sassy and Walters are waving to us from Maye's ship."

"Yeah, I see both of them," Gogoj answered from the turret. "Sassy's sticking his tongue out at me. If I hadn't bet the jerk that I'd splash at least two more Zeroes than him, I'd give him a burst from these .50s. I'm going to enjoy spending his pay."

"I don't know. Lieutenant Muri said we're probably going after a merchant ship. There might not be any Zekes nearby,"

Gogoj glanced down at him. "If there're none for me to shoot, I reckon there'll be none for Sassy to cut loose on either."

Or me, Melo thought. He bent over his right .30-caliber and carefully tested the action a few times. He reached up, pulled down one of the feed belts from an overhead ammo box, and inspected it. The ever-present rag appeared from out of his pocket, and he carefully wiped off a few granules of sand. Undoubtedly a souvenir of Midway Island, the sand was sure to play hell with his weapon. The Brownings were bad enough about jamming without

216

extra help. He threaded the belt into the gun and then repeated the process with the left side weapon.

"Hey, Sarge," he called up to Gogoj, "you might want to check your ammo for sand."

Gogoj glanced down and nodded in comprehension. Melo moved aft between the swinging guns to Ashley seated on his tail gunner's stool. He grabbed Ashley's shoulder and leaned over to speak into his ear.

"You might want to check your stuff for sand."

Ashley offered a thumb up, and Melo retreated to his own station. He looked out first one gun port and then the other, wondering what combat would be like. The stories the veterans of Pearl Harbor and Coral Sea had told filled him with anxiety but also instilled a strange sense of curiosity. Running a deadly gauntlet of bullets and shells tearing flesh, mangling limbs, and killing men was no game, not even to a young man who believed in his own divine immortality. There does exist in each of us, however, a need to prove our courage and the will to fight in the face of danger, he thought. I can't deny the strong desire to confront my fears. Will I succeed or fail in this ultimate test of manhood?

"Get ready." Muri's voice came over his intercom headphones, "The Jap fleet's up ahead."

The pounding of his pulse drummed an accelerating tattoo in his head. He wiped his mouth with the back of a sleeve and then reached out to charge both Brownings.

"We see the carriers up ahead." Pren took over the commentary. "Captain Collins is leading the formation in."

"We've got Zeroes on our tail!" Ashley shouted.

"I see 'em, too," Gogoj echoed. "There must be two dozen of 'em!"

As the Marauder suddenly pitched into a steep dive, Melo sprawled against his gun. His stomach fought to remain at altitude, sending a harsh wave of nausea washing over him. He struggled upright and then fell over backwards when the aircraft leveled off. A staccato rumble from the turret added to the deafening din as Gogoj cut loose with the twin .50-calibers.

"If only mom could see us now!" someone, most likely Pren, yelled over the intercom.

Melo leapt over to the left gun; his hands latched onto the spade handles. His finger settled instinctively on the trigger as his eyesight swept the sky seeking a target. A flash in his peripheral vision drew his attention to the five o'clock position. The sudden dive and increase in speed had allowed the faster B-26s to blow past the Avengers. Seizing the opportunity, a horde of Zeroes pounced on the slower aircraft and pummeled them with a lethal combination of 7.7-mm bullets and 20-mm cannon shells. He watched in morbid fascination as first one and then another of the Avengers spiraled away in flames. He flinched and grabbed his throat as a third lost a wing to the fusillade of lead. It did a cartwheel into the choppy water, tossing up geysers of foam and hunks of twisted metal.

A twinkling blur flashed by as a Zero zipped past. The sound of gravel rattling on a tin roof heralded enemy slugs tearing into the Marauder and caused Melo to duck. Dazed, he was brought upright by the steady rumble of Gogoj's .50s. Sweaty palms gripped the comforting handles of his left gun as he fought to calm himself down. Another glance out of the window could not wash away the vision of the Avenger careening wildly into the ocean. Melo thought, is this the fate waiting for all of them? I've never seen anything as fast or deadly as the enemy fighters. The stories told by those combat veterans about these Zekes pale in comparison to the reality of one winging your way and hurling death in your direction.

Melo felt the Marauder weaving left and then right and buffeting up and down. He slapped against one fuselage wall and then ricocheted onto the other like a pinball bouncing off the bumpers at Coney Island. He struggled to brace himself. How in the world will I ever be able to aim a gun, let alone fire it, on such a roller coaster ride? I never expected this to happen.

"There's a Zero on our tail!" two voices, Gogoj's and Ashley's, yelled over the intercom headphone.

Melo shot a glance out the left gun port. A Zero hove into view, sliding from side to side on the air currents. His eyes fell enraptured by the winking, blinking balls of light spitting from the plane's wings and nose. The hypnotic spell shattered seconds later as a spray of shot and shell ripped up the tail and tunnel section like a fire axe busting through sheet metal, narrowly missing him.

His finger tightened on the trigger to blast .30-caliber bullets at the would-be assassin. The Browning lovingly bucked in his hands, the throbbing beat a comforting reminder of his fighting back. He chattered away several dozen rounds from the left gun before, as the Zero skidded the other way, swinging over to the right gun and repeating the exercise. Hot, empty brass cases fell in small piles around his feet and bounced out the ports.

A banshee roar from the top turret drowned out the pounding gunfire. Melo glanced back and saw Gogoj drop to his knees on the floor amidst a shower of Plexiglas and metal. Gogoj's body helplessly drummed back and forth in an obscene rhythm with the B-26s spastic dance. Reaching out, Melo helped him stand. Gogoj shook his head, pushed free, and dragged himself back into the turret seat. Looking up, Melo discovered the turret dome had shattered. Sparking wires flapped in the slipstream like tiny flags caught in a whirlwind.

A large, warm drop splashed against the back of Melo's hand, drawing his attention. The crimson blob sliding down his wrist was blood and not his own. He tore his eyes away, shifted them to Gogoj, and did not recognize the hideous mask staring back. Gogoj's face was a shredded, gory mess of hanging skin flaps and rapidly swelling flesh. The relentless wind sucked along by the speeding aircraft blasted through the wrecked turret, turning the myriad weeping scratches into streaming cuts all over Gogoj's disfigured head.

"Sarge!" Melo screamed. "You've got to come down! The turret's shot to hell!"

"Take care of your own damn guns and stop worrying about me! I'm just getting warmed up!"

Melo watched Gogoj fumble with the Brownings, clear a jam, and manage to get one of them popping off a few shots between intermittent problems. Gogoj loudly swore at each interruption. Bloody fingers fumbled with the breech, freed it up, and then squeezed the triggers again. Another splatter of bullets tearing through the tunnel front drove Melo back to his own station. He alternated between guns, firing short bursts at the quick, elusive targets swarming like seagulls around a cannery. The sulfurous stink of gun smoke mixed with Cosmoline and engine exhaust streamed in through the ragged holes, filling the air with noxious vapors. His eyes smarted and then burned. He felt tears streaking down his face.

An explosion rocked the aircraft, hurling him against the wall. Ashley bellowed in pain and rolled backward out of the rear turret. His scarlet-stained hands clutched a shredded leg. Severed veins and arteries gushed out sprays of blood, open fire hoses pumping from the panicked beat of his heart.

"Ash!" Melo jumped over to the wounded gunner.

"My gun! The fifty!" Ashley raised one bloody finger toward the turret. "Kill that son of a bitch who killed me!"

"Take it easy," Melo shouted over the noise.

"It hurts too much! I know I'm dying!"

One bloody claw clamped onto Melo's shirt and pulled him near. Pleading, child-like eyes stabbed into Melo, knifing a gash into his soul.

"Please throw me out of the plane. Don't let me die like this. *Please!*"

Ashley coughed and passed out. His hands numbed from the guns' vibrations, Melo used his wrists to hoist Ashley under the shoulders. Leaning him against a frame member, Melo noticed his shallow breathing. The young man's face grew pale, and his brow felt damp.

A burst of heat and light accompanied another blast of bullets and cannon shells lacerating the B-26's fuselage. A wicked punch like a blackjack-wielding fist threw Melo a glancing wallop across the skull. He staggered back. Heaved in huge gulps of air. Fought to remain conscious. Shaking fingers reached up to softly caress a deep wound gouged by an enemy bullet. Blood coated his fingertips and ran down his nose and lips. The salty taste mingled with sweat upon his swollen tongue.

Ice-cold rage bred by desperate combat seized Melo's mind and focused his purpose. His thoughts latched onto manning the rear gun, and he fully understood the criticality of fighting off the enemy planes attacking their vulnerable six o'clock position. I can't give those Zekes a clear shot at our tail. They'll flame us for sure.

Melo managed a step, recoiling when another chunk of lead tore into his right arm. The intense pain halted him in his tracks, and knocked him to his knees. Each heartbeat hammered blows against his wounds, spat out precious blood, and weakened him. A welcome veil of gray mist shrouded his vision. Sweet, encompassing darkness reached out to envelop and comfort him. A promise of calming shelter for his wounded body beckoned.

45. KUSAKA
June 04 – 06:45 Hours

Kusaka watched Nagumo pacing the small bridge on *Akagi* and easily read his mood. Nagumo's earlier confidence now shaken with worry, Kusaka wondered what had happened to effect the change. Nagumo's state of mind seems to bend backward and forward with the wind.

"Things are going as planned," Kusaka suggested. "Our attack has certainly ended by now and the planes are headed back."

Nagumo whirled around. "We've heard no reports from our scouts. That doesn't cause concern with you?"

"They've seen nothing to report."

"And the enemy flying boat that's been shadowing us for over an hour? The enemy certainly has more information about us than we have about him."

"Yet the Americans have not attacked," Kusaka countered. "Our strike caught them by surprise as planned. We've destroyed their aircraft on the ground."

"We don't know what's been destroyed. Tomonaga hasn't radioed."

"And I repeat, because there's nothing to report. Things go as planned."

Nagumo waved a hand as if in dismissal and then stepped over to the starboard window. Genda moved next to Kusaka and softly spoke into his ear.

"It's always the uncertainty of things that brings the darkest clouds."

Kusaka's eyesight stayed fixed on Nagumo. "But without the clouds there can be no rain. Such rain may bring a killing flood or a welcome relief from drought. We should be vigilant, not overcome by fear."

"Message, sir." A sailor appeared in the door, bowed, and handed Kusaka a paper.

"Attack completed and homeward bound," Kusaka read. "It's from Tomonaga."

Nagumo turned. "That's all it says?"

Kusaka passed it to him. Nagumo made to speak and then returned his gaze to the window. The long, frustrating wait continues. A coughing roar from below signaled a Zero warming up in preparation of changing the combat air patrol. Kusaka's thoughts drifted to the young men charged with keeping the task force safe. Their duty, though not desired like that of escorting the air strikes, was equally important to the success of the operation. May their skills remain untested and unneeded this day.

"Another message, sir." The same young sailor stood in the door, slightly flushed. He handed the note to the closest man, Genda, and left.

"Tomonaga advises another attack wave is needed against Midway," Genda read aloud.

Nagumo's head lowered and his fingers alternately pinched and released his nose. "As I suspected."

"We knew going in that one attack would not totally destroy the enemy installation," Genda said. "We should follow through on our contingency plans to make another strike."

"You forget—"

The sound of gunfire interrupted Kusaka and drew everyone's attention. *Akagi*'s intercom came alive with a bugle's blare, sounding an air-raid alarm. The deck pounded from the vibration of a multitude of feet heading for battle stations. A gut-wrenching turn followed by increasing speed signaled the huge vessel taking evasive action.

"Where are they?" Nagumo demanded as he bent down to peer into a pair of pedestal binoculars and scan the threatening sky.

"There!" Genda pointed to port at the bursts of smoke thrown up by the anti-aircraft fire.

Kusaka trained his own glasses in that direction and focused on a group of aircraft coming in low for a torpedo attack. Studying them closely, he could not recognize the type at their current distance. A group of dots appeared above and behind them, growing larger and larger and into a flock of Zeroes. Like angry birds protecting their nests, they bore in. Their talons were ribbons of shot and shell raking and clawing at the enemy planes. One after another, they fell from the sky. The aircraft were now flaming funeral pyres, their final resting-place the cold Pacific waters. The Zeroes unmercifully mangled them into fiery pieces until a single shot-up survivor remained. Somehow, it managed to veer off before releasing its torpedo at the nearest ship. The alert captain easily turned away from the slow weapon and it harmlessly chugged past. Beaten and battered, the damaged plane hugged the waves, accelerated, and ran for shelter. The Zeroes declined the chase to zoom off in search of other prey.

Kusaka frowned at the cheers ringing out from the air-control platform below each time an enemy plane went down. Respect, not joy should greet any man's death no matter the cause or his station in life, he thought. He lowered the binoculars to wipe his sweaty forehead.

"Get every available fighter into the air now!" Nagumo came to roaring life.

A runner bolted away carrying the command. Kusaka took note of the renewed fire in Nagumo's eyes and hoped it was there to stay. The moment has arrived. We must all conduct ourselves as warriors now.

"There," Nagumo said to Kusaka, an accusing finger pointing out of the window. "There are the American aircraft you believed destroyed at Midway. You assured me of that. Well, this is the philosopher in me speaking. Take nothing for certain or for granted in combat. One does so at his own peril. Confirm everything. *Everything.*"

"All is not lost nor should we react as if it is, sir," Kusaka replied. "The advantages in machines and men still remain with us, not the enemy. Our forces here shall complete the job started by Tomonaga."

"Enemy medium land-based planes approaching low at twenty degrees to starboard!" a lookout on top of the bridge bellowed.

Kusaka whipped the binoculars up and spotted the in-coming aircraft. Arranged in a single-file formation, they did appear to be medium bombers, but of a type he did not recognize. He wondered, why are they flying so close to the water? Trying to avoid anti-aircraft fire? They'll never be able to attain enough altitude to drop bombs in the midst of *Kido Butai.* If they're not intent on bombing, then what? A torpedo attack? Would medium bombers make a torpedo attack?

Zeroes arrived to tear into their midst, attempting to scatter them. Streaming, dotted lines of tracer rounds punctuated with cannon shells slashed the enemy aircraft. The larger bombers bucked and bounced, trying to shrug them off like oxen, annoyed by a swarm of flies, tossing their heads. Kusaka watched the hellish onslaught dealt by the fighters, thinking, yet, they ignore the damage. They continue coming toward us.

"What are they?" Genda was next to him. "Can you tell?"

Kusaka shook his head. "They appear to have torpedoes slung underneath and are coming in too low to bomb. I didn't know the Americans had multiengine torpedo planes."

A scarlet-hued flash heralded the fatal wounding of the first enemy aircraft. Roaring flames dashed along its fuselage as it spun away and blasted into the water. A tremendous geyser of steam and debris soared skyward to mark its passing. Closing up their formation, the other bombers continued approaching.

And still they press forward, Kusaka thought. What drives them so?

The great mass of protecting vessels surrounding the carriers volleyed a fierce barrage of anti-aircraft fire. Tall columns of colored water and spray erupted in front of and around the approaching planes, making them weave and dodge to avoid a collision. Obscene rainbows, cast by the identification marker die mixed into the shell compound, painted the heavy air. Kusaka watched in growing admiration as the lead bomber continually disappeared behind an enormous waterspout to reappear after careening around it. The other enemy planes latched closely onto his tail. Like ducklings following their mother, he thought. No questions asked, just follow and try to keep up. He felt a guilty smile creep across his face. These Americans possess impressive flying skills.

As the aircraft drew closer, the gunfire rose in frightening intensity, a solid wall of noise that one could bounce against, and it set Kusaka's ears ringing. He grimaced, fighting the pain, but kept his eyesight focused on the terrible scene unfolding. Gun smoke and ship exhaust fumes poisoned the air with a harsh, oily odor he could taste. The bombardment grew larger and larger, overwhelming his senses and turning the bright sky into a dark, colored haze of exploding shell and smoke. A lethal rain of metal pummeled the enemy planes and rent huge gaping holes in their fuselages. He stared in open astonishment as they flew on through the man-made hell, determined to complete their mission.

46. MELO
June 04 – 07:15 Hours

"NO!"

Melo surged upright and staggered toward the tail gun. The B-26 bucked again, tossing him against the ammunition boxes. His arms flailed, grabbed at the dangling belts for support. Lightning struck his side with blinding pain. His eyes popped open. One hand dropped down to touch, coming back smeared with blood. Empty stomach notwithstanding, he bent over and dry-heaved. The spasm subsided as he wiped his mouth with the back of a hand. Moisture-filled eyes drew a bead on the tail position. Ears clanging with the unholy clamor of combat, his sense of smell deadened by the overload of metallic odors, he pressed on.

Flaming shell fragments peppered his left leg, forcing a scream from his lips. Another wave of nausea choked it off. He stood braced against the bouncing aircraft and forced himself to look. A shredded trouser leg revealed the gory extent of the damage. Numbed by pain and exhaustion, his body reduced to a scarlet-streaked nightmare, he ignored it all. He fell to his knees. To abandon his crucial mission was not an option. He dragged his way along the floor.

Crawling into the tail section, he grabbed onto the Browning's grips to pull his battered body onto the seat. A dark blur clouded his vision as he tried to aim the gun. Panic seized him. He frantically blinked, trying to clear his sight. The left eye burned and wept as he thought, what is it? What is it? A palm reached up, rubbed his forehead, and extended outward to reveal blood. The head wound's draining into my eye. That's all it is. Calm down. Take it easy. He squeezed the eye shut for a few seconds. Tears washed it until sufficient sight returned, and then he banged off a long stream of lead at an approaching Zero until the gun jammed.

He cursed while his fingers desperately clawed at the Browning's mechanism. The bolt freed up and then retracted home with a gratifying *clack*. Easy does it, he thought. Pace yourself firing. Don't allow excess heat and burnt powder to foul the gun's action. He started popping brief bursts at the pursuing fighters. Allowing for proper deflection, he skillfully walked .50-caliber tracers into the nearest Zero. Large hunks of metal blew off as the damaged plane veered away. Without pause, he turned the gun on another. The unrelenting firepower of the Browning hammered a lethal message home . . . to approach too close was to die.

A commotion from behind made him swivel his head. Gogoj fell onto the rocking, bloody floor again. He rolled up into a seated position, dug something out of his tattered face, and tossed it away. With a roar and a curse, Gogoj struggled back into the turret.

Tracer rounds punctured the tail section, stabbing into Melo. Searing agony rippled across his backside and bent him over. His mind screamed, *I'm on fire! I'm on fire!* Fumbling fingers sought and found a burning seat cushion. He pitched it out of the gun port and watched in angry frustration as the howling air currents pushed it back inside. It struck his chest, igniting his oily clothes. *Sweet Lord help me I'm burning alive!* Again, he clutched and tossed it below the turret. Blistered hands slapped out the flames licking his heavy coat.

Panting for breath, he sagged backward against the aircraft's frame. Choking smoke mixed with the stench of burnt material and scorched flesh filled his lungs. I'm suffocating, he thought. A deafening tumult of explosions heralded hot metal tearing large holes in the B-26. Amid his growing physical agony, random thoughts stippled his mind. This is insane. Gogoj is dying. Ashley's already dead. Someone has to do something.

I have to do something.

Aching fingers fell against the intercom switch and flipped it on. "We need help back here!"

Silence greeted the call. He tried again.

"Somebody help us back here!"

No response.

The intercom's dead, he thought. Most likely destroyed by gunfire. More bullets and tracers splattered around him. Another small blaze flared up, which he extinguished with the back of a hand. I have to get help. Tumbling out of the turret, he painfully made his way through the tunnel. Each step was a fight against the rocking, weaving, heaving, falling aircraft. He staggered like a drunkard, colliding against things and rebounding off. My body aches like one large bruise, he thought. The plane's shot all to hell. Those Japs are giving us the business.

He stuck his head through the circular hatch into the radio room. His hammered body cramped up, forcing him to wiggle through and drop down the small ladder onto the floor. Landing on his sore arm and shoulder, he groaned but managed to stand. A scared-looking W. W. Moore seated at his table dropped his pencil and tried to rise and help. Melo violently shook his head, knowing the navigator must remain at the charts. Stalking forward like a mummy in a horror show, Melo reached the other end. He mounted the steps until his head entered the cockpit.

"Lieutenant," he said, clamping a bloody hand on Muri's shoulder, "we need help in back. I think Ashley's dead and the Sarge is badly wounded. There's also a fire in the tail turret."

Muri glanced at Pren. "Go!"

Melo lowered himself and watched Pren unbuckle and then scramble down the ladder. Summoning his waning strength, Melo managed to follow the copilot toward the rear. He arrived inside the tunnel to see Pren wedge himself into Ashley's blood-smeared seat and grasp the Browning handles. Melo slid to his knees behind him, prepared to pass ammo.

The gun barrel tilted upward. Pren squeezed off a quick burst at a Zero making a diving pass. Looking over the lieutenant's shoulder, Melo saw the enemy plane flash past. It's after a different target, he thought. He watched a vicious storm of bullets and exploding shells jar a trailing B-26. A roar of thunder and flash of lightning preceded the Marauder's bursting into a raging fireball. It keeled over, fell away, and detonated against the ocean.

"Damn!" Pren said.

Pren blasted off a few more rounds and then eased up on the trigger. They both noticed the Zeroes falling back.

"What gives?" Melo asked.

Moments later the question was answered. Intense anti-aircraft fire rocked and shook the Marauder. They looked down and saw huge colored waterspouts thrown up by exploding shells erupting on each side. Through the swaying, swerving motion of the aircraft, Melo knew Muri had his hands full dodging the walls of water. To hit one at their speed would be like slamming into a concrete barrier at over two hundred miles an hour.

Pren shouted over his shoulder. "That Muri's a hell of a pilot, isn't he?"

"Yes sir, he is indeed."

"Gogoj looks bad but he's still working his guns," Pren added. "I tried to get him to come down and he told me to worry about someone else. These Japs have severely pissed him off."

Melo's arms shot out, grasping the walls to keep from sprawling onto the floor. His right arm throbbed with the effort and he felt the bleeding begin once more. A movement in his peripheral vision drew his attention. He looked at Ashley and felt like cheering as the young man stirred, trying to sit up.

"Ashley's alive," he told Pren.

Pren glanced back at the wounded tail-gunner. "Find something to tie around his leg and clamp off the bleeding."

Fumbling with his belt, Melo slid over to Ashley. His eyes fell upon Ashley's mangled leg. Thoughts of raw hamburger came quickly to mind. He tasted bile and stifled a retch. Head turned, he looped the improvised tourniquet around Ashley's upper thigh and pulled it tight through the friction buckle.

The B-26 heaved again, tossing Melo flat onto his back. Glancing up, he noticed Ashley's teeth clenched and his pale face pinched up in agony. Ashley's chest heaved once or twice and then settled down. His eyes flew open. They look clear, Melo thought. Clear and angry.

"Who's firing my .50?" Ashley asked.

"Lieutenant P. Moore."

"Let's get those bastards," Ashley said, trying to stand.

The pain must be excruciating. Melo felt new respect for the gunner's courage. Ashley has faced down his fear and emerged victorious, Melo thought. Dear Lord, help me do no less.

The aircraft suddenly lifted a bit and then angled upward. The thunderclaps of flak rose to an ear-splitting crescendo like a line of belching cannons surrounding the B-26. Melo scooted to the left gun port, banged against its sharp side, and moaned in pain as flaming knives ripped down his right arm. His face slid past the Browning's barrel and eased through the rectangular opening. He looked down. His mouth dropped open in shock. The tang of blood settled on his tongue as the B-26 skimmed over an enemy carrier's flight deck. A red circle larger than a Ferris wheel glared up at him and seemed to stare. Reflexively, he snatched back inside, expecting to feel the fuselage bottom scrape the wooden surface. Fighting to catch his breath, he heard Pren firing away on the Browning.

"My Sweet Lord!" Melo shouted.

"What?" Ashley asked.

Melo blinked and shook his head. "Trust me . . . you don't want to know."

He felt the B-26 nose lower, picking up speed. The skidding and dodging renewed in greater intensity. Melo vibrated rapidly against the sticky floor. Sparks of agony zipped across his body. A flash of relief coursed through him. *We've launched the torpedo,* he thought. *It's the only way that we could fly this much faster.* The unrelenting racket of exploding flak, racing engines, and howling wind now joined by the buzzing of millions of angry lead hornets forced a silent scream from his lips. Daylight streamed into the compartment as more showers of bullets and shells tried to kill the Marauder. Pren's machine gun thundered in response, seeking to keep the Zeroes at bay. Melo fought the panic. *Damn not fighting back,* he thought. His gaze fell onto one of the .30s. Maneuvering around, he grasped the handles.

"Give me a hand!" Ashley called.

"What?"

"Help me over to the tail and I'll pass ammo to the lieutenant."

His surprise over Ashley's request quickly dissolved. *Logic and sanity had abandoned the embattled aircraft a long time ago,* he thought. He extended his good arm and helped the groaning man crawl over to lie on the floor behind Pren. Ashley reached out, pulled a .50-caliber ammo box close, and worked a belt free.

Melo fixed his attention back on his guns. He fumbled with one-handed firing, loading, and then cursing as he cleared jams caused by the overheating weapons. The B-26 skipped along, occasionally sending him flying against a wall, impacting with a moan of pain. Bullets more often than cannon shells now continued to dot the aircraft in drunken patterns of lines and holes.

An eternity, perhaps merely a matter of minutes, passed before the noise and pounding lessened. A blistered finger remained locked on a Browning's trigger for several seconds after the ammo was exhausted and full consciousness returned. Relief mixed with caution eased his muscles. He realized no one was shooting at them. Head lowered and eyes closed, he silently prayed, *dear Lord, let it remain this way.*

47. KUSAKA
June 04 – 07:15 Hours

Kusaka staggered a few steps as *Akagi* turned toward the approaching enemy aircraft presenting a smaller target. He watched as three of the battered, tattered medium bombers continued winging toward the carriers intent on launching their torpedoes. Frantic Zeroes, having retreated earlier from the tremendous volume of friendly gunfire belching forth from the screening vessels, now ignored the threat. They dove in, blasting away at the deadly intruders.

The deep Pacific waters already littered with destroyed enemy aircraft, Kusaka wondered at the Americans' tenacity. We slaughter them with ease, yet still they come, he thought. Seemingly oblivious to the certain death awaiting them. Almost contemptuous in their disregard for our defense. Are they arrogant? Stubborn? Fools? What kind of men are these?

The lead aircraft closed to within a thousand meters before releasing its torpedo. It splashed down and disappeared from view, running toward its intended target. The unburdened plane skittered away across the wave tops with enraged Zeroes hounding its tail. Kusaka's eyesight remained locked in place, waiting for the weapon to reappear when it neared *Akagi*.

The huge ship made another hard turn, veering away from the oncoming torpedo. Kusaka lurched sideways into Genda, releasing a groan of pain from the young officer. The torpedo chugged past, missing the carrier and leaving a trail of bubbles in its wake. Cheers and clapping drifted on the combat-torn wind, falling silent as the second enemy plane bore in. The defensive gunfire increased in volume. A mountain of shot and steel sought to destroy the attacking aircraft. Amidst the panicked frenzy and close quarters, friendly fire struck neighboring vessels. Kusaka winced at the number of stray rounds zipping between the ships. This is utter madness, he thought. We could be wounded or killed at the hands of our fellow countrymen.

His vision returned to the attacking aircraft. Impressed with the pilot's skill, Kusaka knew somehow that this man dared to waltz among tigers. He's making a much closer approach before dropping his weapon. He has no fear. Intent on his deadly purpose.

Ears and body pounding from the riotous noise, Kusaka opened his mouth, trying to relieve the pressure. He thought, how could anything or anyone survive such relentless fire? It's not humanly possible. Are the Americans resorting to suicide attacks in desperation? Does their martial spirit allow for such acts?

Within five hundred meters of *Akagi*, the torpedo fell free, skipped once, and then started its run. Kusaka reached out to grab the wall, bracing himself against another sudden turn. Slight motion in the corner of his vision lured his eyesight to a pair of dividers skidding across the small chart table. They fell to the floor in silence, the soft clatter absorbed by the racket of battle.

With one hand, he hoisted the binoculars, focused on the cockpit of the now accelerating aircraft, and plainly saw the pilot straining at the controls. That answers my question about suicide attacks, he thought. This man wants to live. Muffled cheers rose to the bridge. Kusaka knew without looking that the enemy had missed again. Their weapons are unworthy of their courage. Wish that they never gain the swords equal with their desire to use them.

The airplane's nose lifted, and it screamed down *Akagi*'s flight deck. The screening vessels' and pursuing Zeroes' guns fell silent as it flashed by the island structure. The brief pause proved deadly. The bomber's rear gunner cut loose a spray of large caliber bullets. Tracers cut a fiery path into an anti-aircraft gun mount. Unprotected flesh splattered in crimson spray as rivets of lead mowed men down.

"*Look out!*"

Kusaka's vision shot to the window. The third enemy plane, forgotten during the last few minutes, loomed into view. It's heading straight for the bridge, Kusaka thought. It can't miss. No time to run. May death take me quickly. Instinct took over. He ducked, yet his eyesight never strayed from his killer. The aircraft rumbled past mere meters away, miraculously missing them. Propeller-generated turbulence shook the bridge, rattling the windows. Sweeping by, one damaged wing sheared off. The doomed plane flipped end over end, scattering into hundreds of pieces, erupting into a gigantic burning mass of twisted metal.

Kusaka stared at the shattered debris and flaming oil floating on the boiling surface marking the final resting-place of a brave warrior. *These Americans fight like samurai. I never expected such resolve from those raised in such a decadent lifestyle. I wish him peace. May his next life profit from the courageous sacrifice made in this one.*

The noise died away. The fleet's guns fell into a nervous silence. Kusaka checked his body, expecting to find a wound. Nagumo grunted; Kusaka saw him staring down at the bloody carnage near the battered gun pit.

"An amateur effort at best," Kusaka heard Genda say. "There was no coordination between the two groups of aircraft. They released torpedoes at too much distance. All approached from the same side. Our pilots would never make those types of mistakes."

Kusaka covered his eyes and rubbed his forehead against a sudden pain. "The mistakes made are overshadowed by the sacrifice offered. Cowards do not die such deaths. They deserve our respect if not our pity."

"Wisely said," Nagumo agreed.

Genda glanced at Nagumo. "I meant no disrespect to their brave spirits. I felt it my duty to point out the enemy's tactical errors. They have learned nothing about the proper way to fight a naval war."

"Yet, we may profit from their example of the proper way to die," Kusaka offered.

"They also present a serious threat to this task force," Nagumo said. "Midway must be immediately attacked again. This validates Tomonaga's request."

"And where will you draw the aircraft from to make this attack?" Kusaka asked. "You forget the point that Admiral Yamamoto stressed. Fleet doctrine states one-half of the carriers' strike forces must remain in reserve and loaded with ordnance for attacking enemy ships. Besides, there's no guarantee another attack will do any better."

"But these are our best pilots," Genda reminded. "Egusa is standing by, waiting his chance. His group will easily finish the job that Tomonaga's attack started."

"And what would you tell Admiral Yamamoto should the enemy fleet appear while all of our aircraft are attacking Midway?" Kusaka asked.

Genda crossed his arms over his chest. "Given the circumstances, I'd tell him it was the right thing to do. Our scout planes should've reached the furthest extent of their search patterns by now. They have reported nothing. Our submarine picket line is silent. We must address the immediate threat facing us. Admiral Nagumo is correct. These attacks and Tomonaga's message prove Midway must be neutralized."

Kusaka cast a quick look over at Nagumo and found him studying the deck. I'd not wish to be standing in his shoes, Kusaka thought. Yamamoto watching over his shoulder, waiting for a mistake. Enemies before him and comrades bearing daggers following close behind. Yet, Genda's words are very persuasive.

Kusaka nodded. "Your thoughts are well considered and logical. I agree we should strike Midway with the reserve force."

Nagumo's head jerked up, and he gazed at them. Kusaka read indecision and hesitation in Nagumo's eyes and facial expression. He's not convinced, Kusaka thought. Nagumo had voiced the necessity of repeating the Midway attack and is now questioning his own statement. This must be decided quickly. The sands of time trickle faster and faster. The sounds and activity of the huge ship recovering from the enemy's attack faded into the background as they faced off.

"That will require rearming the aircraft with contact bombs," Nagumo reminded. "It will take time to do this. Time that I do not wish to waste."

Genda shrugged. "It must be done."

Nagumo motioned toward Kusaka. "And what of Admiral Yamamoto's order to follow fleet doctrine? Our reserve force is to be maintained in case enemy carriers are located. He allowed for no deviation from his plan."

"Admiral Yamamoto is not here," Kusaka answered. "You are in command and must respond as circumstances dictate."

"Look around you." Genda pointed out the window to the damaged gun mount. "Midway can still strike back at us. It must be neutralized before we proceed. You made the same observation mere minutes ago and were correct in doing so. Our mission is clear . . . reduce Midway to rubble."

Nagumo glanced once more out the window and sighed deeply. He remained silent for a few long moments, and then slowly nodded.

"Signal the message to the rest of the fleet. Planes in second attack wave prepare to carry out attack on Midway. Re-equip yourselves with contact bombs. Notify when ready to depart."

Kusaka licked his lips. The decision is made, he thought, and it's the logical one. May it also prove to be the correct one.

48. BEST
June 04 – 07:15 Hours

Best sat at his desk in front of the ready room, trying to concentrate on plotting the latest enemy sighting. His squadron filled the small area, some stretched out in blissful sleep, the others nervously talking and laughing. The waiting's always the most difficult part, he thought. Whether it be waiting to become a father or waiting to enter battle. He chuckled at the thought. That's one hell of an analogy . . . comparing bringing life into the world to sending life out of the world. I've been at war for too long.

An odd motion passing by the door caught his attention. He got up, stepped outside, and saw Gene Lindsey gingerly moving down the corridor. He noted Lindsey wore a flight suit, and thought, Gene was lying in a hospital bed yesterday and today he's prepared to lead his group on the attack? What is he thinking?

"Gene!" he called out.

His hail brought the shuffling figure to an awkward halt. Lindsey slowly turned and seemed to force a smile.

"Are you ready to do this thing?" Lindsey asked.

"I am. Are you?"

Lindsey offered a half shrug. "Just waiting on the final word to go. These false alarms are annoying, aren't they?"

"You can't be serious about flying." Best locked eyes with Lindsey. "You can barely walk. I don't see how you'll ever mount a cockpit. You have no business in combat."

Lindsey glanced down and seemed to gather himself. He looked up at Best, his face a stone mask of defiance. Just like a figure on Mount Rushmore, Best thought.

"Make no mistake, I'll get into my cockpit if I have to crawl along the wing and pull myself in. I'm not about to miss out on this one. I'm a little sore, but I can still pilot an airplane and drop a torpedo. I will lead my squadron in."

Lindsey turned and began to move off.

"Why, Gene?"

Lindsey paused but did not look back. A sudden blaring of the intercom advising all pilots to stand by for orders rang down the corridor and echoed away.

"Because it's what I've . . . what we've *all* been trained to do. This is the real thing. How can I live with myself if I allow it to pass me by?"

Best squeezed his eyes tightly shut, caught up in the moment. They flicked open to see Lindsey enter his squadron's ready room. Best's thoughts drifted a lifetime away to Hawaii. He pictured his wife and child peacefully wrapped in sleep's dark embrace. Safe and secure, he thought, because of men like Gene Lindsey. Where do they come from?

Best thought of how his wife had never discussed combat nor his part in it. Never broached the subject of his possibly dying in battle. Yet it hung between them, like the smoky veil between darkness and sunrise. What was she thinking as he returned to the war once again, turning his back on the ones that he should hold closest in his heart? The letter he had found last night tucked safely away at the bottom of his seabag had answered his question.

Watching as you walk away
I wonder will you
come back to me someday
Your back straight
with your head held high
Never looking back
at what you are leaving behind
I know that you struggle inside
torn between duty
and wanting to stay by my side
A promise you made to us both
secured by a spoken oath
to love, honor, and cherish me
to protect her whether by land or sea
and when to duty you are called
you have to leave behind us all
For that is what allows us to be free
so that I can always be me
I hope that when
you are far away and alone
wondering about me
that you know
I am praying for God to watch over you
while I am absent from thee

That one day you will
once again walk through my door
For that is the way it is
when you are an American Soldier
going off to fight a war.

Now I know that she understands what's at stake and accepts the consequences. Because of men like Gene Lindsey, I have faith that I'm doing the right thing. Faith enough to perform my duty without pause. Thank you, Gene.

* * *

Best placed a foot into the access hole beneath his cockpit and paused to watch McClusky's Dauntless circle overhead waiting for the rest of the SBDs to launch. If any man can handle a dive bomber like a fighter, Wade's the one, he thought. He settled onto his parachute pack lying on top of the metal seat and worked with his crewman to strap and buckle in. Finished, the young sailor gave his helmet a quick tap.

"God speed, sir," he shouted over the incredible noise of the flight deck.

Best glanced his way and winked. Reaching out, he switched the radio knob to the intercom position. A faint *beep* in his headphones indicated the unit coming to life.

"Well Murray, this is it."

In the radioman/gunner's seat behind his, Murray responded, "Aye, lieutenant. Let's give them hell."

The rumble of engines further up the deck drew Best's attention to starting his own. A quick look over the side revealed his deck-handling crew turning the large propeller by hand to prime the 1000 horsepower engine. After four or five revolutions, they cleared away, and he engaged the starter. With a blinding belch of blue smoke, the Dauntless awoke to snarling life. Its heartbeat was a heavy, pulsing vibration sending a paradoxical mixture of thrill and comfort through him. Inside the cockpit, he felt like a baby enveloped in a crib, the Wright Cyclone engine humming a familiar lullaby. Best's eyesight ratcheted over the controls, noted gauge readings, switch and lever positions. He went through the familiar preflight routine, mentally marking the checklist.

He fixed the oxygen mask loosely to his face and inhaled the familiar odor of rubber mixed with exhaust smoke. A quick glance off into the distance revealed the endless watery horizon. Best thought, the enemy's lurking out there poised to strike. We've only to find him, dive down, and drop our bombs. Killing people is such an easy thing. You simply ditch your moral beliefs for a short time. Convince yourself that either the enemy or you must die. Take comfort in the fact that we didn't start this war.

"Lieutenant, I believe we're next." Murray's voice returned his attention to the idling aircraft.

Best sought and located the launching officer, Fly 1, and followed his directions in taxiing the SBD into takeoff position. Standing near the front of his aircraft and holding a white wand in his right hand, Fly 1 raised it straight up and feverishly twirled it. Best took the signal, confirmed the brakes were applied, and revved the Cyclone up to full power. A scan of his instrument panel and gauges revealed everything to be normal. Glancing out, he gave a thumb up indicating his readiness. Fly 1 looked down the length of the flight deck, making sure it was clear, and dropped the wand to point straight ahead.

Best released the brakes, felt the heavy aircraft lumber forward and slowly gain takeoff speed. He held his breath and thought, it always seems like the plane will never lift off. I can picture it rolling right on over the end and plunging into the water. It's no wonder that some of the pilots leave the laces out of their shoes. Makes it easy to kick them off when you're treading water. The flight deck end is coming up fast. I'll have to scramble out in a hurry . . . I hope Murray can, too. This loaded bird won't float for long. His right hand was poised to drop the stick and release his seat belts when he felt a rising sensation as the landing gear finally cleared the wooden surface.

"Lieutenant, does it ever seem to you like we aren't going to make it into the air?" Murray called from the rear seat.

"What's wrong? Can't swim?"

"Just to the extent that I can drown."

"And you joined the Navy?"

"At the time, it seemed like the safest choice. Now I'm not so sure."

"I'll try to keep your feet from getting wet."

One hand automatically shifted to the landing gear selector lever and moved it into the *UP* position. He depressed the engine pump control handle and held his breath for a few long seconds.

Horror stories sprang to mind of unfortunate pilots whose wheels would not rise electrically or manually and then collapsed when the pilots attempted emergency landings. The subtle bump as the gear fully retracted came as a welcome feeling and allowed an intake of breath. The Dauntless continued flying a straight line for another few hundred yards to build up sufficient air speed before he eased into a starboard turn.

Best's vision swept upward and latched onto the other SBDs assembling into attack formation. The morning sun briefly reflected off the ocean below, drawing his attention to the armada of ships awaiting their return. With my shield or carried on it, he thought. How would that translate into an air battle? With my parachute or wrapped up in it as if in a shroud. A morbid thought. Should I not return, there will be no shroud. I'll be strapped into this seat for eternity.

49. SPRUANCE
June 04 – 07:30 Hours

"What in the hell is taking so long to launch this attack?" Browning roared.

Standing under the shade of his flag shelter, Spruance took note of the calm flight deck and sympathized with his chief of staff. What was indeed taking so long? Surprise was their biggest advantage. Surprise allowed for making the first strike. Striking first greatly increased the chances for success. In fact, without surprise, defeat almost certainly ensued.

Spruance trained his glasses on the sky and swept them around the strike force. *Hornet* was maneuvering out of the wind and back onto base course. Mitscher has completed his launch, he thought. The squadrons would assemble and head out. Head out to what? Does it matter? It certainly does if *Enterprise*'s groups fail to join in. Amply warned by a small opening attack, the enemy wouldn't take long to respond. The firepower of four Japanese fleet carriers is terrible to contemplate. Nagumo would lay both our task forces to waste. Virtually wiping out the entire American aircraft carrier strength in the Pacific with one massive air strike. I can't let that happen.

"Bill," he said, addressing Oliver, "I want to know what's taking so long to finish this launch. Now."

"And I want to know the same thing," Browning said.

Spruance shot Browning a quick look and noticed him glance away. Always wanting the final word, aren't you? Spruance thought. Patience, don't leave me. This battle's just beginning.

"By all means, ask for both of us," Spruance said.

"Aye, sir." Oliver picked up the phone and spoke into it.

"You're worried?" Murray was at his side.

"We can't afford for Nagumo to catch us with aircraft on our decks. So far, we've been lucky to avoid detection. We can't waste this opportunity, nor will our luck hold out. Being this close to hostile territory, you can bet he has patrol planes out searching for something like us. It's not *if* Nagumo will find us . . . it's when and how quickly will he be able to strike us. We *have* to take some of his pieces off the board. Quickly."

And what condition will Nagumo's forces be in? he thought, but he didn't say it. There's been a lot of radio traffic on Midway's air frequency, but it's impossible to decipher what's happening. Have they damaged the enemy fleet? If not and our attack fails to mount properly, there'll be the devil to pay. Nimitz's worst nightmare could come true.

"Admiral," Oliver said with his hand cupped over the mouthpiece, "due to the heavy bomb load and the need for extra room for takeoff, the crews could only spot a few planes at a time. They also had a TBD break down and clutter up the flight deck, but it's been cleared away. Things should begin picking up speed very soon."

Spruance bit his bottom lip, thinking, I can't wait for *soon*. *Soon* might be too late. I want these decks cleared immediately . . . or?

"Miles?"

Browning turned to face him.

"I'm thinking we signal McClusky to proceed with what he has. *Hornet*'s groups are on their way and *Enterprise*'s must be close behind. I want a massive, concerted attack that's difficult to defend against, not a bunch of individual elements the enemy can pick off at leisure."

Browning took a moment before replying, "I agree. The SBDs are ready to leave and they're carrying the heaviest ordnance load. It's a lot better than nothing."

Spruance motioned to Oliver. "Signal McClusky to proceed on mission assigned."

Without acknowledging, Oliver snatched up the phone and spoke into it.

"It's done, sir," he said after hanging up.

Spruance scanned the skies. A few minutes later, the sight of the SBD formations retreating into the distance rewarded his efforts. He lowered the binoculars, thinking, hopefully they won't arrive too late.

The drone of departing aircraft continued as first the Wildcat escorts and finally the TBDs made their way down the flight deck and into the air. Spruance watched each one and offered a silent prayer for the men inside charged with such a monumental task. How many of them even know how important this moment is? Few, I'd guess. Most if not all are more concerned with the impending combat. Performing their duty and staying alive while doing it. I can't say that I blame them. But, what they do today is critical to the future. Nimitz was adamant about that. The course of this war depends on them.

"Admiral, we've received word that a Japanese scout plane is on the horizon," Oliver said while hanging up the phone.

Browning spun around and bellowed a curse. "I knew this would happen! Time's run out on us."

"Have we been spotted?" Spruance asked.

Oliver looked at him. "I'd say so. Plot reports the Jap plane's been hanging around too long not to have seen us, sir. Communications is also picking up radio transmissions."

Browning looked up at the now forbidding sky. "Why in the hell can't our CAP find this bastard and flame him?"

Spruance glanced at Browning. "For the same reason that our PBYs give them fits . . . excellent pilots. Survival of the fittest, Charles Darwin would say. The poor reconnaissance pilots don't last long."

"Do we break radio silence and notify Pearl, sir?" Oliver asked. "Give Admiral Nimitz a head's up?"

"Not yet. As far as I'm concerned, until the enemy attacks us we're not spotted. Have a signal sent to Admiral Fletcher advising him of the fact."

"*Yorktown*'s out of sight, sir," one of the combat talkers said. "We can't blinker them."

"We could try to raise him on the TBS," Murray offered. "The Japs shouldn't be able to intercept that."

Spruance thought for a second. Regardless of the enemy snooper, I'm not prepared to risk breaking radio silence. Surely, *Yorktown*'s radar picked up the contact and Fletcher knows. But if he doesn't? Communication is the key.

"Send an F4F and have the pilot drop a message," Spruance told the talker.

He raised the glasses and paused. "Notify *Hornet* to disperse but to try to remain within range if possible. I don't want to make things too easy for Nagumo."

"Aye, sir."

Nimitz's plan is in motion, he thought. I've done all that I can. Our fortunes now rest in the hands of our pilots and gunners. Let the battle commence.

50. BROCKMAN
June 04 – 07:50 Hours

"Down periscope!" Brockman snapped the periscope handles up. "Take her down. Ahead full! Make your depth one zero zero feet!"

He heard the orders relayed to the control room below where Hogan oversaw the actions of the hydraulic manifold operator and the two planes men. The deck sharply declined, forcing him to reach out and grab the periscope stack for balance.

Overhead, a low rumble escalated into a furious howl. The rattle of gunfire preceded the angry whine of bullets zipping through the water. He glanced over to Benson at his chart desk next to the TDC station and noticed him hunching his shoulders. Trying to bury his head between them, Brockman thought. Can't say that I blame him. I often wish I were a turtle, too.

"Looks like we're near enough that they've finally took notice." Benson said.

"We can't attack columns of smoke. You know we had to close the distance between us and them."

"Uh, huh. Who did you anger up there?"

"A patrol plane spotted the periscope and made a strafing run. I caught the glimmer as sunlight reflected off its wings. It was a lucky thing."

"You couldn't give a fellow a warning? This is the only clean pair of dry pants I've got."

Brockman had to smile. "Next time."

"Any chance of taking a shot at one, sir?" Lieutenant Lynch at the TDC asked.

"That's what we're here for."

The deck slowly leveled off as Hogan called up, "Depth now one zero zero, sir."

"I've got pinging, sir," Woods, the sonar operator, advised.

Brockman stepped closer to the sound station next to the periscopes and watched Woods adjust the hydrophone's steering handle.

"I'd calculate about two thousand yards' distance and moving in slow circles," Woods continued. "I've a lot of other screws moving in various directions and speeds."

Brockman rubbed his chin, felt a sudden urge to smoke, and thought, what did I expect? Raise a periscope in the midst of this many Jap ships and I'm bound to attract attention. Now I'm left with a decision. If we stay down, we're safe and can creep away. The enemy's too busy with what's going on up top to worry about us. All we have to do is tuck our tail and run. That's the smart thing to do.

He sensed the men studying him and could almost read their thoughts. The doubts about *Nautilus*'s ability as an attack boat. Too big and too slow, some said. Roy and I had discussed it. We'd heard the talk, too. What could Admiral English expect out of us? We can sneak off now and make a contact report. Let our surface and air units deal with the enemy.

Cuttlefish came to mind. He had tried not to question Spike Hottel's actions. Not until he faced the same circumstances. Now he did. *Cuttlefish* stayed under and lived to fight another day. Did Spike do the right thing? Brockman still couldn't–wouldn't judge another skipper's choices. I must make my own decisions. Not worry about someone else's. He turned around toward the periscopes. We came to fight. Fight we shall.

"Helm, slow to one-third," Brockman said to Yates. Yates stood manning the conning tower helm station located next to the front wall.

Walking over to the ladder rail, Brockman called down. "Dive, make your depth six five feet."

Hogan echoed the order and the boat started inclining noticeably. Brockman automatically leaned into it as he moved into position behind the attack periscope. He tensed, waited for the boat to level off and tried to picture the scene up top. Destroyers racing around trying to locate *Nautilus* along with aircraft skimming over the wave tops searching for any sign of the submerged threat. The enemy now warned of *Nautilus*'s presence, a feeding frenzy certainly stirred the water. Like sharks after blood, he thought. Each one wanting to make the kill.

"My speed is one-third, sir," Yates said.

Brockman's eyesight darted to the quartermaster of the watch, Crenshaw, who served as periscope assistant. "Keep a close eye on me, chief. When I slap these handles up, you drop the thing fast. Don't wait for the order."

"Aye, sir."

"Depth is six five feet," Hogan called up.

Brockman braced himself and squatted. "Up scope." As it rose, he dropped the handles and paralleled its movement. First faint light and then a viscous blending of colors and shapes filled the view as the periscope head broke the surface. He quickly did a 360-degree scan looking for a predator within striking distance and noticed a cruiser prowling nearby. The view rotated further and focused on a formation of four vessels before concentrating on the largest ship in the group. He took a mental photograph of its structure and slapped the handles up.

"Down scope!"

Crenshaw watching his every move, the periscope dropped before the words left his mouth. Brockman joined Benson at the desk and took the offered book identifying Japanese shipping types. He flipped pages, fingers weaving over the silhouettes, and tried to find a match with the vessel above. The hunt ceased; he turned the book around.

"*Ise* class battleship of 35,000 tons," Benson said, reading the information. "I'd say that's a target worth attacking."

"That's the big leagues," Lynch added. "Almost as good as an aircraft carrier."

"She's not alone," Brockman responded. "Looks like three cruisers keeping close company."

He thumbed through the pages, again searching for a picture resembling the ship actively searching for *Nautilus*. Settling on a *Jintsu*-class cruiser, he pointed it out to Benson and Lynch.

"The *Jintsu*'s stalking us," Brockman said.

"Any chance of getting a solution and shooting at more than one?" Lynch asked.

Brockman thought, shooting at more than one? It would be nice to do so. *Nautilus*'s first score not one but two of the Imperial Japanese Navy's ships. The crew would love it. It'd make a hell of a great patrol report. However, the periscope time I'd need to acquire the data for two setups for the Torpedo Data Controller to use . . . I can't disregard that. It's the old risk versus reward decision. In this case, the risk's too high. One battleship's reward enough.

"Too much exposure time for the necessary observations," Brockman answered. "Let's sink the *Ise* and then worry about a cruiser."

"Sounds like a plan," Benson echoed.

"Helm, make your bearing three five zero. Ahead full."

"Let's move ahead of her and pop up for another look," he said to Benson.

"And the sound from our screws?"

"They're making too much noise themselves to notice us. It'd take direct pinging. We should hear that approaching in time to stop."

That balance of risk versus reward, Brockman told himself again. Never forget this. *Nautilus* must get to the right place at the right time without undue risk. He studied the chart, wondering, where are the enemy carriers? With so much firepower above, they must be near. I'd love a shot at one of those.

Brockman moved back to the periscope and glanced over at Crenshaw.

"You know the drill."

Crenshaw smiled.

"Helm, slow to one-third."

"Slow to one third," Yates answered.

Brockman waited, sensing the boat slowing. Mustn't make it easy on them to spot us by feathering a wake with the periscope mast, he thought. The Jap lookouts seem sharp enough as it is. A quick peep should be enough. Just need to know if she's still where I think she is.

"My speed is one-third, sir."

"Up scope."

He rode the periscope up and waited until the lens washed clear. An ominous, metallic spark burst against the sky, registering on Brockman. *Nautilus* sighted, he heard the airplane's engine change in pitch and intensity. He slapped the handles up, leapt away from the vision of the attacking aircraft.

"Down scope! Take her down! Make your depth nine zero feet. Right full rudder. Ahead full."

Again, Crenshaw anticipated the order and had the tube safely buried in its well within seconds. Brockman grabbed hold of the bulkhead as the deck sloped sharply downward and the boat veered left. The question came to his mind, was this another strafing or—

Shock waves from an exploding bomb shook the boat. Paint flakes and cork pieces showered down, filling the air with thick

247

particles of matter. An odor of charcoal and lead defined the thick air. The lights blinked, radiated back into full brilliance. Brockman covered his mouth and coughed. It's damn sure *not* another strafing, he thought. His ears rang from the concussion as a threatening ping stabbed through the ocean, seeking its prey.

"Slow to one-third. Rudder amidships."

He stepped over to Woods.

"Sound?"

Woods settled the earphones in place and turned the directional wheel.

"I've one . . . no, two sets of echo ranging. They're slowing to listen for returns."

Brockman glanced over at Wetmore, the combat talker, standing behind Yates and wearing a sound-powered phone.

"Rig for depth charge attack. Rig for silent running."

Brockman's focus returned to Woods at the sound gear. The bomb was close and a warning, he thought. We tread a thin line. A line between success and failure. How do I measure success? Sinking ships is the common answer. Perhaps, in a situation such as this, adding to the confusion of battle equals success? Distracting the enemy from concentrating on other matters? Who is to say? The measure of failure is simple in comparison. To fail is to die.

Woods snatched the headphones off. "Depth charges in the water!"

Brockman rushed to the ladder railing, and bellowed, "*Standby for depth charging!*"

51. HENDERSON
June 04 – 07:50

"There are rising smoke columns back toward Midway," the unidentified voice keyed over the radio. "Looks like the Japs have made it to there."

"I wonder if we'll have a place to land when we return," another said.

"Stay off the air until we need it," Henderson responded. He flew to the side of his group's formation, keeping a close watch on the inexperienced pilots. His eyesight constantly cycled between the ocean and sky, seeking the enemy in either location. It's going to be soon, he thought. I can feel it.

Taking a quick moment to acknowledge his men's efforts, he felt pleased. So far, we're maintaining flight discipline. No one has strayed or fallen behind. We should arrive over the target together. Not bad for a squadron of Marines making their first attack in SBDs. These men have learned their lessons well. Give them some time and additional training and they'll be the equal of any bombing group in the Pacific.

The familiar smell of exhaust mixed with sweat served to settle him. A review of his indicators and gauges bore more good news. Pressures and temperatures normal or within safe operating ranges, fuel supply is ample. This Dauntless is one hell of a good aircraft. All I have to worry about is locating the Japs and pressing home our attack. The rest will take care of itself.

His vision swept the sky and noticed the rising sun. An image of renewal and beauty, he thought. Except when colored blood red and spread across a white background. Damn those Jap bastards for profaning the thing.

Another glance at the squadron formation revealed no problems. Concerned with the pilots' inexperience in the new aircraft, he had made Captain Richard Fleming navigator of the lead group. All the men have to do is follow Fleming, he thought. Just concentrate on flying the SBD and not worry about the route to take.

His mind drifted to Norris and the Vindicators following behind. I hope that Ben's green flight crews are hanging together. We need to hit those carriers with everything possible. Perhaps my bunch can disperse the Jap fighter screen and take some of the heat off the Vindicators when they arrive to attack. At least give them a fighting chance.

Something below? A sudden crease between thin wisps of cloud revealed white lines carved into the water's surface . . . tracks left by ships' propellers. Binoculars raised, he made out the forms of two enemy carriers making way. Jackpot!

He picked up the microphone and keyed it. "Fleming from Henderson, look off the port bow. Spotted two enemy flattops. Am assuming position to mount the attack."

"Henderson from Fleming. Roger. Lead the way."

Here we go, Henderson thought. Time to start dropping altitude and line out for the bombing run. I must keep everything simple. Bear in mind that this is the first combat for most of these men. A small knot of fear gathered inside his stomach that he briefly acknowledged. The fear is natural. Nothing to concern myself with. Remain focused on making a successful attack. Trust that our training will guide us through.

Henderson switched to the interphone. "Get your gun ready, Reininger. I've a feeling we're about to have company."

"Yes, sir. I'm primed and ready."

Henderson advanced the Dauntless' throttle and guided his aircraft into the lead position. The increased roar from the engine added to the howling wind flowing over the open canopy. Pausing to wipe his goggles with the back of a sleeve, he focused on the inviting targets below. A few puffs of ack-ack fire reached up to pepper the sky around them. They've spotted us, he thought. The Zekes will be on us soon, guided by the shell explosions. No sense in dallying around. Head for the closest flattop and make it count.

"Squadron from Henderson. Attack the two enemy carriers on the port bow."

He eased the aircraft into a wide let down circle, trying to place the sun behind their backs. Every precaution helps . . . makes it just a little harder on the enemy to spot us. Gives us a small edge in reaching drop position before–

"*Here they come!*" the radio trumpeted.

The empty sky filled with a horde Japanese fighters. Like giant enraged bees, they swarmed around and through the SBD formation. Wings and noses twinkled with machine guns and cannons firing; curving lines of tracer and shell shot carved into the American ranks. Stay together, Henderson silently implored. Not much farther now.

Henderson heard Reininger returning fire from the rear seat and felt the SBD vibrating from the recoil. The combat odors of hot metal and burning gunpowder reached out for him. He struggled to tune out the noise and confusion, steadily concentrating on making his approach glide. Focus. Stay the course. Focus. Show these young guys how it's done.

Blasts of smut and paint splattered the sky as enemy ack-ack clawed upward after him. The Dauntless pitched and reared in the explosions' wakes, trying to tear loose from his grip. Fingers and arms growing numb from the exertion of maintaining control, his ears rang from the unrelenting racket of battle. It sounded as if loaded machine guns were pressed against each side of his head with their triggers held down. Ignoring the confusion and pain, he fought to maintain focus. His eyesight stayed locked onto the fleeing carrier as he lumbered toward it. Feet became miles; seconds became hours, as fighting raged through the skies surrounding him.

He chanced a glance over a shoulder and proudly noticed the squadron staying intact behind him. Good men, he thought. Hang on. Not much farther now. Allow your training to take over and you will be successful. Just follow me.

Another Zeke slashed by in front of his SBD's nose. His propeller raised a painful clatter as if it were chewing a bucket of rivets. A flash to his left revealed his wing shot full of holes and burning. Oily smoke filtered into the cockpit, causing a cough and burning his eyes. Tears of rage wet his cheeks. He latched tighter onto the stick as the SBD attempted to roll in that direction. Can't stop. I have to keep going. Keep the men on course. Not much farther. I can see my drop point.

Whip cracks and whines announced bullets zipping through the air, ripping into the canopy. The Plexiglas cracked. Damage holes resembling spider webs splattered with blood obscured his vision. Blinding pain stabbed into his right arm and shoulder, jerking the stick out of his hand. He felt the plane roll over. A glimpse of sky below. He briefly acknowledged the world turned upside down. Nausea gripped him. Vertigo took command of his senses.

Home.

52. KUSAKA
June 04 – 07:55 Hours

"An urgent message, sir," the runner shouted to be heard over the noise on the bridge.

Kusaka threaded himself through the tight quarters. He took it and scanned the words. As he read, a gauntlet of iron grabbed his heart and squeezed. He looked up at Genda and Nagumo and forced a swallow down his now thickened throat.

"*Tone*'s scout No. 4 reports enemy surface units in position bearing 10 degrees, distance 240 miles from Midway. The course is 150 degrees and the speed in excess of 20 knots."

"Enemy surface units?" Nagumo boomed out.

Even amidst the chaos, his question registered on all. Anxious faces turned toward Nagumo. He took the note, devoured the contents, and glanced at Genda.

"Scout No. 4 should have reached this position some time ago. Why the delay in transmitting this? What type of surface units?"

Genda shook his head and stammered, "I . . . I don't know, sir. Some unforeseen problem? But we must find out."

"Yes," a visibly agitated Nagumo responded. "Immediately. Immediately."

Genda turned to the runner. "Send this urgent reply, 'Retain contact and identify ship types and numbers.'"

Kusaka silently observed, trying to rein in his rushing emotions. Concentrate on the breath, he thought. Do not become distracted or lose focus. The enemy has made several attacks to no avail already. There's no reason to believe he'll fare better with surface units. However, if there are aircraft carriers poised on our flank?

"Suspend rearming the planes immediately!" Nagumo's voice sliced through the noise.

Genda and Kusaka crowded closer to Nagumo. They waited while Ono calculated the enemy's position at the small plotting table. Finished, Ono exhaled deeply and looked up at them. The look on his face flashed fear into Kusaka. Things are coming undone.

"A little over 200 miles from us."

"They're within our striking distance," Genda remarked.

"As we are within theirs," Kusaka countered.

Genda ignored Kusaka to fix his attention on Nagumo. "Only if they have an aircraft carrier. This report says nothing of the sort."

"This report says nothing at all," Kusaka said, already straining over the din, elevating his voice another notch in volume and intensity. "It's hard for me to comprehend an enemy task force this far from land-based protection not being accompanied by at least one aircraft carrier. The Americans would not make that mistake. Surely, they've learned from the example of the British Battleships *Prince of Wales* and *Repulse* of the fate that awaits surface vessels targeted by aircraft. Both were easily sunk in the Gulf of Siam."

"Midway offers protection."

"Minimal, and with very limited coverage."

Genda fell silent. For the first time, Kusaka felt the growing tension between them on the cramped bridge. They were not alone and should not comport themselves as if they were. Kusaka motioned; their heads bent closer to Nagumo.

"Admiral Kusaka is correct," Genda said. "There could be at least one enemy aircraft carrier. If there is, so much the better. We'll annihilate them now if the opportunity exists. That conforms to Admiral Yamamoto's plans."

"That is possible if we act quickly." Nagumo rubbed his jaw. "What do you suggest, Genda?"

Again, the rumble of gunfire—this time more distant—interrupted. Kusaka rushed in its direction and found an open spot near the starboard window to search the skies. Colorful, cottony puffs of exploding anti-aircraft shells drew his focus. *Hiryu* appears to be the target, he thought. He located a flight of enemy dive bombers approaching the carrier at a shallow angle. Puzzled, his binoculars lowered and then snapped back into position. Much too low for a diving attack and the improper position for launching a torpedo, he thought. What new tactic is this?

The waiting Zeroes rained down like a willow tree's sad branches. Bullets and cannon shells pounded destruction into the enemy aircraft. A thunderous cheer went up from the crowd below *Akagi*'s bridge each time a burning enemy plane crashed into the waves. As Kusaka watched, realization of the enemy's tactics dawned. Glide-bombing against this enormous strike force? Who could conceive of such a thing? What madness is this? These slow flying aircraft provide easy prey for our gunners and fighter pilots.

"I don't understand these Americans," Genda said. As if reading Kusaka's mind, he added, "Why would they not dive to make their attack? It's much more difficult to defend. They've no chance at all by glide-bombing."

Why not indeed? Kusaka thought. Though explosions splattered the ocean around *Hiryu*, none hit. One particularly brave American, aircraft smoking, released his bomb at almost minimum range and then made a strafing pass over the carrier.

Head pounding and ears ringing from the noise, Kusaka caught his breath as the final enemy plane vanished from view with Zeroes hounding his tail. The stench of salty humidity and human sweat warred against his nose, stung his eyes, and deadened his senses of smell and sight. A growing feeling of panic threatened to manifest itself upon him. He clutched the window frame and counted breaths, angrily trying to regain his compose. I've no time for such foolish behavior, he thought. The enemy is here. The battle will not wait. I'm in need of my full mental faculties.

"Enemy force is composed of five cruisers and five destroyers." Genda was speaking.

Kusaka's eyelids blinkered open and saw the message in Genda's hands. He thought, no enemy carriers? Can it really be true? Can we return our attention to Midway and deal with this surface force later?

"*Tone* also answered that Scout No. 4 was nearly thirty minutes late in catapulting off. The message doesn't offer an explanation."

"I thought as much," Ono said. "The omens remain strongly in our favor."

"I agree," Genda echoed. "The enemy has made three attacks and damaged little. The battle is now ours to win."

Nagumo pointed a hand toward the window. "Damaged little but disrupted much. The fleet is now scattered and our fighter umbrella has dispersed and is low on ammunition. This situation must be resolved at once."

Genda turned to a runner. "Message the fleet to reassemble. Have adequate fighter reserves dispatched to relieve those on station and allow them to refuel and reload."

The sailor bowed and hurried off. A frowning Genda looked at Nagumo.

"The fighter reserves were sent airborne already. We'll have to draw from the planes assigned to escorting the attack force. We need time. Time to—"

Thunder cracked nearby as if on schedule. Kusaka glanced out the window at *Tone* assaulting the heavens with painted blossoms of smoke and metal. *Soryu*'s turn before the executioner had arrived. Shredded columns of water colored in various hues and topped off in smoky gray pillared up around the dodging carrier. *Soryu* vanished behind a screen of spray, an apparent victim to enemy bombs. Several tense moments later, *Soryu* emerged unharmed and making full steam.

"High-altitude enemy bombers," Genda explained. "Our anti-aircraft fire will never reach them, but it's nearly impossible to hit a moving target from such height. They should be easy to evade."

The morning's exercise has taken its toll, Kusaka thought. Exhausted gunners do not respond with the same accuracy and zeal as rested ones. The task force as a whole shows visible signs of combat fatigue. Yet, the enemy continues to come. How much more can we endure? How much longer before some of them pass through our wall of iron to sow destruction upon us?

"Lieutenant Tomonaga is signaling for permission to land," Genda had to shout. "His planes are running low on fuel."

Kusaka watched more enemy bombs erect a picket fence of billowing water fountains around *Hiryu*, and thought, Tomonaga now? How can we expect to land airplanes in the middle of all *this*? Recovery efforts will leave our carriers completely vulnerable to enemy bombs and torpedoes.

Then as abruptly as the enemy arrived, it disappeared. The bridge fell strangely quiet to a level at which one could hear his own thoughts. The men glanced at each other, happy to be alive yet wondering how they had managed to remain so, Kusaka thought.

"Message, sir."

Kusaka was closest to the door and took it. He opened it, read through, and covered his eyes. He was right the first time.

"The enemy is accompanied by what appears to be a carrier bringing up the rear," he advised.

"A carrier?" Nagumo spun around. "It says a carrier?"

Kusaka passed him the paper. Nagumo's lips moved in time with his eyesight down the page. His nostrils blew and his eyebrows pitched upward as he handed the message to Genda.

"This settles the question about attacking Midway again," Nagumo said. "We must deal with this enemy carrier. Nothing bears greater importance now."

"But what of Tomonaga's group?" Genda pointed out. "If we launch an immediate strike, they'll run out of gas and have to ditch. We'll lose half of our available aircraft. The attack complement of four carriers will be reduced to that of two."

"There's also the question of making an attack without proper ordnance loaded out," Kusaka joined in. "We're well along in the process of rearming with contact bombs for a land target. To attack ships we need torpedoes and armor-piercing bombs."

"Enemy dive bombers!"

The lookout's cry sent them into immediate action. Captain Aoki shouted a hard over to the helmsman. The officers staggered, lurched, and fought to maintain their balance as the deck tried to tilt out from underneath them. Feeling his stomach heave, Kusaka fought down the urge to vomit.

"They're after *Haruna*!" someone yelled over the roar.

Kusaka searched the sky over *Haruna* and located the plunging airplanes. The angle too shallow for a normal dive, he quickly realized this group was also glide-bombing. What are these Americans thinking in using such a foolish tactic?

"Can you believe this?" Genda was at his side. "Another enemy squadron attempting a glide-bombing attack. It's as if they have no regard for their lives . . . like they wish to be shot down. Are they that desperate?"

"Perhaps not," Kusaka answered. "Our fighters are having more difficulty with this group. I believe that most if not all will complete their bombing run. I fear for *Haruna*."

They fell silent for a moment, watching the unfolding drama. The protective screen of Zeroes appeared disorganized, almost tentative as they worked in among the assaulting bombers. The rear gunners looked to be easily holding them at bay while the pilots completed their drops. Explosions spewing huge fountains of water dotted the sea around *Haruna* as she bravely sailed onward.

"You're right," Genda shouted over the noise. "Our fighter pilots are having difficulty. They've been in constant action for almost four hours. Fatigue could be affecting them."

Fatigue will affect all of us, Kusaka thought. Is there no end to these attacks? He pasted his eyelids shut for several long moments and then slowly pried them open. He focused on breathing as he watched the old battleship continue to wage combat against the enemy aircraft. Wreaths of smoke and bursts of metal jolted the attacking aircraft, spoiling their aim. The retreating enemy hugged the ocean tightly, denying the Zeroes a chance to get underneath to their unprotected bellies. Dismayed, Kusaka noticed nearly all of them escaping.

The storm quickly passed; the tempest calmed. Kusaka tried to relax, but kept returning to the same troubling thought. How much longer can we keep this up? With each attack, the Americans appear to be getting stronger. We grow weaker, less focused on our task.

He glanced over at a now visibly disturbed Nagumo. He looks much older, he thought. As must I. Nothing in this war so far could have prepared us for this. However, I shall not allow this worry to consume me. I will take heart and logically examine the situation. Five attacks of different variety, and we remain relatively unscathed. Perhaps Nagumo's omens did not bear ill tidings after all. Genda was correct. These Americans are a brave but foolish bunch attacking in such unorganized fashion. May they not learn from their deadly mistakes. Yet . . . I fear that they will.

And they continue to attack.

"Admiral Kusaka." A runner was at his elbow. "An urgent message from Admiral Yamaguchi."

Kusaka took the note, thinking, Yamaguchi? Do we not have enough trouble without Yamaguchi's fiery rhetoric? He read the words and found what he'd expected. Yamaguchi's a fool with important friends . . . a dangerous combination.

"What does it say?" Nagumo's strained voice sounded barely audible.

"He wants you to launch an immediate strike against the enemy carrier with everything available that can fly."

"Has he learned nothing at all from this?" Genda said. He raised an arm and pointed a finger toward the window. "This is what happens when bombers and torpedo planes try to attack without fighter escort. A multitude of aircraft shot down. Dozens of lives surrendered in vain. Nothing to show for the effort. Is he blind?"

"We must not make the same mistake as the Americans," Kusaka agreed. "Doing so invites disaster. We'll be throwing away planes and pilots in the same fashion. We should delay for a while. Recover all of Tomonaga's planes and the escort fighters now protecting us. Then send out a balanced, coordinated strike."

"And in the meantime?"

Nagumo's tone presented a challenge, one Kusaka did not expect. Kusaka pulled back his shoulders and locked onto Nagumo's eyes with his own.

"Use the time to rearm the second wave with armor-piercing bombs and torpedoes for use against the enemy carriers. With the correct launch sequence, we can launch our strike while the fighters are refueling and rearming. They can easily catch up to the slower bombers and torpedo planes."

Nagumo dropped his eyes to the deck; his fingers pinched and released his nose. Kusaka could feel his conflicting thoughts and felt sympathy. Yamamoto is always standing behind Nagumo, he thought. It's hard to see the sun when one constantly walks in the shadow of another.

Nagumo looked up at Genda. "What do you think?"

Genda glanced at Kusaka and then back to Nagumo. "Our first priority should be Tomonaga and his group. Nothing else is more important. We should do as Admiral Kusaka suggests, not Admiral Yamaguchi."

Nagumo looked at the message and then up at his two officers. "Make it so."

53. BROCKMAN
June 04 – 08:10 Hours

Brockman's hands clamped onto the tubular rails. A distant booming radiated outward, bobbled the boat, and kicked up more debris into the air. He could hear–*feel*–a wicked throbbing, beating at the water, drawing closer and closer. Crescendos of noise, evolving in pitch, and now a swishing sound.

Swish—Swish—Swish!

Violent shock waves of destruction clanged against the metal hull. Giant, enraged hands reached out to hammer and shake the boat's protective shell as the depth charges detonated.

Whack—Whack—Whack—Whack!

Long minutes tugged past accompanied by more explosions. Brockman's fingers and arms grew numb and his muscles sore from hanging on to prevent himself from flying around like a ragdoll. Pops and the harsh smell of sizzling wire accompanied light bulbs bursting. Spots of darkness dotted the conning tower, killing their shadow images. The ruthless racket nurtured aches in both the ears and head. A lifetime of bitter reflection rolled past before the clamor slowly subsided and the rolling thunder receded.

Brockman pried his grip free and moved over to the chart desk. Benson, hands fastened to the top, offered a thin smile.

"So *this* is what enemy depth charging feels like," Benson said. "It's much more impressive than the ones our destroyer dropped near us so we'd know what to expect. Our boys can't do justice to this."

The chronometer clicked off a few more revolutions before Brockman concluded the attack had ended. The noise died away, replaced by an incessant hum from outside the hull. Brockman's sight drifted upward onto the hatch. What in the world is that? It can't be one of the deck guns. Nothing on the bridge makes a sound like that. The only other things up there are the deck torpedo tubes.

"Sound," Brockman said, addressing Woods, "where's that noise coming from?"

Woods cradled the headphones back into position. He listened for a few seconds and glanced over at Brockman.

259

"It seems to be coming from one of the deck tubes, sir. I think we've got a torpedo running hot inside one of them."

Brockman faced Benson.

"Retaining pin sheared off?" Benson guessed.

"I think so. We're probably streaming up bubbles, too."

Benson grimaced. "As close as those ash cans are dropping now, the Japs don't need any help in locating us."

Brockman rubbed the back of his neck, shrugging tired shoulders. What more can they dish out at us? They've strafed us. Bombed us. Depth charged us. Hounded and pounded. And we've done nothing in return! We've simply absorbed the blows . . . turned the other cheek. We've made no attempt to strike back.

It is time we do.

"Sound, report."

Woods manipulated the steering handle and leaned into his board. Sweat stung Brockman's eyes and dripped onto the deck. It didn't take long for the temperature to soar inside a boat buttoned-up and silenced-down for depth charging.

"I'm sorry, sir, I've never heard anything like this. There are high and low speed screws all over the place. It's hard to line out on a single contact."

That's it then, Brockman thought. I must risk another peek up top to fix location on the *Ise*. Along the way, we'll have to avoid collision with anything scurrying around on the surface. That could work out to our advantage. All of those waves and wakes churning up the water should make it difficult to spot our periscope or any bubbles streaming up from that hot torpedo on deck.

"Dive, periscope depth."

Brockman returned to the attack scope. Crenshaw took his position nearby, prepared to read off the information from the periscope's stadimeter and bearing ring.

"TDC, stand by for data," Brockman said.

"Stand by for data," Lynch repeated.

Brockman felt a thrill surge through him as he waited on the boat to settle out. He rubbed the back of his aching neck and thought, this is it. What we've trained for the past few months. Firing live torpedoes at an enemy vessel. Kill or be killed with the push of a button. All of the training and drills lead up to this moment.

"Periscope depth, sir."

"Up periscope."

He allowed it to break the surface and then said, "Stop."

Metallic thunder ripped the air and resonated throughout the boat. His eyes, glued to the eyepiece, strained as he willed the lens to clear. A world of dazzling light and insane chaos filtered through, stunning him. Ships wove past on all sides, circling, veering, anything to place distance between themselves and *Nautilus*. Geysers spouted out of the ocean as the *Ise* hurled broadsides in their direction. He forced himself to ignore the distractions, concentrating on setting up his shot.

"Bearing—*Mark!*" Brockman snapped.

"Bearing three seven zero," Crenshaw said, calling out the reading on the periscope's bearing ring.

"Bearing three seven zero," Lynch echoed.

Brockman focused, centered the crosshairs amidships on the target. A gray-hued waterspout briefly washed out his view. He blinked. The lens cleared.

"Range—*Mark!*"

"Range four four oh oh," Crenshaw advised Lynch who repeated the call in acknowledgment.

"Angle on the bow eight zero degrees starboard." Brockman snapped the handles up.

Crenshaw dropped the scope and relayed the reading.

The TDC must have a target speed to finish its calculation and set up the torpedo shot, Brockman thought. Considering the *Ise*'s bow wake, that Jap captain is pumping out every revolution the ship can turn.

"Speed two two knots," he called to Lynch.

He thought about the extreme range of the target. Two and one-half miles are a long way to track a torpedo. Is it worth the risk? Risk versus reward . . . it always goes back to that. But, we've come too far, risked too much. We can't sneak away without striking back. The morale of this boat depends on us taking a shot.

He wracked his brain double-checking the torpedo firing procedure. What have I forgotten? TDC had the needed data and Lynch was making the computations. I'll take at least one more observation to confirm the solution and then fire. That's following the procedure to the letter. Everything's good.

What about the torpedo tube?

261

"Relay to forward room," he said to Wetmore. "Open outer doors on tubes one and two. Make the tubes ready for firing in all respects. Set depth at eight feet. Set number two tube for one degree offset."

The five-minute wait until making another target observation filled an hour's time. A constant rain of massive shells undoubtedly thrown by the *Ise* buffeted the boat, stirring up a thin haze of dust in the air. Brockman's gaze drifted over each man inside the conning tower, and he tried to gauge the men's emotions. Nothing could be more stressful than combat, and their reactions and actions would determine *Nautilus'* fate. Wetmore, the youngest, peeled the wrapper off a piece of chewing gum and popped it into his mouth. His jaws proceeded to pound the stuff into submission, filling the space with the tangy smell of peppermint, and reminding Brockman of a chipmunk.

"Up periscope. Final bearing to shoot."

The scope snaked up until he called, "*Stop!*" It smelled of metal and sweat, noticeable for the first time. Crenshaw, reading the aiming reticule, guided it to the target's expected position. Brockman waited for the lens to clear, anticipating the view above while he mentally counted off the seconds the scope was exposed. There it was, right where he'd calculated.

"Bearing—*Mark!* Range—*Mark!* Down periscope!"

He spun around to watch Lynch compare the numbers that Crenshaw had called out with the TDC computation. Benson stood next to the torpedo-firing panel, ready to press the buttons. Time leisurely trudged by. Lynch looked up and smiled.

"Bearing agrees with TDC solution, sir."

"Fire one!"

Benson palmed the button. Brockman counted out a spread time of six seconds.

"Fire two!"

An audible "whoosh" followed by the boat lunging accompanied the second torpedo's release. Brockman cursed, anticipating the bad news relayed by Wetmore.

"Forward room reports number one tube failed to fire electrically or manually, sir," Wetmore confirmed.

"One torpedo running hot, straight, and normal, sir," Woods echoed.

"Time to impact, three minutes, sir," Lynch advised.

"Up periscope!"

Brockman braved a quick look around and saw the *Jintsu* belching black smoke headed down their torpedo track. He passed by it, locked onto the *Ise,* and felt a cavern in the pit of his stomach. The battleship alerted, she had turned to port and was now headed directly away. *Nautilus's* torpedo had no chance of striking her. We missed.

"Screws at three five oh relative, high speed!" Woods called out.

The *Jintsu!* Brockman slapped the handles up and leaned back as Crenshaw collapsed the periscope mast.

"Take her down! Ahead full! Right full rudder!"

"True bearing three five five," Woods corrected.

"Dive, make your depth one five zero feet!"

A familiar, menacing sound drowned out Hogan's response.

Swish—Swish—Swish!

Brockman reached out for the railing again and clamped on.

Whack—Whack—Whack—Whack!

His head throbbed, pounding in rhythm with the deadly barrage. More cork and paint chips scaled loose from the walls and ceiling, cascading onto the deck to swirl in puddles of condensation and perspiration. Rubber-sole shoes offered up a sticky *snuck* as they trod across the floor.

Swish—Swish—Swish!

Whack—Whack—Whack!

The ruthless concussion jarred his hands loose and hurled him against the bulkhead. Fighting to remain conscious, he slid down onto the deck.

54. THACH
June 04 – 08:30 Hours

Thach slapped the desktop. He could not—did not—want to believe that he had read the Teletype correctly. Instead of eight Cats escorting *Yorktown*'s strike, he now had six. *Six* fighters to cover a combined attack group of torpedo planes and dive bombers? What in the hell is Arnold thinking?

There's only one way to find out. He jumped up and quickly made his way to the bridge. Entering, he found Lieutenant Commander Murr Arnold, *Yorktown*'s air officer, standing next to Pederson discussing the impending launch.

"What are you doing up here, Jimmy?" Arnold asked. "You should be taking off in about a half hour or so."

"What in the hell's going on with the flight assignments? How did I lose two F4Fs without leaving the ship?"

Arnold raised a hand. "I understand what you're saying, but it's not up to me."

"I need those other two F4Fs. To operate correctly, my defensive tactic depends on groups of four. I believe my tactic is the best chance we have to hold our own against the Japs. Butch O'Hare and I tested the theory. It should work, but I need the planes to find out."

Arnold offered a helpless-looking shrug.

Thach glanced at Pederson. "Oscar, can you help?"

Pederson shook his head. "This is coming down from Fletcher. He and the captain are concerned that, after your group departs, the Japs will suddenly show up here. They're worried about *Yorktown*'s safety. A Coral Sea hangover, I'd say. There's no changing their minds, so the flights go off as scheduled. I'm sorry."

"Do what you can, Jimmy," Arnold added, "and bring your planes back. I believe we're in for a hell of a fight."

Thach snatched a cigarette from his pocket, lit it, and filled his lungs. Blue smoke streamed from his nose like from a dragon exhaling. I wish I *could* blow fire, he thought. Maybe I could light one under some of these ignorant SOBs. He spun on his heels and retreated down to the ready room. Entering, he found the pilots restlessly awaiting his return. Conversation came to an abrupt halt as he stepped up to the chalkboard and wrote down the squadron

264

assignments. Finished, he turned to face the room, stubbing the cigarette butt out in his hand.

"There it is." He jabbed a thumb over his shoulder. "And I had no say in the matter. As far as our duty is concerned, nothing's changed. Bassett, Dibb, and Macomber are up top with me as high escort. Cheeks and Sheedy will provide close lower escort with the torpedo planes. The rest of you will stand by for CAP duty."

He moved a little nearer to the line of chairs and cleared his throat. The moment demanded some type of speech from him . . . but what? After *Yorktown* sailed, their time together was too short and the opportunities to build some type of squadron cohesiveness had proved fleeting. He searched the young faces, thinking, have we come far enough as a team to take on this task? With eight or six Cats in my group . . . does it really matter? Without Don teaching them the beam defense, sixteen might not be enough against those veteran Jap pilots. Our chances are slim. Still, I *have* to say something.

"I don't want any of this lone-wolf stuff from any of you. Wolves don't live very long under the circumstances facing us. Stick together no matter what. It's the best way to survive and protect those TBDs and SBDs. Those Jap pilots we're going up against are good . . . damn good. They've had lots of combat flying time. Many of them have kills to their credit. Some are aces. I don't want any of you to forget that. Those Zeroes are faster and more maneuverable, so do not under any circumstances try to dogfight them. You will lose. Stick together and use the advantages that the F4F does have, such as diving speed and the ability to take damage, neither of which is the Zero's strong suit."

He moved toward the desk and then thought of one more thing.

"Of course, that doesn't mean to go out and *see* just how much damage one of those Cats can take. It means not to panic if a Jap should get you in his sights. Keep your wits about you and don't do something foolish that gets your ass flamed."

* * *

Thach strode out to his F4F and climbed up to the cockpit. He paused before swinging a leg over. Fighting against the urge, he could not prevent his eyesight from straying to the spot where Don's accident had occurred. A warm breeze, stirred up by the carrier sailing into the wind, massaged his face and served to blow

265

the bitter memory back into the past. He thought, no time for that now. His vision made a circuit of the flight deck, and he saw pilots getting into their planes. There'll be others to mourn before this day ends. I'm sick and tired of our guys coming up on the losing end of things.

Seated, he and his crewman secured the buckles and straps. Thach nodded and acknowledged the wish for a safe flight. He went through the pre-flight checklist and inserted a cartridge into the starter breech. Firing the engine off, he gradually brought it up to operating temperature. His sight flicked down to the red gun trigger mounted on the stick as he thought about the new arrangement of six .50-caliber machine guns in the wings. I'd rather have the old configuration of four .50s and more ammunition. The Cat's already too slow. It didn't need the extra weight of two more guns. Seems like there's always someone seated at a drafting board that knows more about what a pilot needs than the pilot himself.

He released the brakes, rolled forward into the takeoff spot, and pulled back on the tail wheel-locking knob. When the Fly 1 officer began rapidly twirling his wand, he accelerated the engine, building maximum RPMs. He felt the tough, stubby plane straining against the brakes, fighting to tear free, and it reminded him of a razorback hog cornered in a thicket by a pack of hounds. The hounds might get the hog but not without losing a few of their own in the effort. This Cat and I will treat those damn Zeroes the same way.

Satisfied the plane was good to go, he motioned to Fly 1. The wand dropped and pointed toward the far end of the deck. The brakes released, the plane leapt forward, rapidly accelerating. The familiar sensation of breaking gravity's chains fluttered through his stomach as the wheels lifted off the deck and the Cat became airborne. Banking away to clear the carrier, he reached over to grab the retractor handle and wind the landing gear up.

The nose of his plane angled upward, he opened the throttle to gain altitude and latch onto the retreating SBDs. His eyesight strained unsuccessfully to pierce the distance but failed to locate the lumbering TBDs leading the way. We should catch up to them with no problem, he thought. I know Lem's bunch is in front of us. A sobering thought came to his mind. The enemy's in front of us, too.

55. MELO
June 04 – 08:45 Hours

The crippled B-26 roared along carrying its wounded crew away from the scene of battle. Pren Moore and Melo ministered to the prostrate Ashley, trying to make him comfortable for the return flight to Midway. The young man now suffering from shock, a dose of morphine given by Pren succeeded in knocking him out. Pren leaned back on his haunches to look at Melo.

"How are you holding up, Melo? You look pretty badly shot up yourself."

"I'm sore everywhere and I believe I'm carrying some fragments," Melo admitted. "Feels like a piece or two passed clean through my side, but I think most of the bleeding's stopped. My hands are burned a little. Looking at Ash and Sarge, my wounds seem minor."

Pren pointed to the gash over his eye. "And that?"

"I've got a headache that I wouldn't wish on Tojo, but I don't think the cut's too deep, lieutenant."

Melo motioned toward Ashley. "What about Ash?"

Moore's brow furrowed as he blew out his cheeks. "He's lost a lot of blood, but your tourniquet certainly helped. Good thinking to use your belt. His leg is . . . I don't know. It's bad. That's about all I can say. We need to get him medical attention and soon."

A deep groan came from the front of the tunnel, and Gogoj dropped off his seat onto the littered floor. He ducked free and glanced around wildly. His face looked as if a cheese grater had rubbed against it. A nasty cackle ripped from his lips to ricochet off the metal-shredded fuselage.

"Scared bastards had enough and ran for home! Don't let those slant-eyed sons of Tojo's whores fool you. They don't want to die any more than we do. Aim a .50-caliber Browning at them and they tuck tail and light out! I fended those brave samurai off with a gun that couldn't fire. You should have seen the looks on their faces. I'd point that big barrel at one of them and he'd haul ass. *Mamasan, save me!*"

Pren moved over next to him. "Are you okay?"

Gogoj's head snapped around, and his frenzied stare latched onto Pren and Melo. His heaving chest gradually calmed. He

267

remained silent for a few moments, the flames of madness slowly dying out on his face. He blinked, seemed suddenly aware of his surroundings, and then glanced over at Ashley.

"Did they kill Ash?"

Pren placed a hand on his shoulder.

"No, he's still breathing. I'm hoping we can keep him that way. He even helped me fire his gun for a while."

A sad smile creased Gogoj's torn features. "That's just like the aggravating little shit. Too ornery to know when he's hurt."

"How about your wounds?" Pren asked.

Gogoj waved his concern away, struggling to his feet. He nodded toward Melo.

"What can Melo and I do to help?"

"Head up front and check with Lieutenant Muri. Make sure he understands how bad the situation is back here. He'll probably need Melo on the radio. I'll keep an eye on Ashley."

"You've got it, lieutenant."

Melo followed Gogoj toward the cockpit. Passing through the bomb bay, his eyes started to burn from the unmistakable vapor of aviation fuel. A sudden thought struck Melo. A leaking fuel tank posed a greater threat than another Zero attack due to the possibility of a spark causing a fire or explosion. How ironic . . . surviving everything the Japs threw at us only to die in a fireball caused by a damaged electrical wire.

They passed through the radio room, where Melo noticed W. W. Moore occupied at his navigator table. Gogoj mounted the steps between the pilots' seats. Melo saw Muri cast a quick glance at Gogoj before his head snapped around and he stared.

"Sarge, you look like a blood-soaked rag. Did you know you're bleeding?"

Gogoj reached up, tried to reattach a flap of skin. "I cut myself shaving. Do you have any tissue?"

Melo smiled in spite of his pain. A sudden thought of Ashley brought him up to the back of Muri's seat.

"Lieutenant, Ash is badly shot up. Lieutenant Moore says we need to get him medical help ASAP. I'm also sure we're spraying fuel all over the fuselage. Wouldn't take much and she'll light up the sky like Chinese fireworks."

Muri spoke over his shoulder to Gogoj. "Sarge, see if you can manually transfer the fuel out of the leaking tanks into the others.

Maybe they're not holed. Melo, try to raise Midway on the radio and get a homing signal. We need some help to make it back at all, let alone in time to help Ashley."

Melo immediately went to his radio and sat down. He frantically twisted the dial, tapping out messages on the transmitter, trying to raise someone–*anyone*. He fought to remain calm. Someone has to be out there, he thought. Someone must hear me calling. Midway's lagoon was full of PT boats, not to mention all the scout planes and the other aircraft flying around. But, what if they're still fighting off a Japanese attack? They could be too busy worrying about their own skins to listen out for us.

He rose halfway out of his seat and banged a fist onto the table. Where in the hell is everybody? A sudden pain jarred his entire body, snatching him back to the harsh reality of his own wounds and the foolishness of his actions. Collapsing onto the stool, he hung his head for a few moments to regain his composure. A tiny idea, nothing more than a worm burrowing into his addled brain, ballooned into a sewer-freed python. The problem isn't that he can't be heard. The radio isn't transmitting. Gunfire or shell fragments had damaged something. Probably the exposed antenna. Just look around at the bullet-riddled shell of this B-26 to see proof.

He glanced over at W. W. and found the navigator watching him.

"What's wrong?" W. W. asked.

"No good, lieutenant, I don't think we're transmitting. I'd be willing to bet the antenna's gone, sir."

"Let me try something."

W. W. pulled his seat underneath the small Plexiglas dome atop the fuselage and climbed on top. He spent several minutes staring outside and then jumped down and returned to his chart.

"I'm thinking I've got a good bearing on the sun," he explained to Melo. "Let me do some head scratching and pencil chewing and we'll see what I can come up with."

Gogoj appeared, wiping his hands.

"Any luck, Sarge?" Melo asked.

"It's wasn't quite as bad as I figured. Those self-sealing tanks did a fair job, but we were trailing fuel. I managed to swap tanks. The others seem to be holding."

"Melo." W. W. ripped a page out of his notebook. "Give this to Lieutenant Muri. I'm thinking if we can get close to Midway, we should spot smoke from the Jap attack."

Melo took the note, not wanting to consider questioning the idea of smoke coming from Midway. After their experience over the enemy fleet, there was no doubt in his mind of what the enemy was capable of doing. Those guys put up one hell of a fight, he thought. We're lucky to make the bell and be walking back to our own corner. After climbing the steps, he handed the page to Muri.

"Lieutenant W. W. says to watch out for smoke, sir."

Melo returned to his seat in front of the useless radio and flopped down. He leaned his head back against the fuselage and then closed his eyes. His flow of adrenaline waned, and the pain started radiating from his wounds. He wished for blessed sleep and was disappointed that the throbbing wouldn't allow it. I can count each heartbeat by the jolt throughout my body. Maybe Pren will shoot me up with a little morphine. He glanced over at Gogoj slumped onto the floor and quashed the thought. Sarge and Ash need the stuff worse than I do. I can tough things out a little longer.

His eyelids sagged as his heartbeat pounded louder in his ears. Ignore the hurt, concentrate on something else. We're headed for home. Away from this place of death. Focus on that thought. A noise attracted his attention. The sound of a strange flute trilled in the distance. He listened closer, thinking, no, not a flute but a whistle. Who'd be playing a whistle up here? He studied the haunting melody, feeling a familiarity in the aimless tune. Angels? Our Guardian Angel? Realization coupled with disappointment dawned on him. It's the wind blowing through all of the holes in the plane as if through an ocarina. The old expression *the sound of combat* has new meaning for me.

"I've got smoke on the horizon," Muri called out.

A few long, tense minutes passed and then, "It's Midway and the Japs have damn sure paid it a visit."

Melo considered climbing up and looking out the cockpit but decided against it. The pain grew steadily worse and he did not want to increase the bleeding. His thoughts strayed to the poor condition of the B-26. Fear rose in him once more. How silly! After

270

everything we'd just come through, now I'm going to worry about making a landing? As Pren said, *Muri is a hell of a pilot.*

"Strap yourselves in as best you can," Muri called back over his shoulder. "I'm not sure what kind of shape the landing gear's in."

"Give me a minute to find my seat aft," Gogoj replied. "I'll try to give the lieutenant a hand with Ash."

Melo glanced up as he lumbered by, feeling a sudden rush of pride when Gogoj's bloody, gnarly hand dropped down on his shoulder and gave it a quick squeeze. He thought, what is it about sharing battle that draws men so close together? Dying is the loneliest thing that a man does, but facing death with companions forms a bond unlike any other.

"Here we go!" Muri sang out.

Melo braced himself, praying for the best. The landing started slowly like a roller coaster and then quickly grew into the wildest, most violent ride he had ever experienced. Snatched and slammed from side to side and back and forth in his seat, he felt the belts jabbing red-hot knives into his wounded shoulder. A rattling uproar grew, ominously reminiscent of enemy gunfire. It hammered his weary eardrums and shook the heavily damaged B-26, trying to tear it into pieces and kill the lucky survivors of the attack. Delirious from the rough treatment and pain, Melo screamed himself hoarse, his throat scraped raw by the effort. Days later the earthquake subsided and then kicked up a few final convulsions before rumbling to a halt.

Reality slowly returned . . . knocked on the door. Door? Melo thought. There's no door here. A squeaking thud and a head grew up out of the floor. It slowly turned, the eyes settling onto Melo and opening wide. The head looked down and spoke to someone out of sight. The words chased away the fog of Melo's nightmare and welcomed him back among the living.

"Give me a hand! We've got some shot up boys in here!"

Melo fought against his belts and managed to raise an arm. He rasped, "Check the aft compartments. There's a badly wounded—" A nasty cough choked off his words.

"Buddy, if someone back there looks worse than you, I'm not sure I *want* to see him."

The head dropped down through the floor hatch. Melo drew a deep breath and fumbled with unlatching himself. Successful, he glanced over at W. W. and saw him stirring.

"Everyone okay?" Muri stepped down the cockpit ladder with Johnson following. Melo stood, felt the B-26 twirling around trying to throw him again. In a flash, W. W. and Muri were at his side, bracing him upright. He drew in a few deep breaths before regaining his balance.

"I'm okay," Melo said. "I just want to get outside for a few minutes."

Muri smiled and helped him over to the hatch. "Don't we all?"

The four of them emerged from beneath the plane, stepping out into the daylight. Pren and Gogoj walked up from the rear. The smell of smoke and destruction hung heavy in the air, not only from the B-26, but also from the damaged buildings surrounding the field. Two husky, sweaty Marines marched by carrying a pale but breathing Ashley on a stretcher. A medic holding up a plasma bottle connected to Ashley's arm glanced at them.

"It looks pretty bad, but I believe he'll make it," he said. "From the looks of things, the rest of you could use some attention, too."

Muri held up a hand. "We'll be along in a minute."

They walked and limped around the sad, battered aircraft counting bullet and shell holes. Leaking fluids stained the sandy ground, stirring up small puffs of dust. The propeller blades looked like a rat had gnawed on them, and the wings resembled coffee strainers. Melo shook his head, thinking, how did this thing ever get us back here?

The blood-splattered, burnt rear turret brought them all to a halt as worshipful thanks flowed freely from each man.

"Susie-Q, beautiful Susie-Q," Muri said. "What have they done to you?"

"Frank!"

Melo saw a familiar face approaching.

"Steve, wasn't it?" Melo asked.

"Yeah, I met you at the beer shack last night. Pauly told me about you. Said he was going to say a prayer for your safe return. I'd have never believed it of him 'til I saw him drop to his knees when your group took off."

"I'm grateful. Where is the big guy?"

Steve pursed his lips and looked away. Melo understood. Pauly's wish for combat had come true.

"How?" Melo asked.

"A bomb landed in his ammo pit."

Melo's head dropped. "Damn."

"I wanted you to know and to tell you that you were one of the few people Pauly ever warmed up to, specially that fast. He didn't make friends easily."

"Thanks, I appreciate that. Pauly was something else."

Steve started away. "Yes, he was. Take care of yourself."

Someone was next to him . . . Muri. "Are you going to make it?"

Melo looked up and nodded.

Pren appeared. "The word is none of the other Marauders have returned. For that matter, not much of *anything* else has made it back. I do believe that I now know what hell is like."

"I hope we did some good," Muri said. He glanced at Melo. "Did you see if our torpedo got a hit?"

Melo sighed, shook his head. "No sir, but we returned here. Right now, I'm thinking that's enough to be thankful for."

Melo walked a short distance away and stared at the small beer shack. I have faced real combat, he thought, and I'm ashamed at my eagerness for it. I'm grateful to be alive. God help us to end this senseless slaughter. By His mercy, we'll end it soon.

56. WALDRON
June 04 – 08:45 Hours

Waldron sat in the cockpit of his cruising Devastator and silently fumed, thinking, two Jap carriers lying unawares within striking distance and we're heading off in the wrong direction. What is Ring thinking? You can't count on the enemy sitting motionless in the same spot for over an hour. It doesn't make sense. After launching his aircraft, Nagumo had moved closer to Midway. When his patrol planes spot our task force, he'll want to head northeast and close the distance. We're flying too damn far north to cut his trail!

Glancing out of the open canopy, he looked at his squadron tucked carefully into formation following his lead. He felt the anger rise. All that training, preparation, and now we're denied our chance to join the fight? I have to make Ring understand. Damn this radio blackout! This truck of an aircraft won't allow me to catch up and hand-signal to him.

Through his parachute pack, the seat grew warm. He wiggled, shifted his position, and tried to concentrate on the mission. I'm an officer. My first priority is to maintain discipline by following orders. A professional military can't exist without discipline. Otherwise it's just a mob. We do things the correct way . . . by following orders.

One gloved hand hovered over the radio microphone, almost anticipating his next move. Damn a radio blackout! I've a duty to follow orders but I've also a duty to attack the enemy. *That's* the reason we're out here risking our lives . . . to attack the enemy. Ring's leading us on a wild goose chase . . . keeping us from attacking the enemy. He's refusing to allow us to do our duty.

Not if I can help it.

He picked up the microphone and keyed it. "We're heading the wrong way."

He waited, thinking, short and sweet. That's the way to do it. No radio call signs or unnecessary traffic. Ring knows who transmitted. I'm giving him a chance to correct his mistake. I hope he'll take it.

The plodding TBDs dragged a few minutes past bringing no response. His frustration grew. I should've known. I don't believe it, but I should've known. How can a war between two countries rate as a lower priority than a disagreement between two men? This is insane.

"I know where the damn Jap fleet is," he transmitted again.

"You fly with us." Ring's unmistakable voice cut through the warm airwaves. "I'm leading this formation. You'll stay with us."

Stay with us, Waldron thought. He's leading us to nowhere and we're supposed to blindly follow? How stubborn can a man be? We'll never stumble onto the Japs. There are four or five enemy carriers out there and we need every advantage. We're giving up this precious opportunity to attack first. One-third of Nimitz's carrier strike force pissed away because of one jackass. Damned if I'll be a party to it. My primary duty is to attack. I will attack.

He started to raise the microphone but hesitated. And if I'm wrong? If we head off on our own, miss the Japs and Ring does find them? We'll all face a court-martial on multiple charges. Refusing to obey orders . . . possibly desertion and anything else the JAG could come up with. Given the circumstances and that we're in a time of war, the penalty could be execution.

If I'm wrong.

Staying with Ring is the safe bet.

Either way, it's a hell of a gamble. My career, possibly my life, or doing my duty.

If I'm wrong.

I'm *not* wrong.

He raised the microphone. "The hell with you."

The Devastator slowly banked to the left, heading away from Ring's groups. Waldron glanced over a shoulder and was gratified to see his men following. Good old Tex, he thought. He's keeping the boys with me just as I told him to. At least *Hornet*'s air strike won't be a total waste. Torpedo Squadron 8 will join battle with the enemy. We will be heard from today.

* * *

"Skipper," Dobbs said over the interphone.

"I see him." Waldron's constantly sweeping eyesight had noticed the lurking aircraft tailing them. He keyed the microphone and transmitted, "There's a fighter trailing us."

He thought, that Jap's radioing our position back to his fleet. So much for our chance at surprise. What I wouldn't give for just one

275

Wildcat escort to shoot him down. To hell with it. We'll make do with what we have.

Thin, floating pillars rising on the horizon drew his attention. He smiled, rubbed his dry mouth with a cupped hand. *Just like I figured. A Sioux is good at reading smoke signs. That one says, Target in sight.*

"Look sharp, boys, the enemy's up ahead. Everyone keep your head on a swivel. You can bet we're about to have company."

He lowered the mike and then remembered one more piece of business.

"Stanhope from Johnny One. Enemy sighted."

He waited but received no response. *Damn him,* he thought. *He must hear me.*

"Stanhope from Johnny One," he nearly shouted. "Answer. Enemy sighted."

"Bandits, Skipper," Dobbs called out. "Six o'clock high." The coughing rattle of his twin .30-caliber machine guns punctuated the message. The Devastator vibrated in rhythm with the Brownings.

Over the deep bass rumble of the TBD's underpowered engine, Jap bullets split the air with angry whip cracks. He chanced a glimpse to the rear and noticed a swarm of Zeroes winking at him, hurling shot and shells his way.

Waldron felt an icy calm descend over him as he keyed the microphone. "We're going in. We won't turn back. We will attack. Good luck."

He fought the controls, searched in vain for some maneuver, *any* maneuver, to throw their attackers' aim off. Bullets and shell fragments stitched crazy designs across the fuselage and wings. Death had come to the South Pacific in the form of an agile fighter aircraft ironically given the innocent name of *Zero*.

A comet falling from the heavens caught his eye. "Is that a Jap or one of ours?"

"It's a TBD!" someone who sounded like Gay answered.

Waldron led the way down toward attack altitude and leveled off at around 500 feet. Puffs of smoke and the rattle of metallic hail struck the plane as the ack-ack fire snaked out in glowing, deadly ribbons. Waldron rode a bucking bronco, trying to stay mounted to complete his torpedo run. The smell of oily smoke and burnt sulfur masked his face and stirred up a choking cough.

Noise whacked away in his ears like a tom-tom, a sonic rhythm of misery. Burning tears streamed down his face as he blinked, fighting to clear his eyes. Lifting his goggles, he rubbed them with the back of a sleeve gaining momentary respite.

Amidst the chaos, Waldron found his focus and plowed onward. The enemy fleet unrolled in front of him. His eyesight skimmed over destroyers, cruisers, and a battleship before locking onto three aircraft carriers. Bringing his section around, he focused on the nearest carrier. The sight of two Zeroes flaming down briefly sent his spirits soaring.

"There are two fighters heading for the water," he said, breaking into the noisy radio traffic. "Do you see that splash? I'd pay good money to know who did that!"

Double flashes in his peripheral vision claimed his attention. He looked and felt despair as the two closest TBDs streamed smoky trails into the water.

He transmitted, "My two wingmen are going down."

More pounding against his Devastator caused him to drop the microphone. Both hands clutched the stick, grappling with the balky plane. The smoke bellowed forth inside the cockpit as flames mounted his back and gripped him in a bear hug. *I'm roasting alive! Get out! Get out!*

"*Bail out!*" he yelled to Dobbs.

Frightened, bumbling fingers clawed at his belt before managing to free it. He surged up out of the seat, clambered out onto the burning wing. As he glanced down, the realization hit . . . I'm too low to jump.

The ocean reached out to embrace him.

57. BROCKMAN
June 04 – 09:10 Hours

"Sound, has he given up?"

Brockman's hoarse voice disturbed the eerie silence. He sat on the floor with his legs dangling down the hatch into the control room. Head pounding and body aching from the rough treatment caused by the depth charges, he wished the ordeal were over. At this rate, there won't be a spot on my body without a bruise.

Woods listened for a few moments before saying, "Nothing's close to us, sir."

A momentary reprieve perhaps, Brockman thought. Let's see if we can take advantage of the situation.

"Helm, slow to one-third. Dive, periscope depth."

He felt the deck angling up as the boat slowed. Standing, he glanced around and found worried eyes staring at him. He thought, are they losing confidence in me? Am I taking too many chances? At what point do I cross the line between being aggressive and being foolish? It looks like we've poked a stick into an ant bed. The surface is crawling with escort vessels, any one of them more than capable of sinking *Nautilus*. That's a lot of firepower gunning for one submarine. Is the risk more than the possible reward?

"My speed is one-third, sir," Yates advised.

The reward is sinking a Jap carrier and putting a bunch of Tojo's pilots out of the fight, he thought. That's possibly an enormous sum of bombs and torpedoes not used against American ships and land targets. Think of the lives saved. The families back at home who won't have to grieve for loved ones lost. I'm risking the small complement of *Nautilus* for an exponentially greater result gained by completing our mission. With so much to gain, we must accept the risk. It's what servicemen do. *Serve as and where needed.*

"Periscope depth, sir."

He crouched. "Up periscope." Rising with it, he waited until the head cleared, and said, "Stop."

Several quick circuits revealed the immediate area free of threats. His visual transit moved father off into the distance and settled on a huge, unmistakable shape. *Bingo!*

278

"There's one of the carriers that Admiral English was interested in," Brockman said. "Pass that on to the crew," he instructed Wetmore. "We've found what we've come hunting for."

He focused on it, said, "Bearing—*Mark!*"

"Bearing zero one three," Crenshaw said.

"That's relative," Brockman added. "She keeps changing course and is too distant to get an accurate fix."

Brockman adjusted the stadimeter knob under the right handle. "Range—*Mark!*"

"Range one six oh double oh," Crenshaw read off.

"Nine miles," Benson said. "Would you like to take a shot at her just for the hell of it? Throw a little more panic into Nagumo's bunch."

Brockman ignored the comment and continued to study the carrier. No sign of smoke or damage, he thought. Heavy anti-aircraft fire overhead . . . perhaps Midway's attacking? Roy's right, it's a long ways off. There's no way we'll ever reach him submerged. All we can do is—

"New contact! Fast screws at six five relative!"

He shifted the periscope, found the *Jintsu* plowing through the waves headed for them. Enough is enough, he thought. I'm fighting back.

"Bearing—*MARK!*"

"Bearing zero seven zero!"

"Range—*MARK!*"

"Range nine oh double oh!"

"Angle on the bow is port one zero!" Brockman barked, slapping the handles up. "Speed two five knots!"

He heard Lynch echo the call and glanced over at Benson. "The *Jintsu's* coming this way with a bone in his teeth, kicking up ocean. I'm tired of taking a pounding and doing nothing in return."

"Fair enough. What's the plan?"

Brockman removed his soaked shirt and wiped his drenched face. The salty odor stung his nose, mixing with the smell of paint, cork, and unwashed men. He hung it over the rail and turned back toward Benson.

"We're going to give him something to think about . . . slow him up a bit."

"Snap shot?"

Brockman nodded.

"Relay to forward, make tube three ready to fire in all respects," Brockman directed Wetmore. "Make torpedo depth eight feet."

"Generated distance to target's track, three oh double oh," Lynch called out.

"TDC, stand by. Final bearing to shoot."

Brockman heard the echoes of his orders and directed his attention to Woods. "Sound, report."

"Fast screws bearing zero eight five and closing, sir."

Good, he thought. Still coming for us. Don't change a thing. He and Crenshaw took their positions. He squatted, preparing his vision for the anticipated view on the surface.

"Up periscope."

Brockman hung onto the mast, waited until the head surfaced, and called, *Stop!* After a quick area scan, he focused upon the charging *Jintsu*.

"Bearing—*MARK!*"

"Bearing zero seven five!" Crenshaw relayed.

"Range—*MARK!*"

"Range two six double oh."

"Angle on the bow is port four five," Brockman said, moving away for the periscope to lower.

Brockman whipped his head and noticed a shower of salty moisture spraying into the air. The sound of approaching screws pulsed through the boat. He glanced impatiently at Lynch, waiting for him to run the TDC calculations.

"We have a matching solution, sir," Lynch confirmed.

"Fire tube three!"

He heard Benson hit the plunger and then felt the boat react as the fish whooshed out of the tube.

"Up periscope!" Brockman said.

"Tube three fired electrically."

"Torpedo running hot, straight, and normal."

Brockman located the torpedo's wake and watched in disgust as the *Jintsu* sheared away from it.

"He's seen it and is turning away."

"New contact! Screws at two eight zero relative, fast speed!" Woods called out.

Swish—Swish—Swish!

Brockman slapped the handles up and jumped clear. "Take her down! Ahead one third! Left full rudder!"

They're ganging up and surrounding us, Brockman thought. We've made enough trouble to warrant serious attention and have nothing to show for it. Something must give one way or the other and soon. I just hope that it's in our favor.

58. KUSAKA
June 4 – 09:30 Hours

These Americans die like true warriors, Kusaka thought. I watched an entire torpedo squadron obliterated in wasted sacrifice. Fifteen planes and fifteen brave crews gone in just a matter of minutes. Aircraft after aircraft struggling to attack and then exploding into flaming debris . . . raining into the ocean. A killer sky crying metallic tears. All in vain. *Soryu* had easily dodged the single torpedo released.

Still they attacked.

Yet, we doubted their will to fight.

"*Kido Butai* is battling magnificently," Genda said. "The enemy has thrown wave after wave of aircraft at us, but we've suffered no bomb or torpedo hits."

"We've indeed been fortunate," Nagumo remarked.

"Fortunate! Our pilots bravely met the challenge and dealt with it."

Nagumo turned to Kusaka. "There's no reason to maintain communications blackout. Send a message to Admiral Yamamoto. Tell him we carried out the air strike on Midway at 0630. Many enemy shore-based planes attacked us around 0715, but we've suffered no damage. We've sighted an enemy task force composed of one carrier, seven cruisers, and five destroyers. I intend to deal with those ships and then resume our Midway operation."

Nagumo returned to the window. Kusaka made a few notes on a paper scrap and handed it to a runner. Feeling a sudden presence, he turned and found Genda standing there.

"I believe that you've noticed what I have," Genda said. "These Americans fight with much more heart and spirit than we gave them credit for possessing."

Kusaka released a sigh. "For the first time, I've doubts about the outcome of this battle. They never stopped coming."

"Doubts? We've annihilated everything they've sent against us . . . torpedo planes, dive bombers, level bombers, everything."

"And all the while we're prevented from launching a counterattack of our own. There's at least one enemy carrier within striking distance of us, yet we can do nothing about it. Not as long as our flight decks are busy launching fighters to protect us."

"But we're using the time to rearm our planes to attack the enemy fleet," Genda reminded. "A lull shall eventually fall, allowing us a window to retaliate."

"And what will the enemy be doing in the meantime? Just sitting back . . . waiting for our bombs and torpedoes to strike their vessels? Will they not continue attacking while they have aircraft to do so?"

Genda fell silent and joined Nagumo at the window. Kusaka took advantage of the respite to clear his mind. *The strain from the enemy attacks has unsettled my breathing, left me vulnerable to dangerous passions. I must allow the air free passage, fill my lungs completely, and then exhale without interference or conscious thought. I recognize the desire . . . the necessity to return my mind to a state of calm equilibrium. Such equilibrium results in clear thinking. There is no past or future. There is only the present. In the midst of combat, I must focus. I must not compromise my ability for making correct decisions.*

"Admiral Kusaka," another runner said, appearing at the door, "a message."

Nagumo turned a scowling face toward Kusaka, asking, "Yamaguchi trying to take command of *Kido Butai* again?"

"No, sir," Kusaka replied. "There's an enemy submarine stalking our task force."

"A submarine?" The scowl vanished as Nagumo's lips mashed together.

"He's made a nuisance of himself for several hours. We've dropped depth charges, bombs, and fired upon him, yet he keeps popping back up. He's made several failed torpedo attacks. He's causing a disturbance in our ability to hold proper formation. Something must be done to stop him."

"We must maintain our attention on air operations," Genda said. "This must wait."

"And if the enemy manages to torpedo a carrier? We can't simply ignore the threat."

Nagumo held up a hand. "We've more important things to deal with than one submarine."

"*Arashi* has had intermittent contact with the submarine and is presently attacking it," Kusaka offered. "I suggest she maintain contact and keep the enemy too busy to present more problems."

"Leave her post protecting the fleet?" Genda asked.

"That's exactly what she'll be doing. This submarine is every bit as dangerous as a squadron of enemy torpedo planes. We must not take this threat lightly."

"Agreed," Nagumo said. "Send a message to *Arashi*. Detail her to occupy the enemy until *Kido Butai* is safely out of range. Once we open some distance, the submerged vessel will not have sufficient speed to catch up with us."

Kusaka dashed off a quick note and handed it to the runner. Anti-aircraft fire erupting from a nearby cruiser captured his attention again.

"Enemy torpedo planes!" a lookout yelled. "Bearing ninety degrees port!"

Kusaka joined Nagumo and Genda in shifting over to the other side of the bridge. He knelt to place his eyes against a pair of spotting binoculars and easily picked out a formation of planes coming in just above the waves. The early morning sun glinted off their wing tips like sparkling jewels. Yet still they come, Kusaka thought. Can this many planes be coming from Midway, or has the enemy carrier already launched? Where are our fighters?

He felt *Akagi* execute a hard starboard turn to parallel the incoming torpedo planes. The abrupt motion threw him against Genda, knocking both away from their glasses. Kusaka swung back into place and watched as the lumbering enemy aircraft split into two formations. They bore down on the nearest carrier, *Kaga*, maneuvering for position to execute torpedo runs.

"Where are our Zeroes?" Genda asked for them all.

A rumbling roar blew past the *Akagi*'s island followed by another and another. Kusaka smiled, recognizing the sound as fighter aircraft taking off. His eyesight remained fixed on *Kaga*, and he noticed with admiration how her Captain Okada skillfully handled the huge carrier, whipping her through the water like a snake gliding across a pond. Okada and his crew do themselves proud by their efforts, he thought.

A sudden flash accompanied by plumes of thick, oily smoke dissolved the lead enemy plane in a mangled shower of fiery fragments, announcing the arrival of the Zeroes. Maintaining their launching runs, the enemy torpedo planes ignored the carnage and seemed to block out the vision of their comrades falling to their deaths. Kusaka thought, in the face of such furious onslaught by our fighters, they still come. How does one defeat such an enemy?

59. BROCKMAN
June 04 – 09:45 Hours

"Dive, make your depth two zero zero feet!" Brockman shouted.

A tremendous explosion ruptured the ocean outside, hurling Brockman against the guard railing. He felt ribs bruise–possibly crack–and fought to breathe. The deck dropped away from his feet as the boat tilted downward. His hands flailed out for support, sending rivers of pain flooding throughout his chest. The stifling, intense heat compounded his misery; his vision dissolved into a midnight-black curtain as his ears plugged.

Whack—Whack—Whack—Whack!

The crashing clamor flowed up to him from the bottom of a well bringing a tide of nausea with it. Shock dulled his senses as his legs tried to walk away from him. Nothing could train a man for this, he thought. Nothing. We're not fighting . . . just absorbing more and more punishment. For what? It's time to sneak off. Cut our losses before it's too late. My decision is made. Another part of him cried out, am I giving up this easy? I wanted to command . . . act like it!

Swish—Swish—Swish!

"Helm, speed one-third! Left full rudder!" He heard a voice, recognized it as his own, and pulled himself back into reality.

Whack—Whack!

Light bulbs popped. A hard rain of paint and cork poured onto the deck, forming piles of debris. Darkness, broken only by the warming illumination from the various control stations, created a false night inside the conning tower.

"Helm, rudder amidships. Sound, report."

"He's slowed and turning, sir," Woods responded. "Heavy pinging."

"He's alone?"

"Aye, sir and headed back in this direction."

"Rig for silent running," Brockman said, forcing a calm reply. He heard the order softly passed down below and around the conning tower.

A weak flash behind him revealed Benson replacing a light bulb. He offered Brockman a quick shrug. Harsh lighting returned to the sweltering, cramped space as Brockman positioned himself next to Yates.

"Screws bearing one zero five, slow," Woods said. "He's listening . . . hunting us again."

Thrum—Thrum—Thrum. The screws' pitch dropped with the enemy ship's decrease in speed.

"Right full rudder," Brockman whispered to Yates.

The sharp turn should prevent the ship from laying depth charges down *Nautilus'* length, he knew. Evasive procedure number one, present as small a target as possible.

Yates nodded in silent reply. Brockman strained to slow his breathing. Can they still find us? A noise like the sound of steel wool brushing against the hull layered the humid air. Active pinging . . . they're searching. Trying to locate us to deliver the killing blow.

Swish—Swish—Swish!

"Speed full. Left full rudder," Brockman said, thinking, the *Jintsu* won't be able to hear us over the increased noise from his own screws.

Whack—Whack—Whack!

Wicked waves of sound thrashed against the boat, hurling the helpless men around. Brockman landed on the deck next to a clinging Crenshaw. He felt some invisible hand pounding on his sore ribs with a Louisville Slugger and noted the scared look on the chief's face as Crenshaw helped him stand. None of us has ever experienced anything like this, Brockman thought. How much longer can we hold out?

"Screws slowing again," Woods said, continuing the updates in a stage whisper. "He's turning. Now bearing three two zero."

"Right full rudder," Brockman instructed Yates.

Thrum—Thrum—Thrum!

Brockman's head reflexively tilted upward toward the ceiling as if to watch their deadly stalker churn past. No increase in speed? He's not sure where we are? Again, the uncomfortable sound of active sonar beaming through water onto the boat's hull came to his ears. He hoped . . . prayed that somehow *Nautilus* would evade the relentless pursuit. As if by divine answer, the ominous noise receded into the distance without dropping more depth charges.

"Rudder amidships," Brockman ordered before turning to Woods. "Sound?"

Leaning into the set, Woods tuned his hydrophone. Brockman patiently waited and fought to breathe through the pain compounded by the wilting heat and salty humidity. Sticky undershirt and slacks clung to him like a second skin. He glanced around at the others to find exhausted, concerned faces but, thankfully, no sign of panic. Benson caught his eye and winked. Roy is thinking what I am, Brockman knew. This is one hell of a fighting crew.

"He went a ways past this time, sir," Woods said. "There's a turn and here he comes. Bearing two five five, slow speed. Still pinging away like crazy, sir."

Bearing two five five, Brockman calculated. He's tracking farther away from us. He didn't drop depth charges. Now this. Perhaps he lost the scent.

Thrum—Thrum—Thrum.

The enemy ship angled past at a distance, the screws' noise rapidly weakening and then vanishing. Another run without dropping depth charges, Brockman noted. He felt someone standing next to him, and saw it was Benson.

"What do you think?" Benson asked.

Brockman shrugged. "Out of depth charges?"

"Possible, but he didn't drop many. I'm not sure if he expected to hit us or even cared. I thought that he was moving mighty fast to be pinging and listening. He seemed more interested in keeping us down."

That's it, Brockman thought. The Jap captain is trying to keep us pinned down or drive us away. While we're busy dodging depth charge attacks, the carriers slip past. Rattle our hull enough and we'll slink off with our tail between our legs. Make it too rough on us and we'll run and hide. That's exactly how he figured it.

Well . . . he figured wrong.

"Sound, report!"

"High speed screws retreating, bearing one four five," Woods answered. "No other contacts, sir."

"Secure from silent running! Periscope depth!"

As soon as the periscope head broached the surface, Brockman verified the area was clear. He clicked to high-power, focusing on the retreating *Jintsu*. He's certainly going somewhere in a big hurry, Brockman decided. And I know where.

Brockman took his eyes off the scope bumper to glance at the conning tower crew. Sweaty, shaken men looked back. He understood that the past few hours had tried each man's will, tempting him to surrender to his fears. We're all exhausted and could use some rest. The need is plainly evident, like a scar etched on each face. However, I also see something else. I see determination.

"Those carriers are still out there," Brockman said.

"What are we waiting for, skipper?" Crenshaw asked.

"They're getting away," Woods added.

"Plotting a course," Benson said from the chart desk.

Brockman smiled. And I doubted these men and myself?

"Helm, ahead one-third. Bearing one four five." Brockman said. "We're going to let our Jap friend lead us right back to his task force. *Nautilus* will be heard from before this day is over."

60. BEST
June 4 – 09:55 Hours

Best inhaled the oxygen supply, immediately feeling caustic soda burning its way to his lungs. He coughed and gagged, feeling like he was suffocating. Snatching the mask off, he heaved in a great lung-full of thin air as he tried to breathe. He briefly considered going to another canister before realizing there was just one spare. Beautiful, he thought. It's not enough having to worry about attacking the Japanese fleet; now my oxygen could be poisoning me. Replacing the rubber mask, he forced himself to take small, measured breaths while he silently prayed the supply would clear. Violent coughing shook his entire body for the next few minutes and then eased off as the soda dust filtered.

He glanced at his sinking fuel gauges and noted with concern the dwindling levels. We'll have to turn back after a few more minutes of flying. How far is McClusky willing to stretch things before giving up? We don't need to ditch all of these planes out here in the middle of the Pacific. What use will that be?

A flicker of motion from higher altitude caught his attention. He looked to see a B-17 making its way back in the direction of Midway and considered flying its reciprocal heading. He's most likely returning from attacking the enemy fleet, Best decided. We should be able to home in on it if we take the opposite track. It looks like McClusky has the same idea, but are we running out of time?

Check your gauges, McClusky, Best thought. We're nearly to the point of not having sufficient fuel to make it back. I don't relish the thought of putting down in those shark-infested waters below. The faces of his wife and child flashed before his eyes, shaming him. How soon we forget. Here I am talking about doing everything I can to stop the Japanese from taking Midway and then invading Hawaii, yet I'm more concerned for myself. Forget our fuel situation . . . let's find those enemy carriers.

"Sir," Murray spoke over the interphone, "Lieutenant Kroeger on our left wing just hand signaled me he's having oxygen problems."

Best thought, first me and now Bud Kroeger, too. What is it with these oxygen supplies? Is the Navy buying them from Tokyo? Japanese war surplus? Hell. There's just one thing to do.

"Signal him back. Tell him to follow me down to 15,000 feet. We won't need oxygen at that altitude."

"Aye, sir."

Easing the Dauntless into a gentle descent, Best watched the remainder of his squadron follow. He removed his oxygen mask to prove his point, saw the other pilots and gunners do the same.

The radio crackled with a sudden blast of white noise before he heard, "This is McClusky. Have sighted the enemy fleet."

"Attack the carriers! Attack!" Best recognized Browning's voice acknowledging from *Enterprise*.

Best could see the massive assembly of enemy ships spread out on the vast ocean ahead. Screening smoke combined with stack emissions from their increasing speed belched a choking pall over the scene. The Japanese fleet seemed to stretch from one horizon to the other. I've never seen a task force this large, he thought. There is no doubt that hell is waiting for us.

"Wilco, as soon as I find the bastards," McClusky said in response to Browning's transmission.

The SBDs penetrated the outer ring of protection and concentrated on the four carriers. Puffs of black and colored AA fire rose from the screening vessels as the defenders tried in vain to bring down the attacking planes. Best bounced around in his seat, felt the sudden sharp blasts of turbulence from the exploding shells and heard metal fragments rattling against his aircraft. Noxious vapors and the stink of burning paint wafted through his cockpit.

I expected a welcoming party of enemy Zeros, yet we're proceeding without an airborne challenge, he thought. It can't be this easy. The AA's annoying but their aim is so bad it'd take a lucky shot to hit one of us.

"Murray," Best said, keying the interphone, "is it clear behind us?"

"All clear, sir. I was just thinking the same thing. Where are the Jap fighters?"

"Let's hope they don't decide to show up before we're gone from here."

"*Amen.*"

The formation of Dauntlesses droned on toward the two closest carriers. McClusky's in the lead position, Best thought, so he should attack the far target. I'll take the near one. He is used to flying fighters and might not understand bombing doctrine. Perhaps I should radio him of my intentions.

He keyed the microphone. "Wade from Dick, am attacking the nearest target."

Best heard no reply. Maybe McClusky's too busy to acknowledge. I'll signal my squadron to form up for the bombing run. After waggling his wings to draw their attention, he motioned the command. His head swiveled from side to side confirming the proper arrangement of each section. Here we go, he thought. We're in position. My altitude's good. Speed is sufficient. Hand on the dive flap lever. Prepare to open them.

"Okay Murray, read them off every thousand feet," he said through the interphone.

"Aye, sir."

Best pulled the flap control lever to the open position and then reached back to depress the engine pump handle. He froze as a swarm of blue-gray blurs slashed by in front of him, plunging almost vertically toward his intended target below. Damn! What in the hell is McClusky doing? He should have attacked the farther carrier. Best closed his flaps and flicked his elevators up and down to signal his squadron to form up on him. At his dismay, he saw most of them following McClusky's lead. Nearly thirty SBDs are bombing one enemy carrier, he thought. If that one's not sunk, we don't stand a chance of damaging any of the others.

He glanced around to see just his two wingmen remaining with him. There is no way three SBDs are going to destroy an aircraft carrier, but we've come too far not to try, he decided. We're going to give it our best shot. He led his small element toward the next carrier located to the west. The flight deck is turned into the wind, Best noticed. They're preparing to launch aircraft. We can't let that happen. No time for a sequential attack. We'll hit him from our current V formation.

Best keyed his radio mike. "Bud and Fred from Dick. Don't let this one escape. Follow me down."

The group of three SBDs slipped into a right-hand turn and headed toward the bow of the carrier to allow for the longest aiming point. Another quick glance verified that Bud Kroeger and

Fred Weber had held position on both sides of his center. At least *they* can follow doctrine, Best thought. We may do some damage yet.

His mind shifted into automatic as his hands walked through the bombing sequence. A quick glance at the air speed indicator and, *damn*, I'm going too fast to open my dive flaps. Horse up on the stick. Slow her down. Losing some altitude, but I'm okay. Fourteen thousand feet is fine to begin my attack. Bud and Fred are still with me. Here we go. Open the dive flaps, and I feel them digging into the wind . . . slowing the plane. Throttle down. Raise the nose, go into a half-roll, and I'm into the dive.

Dear Lord, guide my hand.

61. THACH
June 04 – 09:55 Hours

Thach watched a cylindrical shape flash by in front of his F4F's propeller and instinctively bumped the stick to avoid it. He thought, what in the hell was that? It landed in the ocean to starboard, throwing up a tremendous shaft of briny water. In quick succession, three more blasts stirred up whirlpools below.

"Squadron from Leslie," Max Leslie said, breaking radio silence. "Keep your hands off the electrical arming switches. Use manual control. Repeat, use manual control."

"Too late, sir," a voice piped in.

More echoes over the radio brought Leslie back on the air. "Knock it off, and the rest of you do what I said. Use manual control for bomb arming."

Thach cursed. We're short four bomb loads and have yet to reach the target. What else can go wrong?

His eyesight constantly scanned the skies looking for any sign of enemy aircraft. The enemy fighter that you fail to see is the one that flames you, he thought. There's no relaxing until the Cat's wheels are back on deck. He thought about the green pilots accompanying him headed for their first taste of combat. How will they fare? Will this be their first and last battle? Will it be my last battle? I'm not immune to death. If it comes, let it be from a better enemy pilot and not because I made a foolish mistake.

His visual circuit paused, having registered something. There are aircraft below. We've caught up with Lem Massey's Torpedo 3. It's time to give Lem's squadron some cover. I just wish it were more. He motioned for Cheek and his wingman Sheedy to assume escort position near the Devastators. The torpedo planes flying much slower, the F4Fs began making slow S-turns back and forth to maintain their pace.

Thach coughed and gripped the stick tighter. Anxiety became palpable as he imagined the sensation of his racing heart hammering against his ribcage. The smell of aviation gasoline and sweat permeated the cockpit. Damp khakis clung to him like a salty outer skin as moisture dripped off his body. He periodically wiped either hand down his sodden pants leg, vainly trying to dry the palm.

Maintain focus and watch on the area surrounding me . . . keep sweeping the sky. Mentally run through my check-off list once more. Gauges and controls are fine. Fuel isn't an issue yet. Guns are switched on and tested. I had each section do the same. Keep watching the sky. *Always watching the sky.*

A change in the Devastators' course instantly attracted his attention, and he glanced at the new heading. Welcome relief mixed with nervous anticipation as he spotted the Japanese fleet in the distance. A waggle of his F4F's wings drew Cheeks' notice and Thach pointed toward the enemy vessels.

Different colors of anti-aircraft smoke created pastel clouds up ahead. *Why are they firing while we're still so far out of range? How much damage can they expect to do at this distance?* The purpose of the gunfire became all too apparent a few minutes later when a large formation of Zeroes, alerted by the shell bursts, swarmed over the American planes. *It looks like a pack of wild starving dogs jumping a wounded animal,* he thought. It took just a few brief, violent seconds for their first victim to keel over and drop toward the ocean. A trail of fire marked its passage. He recognized Bassett's F4F and grimly noted no parachute canopy before the machine disintegrated against the water. *Damn, they flamed Red Dog.*

With an overwhelming number of Zeroes confronting his small group of fighters, Thach sought to join Massey's Devastators and offer them what small amount of protection he could. He quickly descended to 3,000 feet, running into a solid wall of swift enemy airplanes dodging in and out, making firing passes at him. Loud pops rattled against his Wildcat's frame as 7.7-mm bullets ripped holes in it. *I can't reach Massey,* he conceded. *How much more damage can this thing take? I have to defend myself. Hopefully, send a few of these bastards to join Red Dog. Maybe we can tie them up. Keep them busy. Allow the Devastators and Dauntlesses time to drop. But these Jap pilots are good. They know what they're doing. Taking turns and waiting to make their runs. Their coordinated attacks mean a Zero is continually shooting at me . . . a chalkboard demonstration of good fighter tactics.*

He ventured a look at Massey's flight below and helplessly watched as another group of enemy aircraft carved up the torpedo plane squadron. *Lem doesn't have a chance,* he thought. *His damn*

Devastators are too slow and vulnerable. Those Zeroes are like a swarm of bees defending their queen.

A quick glance to his high five o'clock position revealed a Zero diving in and lining up to fire. Thach led Macomber and Dibb into a sharp turn away from the incoming attacker and felt satisfaction as the enemy's tracers streaked past behind the trailing Dibb. Another Zero mounted up to make a run and fared no better as the F4Fs repeated the snaking maneuver.

We're holding our own but making no headway against them, he thought. I need more room to operate, but Macomber is trailing me too closely. We're presenting one big target. It's my fault. I instructed them before we took off to stick together. No lone-wolf stuff. He's following orders, but I must make him understand.

"Brainard from Jimmie," he transmitted, "split out to the left."

He waited, received no reply, and noticed no change in Macomber's position. He tried again. "Brainard from Jimmie. Split out to the left."

They dodged another incoming Zero, and Thach tried motioning Macomber to fall back. The young pilot seemed oblivious to Thach's signals, clinging tenaciously to the lead F4F's tail. Give him his due, Thach thought. He damn sure knows how to follow orders. If I'd just had a little more time to drill them on the beam defense tactic. Or if Don had not been killed . . . no, I'll not dwell on that now. The combat is all that matters.

These Japs are skilled, but I am too. It's time that I showed them.

Or die trying.

62. BEST
June 04 – 10:25 Hours

"Thirty five hundred feet!" Murray called over the interphone.

Best bumped the nose of the Dauntless aside to get a quick view of the Japanese carrier below. A sense of amazement swept through him as he stared at the bright yellow flight deck with a large blood-red rising sun painted on it. It looks like a gaudy advertisement saying, *Here we are,* he thought. I couldn't ask for a better bull's-eye target.

He eased the plunging SBD back to 70 degrees, gave a fast wipe of his right goggle, and locked his eye against the telescopic sight mounted on top of the control panel. The wide safety belt dug into his lap holding him firmly to the seat. At this point in the procedure, a strange sensation of hanging freely in space, almost as if he would fall out of the cockpit, always came over him. He ignored the feeling to concentrate on the task. Centering the crosshairs on a point next to the carrier's island structure, he took faint notice of an unsuspecting Zero taking off from aft of the flight deck passing through his view. A fleeting thought questioned the absence of fighter cover and AA fire. How much longer before they notice us? McClusky's attack should have alerted them.

"Three thousand feet!"

Target's still centered, slight drifting . . . use aileron to compensate. The Japs still don't seem to see us yet. Focus. Remain focused. Speed's increasing. Slight nose buck. Adjust the tab. Squared away.

"Twenty five hundred feet!"

Finally some reaction came from the target as light AA reached upward, followed by a frantic starboard turn. Best bore in, heard the SBDs raising a banshee wail of impending destruction upon the carrier maneuvering below. He noted the vessel completing its turn, now presenting the narrower broadside to the diving bombers and greatly decreasing the odds of a successful hit. It's launching fighters to attack us if we attempt another pass, Best thought. I'd better aim true. Blast it on the first attempt. There might not be a second one.

"Two thousand feet!"

Best anticipated the call; his left hand gripped the double-handled bomb release and gave it a powerful yank. A sudden surge of engine power confirmed the bomb's departure as he quickly retracted the dive flaps, allowing for the pullout. The SBD continued its screaming free fall for another few tense seconds and then curved back to skim over the waves. The whip-like action resulted in heavy G-forces pressing him firmly against the seat like an invisible vise. From prior attacks, he knew what to expect next. The blood vessels constricted and throbbed inside his neck and head, struggling to pump blood throughout his dimming brain. Reality's colors faded into gray. Tunnel vision constricted his view. Blackout. Tunnel vision. Charcoal tints focusing into colors. Normal sight.

A tremendous explosion rent the air, buffeting the plane. A gigantic hand tried to hurl him free of the cockpit and into the cold depths below. He opened his mouth to equalize the pressure in his ears. The harsh stench of sulfur and fleshy taste of brass played hell with his senses.

Best dared a glance rearward at the death he had unleashed upon his enemy and cruelly gloried in his act of blood vengeance for what happened on December 7, 1941. A fiery cloud of devastation towered up from the raging inferno, consuming the carrier's flight deck, mocking God's heaven above. He looked down into the gates of hell, feeling like Lot's wife gazing back upon the awesome destruction of Sodom. *Now I understand her reason for doing so,* he thought. What had General Robert E. Lee said at a similar scene of mass death and destruction? *It's well that war is so terrible else we'd grow too fond of it.* Lord help me, but I am enjoying this.

A covey of Zeroes flashed by without firing a shot, headed in the opposite direction. *They must be after other prey,* Best decided. *I'm glad it's not us . . . pity whoever it is.* He led his formation of three planes wave hopping past another burning enemy carrier, thinking, *Hornet's* or *Yorktown's* attack groups have also succeeded. If we can all make it home in one piece, it has been a good day.

A very good day indeed.

63. KUSAKA
June 04 – 10:25 Hours

As the first fighter roared down the flight deck, Kusaka felt relief. *Now we're making progress. If we can get a few more launched to replace those low on fuel and ammunition—*

"Enemy hell-divers!"

The lookout's shout drove a stake of solid steel into Kusaka's heart. His sight darted upward through the bridge window and centered on the sinister shapes of three dive bombers screaming in for the kill. He stood petrified, unable to tear his eyes away from the birds of prey as three small black eggs fell free of them. The eggs grew to enormous size, drifted and fought against the wind currents, yet they continued on their lethal path aimed directly at him.

Time seemed suspended as death made its lazy way down onto *Akagi.* Kusaka's world dissolved into a flash of demonic light followed by a mountainous explosion of wooden and metallic fragments. A second cataclysmic blast, insanely louder and more violent than the first, seemed to snatch the giant vessel out of the water and then hurl it back down so wickedly as to forever alter the ocean's currents. Kusaka collapsed to his knees, thinking, *grant me shelter–any shelter from this typhoon of fire and destruction.* A sudden gust of hot air cruelly caressed his chilled skin. The stench of roasting ship and human flesh drilled its way into his nostrils, scarring his memory with a wicked smell he would never forget. *We're burning alive,* he thought. *We've descended into the fiery pit. Mercy on us all.*

Kusaka blindly groped for support to pull himself back to his feet. His fingers brushed against and then clamped around something solid . . . a table leg? More explosions accompanied by a furnace blast of wind shook the bridge, blowing out the windows, and tossed him flopping against the wall like a hooked eel cast upon a beach. Cruel, jagged shards of glass knifed through anything blocking their path. Salty liquid rained down upon him, filling his gaping mouth. He struggled to breathe and then spat. Gagged. He wondered, is this . . . blood? No, seawater. Tongues of flame licked at his clothing, seeking to immolate him and make him a fire demon. His panicked mind screamed out, *please deliver me from this nightmare! Is tender mercy beyond my grasp?* Curling into a fetal position, his arms wrapped over his head. Breathing . . . *return to the breathing*, he implored himself. *Nothing is more important now. Only the breathing.*

"Admiral Kusaka?"

A voice followed by a face pierced the smoky, volcanic haze and blurred into reality. A pale Genda, the vision of deliverance, gazed down at him and offered a hand. Kusaka struggled, broke through the mental paralysis, and allowed Genda to help him stand. They leaned on each other for a few brief seconds, sharing their strength and combining their wills until Kusaka broke free.

"Admiral Nagumo?" Kusaka asked.

Genda motioned toward a crippled figure propped up by a binocular pedestal. Nagumo's head tilted to gaze out the shattered window before falling back onto his chest.

Kusaka picked his way across the debris-littered floor of the demolished structure and joined Nagumo at the window. Kusaka's teary eyesight beheld a scene that he knew would haunt him for the rest of his life. Smoke and flames belched forth from a huge hole in *Akagi*'s flight deck near the amidships elevator. The warped elevator platform sagged into the hangar, venting and providing oxygen for the hungry furnace raging below. Mutilated bodies lay strewn about in grotesque positions. Small blasts and screaming men assaulted his hearing. *This is surely hell*, he thought.

"Flood the ship's magazines!" Captain Aoki's voice pierced through the chaos.

Kusaka felt the carrier lurch as it veered to starboard. He staggered a few steps and caught himself as he peered out toward the rest of the fleet. His mouth fell open as a tremendous weight crushed his chest and threatened to stop his heart. Blossoming clouds of gray smoke drifted up from *Kaga* and *Soryu*, staining the heavens above. Flashes of light jumped along their structures, followed by rumbling explosions racing across the waves in a flood of noise. Grief consumed his being. *Kaga, Soryu,* and *Akagi* reduced to flames? *What shall become of us now?*

Kusaka trembled and then came to terms with the situation. *I have a duty to perform. Admiral Nagumo is also required and needed to perform his. A warrior resolute enough to rise and* continue fighting may yet wrest victory from the ashes. He steadied his legs and carefully returned to Nagumo's side.

"Admiral Nagumo, you must transfer your flag. Your station on *Akagi* has ended."

Eyes as dead and black as the shards of obsidian they resembled stared back at Kusaka without comprehending. He shared Nagumo's intense pain but refused to surrender to it. *The battle has not concluded*, Kusaka knew. *Now is not the time to drown oneself in the comforting waters of self-pity.*

"Sir," Kusaka said, inserting more steel in his tone, "you have to move to another vessel and take command of the task force. Most of our ships are still intact and await orders. You must give those orders."

"Admiral Kusaka is correct," Aoki pleaded. "I will take care of this ship. Please, we all implore you to shift your flag and resume command of the fleet."

"My place is here on *Akagi*'s bridge, and her fate I shall share," Nagumo softly said. "It's as things must be."

Kusaka did not recognize Nagumo's voice. He heard something unexpected and remorseless that he had never heard before . . . the finality of utter defeat. *The man has surrendered. The fire of combat has been snuffed out inside him.*

Nishibayashi, Nagumo's Flag Secretary, appeared in the doorway and spoke to Kusaka. "Sir, the passages below are blocked by fire. You must escape by rope through the forward window to the deck. From there, you must descend to the anchor deck. A boat is coming alongside to take you to *Nagara*."

Kusaka cast a wary glance at the small forward window and considered trying to squeeze his large frame through it before turning back to Nagumo.

"Sir." Kusaka raised his voice another notch. "You've heard the reports and know what you must do. It's wrong for you to allow your heart and not your head to dictate your actions at this critical time. You must transfer your flag to *Nagara* immediately. This battle is not over and we must make plans to carry forward."

A brief ember flared up in Nagumo's eyes. He started to respond, the dim light winked out, and he nodded in resigned agreement. *His sense of duty and honor prevails*, Kusaka thought. *May it prove to be enough to reclaim victory from this massive setback of fortune.*

64. THACH
June 04 – 10:30 Hours

"Come on, you bastard, commit yourself," Thach heard himself say aloud. His vision kept flicking to a Zero dancing astern of Thach's formation, preparing to make a rear attack. The Japanese pilot had frustratingly zipped in and out for several minutes to size up the American fighters and appeared to have settled on taking out Thach.

The enemy plane darted forward, setting up for the killing shot. Here we go, Thach thought. Not yet. Not yet. *Now!* Thach jerked the F4F into a sharp right turn away from the Zero. Tracers and 7.7-mm lead ripped through the air space that Thach had vacated.

Again! Thach snatched the Cat back to the left. The Zero zipped by, trying to pull out of its missed pass too quickly. The fuselage rose, filling Thach's gun sight. *Yes!* His index finger squeezed the gun trigger, releasing a long burst of .50-caliber rounds into the enemy plane. The Cat vibrated in synchronism with the cycling Brownings. The smell of smoke and burnt gunpowder drifted into the cockpit. As the Zero climbed away, the heavy slugs ripped a solid pattern of holes along its length. The bullet-riddled machine stalled, sheared off, and plunged into the ocean. That's one, Thach thought. He retrieved a pencil to place a mark on his kneepad.

It's a start, but the sheer numbers against us are overwhelming. If I can just set up the beam defense, it should give us a chance. I can't reach Macomber . . . maybe I can figure out something with Dibb. Place him in the lead position instead of myself.

Thach keyed his radio. "Ram from Jimmie. Pretend you're section leader and move out abeam. Way out."

"Roger," Dibb's welcome reply, sounding like elation over his spot promotion to section leader, came back.

Thach watched as Dibb broke formation to assume station several hundred yards to the right and even with Thach's altitude. Thach glanced back at the pursuing Zeroes, thinking, take the bait you bastards.

As if in response, a Zero nosed down and charged after Dibb, securely latching onto the tail of his F4F.

"Skipper, there's a Zero tailing me!" Dibb called out. "Brush him off!"

"Ram from Jimmie. Swing sharply left now!"

Dibb followed Thach's order and looped back around while Thach did a scissors to the right. The maneuver resulted in Dibb's heading directly toward Thach with the enemy glued to the vulnerable six o'clock position on Dibb's tail. This is like playing chicken in two automobiles, Thach thought, except we're both flying airplanes at over 250 miles per hour. Let's see who blinks first. I'm just as determined as you are.

At the last possible second, Thach ducked beneath Dibb and set up the Zero for an underneath-incoming shot. Thach jerked on the F4F's trigger, bringing the Brownings to pounding, lead-spitting life. Killing streams of tracer fire sprayed between the onrushing planes. Thach smiled, thinking, you're all mine. He calmly stitched his rounds along the Zero's exposed underside and into the engine housing, chewing off pieces of outer covering and cowling. The engine puffed, ignited, and blew up, sending fingers of devouring smoky flame along the plane's fuselage. The burning aircraft zoomed closely by over Thach's cockpit, bathing him in heat. Blanketed in fire, it fell out of the sky as Thach placed another check mark on his kneepad.

Success! I knew it. But that was also foolhardy. I don't believe I'll try it anymore. The beam defense tactic does work, though. We *can* dogfight with these nimble little bastards using it. The old Cat can get the job done when handled correctly.

"Ram from Jimmie. Good going. Let's keep it up."

"Wilco, Skipper."

They assumed position again with Macomber flying close wing support. Watching each other's tail and alerting the other to attacking Zeros by weaving, Thach and Dibb found good chances to fire at the Jap fighters. Their smooth teamwork easily held the enemy at bay. The Japanese appeared to grow frustrated at their inability to shoot down the slower F4Fs and tried to disrupt the defensive maneuver. Another Zero refused to follow Dibb as he turned back toward Thach but repeated the mistake of attempting a radical recovery while making his dive. The Zero loomed upward into Thach's sights, yielding a perfect opportunity for Thach to hammer a long burst along its vulnerable length. The enemy plane bellied up, violently spun away, and slammed into the water.

Thach placed another check mark on his kneepad and thought, why am I doing this? It's foolish, considering I'm not going to make it back. The sky's still full of angry Zeroes, Red Dog is gone, and I can't see Cheek or Sheedy. That just leaves Dibb, Macomber, and me against all these Japs. They hold the advantages of superior aircraft performance and numbers. We're just tying them up while our dive bombers attack. We can't possibly survive.

"Well," he said aloud, "if they're going to get us all, we're taking some with us."

Dibb quickly learned his role while Macomber fell in behind. Weaving back and forth, the F4Fs held their own against the swifter Japanese fighters. After numerous failed attacks, the anger seemed to grow among the enemy pilots. Their passes grew more erratic and hazardous. Ignoring Dibb's plane, one Zero barreled in at Thach and Macomber. The mistake was his last as Dibb took advantage to open up at close range. His Brownings pounded chunks of wing and canopy free, sending the enemy aircraft spiraling into the ocean.

"Ram from Jimmie, good shooting. Let's keep going."

Time became irrelevant as the battle for survival wore on. Taking a brief respite, Thach glanced at the Japanese carriers below and noted the damage delivered by the American pilots. He whooped with joy at each blast shaking one of the huge ships and proudly counted three burning aircraft carriers. Minutes crawled past, bringing fewer and fewer enemy fighters with it. The Zeroes gradually expended their fuel and ammunition and then began drifting away.

"Ram and Macomber from Jimmy," Thach transmitted. "Hell, they don't like it as well as they did. Let's stick together and we might just make it home."

They continued working the variation on Thach's tactic, keeping the remaining Zeroes at bay. The sky finally cleared. The three F4Fs found themselves alone over the crippled remains of a once proud Imperial Japanese Navy Fleet.

We're still alive, Thach thought. That's an unexpected blessing in itself. Those three burning carriers below are the sweetest sight I've ever laid eyes on. He headed his flight toward *Yorktown* and glanced back once more at the wreckage-strewn ocean. The tide has turned, he thought. An ill wind's blowing from a different direction.

65. TOMONAGA
June 04 – 10:50 hours

Tomonaga stood on *Hiryu*'s flight deck listening to Captain Kaku address Kobayashi's attack group. In the distance, the burning shapes of *Akagi, Soryu,* and *Kaga* provided stark proof of the desperate nature of their impending counterattack. It's difficult to believe, he thought. At daylight this morning, we possessed overwhelming air and naval superiority over the enemy. Now we fight for survival against a relentless foe holding the advantage over us.

"I need not tell you this is one of the Empire's darkest hours," Kaku shouted over the noise from the idling aircraft. "Look around you at what the enemy has done to us. We came into this battle with four aircraft carriers. That number is now cut to less than one."

Kaku paused, his ferocious-looking scowl sweeping over the group, and seemed to make certain that he had each man's engrossed attention. The sight reminded Tomonaga of a tiger eyeing its prey, prepared to leap if it moved. Would that harsh looks could win a battle.

"Your bombers and the torpedo planes that will follow are all that Combined Fleet can now employ against the American carrier force. There are no others. It's within your hands alone to retrieve glorious victory from the certain defeat confronting us. The outcome of this battle depends upon how successful you are at performing your duty. The omens have not lied to us over the past six months. We sailed with fate's good fortune. We must only prove worthy of its kind smile upon our efforts."

Tomonaga felt *Hiryu*'s motion change beneath his feet, realizing she was turning into the wind. Launching time grows near, he thought. First Kobayashi's bombers strike to minimize the enemy anti-aircraft fire, and then my torpedo planes provide the crushing blow. We can turn the tide of this battle in our favor. Men control the circumstances that determine the difference between victory and defeat. To credit fate is to discredit ourselves. Our efforts shall reclaim the initiative. The battle is ours to win or lose. There is nothing else. The warrior's will must endure and exert itself.

"You must not act rashly," Kaku cautioned, "and sacrifice yourselves without hope of inflicting great damage upon the enemy. We need each one of you. You must return here, rearm, and continue the fight.

"We're not certain of the enemy's position, but search planes are flying over the suspected area. We should have new information soon."

Kaku stopped once more. The stern visage softened for a fleeting second to look at each man and then reverted to statue-like form. The Stone-Faced One does have a heart, Tomonaga realized. Sending men to their deaths is a heavy burden for anyone to bear without showing some compassion for their sacrifice.

"Prepare yourselves to depart."

Kaku's talk concluded; the fliers dispersed to mount their planes. Kobayashi passed by Tomonaga and halted.

"We shall mark the path for your group with burning enemy ships," Kobayashi said. "Look for the smoke on the horizon."

"You're leaving without a firm target location?"

Kobayashi shrugged. "There's no time to waste. We know we're close to the enemy and have a general heading to fly. The scouting reports will be relayed to us as they're received."

"That sounds like a gamble."

"What else can we do now? We can't sit here and do nothing until the enemy makes another attack on us. They know exactly where we are. They'll be coming back to finish this business."

Tomonaga studied Kobayashi's calm face and understood that he spoke the truth. The Americans would indeed return. Of that, he had no doubt.

"Good fortune flies with you," Kobayashi said, extending his hand.

Tomonaga returned the handshake and said, "And you."

He watched Kobayashi stride over and mount his Aichi bomber. Tomonaga covered his ears and smelled the smoke and fuel fumes as the lead fighter plane bellowed past and leapt into the air. He retreated into the crew pits next to the flight deck and joined the deck crews in offering a silent salute as each aircraft thundered by. As the final bomber rose off the carrier, Tomonaga felt a presence at his side. He turned to find his chief mechanic, Minegushi, nervously watching him.

"Yes?"

"Sir, I beg to inform you that we couldn't seal up the holes in your left wing fuel tank."

"It's leaking?"

The mechanic lowered his head. "We discovered the damage while refueling it. We don't have time to repair it. I am most sorry."

Tomonaga closed his eyes, thinking about the morning's combat. He replayed it mentally. The enemy fighter diving in, attacking from above . . . bullets striking that wing. The brief flames extinguished in the slipstream. Burning fuel. It must have happened then. I forgot . . . should have reported it upon landing. My fault. Minegushi is right. Not enough time to do anything about it now.

Tomonaga reached out and clapped Minegushi on the shoulder. "It's not your fault. I should have said something. Do what you can to make it ready for the torpedo attack."

"The torpedo attack?" Wide eyes looked at Tomonaga. "You can't fly another mission without repairs. You'll run out of fuel before making it back."

"We must have every aircraft making the strike."

"My pardons, sir, but Captain Kaku also said that we must not act rashly. Each pilot must return to rearm and make another attack. You are needed to continue the fight."

"Then you must see that I do. I trust your abilities and skills in repairing my aircraft."

"There's not enough time."

Tomonaga shrugged and then walked away.

"Why do this?" Minegushi called after him.

Tomonaga ignored the question.

66. SPRUANCE
June 04 – 12:00

Spruance looked up as an exhausted Wade McClusky walked into the flag shelter wearing an arm sling.

"You were wounded?"

"Aye, sir. A Zero put some rounds into the cockpit. My left shoulder feels like a sledgehammer hit it. Nothing serious. It's been dressed, and I was given some painkiller."

"You're grounded then," Spruance summed up.

"Aye, sir. I don't know how I could've handled an SBD with a sore shoulder anyway."

"We'll not find out," Spruance said, motioning him to sit. "Who will take your place leading the next strike?"

"Lieutenant Earl Gallaher, sir. He's an excellent pilot and a fine officer. I know he can get the job done."

"Good," Spruance said, before he changed the subject. "What happened out there?"

McClusky moved to a chair near Spruance. He softly groaned as he lowered himself into it. McClusky's in more pain than he wants to admit, Spruance thought. He glanced around the flag shelter to catch Oliver's attention.

"Have someone bring us some coffee."

"Aye, sir." Oliver disappeared.

"Go ahead, Mr. McClusky."

"We had a hard time locating them, sir. They weren't where we figured they'd be. I didn't think we had enough fuel to do much looking so I modified a box search pattern. I guess we had a little luck or divine guidance because we came across a cruiser headed northeast. He had a bone in his mouth as if he was in a hurry. What he was doing out there all by himself I've no idea. It seemed like a safe bet that he was headed to Nagumo's force. We just followed him right back to the rest of the Jap fleet."

"Good thinking."

"Thank you, sir."

A steward appeared and placed a coffeepot, china cups, and service down on a small side table. He poured a cup for each officer, stirred in the requested cream and sugar, and passed them out.

"Will there be anything else, sirs?" he asked, addressing the room in general.

"Not right now, thank you," Spruance answered.

A surprised, pleased look flashed across the steward's face at Spruance's word of thanks. I'd hate to think that I'm the first admiral to acknowledge this man, Spruance thought. I guess it's not Bill's fault. He's fought this war since day one . . . hasn't had time to think about much else. Still. . .

"What were the Jap defenses like?" Browning took advantage of the momentary pause while the steward left.

"I can't speak for the others, sir, but my group went in virtually unopposed. I don't know what happened to the Jap air cover. They were absent while we made our bombing runs, not that I'm complaining. They didn't show up until we headed back here. I played a little game of tag with two of them while my replacement gunner shot one down and chased off the other."

"Your replacement gunner?" Spruance asked.

"Radioman Chochalousek," McClusky answered. "My regular radioman broke his glasses this morning and couldn't make the trip. Bombing 6 offered me Chochalousek to take his place. He's green, but fresh out of aerial gunnery school. He seemed like just the fellow that I needed and he certainly proved himself."

"I agree." Browning broke in again. "Sounds like some fine shooting on his part."

Spruance chose to ignore Browning's comment and said, "What about the damage done to the enemy carriers?"

"I saw three of them burning, sir. I'm certain that Best hit a different one than I did. That leaves *Yorktown* or *Hornet* accounting for the third."

"And the torpedo planes?" Spruance asked.

McClusky lowered his head and sadly shook it. "From my vantage point and by the radio traffic, they were butchered. Those Devastators didn't stand a chance against the Zeroes. I hope I'm wrong, sir."

Spruance fought to keep the dismay from showing on his face. "As do I."

He paused for a moment to collect his thoughts. I doubt that McClusky's wrong, but I can't grieve now. There's still a battle to win. We mustn't let their sacrifice be in vain.

"Did you see any other carriers?" Spruance asked.

"There was a fourth flattop located at a distance from the others. I didn't see anyone striking it before leaving the area."

"Anything else you'd like to report?" Spruance asked.

Spruance noticed McClusky hesitate and glance over at Browning. Something's wrong here, he thought. Something is bothering McClusky that he doesn't want to talk about. I intend to find out what it is.

"Go ahead." Spruance nudged him. "You look like you have something to add."

"When we returned from making the attack and reached Point Option, the task force was not there. The rendezvous location was not where I expected. After all we'd been through, that came as quite a shock. I was lucky to raise *Enterprise* and be guided home before running out of gas."

"It changed from the original designation?" Spruance sought clarification.

"No sir, there was no Point Option given before we left. I followed standard procedure and calculated it on the premise that *Enterprise* would continue to close on the enemy carriers at high speed."

"It was necessary to veer off course and turn into the wind occasionally to carry out CAP activities," Browning broke in to say.

"Is there any reason why that could not have been relayed to our pilots?" Spruance directed his words to a flustered-looking Browning. "I'm sure Mr. McClusky would have appreciated the information."

"I was . . . observing radio blackout, sir."

Spruance fought to maintain his calm composure and mask his face. Now is not the time or place to have this discussion, he thought. Browning knows that I'm displeased. That will have to suffice for the moment.

"Thank you, Mr. McClusky," Spruance said. "You are excused to return to your pilots."

"Aye, sir." McClusky saluted and left.

Spruance thought, three enemy carriers burning and one unaccounted for. I still have aircraft missing . . . must refuel and rearm those that have returned. Perhaps now is the time to pull back and regroup. Check with Admiral Fletcher and see what he's thinking. Plans must be made—

"Sir," the combat talker called out, "*Yorktown*'s under attack by enemy dive bombers!"

Spruance rubbed his chin. That settles things. One more undamaged enemy carrier waits out there and is capable of striking us. We can't retreat now. We must find her and sink her or else this battle might still be lost.

67. FLETCHER
June 04 – 12:00 Hours

"Admiral," Buckmaster said, standing in the doorway of flag plot, "Jimmie Thach is here and wants to report."

A seated Fletcher glanced up. "By all means, bring him in."

He rose and returned Thach's sharp salute. "I'm glad to see you made it back, Jimmie."

"Thank you, sir. The men did a good job and we had some luck."

"How many did you lose?"

"I saw Edgar Bassett go down–no parachute. Dibb, Macomber, and Cheek are all below. I don't know where Sheedy is."

At the mention of Bassett's death, Fletcher fought to maintain a placid expression on his face. Wouldn't do to show too much emotion over the loss of one man, he thought. Too many good, young men have already died and will die today. I mustn't grieve over just the one. But it still hurts. It hurts like hell.

"How did you do?" Fletcher changed the subject.

"I flamed three Zeroes . . . saw them hit the water. Dibb put one down and I'm thinking Macomber can claim a probable. I noticed a lot of damage on the one that he shot at. Those Jap fighters, as quick and nimble as they are, won't stand up to much .50-caliber fire."

"That's quite an accomplishment. It's not often you hear about Grummans besting Zeroes."

Thach's tired-looking face grew solemn. "We used a variation of a new tactic Don Lovelace and I worked on. Like I said, we also had some luck."

Just leave it to Jimmie to find a way to match up with those damn Zeroes, Fletcher thought. News like this should cheer up our fighter pilots. They've been behind the eight ball too long against those Jap fliers.

"Admiral, I saw three large enemy flattops burning," Thach said.

"Three carriers burning?" Fletcher asked, thinking, could it be true? Had Chet gambled and won such an incredible victory?

"Aye, sir. We hit them hard and made it count. I'd say all three are out of commission."

Fletcher slapped him on the shoulder. "Good." He felt happy for the first time in days, thinking, three top of the line enemy carriers out of action. I doubt if anyone ever envisioned this much success. Not even Chet.

"Can you show me the location on the chart?" he asked Thach.

Thach led him over to the chart table, spent a few moments studying it then pointed to a spot northwest of Midway.

"Right in this general area, sir. I can go and retrieve my plotting board and narrow it down a little. The fact is, I was kind of busy at the time to make good notes."

"I understand, and that's not necessary," Fletcher responded. He understood that Nagumo's massive fleet had taken the measure of all the pilots and crews today.

"Sir, I'm sad to report that Lem Massey's bunch was slaughtered. They never had a chance against the swarm of Zeroes that jumped us. It reminded me of being inside a beehive."

"All of them?" Fletcher hated to ask.

Thach blew out his cheeks. "I stumbled across two of them making their way back to *Yorktown* and provided escort until they cleared the kill zone. I didn't see any others, sir."

Fletcher shook his head and muttered a soft curse. The sad news just keeps coming. It's difficult to enjoy our success while thinking about the lives lost in the process.

Another question struck him. "Did you see a fourth carrier? Admiral Nimitz figured Nagumo's Task Force had at least four and possibly five carriers in it. He's been pretty much on the money with all of his information."

Thach frowned. "No, sir. I'm not aware of nor did I see a fourth flattop. That Jap fleet was well dispersed. It's possible another carrier could have been hidden over the horizon."

"I'm taking no chances," Fletcher said. "*Yorktown* launched 10 SBDs a short time ago to search the north and northwest quadrants. If there's another enemy carrier out there, they should locate her."

"Aye, sir."

"By the way, the CAP pilots you left behind are doing a fine job of guarding the fleet. Your replacement XO is really on the ball."

"Thank you, sir. I'll pass that on to Lieutenant Leonard."

Fletcher motioned him toward the door. "You'd better get below. Check on your men and aircraft. I've an idea we'll need you again before this day's over."

Thach saluted and left.

"We've got a large group of bandits coming in from the southwest, sir," Yeoman Newsome said from his station near the intercom. "Approximately twenty-five miles out and closing fast."

There's my proof of the fourth enemy carrier, Fletcher thought. These bandits certainly didn't fly all the way here from Japan.

"What's the status of our combat air patrol?"

Newsome spoke into his microphone, listened for a few seconds, and glanced up at Fletcher. "*Yorktown*'s launched a dozen F4Fs. Lieutenant Commander Pederson is trying to direct them toward the incoming attack. No word on how many of the F4Fs have responded." Newsome pressed a hand against his right headphone, unconsciously nodded to the incoming message, and continued, "One of the CAP pilots notifies there are eighteen Japanese planes heading for us, sir."

"Come on boys, get them!" Pederson's voice blasted out from the overhead speaker tuned to the fighter director transmissions.

He sounds like a football coach cheering on his squad, Fletcher thought. I guess a little pep talk can't hurt. Let's win one for the home team. Still, eighteen Japs against maybe a dozen F4Fs isn't good odds in our favor. Some of them are bound to slip through. He walked over to remove his doughboy-style helmet from its wall peg and put it on. Lewis saw what he did and followed suit in donning his own helmet.

"Let's get a message to Spruance to dispatch any fighters that he can spare to help out *Yorktown*'s group," Fletcher instructed Lewis.

Fletcher returned to the chart table and bent over it. Marking the position of the incoming attack, he tried to correlate it to the location of the burning enemy carriers sighted by Thach. The sound of distant anti-aircraft fire from the escort screen kicked off a steady rumble that he knew would gradually grow into a continuous thunderstorm of noise.

"Admiral," an aide said as he stuck his head through the open door, "the attack is coming in on us, sir."

Fletcher lifted his hands up and straightened his helmet. "Well, I'm wearing my tin hat. I can't do anything else for now."

Fletcher, Lewis, and the other members of his staff moved outside onto the flag bridge to watch the aerial battle. Like a well-rehearsed troupe, the enemy aircraft scattered to form several separate strike groups and attack *Yorktown* from different directions. Grumman Wildcats pounced upon the incoming dive bombers like their namesake mauling its prey. In a few quick moments, smoke and flames heralded the long fall into the ocean as one after another made the ultimate sacrifice for his Emperor.

"*Starboard incoming!*" an anonymous lookout yelled from above.

Simultaneously, the entire starboard-side array of automatic weaponry blasted into furious life, casting up a hellish display of tracer rounds, gun smoke, and deafening racket. Fletcher's nose and eyes burned from the suffocating vapors. He clamped his mouth tightly shut, tried not to inhale more than necessary. The infernal noise grew painfully louder; his ears thrummed from the aural assault.

Lewis pointed and Fletcher looked up, spotting a diving Jap plane. Glowing chains of yellow AA tracer fire danced along its length, fracturing the aircraft into three separate whirling pieces. Its bomb, wrenched free by the fatal damage, drunkenly tumbled down and slammed against the flight deck aft of #2 elevator. The resulting explosion ripped a gaping crater into the deck. Huge sections of flaming shrapnel blew through the nearby gun mounts, hewing men down. A gagging odor of brimstone and scorched flesh latched onto the generated whirlwind to force its way into Fletcher's lungs and pores. An unclean feeling washed over his body and left him wiping his hands down the length of his exposed arms. He gagged, quickly pinched his nose, and fought the urge to vomit.

Shrill whistling marked the passage of more bombs raining down on *Yorktown*. A direct hit or near miss proved equally effective at damaging the great ship and killing men. Fletcher pitied Buckmaster who was straining to direct the helm in evasive maneuvers, trying to avoid the Japanese planes. Fletcher stumbled back and forth, struggling to remain upright against the vessel's random twists and turns as concussive waves of destruction blanketed *Yorktown*. He braced himself against the ship's railing and watched in shamed respect as another enemy dive bomber pushed through the F4Fs and iron curtain of AA fire, delivering its

315

lethal payload. He grudgingly admitted, these fellows know their business and aren't afraid to conduct it.

A jolting impact flung him away from the rail and bounced his helmeted head off the back wall. Something wet leaked down the side of his face. His fingers explored, found a small trickle of blood from a cut scalp. The old tin hat had saved him from serious injury, he thought. He glanced around to check on his staff. Lewis returned his look with a small nod, his eyes growing large at the sight of Fletcher's face.

"Are you hurt?"

Fletcher considered the casualties and serious wounds that the enemy bombs had littered *Yorktown* with before shaking his head. "Just a scratch."

Fletcher's vision returned to the carnage below. The stink of burning paint and smoldering grease compounded with salty air leached into his hair and clothing to spread a tangible layer of destruction on him. I'll never be able to wash all of this away, he thought. I'll carry the memory like a scar.

The numbing din of gunfire and explosions thankfully subsided as the enemy planes either blasted into the ocean or vanished into the distant skies, the smoking mass of *Yorktown* left behind to lick her wounds and prepare for the next attack.

Fletcher leaned out, assessed the grisly toll, and thought, we must find that last enemy carrier before *this* is repeated.

68. TOMONAGA
June 04 – 13:00 Hours

Tomonaga stared at the growing columns of smoke smudging the horizon, and thought, three of the Emperor's carriers reduced to ruins. Dozens of our aircraft destroyed and hundreds of men killed. This attack must not go unpunished. In missing *Hiryu*, the enemy has made a fatal mistake. We can still strike back. Vengeance rests in the hands of the man wielding the sword and willing to strike the blow.

He glanced around at the small group of men gathered on the flight deck with him. This morning our air strike darkened the skies with a typhoon's fury, he thought. Now we comprise little more than an afternoon's shower. However, even a single cloud can possess a lightning bolt.

His attention drew upward to the bridge level, and he was not surprised when Admiral Yamaguchi stepped out to address them.

"You are truly the last hope for Japan and must do your utmost to succeed," Admiral Yamaguchi said. "We've learned from a captured American flier that *Hiryu* faces not one but three enemy carriers. We've hit one of them and left it burning. It's crucial that you attack another and lower the odds against us. With their numbers reduced to one, we will be back on equal footing. We can regain and hold air superiority until Admiral Yamamoto's Main Battleship Force arrives to join the combat. Victory is still within our grasp if you will but seize it."

Yamaguchi faltered, and he paused to wipe his brow. The realization of our dire situation is sinking in, Tomonaga thought. We're outnumbered more than two to one and reduced to a handful of planes. He is indeed correct. What we do now will determine the outcome of this battle.

"You must find and attack the enemy carriers that haven't been hit," Yamaguchi implored. "Attack the ones that haven't been hit."

Yamaguchi raised both arms and shouted, "Ten thousand years to the Emperor!"

Echoing his cry, the fliers dispersed and headed toward their aircraft. Yamaguchi climbed down, approached Tomonaga, and extended his hand. Tomonaga returned his firm grip. He took the opportunity to study Yamaguchi's anguished eyes, able to read the emotions buried within. He aches for the chance to strike a blow, Tomonaga thought. His place isn't here on the deck of a ship . . . it's facing the enemy with a sword in his hands. To live or die while cutting down his foe. This is the warrior's way. I should learn from his example.

"You won't be flying with your usual observer?" Yamaguchi asked.

"No sir. Hashimoto is second-most senior to me. I thought it best to send him with the inexperienced crew of another aircraft. Ensign Akamatsu will accompany me."

"As you wish. I understand that your aircraft is damaged and not capable of returning."

"Our scout reports that the enemy is near. It hasn't taken Kobayashi's group long to return, so it must be true. I should be able to make it back."

Tomonaga knew Yamaguchi did not believe him. I don't believe it either, he thought. What other choice is there? It's imperative that every remaining plane goes out on the strike. We must attack the enemy with everything we have left.

Yamaguchi's glistening eyes seemed to search his. "You're sure of this?"

"It must be."

"I'm reminded of something Admiral Yamamoto said," Yamaguchi said as his head turned toward the ocean. "During the discussion leading up to our attack on Pearl Harbor, he predicted that our forces would run wild throughout the Pacific for six months. After that, the American industry and resources would allow them the upper hand. He had spent a lot of time in the United States and appreciated its potential to raise enormous armed services and fully equip them. We have six months to bring them to negotiations on our terms. Six brief months. After that, they will hammer us down in a war of attrition, he predicted."

He looked at Tomonaga. "It's almost six months to the day of December seventh. Pearl Harbor awakened a giant and filled it with a terrible resolve. Those were Admiral Yamamoto's words– not mine. We mustn't lose in this manner, at this time and place. To do so could lead to the fulfillment of his prophecy. We must regain some of what we've lost."

Tomonaga fell speechless and could only nod.

Yamaguchi appeared to force a smile. "I'll gladly follow you," he softly said.

His words are not meant for the ears of others, Tomonaga knew. He doesn't posture. His emotions are real. He has no desire to steal this moment away from the brave warriors tasked with making the attack. I feel a growing respect for the admiral. Grandfather would have been honored to call Yamaguchi his friend. Tomonaga stepped back, bowed, and saluted. Yamaguchi acknowledged his salute with a bow, turned, and walked away.

Hachiro came running up, pointing at his own aircraft. "Please, sir, won't you honor me by trading planes? Allow me to fly the damaged plane. You must return to lead more strikes against the enemy."

Zenkichi and Yukio joined Hachiro in offering to switch aircraft with him. Yukio implored, "Take my plane, sir. We can't take a chance on losing you."

Tomonaga felt a momentary flash of annoyed anger that he repressed and managed to grin. "My life is no more valuable than any other's. I thank you all, but I should be able to make it back. The Americans are only 100 miles away. If we're forced to ditch, my crew and I will swim back to *Hiryu*."

Nervous laughter passed through their ranks until Zenkichi asked, "And if you can't? What then?"

Tomonaga looked at each man in turn. "I'd expect each of you to exert your wills in service to the Empire. Let not my death . . . let not any of the lives ended on this day be in vain."

Hachiro extended both hands toward him. "But, sir— "

"Enough. Mount your planes and prepare to take off. The enemy is out there. Let's not keep him waiting."

He quickly strode away and climbed into the cockpit of his Nakajima Ninety-seven. Minegushi reached over to help strap him in. Finished, the mechanic pressed something into Tomonaga's hand and then scrambled down. Tomonaga looked to find a dried narcissus flower nestled safely in his palm. He glanced up to find Minegushi watching him. He raised the petals to his nose and inhaled the memory of the blossom's fragrance. Japan calls out to me, he thought. How will I answer her?

His eyes drifted to the left wing and its empty fuel tank, thinking, by flying this plane am I sacrificing all in a foolish attempt to honor my ancestors with a selfless act? Perhaps my arrogance makes me think that so much depends on me. He looked at the flower lying in his lap. No, I mustn't have that attitude. My duty's clear. There's nothing to question. The men need to see the identification stripes on my Nakajima's tail . . . to know their leader is sharing the danger by his own actions. I'm willingly accepting the risks to serve the Emperor, *like a noble samurai*.

69. FLETCHER
June 04 – 13:00 Hours

His ears ringing with the attack's echo, Fletcher retreated into flag plot. Columns of strangling smoke streamed up from every opening below to fill the space, driving them all back outside. That air no better, Fletcher turned to his gagging, coughing staff.

"Let's get down to the deck where we can breathe."

The small group descended to the flight deck, emerging onto a world of utter chaos. A stab of pain knifed into his heart at the sight of tarp covered bodies near the port side gun mounts. Offering a silent prayer, Fletcher carefully maneuvered through fire hoses and harried damage control parties to a relatively calm spot on the stern. His stinging vision made a slow circuit of the struggling carrier, registering each nightmare sight. Destroyed equipment and blood-splattered material lay tossed about as if ripped free by some enraged giant. Expanding clouds of smoke bled from every pore of *Yorktown*, resembling a massive thunderhead building up for a deluge. Sailors ran, stumbled, feverishly dug through the wreckage, and shouted as they tried to extinguish the fires and help the wounded. His senses and emotions assaulted by the scene, Fletcher fought to maintain his quiet composure. A sudden flash of unmerciful memory visualized a picture of the doomed *Lexington's* death throes before it went under at Coral Sea. The haunting parallel image snapped his eyes shut.

This isn't my fault, he told himself. I did the correct things that needed doing without hesitation. Blame a dangerous, determined adversary and the fortunes of war. Men die and ships sink . . . it's the nature of the beast.

Curse this damn war.

"Admiral Fletcher, sir." A sooty Kiefer, his voice raised to be heard over the racket, appeared to snatch him back into the moment. Kiefer's jolly disposition subdued, Fletcher read in Kiefer's face the same anguish he felt.

"Report," Fletcher croaked, shocked at the raw sound from his smoke-ravaged throat.

"The damage is bad but manageable. Most of the fires below are under control or soon will be."

Kiefer motioned toward the frantic activity behind them. "The flight deck repairs should be completed in less than an hour. The men got right on it."

"What about propulsion?"

"Five of the six boilers were snuffed out, most likely from a bomb concussion. Captain Buckmaster is directing the repairs and setting priorities. Preliminary observations suggest we should be getting back underway before too long. There's no idea of how fast she'll go, but we'll be moving, sir."

Cautious hope surged through Fletcher. After all of *this*, the ship still has life and fight left in her? Bless you *Yorktown*.

"You have a good crew, XO," Fletcher noted.

"We have a *damn* good crew, sir. We're still in this fight."

Fletcher thought, so now what? Stay with the stricken *Yorktown* and hope for the best? Move my flag and face accusations of abandoning ship too soon? That bunch back in Washington would love to put *that* on my record. *Fletcher bails again at the first sign of trouble.* I'll not give them the opportunity.

"Admiral, may I?" Lewis spoke up to ask.

"By all means," Fletcher answered.

Lewis addressed Kiefer. "Do we have adequate communications established with the rest of the fleet?"

Kiefer shook his head. "No, sir. The smoke's too thick in the communications center to get back in there and assess the damage. It's doubtful we can blinker through this cloud covering us. It'd be hit and miss. Radar's also out."

"So we're deaf, dumb, blind, and dead in the water?" Lewis summed up.

A tired-looking, impish grin, quickly stifled, bent Kiefer's lips. "I'd say that's the way of it, sir."

"Thank you." Fletcher broke in. "You may return to more pressing duty."

Kiefer threw a precise salute and hurried off. Lewis motioned at Fletcher to step away from the other officers and followed him to the far side of the flight deck.

"You must move your flag to another ship that can provide mobility and communications," Lewis advised.

Rubbing his sore head, Fletcher stared out over the hostile water and considered the situation. I owe *Yorktown* a fighting chance to get through this. She was there when I needed her. She made it through the Coral Sea and out here to strike a blow. I should return the favor. The men would expect as much.

Fletcher shook his head. "Not yet. The time's not right. I'm not that desperate."

Lewis's mouth worked in and out for a few seconds as if he were fighting for the right words to say. You'd think after all that we've been through Spence would speak his mind, Fletcher thought. Maybe he needs a little prompting.

"Let's hear it, Spence. You've never been one to hold back an opinion."

"It is imperative that you establish command elsewhere," Lewis blurted out. "*Astoria* is close by. You should transfer your flag over to her."

"Like a rat off a sinking ship?" Fletcher immediately regretted saying it.

"No, *sir!*" Lewis seemed to bristle, and he bit off his words. "You're responsible for both task forces . . . including *Enterprise* and *Hornet*, not just *Yorktown*."

Lewis pointed at the damage control parties hustling around, fabricating fast repairs. "This should prove that Nagumo is still capable of causing tremendous harm to us. The Japs will be coming back looking for Spruance's carriers."

Chastened, Fletcher fell silent. He took one last look around and thought, Spence is right. There's no time for personal issues or remorse. This battle's far from decided. There's another Jap carrier out there still posing a threat. There's also a huge surface fleet with it that's capable of doing tremendous damage to Midway or us.

"Notify *Astoria* to send a boat over," Fletcher said. "We have a job to finish."

70. SPRUANCE
June 04 – 13:30 Hours

Spruance, Browning, and Oliver stood inside *Enterprise*'s flag shelter watching distant clouds of anti-aircraft fire dot the sky over *Yorktown*'s position. Frustration gnawed at Spruance. I can't even steam in that direction and help until we recover all our strike planes. All I can do is stand here hoping for the best. His heart sank as a heavy pillar of smoke rose up to smudge the horizon in ashen shades.

"Sir, Admiral Fletcher is requesting fighter support for *Yorktown*," a yeoman said from the doorway.

"Notify Lieutenant Commander Dow," Spruance responded. "Have him send over all the aircraft we can spare."

"Aye, sir."

Spruance thought of Fletcher and his ordeal at Coral Sea. *Lexington* sunk and *Yorktown* limps back to Pearl needing extensive repair. Now *Yorktown* has been struck once more. I can't imagine reliving such a terrible scene. He certainly deserves better than he's been receiving lately. I have to do more to help. Send more than aircraft.

"Bob, let's get some surface support headed that way. We'll increase their anti-aircraft fire. Dispatch the cruisers *Vincennes* and *Pensacola* and the destroyers *Balch* and *Benham* to assist."

Oliver ducked inside to deliver Spruance's orders.

Buracker appeared. "Admiral, Dick Best confirmed there's another Jap carrier out there. He's urging that we attack immediately."

Spruance maintained his impassive demeanor, thinking, first McClusky informs me, then *Yorktown* comes under attack, yet I'm *still* advised about a fourth enemy carrier and the need to attack it? What other conclusion could I draw? Do they think I'm not paying attention to what's going on? Feeling anger building, he purposely inhaled deeply and slowly exhaled.

"Sir," Oliver returned to say, "we're missing ten torpedo planes and eighteen bombers. There's no word about what might have happened to them."

Spruance thought, no word? McClusky believes the enemy annihilated the torpedo planes. That accounts for them. What I don't understand is how those eighteen SBDs disappeared. McClusky said they attacked virtually unopposed and easily drove off the enemy pursuit. So where are the rest of those dive bombers? Given their low fuel levels and their lack of knowledge about the location of Point Option, the logical conclusion is that they had to ditch. McClusky mentioned that he had barely made it back. That should never have happened. I'm rapidly losing confidence in Browning and his air staff. I must pay closer attention to their decisions. Ask more questions of them.

Spruance leaned back, closed his eyes, and softly massaged his throbbing temples. The intense noise of combat operations whaled away on his hearing as if he were standing with his head leaned against an airplane engine while the pilot jammed the throttle wide open. The intercom constantly squawked . . . summoning or advising. Over the ceiling loudspeaker, the flight director and airborne pilots maintained a static chatter. The throaty bass bellow of aircraft taking off and landing added to the racket and unleashed a sustained barrage of noise against his buzzing eardrums. He instinctively acknowledged messages demanding his immediate attention or issued orders, all the while withdrawing behind his inner sanctuary of concentration.

Spruance thought, that fourth carrier is out there, but where? It's been over two hours since the last visual location. He's had plenty of time to move and will have more time before we're ready to launch another strike. Sinking that carrier takes top priority. There's no debate on that. But I can't send a flight out without telling them where to head. However, if I wait too long? *Yorktown*'s smoking and seems badly damaged. *Enterprise* and *Hornet* have lost a large percentage of their dive bombers and torpedo planes. Despite our leaving three enemy carriers burning, this battle could still turn against us.

"Sir." Browning was at his side, "We've got to launch an attack against that last Jap carrier now. We can't afford to wait."

Here we go again. Spruance dropped his hand to glance up at Browning.

"Where would we send them to?"

"Sir?"

"A destination for them to head," Spruance patiently explained. "It's a big ocean out here."

Browning offered him a puzzled look, and Spruance could sense the man's growing frustration. He's trying to decide if I'm patronizing him, Spruance thought. Let him wonder. Spruance focused on maintaining his stoic facial expression, determined to conceal his true thoughts.

"Well, I . . . I'd send them out to the last contact location."

"Indeed." Spruance replied. "You do understand our last contact with the enemy is over two hours old?"

Browning's lips vanished from sight for a brief moment before he replied, "They can't have gone very far. We should be able to spot the exhaust smoke from their stacks and home in."

"Spot their exhaust smoke? Is that your suggestion? What about all the smoke from those burning carriers out there? I would think that might hamper attempts to locate stack smoke. Then there's the matter of four hours."

"Four hours?" Browning's voice sounded wary.

"Even if we did launch whatever aircraft we have ready right now, four hours will elapse between the time our first strike left the attack location and the time the second strike arrives. That enemy carrier has a good deal of head start on us. By now, they certainly know they're facing a multiple carrier group with more aircraft available to use. I find it hard to believe they're hanging around waiting on us to return and finish the job of sinking them."

"Sir," Oliver interrupted to say, "we've lost radio contact with *Yorktown*. One of our fighter pilots is in the area and reports heavy smoke and no movement."

Spruance instantly shifted attention to the problem at hand. "Have Dow assume control of *Yorktown*'s CAP. Notify her pilots to use *Enterprise* or *Hornet* as home base until further notice."

"Admiral, this should serve as a warning to us," Browning said, pressing the discussion. "That Jap carrier is more than capable of doing tremendous damage to both task forces. We must take the initiative and launch now."

Spruance held his silence, thinking, is Browning correct? Am I making the wrong decision? This morning I sent out every aircraft both *Enterprise* and *Hornet* had based on one questionable scouting report. Now I've a better approximation of the enemy's position but I'm delaying action. However, circumstances evolve during a battle. Earlier it was imperative to make the first strike against an unsuspecting, numerically superior enemy fleet. That

326

was the time to gamble and, thankfully, it paid off. Three of those carriers are heavily damaged and burning. Now is the time for studied caution. I will attack but only when I know where to send my aircraft.

"Admiral?"

Spruance detected annoyance in Browning's voice and restrained from showing his own growing impatience. The man's just trying to do his duty in advising me as he sees fit, he thought. I don't want a staff that's afraid to voice its opinion, but I'm in command.

"We'll send off our next attack when we receive the enemy's current position."

"Fine, sir, but I'd not want the responsibility for whatever results from this delay."

Spruance glanced up at him. "The responsibility isn't yours . . . it's all mine. We'll attack when I give the order."

71. BROCKMAN
June 04 – 13:30 Hours

Brockman peered through the periscope and could not believe his eyes. The damaged carrier they had trailed for the past three hours had stopped. He studied it through high-powered magnification, noted it sitting upright and floating high on the water. It doesn't seem to be listing and no fires are visible. He panned the length of the ship and marveled at the destruction wrought on her topside. Focusing backward, he noted several small boats bouncing around her bow while two cruisers stood nearby as escorts.

"Roy, take a look," Brockman called Benson over.

He stepped back and allowed Benson to take his place. A low whistle escaped the XO's lips as he peered into the eyepiece.

"What's keeping that thing afloat?" Benson asked. "Our flyboys did one hell of a demolition job on it. The entire upper sections are gone."

"I don't think the hull's damaged because it seems to be riding on an even keel. Most probably, bombs did most if not all of the damage, and they're not likely to tear holes in the hull. What's bad for us is it looks like they're rigging a towline. If they manage to get it into dry dock, they'll rebuild it. We'll have to deal with it again somewhere down the line."

Benson turned to look at Brockman. "We can't let that happen."

Brockman glanced over at Lynch. "Bring me the aircraft carrier identification charts."

Lynch retrieved them from the navigator's desk. Brockman took another long look through the periscope and then thumbed the pages. Pausing at one silhouette, he compared it with the periscope view and moved away to allow Benson to see it.

"I'm thinking that's him," Brockman said, passing Benson the identification card. "What do you think?"

Benson shifted between the silhouette and periscope several times before shrugging. "It's kind of hard to tell by the shape he's in. Hell, it's hard to tell if the thing is an aircraft carrier by the shape he's in. It could be the world's largest fishing sampan."

Brockman nodded to Lynch, who also alternated looking between the periscope and pages. After several long moments, Lynch rubbed his eyes while closing the book.

"Island on the starboard side . . . *Soryu* class, I'd say," Lynch pronounced.

"You agree with me," Brockman said.

"I'll go along with both of you," Benson said, making it unanimous. "Make a note of that, Mr. Wetmore. One *Soryu*-class carrier sitting idle right in front of us."

"Aye, sir."

"We've got three good targets to attack," Brockman said, "and full tubes both fore and aft. Which do we hit first?"

"The carrier's not going anywhere," Benson offered. "We could go after the cruisers and come back for him."

"And the batteries? We've used up a good bit of juice as it is. Those cruisers are a couple miles farther out. We'll drain the batteries trying to catch up to them."

Benson removed his hat and ran his fingers through his damp hair. "You're right. I don't think it's possible to overtake them. They'll just keep circling around the perimeter out of reach."

"I agree."

"The carrier?" Benson asked.

"It's the smart move. He's a sitting target and still presents a threat as long as he's afloat. The Japs are doing their best to save it. We can't let that happen."

"Sound, report," Benson said to Woods.

"Two sets of screws at two two five and two four zero. Slow speed, sir."

"Helm, ahead one-third," Brockman ordered.

He returned to the periscope, spending the next several minutes taking sightings and double-checking them against the identification cards. It is difficult to tell, but that has to be *Soryu*, he thought. He rotated over to verify the positions of the cruisers. They seem oblivious to our presence. Our luck is holding.

Lowering the scope, he stood watching the minute hand creep around his watch dial. Slow and careful will get the job done, he thought. Set the shot up and make it count. We've come too far to get in a hurry and make a foolish mistake. Should they spot us before we shoot, those two cruisers will present tough opposition. I'm not certain that this boat and crew can withstand another long depth charging today . . . not without doing some damage to the enemy in return. Morale is low as it is.

"Stand by TDC for target readings," Brockman said while squatting in front of the periscope. "Up scope!"

Clapping the handles down, he moved in unison with the rising tube. The view grew lighter until the head broke the surface. The liquid picture slowly cleared as the water ran off the periscope lens. He increased magnification and blinked when the stationary target seemed to leap toward him.

"Bearing—*Mark!*" Brockman called out.

"Bearing zero zero five!" Crenshaw read off.

"Range—*Mark!*"

"Range three five double oh!"

"Angle on the bow is port ninety, and target is stationary." Brockman clapped the handles up as he spoke and watched the periscope shaft retreat into its well.

He heard Lynch at the TDC echo the readings. A sudden thought struck him and caused him to glance over at Wetmore.

"Ask forward torpedo room if the problem with number one tube is repaired," Brockman ordered.

"Forward room, is number one tube repaired?" Wetmore relayed. A slight pause followed, and then he looked up at Brockman.

"Aye, sir, as far as they can tell. They won't know for sure until we attempt to use the tube."

"Let's find out. Make tubes one through four ready in all respects. Set torpedo depth for eight feet."

"Sound, report," Brockman said to Woods.

"Two sets of screws maintaining distance from us, sir. They seem to be passing back and forth along a straight bearing."

"They're not aware of us?" Brockman asked.

Woods shook his head. "No, sir. I don't think so."

"Up periscope!" Brockman ordered. He made a double sweep of their surroundings, verified the cruisers' locations, and focused back on the carrier.

"Bearing—*Mark!*"

"Bearing zero zero five," Crenshaw relayed.

"Range—*Mark!*"

"Range three four five oh."

"Angle on the bow is port ninety and target is stationary," Brockman said as the scope lowered.

"We have a solution that agrees with observation, sir," Lynch advised.

"We can't get a setup much better than that," Benson observed. "A straight shot at a stationary target. The only thing that comes close would be catching the *Soryu* tied up at the dock with an enormous bull's eye painted on its side. Hell, it's almost too good to be true."

Here we go, Brockman thought. A chance to make up for those earlier misses. A large target, especially an aircraft carrier, dead in the water is every submariner's dream. Roy is right. We're in perfect position to nail it. Let's make the best of this opportunity.

"We're going to shoot a spread of four," Brockman announced. "The carrier's stationary and the angle on the bow are set, but I want to check scope and TDC bearing and range before each one. Once we begin, I want no interruptions until that last fish is on its way. Let's do it like we've drilled . . . no mistakes. Final bearing to shoot number one."

He waited a few moments while Wetmore passed the order throughout the boat and then looked at Crenshaw.

"Up scope!"

The *shwick* sound of the periscope extending jumped out at him.

"Bearing—*Mark!*"

"Bearing zero zero five!" Crenshaw called out.

"Range—*Mark!*"

"Range three four double oh!"

Brockman could hear Lynch's fingers dancing away on the TDC. He felt the air poised, anticipating his next command.

"Solution agrees!" Lynch confirmed.

"Fire one!" Brockman said, focusing the scope again. "Bearing—*Mark!*"

"Bearing zero zero five!"

"Range—*Mark!*"

"Range two nine seven five!"

Another pause and then, "Solution agrees!"

"Fire two! Bearing—*Mark!*"

"Bearing zero zero five!"

"Range—*Mark!*"

"Range two five five oh!"

Condensation mixed with sweat dripped into Brockman' eyes. He blinked to clear them.

"Solution agrees!"

"Fire three! Bearing—*Mark!*"

"Bearing zero zero five!"

"Range—*Mark!*"

"Range two one six oh!"

Brockman searched for and located a torpedo wake heading toward the carrier. Right on target, he thought.

"Solution agrees!"

"Fire four!"

The boat shuddered one final time, and Brockman instantly realized that something was wrong. Did I feel four torpedo releases? I was so involved in the setup . . . could I have missed one?

"Three torpedoes running hot, straight, and normal," Woods said, confirming his suspicions.

"Sir," Wetmore said, "forward advises that number one tube failed to shoot electrically or manually."

Brockman sighed. Three will have to do. Those cruisers will be on us before we can maneuver the boat for a stern shot. He remained focused on the torpedo tracks, silently wishing them onward. His eye watered and stung from straining so long.

Brockman knew that Benson's eyesight was fixed on a stopwatch, heard him advise, "Not much longer now before the first one should reach the target."

As the first fish neared the carrier, Brockman sucked in a deep breath and held it.

"Right about *now!*" Benson sang out.

A mass of flames roared up from the bow and spread amidships. Bull's eye, Brockman thought.

"Sound, report," Brockman said, turning toward Woods.

"There's a great deal of noise coming from him, sir. It's hard to single out individual sounds."

Brockman peered back into the periscope and noticed figures going over the side of the carrier like rats out of a sinking ship. The small boats dropped their towing lines to scurry out of harm's way.

"Roy, have a look," Brockman offered.

332

He moved back and then motioned the others to take a quick peek. Benson maneuvered the periscope, whistled softly, and leaned back out of the way for Lynch.

"No explosions?"

Brockman shrugged. "I watched the torpedo wakes all the way, and he started burning like that after the first one struck. It happened right at the end of the calculated run time by your stopwatch. It can't be a coincidence. I don't know why we didn't hear anything."

"Water density interfering with sound waves?" Benson offered. "That could muffle the noise."

"I've read patrol reports of such a thing," Brockman agreed.

Lynch slapped the handles up and leapt clear.

"Skipper, cruisers headed this way!"

"Sound contacts closing in!" Woods echoed. "Active pinging!"

"Down scope!" Brockman roared. "Take her down fast!"

He gripped the periscope mast, bracing himself against the sudden decline angle on the boat's bow. Foolish, he thought. Waste time admiring your efforts, forgetting the carrier had escorts.

"Let's go deep," he called down to Hogan. "Make your depth three zero zero feet! Rig for silent running!"

They could all hear it now: the unmistakable sound of two sets of screws bearing down upon them. The noise of pebbles gently rattling on the hull made his skin crawl with the realization that the enemy's active sonar had locked onto them. There'll be no hiding from them this time, Brockman thought. They're full of rage. And they're concentrating on killing this submarine that has hounded them all day.

72. TOMONAGA
June 04 – 14:30 Hours

Tomonaga scanned the ocean, expecting to see the burning carrier left by Kobayashi's attack. The other enemy vessels should be near the same location or at least in sight of it, he thought. I should be at the position now. He cursed the necessity for flying close to the water to avoid detection, because it sacrificed vision range for stealth. *Hai,* but the enemy's close. I can feel his presence. I sense the hatred fueling his purpose.

His thoughts drifted to Admiral Yamaguchi's admonition that it was necessary to attack a different target than the one Kobayashi's group had damaged. Kobayashi had fulfilled his mission. Victory depends on our destroying another of the enemy's carriers. We must do this. To do so lowers the numbers against us. It allows us to maintain an airborne presence while our superior surface fleet closes on the rest of the enemy's task force and engages it in final combat. Admiral Yamamoto shall have his great sea battle against the Americans. The enemy is no match for our skill in ship-to-ship combat. Good fortune and victory will yet be ours.

He allowed but a brief glance at the rapidly falling level in his fuel tanks. It's dropping quickly as I knew it would. There's no controlling certain things. At least the left wing had stopped streaming flammable spray a short time ago. One tracer round coming too close could have touched off an inferno . . . flamed me before I had a chance to drop my torpedo. Denied me the right to strike one final blow. To suffer a martyr's death instead of that of a warrior.

His eyesight made a quick circuit of the menacing sky. The sun seemed to stare back at him like an accusing eye, questioning his desire and commitment. *Will you allow the enemy his triumph without fighting back? To dishonor you and your house? Does the Code of Bushido meaning nothing to you? Who is your master?*

Ship masts rose on the horizon like a winter's trees against a December sky revealing a screen of escort vessels. He noticed they formed a cocoon around a moving aircraft carrier. The carrier is not burning, nor is it slowly steaming, Tomonaga thought. It does not appear damaged, but I see no sign of Kobayashi's victim. From the position given, it should be near this location. I don't understand. Could it have sunk so quickly? Gone under without leaving any trace such as survivors or a field of debris? How can this be? Stuttering gunfire from attacking enemy fighters dismissed the questions from his mind. *I have a visible target to destroy. Nothing else matters.*

"Send a message, Murai," he said to his radioman. "Take position for attack formation."

His attention focused on reaching the ideal release position, ignoring the rattling from Murai's 7.7-mm. machine gun. Fiery bursts of tracer sliced through the air seeking to chew the life from his plane. A friendly Zero, cannons blinking, flashed over his canopy headed in the opposite direction. The amber glow from metallic fire accompanied his passing.

"Hai! Good shot! Watch him burn!"

Tomonaga heard the radio transmission and realized the Zero had shot down the enemy fighter. He thought, *another brave warrior fulfills his duty. How many others on both sides will join him and Kikuchi before this day is over?*

"Send this message, Murai. Attack!"

The small wave of torpedo bombers divided into two sections. Tomonaga banked the Nakajima, leading his group toward one side of the large vessel, knowing that Hashimoto would circle his aircraft around to the other. *Hammer and anvil,* he thought. *Position ourselves on both beams of the target to make our runs. Some of us are sure to get through. The enemy can't dodge in two different directions at the same time. Just one well-aimed torpedo in the right place can cripple a ship and even the odds facing them. Battles are won on such small things as this.*

The stink of body odor and fuel oil dulled his sense of smell and filled him with shame. *How long has it been since I have taken a proper bath? There was little time this morning, and my thoughts were occupied with leading the attack on Midway. A poor excuse for a samurai to ignore his cleansing before battle.* The occasional sulfurous stench from burnt gunpowder mixed with the hostile atmosphere. *The stink of death and dying,* he thought. *Stink? No. Sweet fragrance. Like a lotus blossom for a warrior intent on the kill. I glory in it.*

His descending aircraft leveled out at around 60 meters and zipped through the screening vessels. Up ahead he spotted a small gap opening between a cruiser and destroyer and aimed for it. A percolating wake brewed up around the larger ship as it churned around trying to bring a broadside array of weapons to bear on Tomonaga's fleeting plane. Stuttering trails of tracer zipped past his canopy as he barreled past, boring in on the target.

The Ninety-seven suddenly snorted and jerked, a victim of the indiscriminate anti-aircraft salvos. Squealing shells slammed into the water in front of him, throwing up huge fountains of killing density. His skilled hands manipulated the aircraft, weaving in and out, dodging the frothy towers. He stomped on the rudder to veer around a geyser erupting directly in front of him. The aircraft's propeller sheared through a thin sheet of water as the Nakajima's engine roared in defiance of the enemy's determined defense. A bird of prey screaming at its intended quarry, Tomonaga thought. It shall not be denied its kill.

Tomonaga inhaled salty smoke, tasted fear on his tongue, and felt his guts trying to heave. I've never endured gunfire this overwhelming nor faced a foe who was consumed with such murderous intent. These Americans are not the cringing cowards that I'd been taught to expect. It's almost too much to bear. Ignoring the rising wave of nervous panic, he locked onto the enemy carrier looming ahead. A destroyer appeared from out of nowhere blocking his passage, its automatic weapons blazing away at his incoming torpedo plane. His Nakajima twisted and jerked in pain as the bullets tore into it. It gently lifted, brushing over the destroyer's outstretched mast. Flames of gunfire stabbed into his aircraft as he blew by, tracking him toward his target. An avenging whirlwind riddled by bullets, the Ninety-seven maintained its steady course.

Don't fail me my friend, Tomonaga silently implored the aircraft. We're too close to give up. Together we can–we *shall* endure to strike our enemy. We shall not be denied the opportunity. There's no escaping us now.

Directly ahead, he noticed an enemy Wildcat fighter in perfect position making a pass at him from the side. His vision registered the tracers crossing in front of his aircraft, but his hands remained steady on the controls. He solemnly accepted the necessity of flying through the killing streams of lead. Swerving off now would prevent me from making an accurate torpedo drop. My life's purpose comes down to this single moment. There will be no second chance. The bow is drawn. All I need do is loose the arrow.

I am the archer.

73. THACH
June 04 – 14:30 Hours

Thach stood on *Yorktown's* smoking flight deck surveying a scene of total chaos. A horde of young men dressed in different colored jerseys, greasy dungarees, and fire protection suits dashed around making hurried repairs or securing flammable materials. The odor from dozens of different burnt materials mixed with various shades of smoke to fill his lungs with a choking mixture of unhealthy vapor. He coughed, gagged and wiped his agitated eyes with the back of his sleeve. If this is what *Lexington's* final hours were like, I'm glad that I missed it, he thought.

A haggard Kiefer emerged from out of smoke and walked toward him. An uncharacteristically grim face greeted Thach as Kiefer removed his helmet to wipe a sweaty brow.

"What do you think, Dixie?"

"We're almost there and should be able to launch within a few minutes," Kiefer replied while glancing around. "There's just . . . an incredible amount of smoke and bomb damage. Thank goodness, the fuel lines were drained and purged or else we could have been blown to the moon. I can't believe how much this old girl can take. Damn near sunk at Coral Sea and now this."

"She's a fighter," Thach agreed.

"That she is and so is the crew. I couldn't be prouder of the way these men have responded. Thanks to them, we should return to operations soon."

"Everyone's doing his job, no doubt about it."

"That and more. I've lost track of all the actions that I've seen deserving of medals. It makes me feel good being part of this team."

"How about fueling my fighters?"

Kiefer cocked his head. "We've sustained damage near the main fuel station, and things are going slow. We're doing what we can. There's the danger of igniting a fire, so we can't go too fast in making repairs. I'll go try to hurry the boys up a little."

"Thanks, Dixie. Keep your head down and don't get excited."

Kiefer seemed not to hear and hurried away. Thach turned and walked toward his waiting plane. Spotting Tom Cheek standing among a group of pilots, Thach waved him over.

338

"There's no telling how soon the Japs will return," Thach said. "I doubt we'll have time to refuel everything. I only want the Cats that have at least thirty gallons of gas manned and ready. It won't be many, but it'll be better than none at all. We have to do something to help out with the situation."

"Aye, sir, I'll pass the word."

Thach climbed inside the cockpit of his F4F and willed the wind to blow. Canopy opened, the steady breeze licked his face, teasing him with the enticing promise of taking off. He thought, I don't care if it's *Yorktown's* gaining speed or God that causes it, but I need more airflow streaming down this deck to get my Cats airborne. I'll not stand helplessly by and watch this ship attacked again. The next time the Japs come, I'm going to do some shooting.

"Sir," Cheek, who stood on the wing root, leaned in to say, "There are incoming Jap planes, and Commander Pederson advises we're going to have to stop refueling. He wants to know if you're willing to go as you are."

Willing? Thach thought. Is he serious?

"Hell yes, I'm willing if there's an incoming attack! Get these birds airborne!"

Cheek grinned, clapped him on the shoulder, and climbed down. Thach watched him speaking to the deck crew while pointing toward the F4F. Let's get this thing cranked and warmed, Thach thought. Every second of delay works to the Japs' advantage.

Thach went through the preflight checks and watched his crew rotating the propeller a few turns by hand to circulate the oil. At his plane captain's signal, he fired up the ignition. The Pratt and Whitney radial engine barked, coughed, and then exploded into snarling life. Thach opened the throttle for a few moments to check his pressures and temperatures before allowing it to settle into a loud purr.

He looked at his fuel gauge with dread. Only about thirty gallons like the rest of my guys. That won't allow for much flight and fight time. What does it matter? The Japs are already into their runs. I'll have to scramble to get enough altitude and speed for immediate attack. Thirty gallons should make the difference.

Thach caught Fly 1's notice and raised his hand, signaling he was ready to take off. Fly 1 checked that the flight deck was clear and then flagged Thach to go. As the F4F blew past, Thach noticed the deck personnel standing and waving clenched fists, their mouths open as if shouting. We're all making this fight together, he thought.

Thach mentally prepared for immediate combat, knowing the enemy was already bearing in as he pushed the plane for altitude. Curving around in a gentle circle to the right, he headed toward *Yorktown's* stern. He hand-cranked up the landing gear and charged and tested his guns, all the while keeping his vision sweeping the dangerous sky.

The chilling sight of enemy airplanes dodging their way through *Yorktown's* screening vessels grabbed his attention. Seeing the Jap aircraft separate into two groups, he decided to focus on those targeting *Yorktown's* starboard side as she sluggishly tried to flee. His thoughts flashed onto the men he had left behind on her vulnerable deck. Dodge, *Yorktown*, dodge! Don't give these bastards a clear run at you. Give me a few moments of time and some altitude. I'm coming to help. He realized that he was leaning against the belts, trying to urge the stubby aircraft higher.

Locking in on the lead Nakajima, he noted the deadly Long Lance torpedo slung beneath its belly and understood the massive amount of destruction one could cause. In the poor shape *Yorktown's* in, that thing could finish her. This one's mine.

Thach used his slight height advantage to roll into a beam run on the Nakajima's right side. He powered the F4F in low and steady, allowing himself the best chance of striking the target. Breath held, he anticipated the aircraft crossing in front of his plane's nose and prepared the deflection shot. His finger squeezed the trigger a fraction of a second before his prey zipped past. Flickering streams of .50-caliber tracers arced gracefully through the air, curving into the target streaking by. Staccato ropes of steel-jacketed lead ripped into the Nakajima's uncovered fuselage, blowing large pieces free. The enemy plane rolled over slightly as the slugs chewed into it, exposing its far side to damage. The F4F vibrated and slowed with the kickback from the hammering Brownings. Thach continued raking the enemy plane until it cleared his field of fire.

Completing his pass, Thach turned back to look. The Nakajima's left wing blazed, the intense heat and flame melting away the outer covering and exposing the frame. The enemy plane wobbled and dipped and then straightened out. He watched in frustrated admiration as the enemy pilot struggled to complete his run and succeeded in releasing his torpedo. Thach cursed, thinking, what do I have to do to stop this guy? Flame his aircraft, destroy a wing, and he *still* drops his fish. What drives a man so?

74. TOMONAGA
June 04 – 14:55 Hours

His open canopy shattered as flaming spears of agony tore into Tomonaga's body and nailed him deep into the seat. Waves of blindingly intense pain radiated throughout him, threatening to overwhelm his system and knock him unconscious. His peripheral vision registered the damaged left wing burning, and he thought, it's heaven's blessing that fuel tank is empty. Full, this aircraft would now be a funeral pyre. I can continue onward.

The stink of blackening, melting paint and roasting metal filled his nostrils. He gagged and twisted in the seat. More red-hot spikes drilled into his torn flesh. A burst of crimson splashed against the cockpit walls, covering the instrument panel. He fought to remain upright . . . to concentrate on his task. Focus. Don't lose focus. But it's hard to see. Where am I headed? A bloody hand–his?–extended and clawed at the fractured windscreen trying to wipe it clear. Sticky blood smeared, spreading a reddish veil over the surface.

Where am I headed?

"Akamatsu, where are we?" he called over the speaking tube.

No answer.

"Murai?"

Silence. Enemy bullets have done their job. I'm now alone.

Dark threads stringing out before his eyes fattened into huge ropes, blocking his vision. He wrenched his eyelids fully open, washing them with harsh sunlight. Something large loomed up out of the bloody mist ahead. His retreating mind barely recognized the enemy carrier silhouetted before him. Soothing darkness reached out to comfort him. Allow me to rest for just a moment. That's all that I ask.

No! No! I've come too far. I'm much too close. I won't quit now! Maintain focus on my task. I can see it. I can strike it.

I am the archer.

My wings aren't level . . . I must correct. Nothing shall throw off my release. The spirit of combat inhabits me. It guides my way . . . lights my path. The bow is drawn. The arrow aimed. Closer. Move closer. The target flees but can't hide.

Anti-aircraft fire pounded the oxygen out of the air, shaking the plane like a crocodile snapping its tail against the fuselage. Daggers of noise stabbed into his eardrums, seeking to puncture them. The dragon speaks, he thought. Roars its defiance into my soul. He opened his mouth, relieving the pressure, but refused to surrender to the pain. Closer . . . closer. Smell the enemy. See the enemy. Kill the enemy.

I am the archer.

Strike, samurai, strike! Fading fingers fumbled over the torpedo release, succeeded in grabbing it, and then viciously yanked. A divine sensation of peace washed over his body as he felt the torpedo drop and the Ninety-seven rise. It is done. He leaned back against the wet, clinging seat and relaxed. A vision of his grandfather swam into view.

Tomosan, whom do you serve?

He felt a smile part his lips. I serve Japan, grandfather. I am her native son.

Tomosan, you did not forget the spirit of combat?

I did not. I have kept the reality of death in mind.

A corkscrewing motion snatched the plane out of his control. His eyelids snapped open. A brief image of his hanging upside down flashed before his eyes.

75. THACH
June 04 – 15:00 Hours

Thach watched in grim relief as the stricken Nakajima's damaged wing folded, rolling the aircraft over upside down and into a fiery impact with the ocean. Flaming fragments of debris exploded in a shower of emerald spray and froth. He lifted a gloved right hand to his brow, offering a final salute to a brave, determined pilot. One last quick glimpse at its tail section revealed three broad yellow identification stripes before it vanished beneath the hissing, spitting waves.

A loud pounding, jarring sensation snatched him back into the present moment. Pay attention, Jimmie! He yanked backward on the stick and barely managed to sheer away from *Yorktown's* rapidly approaching starboard quarter. Vicious streams of anti-aircraft fire lashed out at him as the carrier fought to save herself from the attacking enemy planes. Get the hell out of here! Thach thought. He headed for the safety of higher altitude, noting Leonard hot on the tail of another enemy plane coming in on *Yorktown's* port bow.

"Take him down, Bill," Thach heard himself say. "Don't let him get *Yorktown!*"

Thach saw welcome sparks of tracers arcing out from Leonard's guns and dancing along the length of the torpedo plane. Its underside flickered, smoked, and then burst into flames. Leonard eased upward and away as the Japanese aircraft buried its nose into the ocean well short of *Yorktown.*

Leonard seemed to catch sight of Thach and waggled his wings before roaring off in search of more prey. Good job, Thach thought, before *Yorktown* drew his attention once more. Concern became dismay as a large geyser erupted from the carrier's port side, heralding the first torpedo strike. The ship shook visibly from the impacting explosion and immediately started to list.

Yorktown, how much more can you take? Thach wondered. The Japs did their best to sink you at Coral Sea. A fast repair at Pearl, and you were right back into battle with a cobbled-together group of pilots. A short time ago, bombs left you dead in the water. A super job by the crew got you steaming again, back in the fight. Now this. Haven't you suffered enough?

Another towering waterspout next to the carrier drove the spear point deeper into her metallic heart. One more Jap torpedo finding the aim and distance. Thach bit his bottom lip, trying to remain calm. They're as determined as we are to see this thing through. Thach pulled his vision away from the miserable scene. The war won't wait. Time to get busy. Take out a few more of Nagumo's pilots.

Eyesight sweeping the violent horizon, he spotted a lone Zero ahead and slightly above him. If I can surprise him, he's mine. The Cat crept forward, prepared to pounce. The enemy plane slowly filled the gun sight as he flexed his fingers preparing to fire. Just a bit closer, he thought.

What in the—? The Zero had vanished from view. His head snapped up as he registered it looping overhead to get into the kill position behind him. He jammed the throttle open in a vain attempt to escape. The F4F jerked as slugs chewed into its tail. Damn! I can't operate the beam defense by myself. I'd better get the hell out of here. There's a cloud. I'll lose him in there.

The Wildcat plowed into the vaporous mass. As if in a heavy fog, Thach's canopy blanketed over in the mist. Easing back on the F4F's speed, he cruised along taking full advantage of the refuge. His plane emerged a few minutes later into a sky empty of enemy aircraft. More F4Fs circled around the crippled *Yorktown*, maintaining a tight vigilance.

Good work, he thought. A sudden sensation of a presence joining him brought Lovelace to his mind. We couldn't have done it without you, Don. Rest in peace.

76. BEST
June 04 – 15:00 Hours

Best sat at his desk in the ready room reviewing his notes from the morning's mission. Just three other SBDs had returned, he thought. Did this tragedy really happen? Three planes remained out of an entire squadron of fifteen. A glance around at the empty seats quickly dispelled any doubts. The two remaining pilots were trying to rest. Best saw that the constant noise and smell of smoke and oil served to keep them suspended in an exhausted, agitated state of readiness. We're all at the point of collapsing, Best thought. Will this day ever end?

A sudden twinge of longing drew his hand to his shirt pocket. He removed a worn photograph of his wife and child and felt a smile form upon his lips. I wonder what they're doing right about now. He glanced at a blank sheet of paper nearby. Maybe I should write a quick note to my wife. I'm just thinking of you as I wait for the war to call me back. I miss you both. Kiss the baby for me. I'll be home soon. God willing, I'll be home soon.

No. Now is neither the time nor the place. Distractions like this in the middle of battle will get me killed. You can bet those Jap fighter pilots aren't thinking about home. Tonight, when this is over, I'll reread her beautiful words and find my own way to reply. To thank her for easing my burden and mind. I'm no hand at poetry but I'll think of something to write. For the moment I should keep my head focused on combat lest some Jap take it off.

"Dick," Gallaher said from the doorway.

Best smiled. "Any news?"

Gallaher shook his head. "I just came from the bridge. Admiral Spruance is planning to launch an attack against that fourth Jap carrier but not until he has a firm sighting report. I'm thinking that he and Browning are at odds about it. I'm glad the admiral is sticking to his guns. I'd hate to go dashing off without a clear idea of where I'm headed."

"So would I." Best motioned toward the sparsely filled room. "We're down to just a few pilots. I won't have much of an attack group."

"He knows, but there's no choice. *Yorktown*'s been hit and left burning. We've got to find and sink that last enemy carrier."

"How's Wade?"

"His shoulder's sore and he's grounded. I'll be leading things this afternoon."

"Let's hope that you do a better job of following doctrine."

"What do you mean?"

"I almost collided with Wade when he dove on the carrier that my group was supposed to attack. You understand bombing doctrine. You know what I'm talking about. As lead group, his bunch should have targeted the farther carrier. He dove on the near one and most of my guys went with him. It's lucky that a few of them stayed with me and that we managed to hit that second flattop."

Gallaher grimaced as he stretched his back. "I guess you're right, but let's give Wade a break. He's new to flying SBDs and in leading bombing attacks, but he's the reason we located the Japs. Wade spotted the wake of a Jap cruiser in the water and figured he was heading back to the main fleet. So Wade decided to follow him. It's a good thing that he did. If he had given up when our fuel ran low, we'd have missed the fight just like *Hornet*'s boys did."

"*Hornet*'s groups missed out?" It was the first Best had heard of this. "How did that happen?"

"The talk is most of them either ditched or landed at Midway without even seeing the Japs. All except the torpedo planes that is. Thank goodness, Wade's actions kept the same from happening to us. Without him leading us, there might be two more undamaged Jap carriers aware of our presence and launching attacks. This battle could be a defeat for *us* instead of Yamamoto."

Best dropped his head and considered Gallaher's words. McClusky had indeed kept searching when the rational thing to do was to return to the *Enterprise* before they ran out of gas. McClusky correctly figured the area to reconnoiter and also spotted the Jap ship making its way back to the carriers and decided to follow it. Not a bad day's effort for anyone.

"Any word on how our torpedo group did?"

Gallaher grimaced. "Lindsey and most of his boys were shot down."

"Damn."

"How are your guys holding up?" Gallaher changed the subject.

Best nodded toward the reclining figures. "Dead tired . . . those that are left."

347

He realized his unfortunate, ironic choice of words and was gratified when Gallaher ignored the gaffe.

"I'd like to get some rest, too, but I figure we'll be called before long. No sense in getting comfortable—not that I could." Gallaher awkwardly stretched again.

"Are you okay?"

"I wrenched my back a little but I'll make it. I'm not about to miss out on the finish, not when we're so close."

A sudden clacking from the Teletype machine seemed to confirm Gallaher's expectations. The noise had the effect of a bugler blowing reveille throughout the room; chairs plopped down, boots hit the deck, and the men reached for their plotting boards.

"This is it," Gallaher said. "I'd better go join my guys. See you on deck."

"Go with God."

Gallaher nodded, said, "You too," and disappeared.

"*Now hear this!*" The intercom caught their attention. "This is Captain Murray. I just wanted to congratulate you on the successful attack this morning. I'm proud of each one of you. However, the job's not finished. We've finally located the fourth enemy carrier that recently bombed *Yorktown*. She's a threat as long as she's afloat. We're depending on you and *Hornet*'s air groups to sink her. You've received your navigation data. Lieutenant Gallaher will be leading the attack. All aircraft will form up on him. Good luck and God speed."

"Okay, you heard what he said," Best said, addressing his tiny group. "Let's try to stay together. Follow my lead. It's hard to say what's going to happen, so let's be ready for anything."

"*Pilots man your planes!*"

The muted sound of men gathering their equipment and making for the door mocked him. This morning I couldn't hear myself think when the squadron left for the flight deck. Now I believe you could bounce an echo off the rear wall. I hope it was all worth it.

His vision dropped to the small photograph nestled safely in his palm before he tucked it away. These things I do in remembrance of you, amen.

348

77. BROCKMAN
June 04 – 16:00 Hours

Swish—Swish—Swish!

Brockman held on to the periscope housing and braced himself for the next round of depth charges. Sweat burned his eyes and soaked through his undershirt.

Whack—Whack—Whack—Whack!

More paint chips and cork showered down upon the anxious men as the boat tossed about. The stink of burnt electrical wiring, sweat, and fear made the dense air almost impossible to inhale. Brockman's tongue felt swollen inside his dry mouth. He forced a swallow, thinking, how much longer can this go on?

He glanced around at the other men fighting to remain at their stations in spite of the hellish assault. Through the dim emergency lighting, they appeared as dark specters, their true nature betrayed by the outstretched arms and legs straining to hold on.

Swish—Swish—Swish!

Here we go again. I guess those cruisers have a lot of anger to blow off. Allowing us to attack one of the Emperor's carriers right underneath their noses has shamed them both. A Jap would rather die than be dishonored.

Whack–Whack-Whack-Whack!

Each explosion radiated killing force throughout the surrounding sea. Violent concussion battered the bruised hull, threatening to rip it open. Brockman fought down a steadily rising terror by trying to calculate how much damage *Nautilus* could withstand. Much more than this, he tried to convince himself. These larger boats are constructed rock-solid. The depth charge hasn't been made that can sink one. It might damage one . . . but that would take a lucky, direct hit.

Swish–Swish–Swish!

Thank goodness, they're still depth charging too shallow. Perhaps the Japs are not aware our boats can reach three hundred feet deep. Let's hope they don't figure it out.

Whack—Whack!

The boat bucked and shook against the turbulence as Brockman glanced up at the ceiling. Just two that time? Could

349

they be running out of depth charges? Tired of hunting for us? We should be so lucky.

"Sound, report," Brockman stage-whispered to Woods.

"Propeller noises all over the dial, sir," Woods responded in kind. "I can't—"

A clanking sound vibrated along the hull and silenced Woods. Brockman looked back at Benson and then over at Woods.

"What was that?" both officers softly asked.

Woods did not respond, but adjusted his controls.

Thud—Thud! Two heavy objects bounced off the deck. Brockman wondered, have we strayed too close to the sinking carrier and caught some of the debris, or were those unexploded depth charges?

"Give me a damage report," Brockman said to Wetmore.

Someone . . . Benson, brushed against his shoulder.

"What are you thinking?" Benson asked.

"The first noise, I don't know. The last two sounds could have been dud depth charges."

Benson softly clucked his tongue. "I was hoping you had a different explanation than mine. After all those good ash cans they dropped, it's nice to know they can make duds, too. "

"Just a few small leaks and some blown light bulbs, sir," Wetmore relayed. "Lieutenant Hogan advises that everything is under control."

"Skipper," Woods called out, "high speed screws moving away from us. True bearing three two five. Range one five double oh and increasing."

Brockman exchanged glances with Benson.

"Is it really over?" Benson asked.

Brockman shrugged. "Sound, anything else sneaking around up there?"

"It's hard to tell, sir. There's a lot of background noise coming from the Jap carrier. I don't hear any more screws."

Benson blew out a long breath and flung perspiration off his arms.

"All that sweat's not a result of the heat," he said. "I'm hoping that sweat is the *only* reason my pants are wet, too."

A welcome ripple of laughter swept through the conning tower. Leave it to Roy to know the right thing to say to lighten the mood,

Brockman thought. He's going to make a damn good skipper of his own boat.

Brockman spoke to Wetmore. "Secure from depth charge, silent running, and general quarters, but let's remain close to battle stations. There may be another *Jintsu* lurking around."

"Aye, sir," Wetmore replied, before relaying the message through the phone.

"Why did they give up on us?" Benson asked. "They must have known that we were pinned down and certainly had ample motivation to sink us. It just doesn't make sense."

"Maybe it does," Brockman argued. "We have one sinking Jap carrier here. From the billows of smoke on the horizon, it's very likely that one or two more of them are in serious condition. Those Jap skippers hunting us could have reached the sudden realization that they're absent of air support. I'm thinking that might give them an entirely different outlook on things, and they might be trying to catch up to the remainder of their fleet."

"Safety in numbers?"

"You've got it."

Benson shrugged. "Seems like as good an explanation as any."

"While it's quiet, I'm going to check on things below and pass the word. You have the con."

Brockman mounted the ladder and descended into the control room. Hogan met him at the bottom.

"Good job," Brockman said. He turned to the rest of them. "Good job all of you. You did *Nautilus* proud."

"Did we finish sinking that carrier, sir?" Hogan asked.

"As good as. We kick-started the fires on her, and she was burning out of control the last I saw."

A cheer greeted his words and swept throughout the boat as the news filtered through each compartment. Brockman found himself shaking hands with each happy sailor.

"This is one hell of a first combat patrol, sir," Hogan remarked. "And we're just getting started."

Brockman nodded, finding himself drawn back into the reality of the moment. The patrol was indeed just getting started . . . as was this damn war. They still had a long, hard sea to sail.

78. KUSAKA
June 04 – 17:00 Hours

Kusaka read the message and glanced over at an agitated Nagumo standing by the bow window of the light cruiser *Nagara*. He continually swept the skies with a pair of binoculars gripped tightly in white-knuckled fists as if fearful of another enemy air strike arriving at any second.

"Sir, Admiral Yamaguchi advises that the second attack wave confirmed two torpedoes impacted an enemy carrier."

Nagumo lowered his glasses and turned to look at Kusaka. Cautious optimism briefly flickered across his somber features.

"Tomonaga located a different carrier to attack?"

Kusaka glanced down at the page and back up at Nagumo.

"Lieutenant Hashimoto observed two direct hits on an *Enterprise*-class carrier, not the same one as was earlier attacked by Kobayashi's bombers. He says this carrier was underway and conducting air operations."

Nagumo's eyes narrowed. "Hashimoto?"

"Lieutenant Tomonaga's plane was seen being destroyed."

"Tomonaga is gone?"

"Yes, sir."

Nagumo sighed and then shook his head. "We've lost so much during this long day. Kobayashi . . . Tomonaga. All of those brave fliers and sailors that died on our damaged carriers. Rivers of tears will soon flow throughout Japan."

"The day is not done," Kusaka reminded. "With two torpedoes in her, that second enemy carrier is certainly incapacitated if not already sunk. We've taken two of their carriers off the board. There's still a chance for us to inflict greater damage on the enemy."

"And what about that last report by *Tone*'s scout plane made after Tomonaga's torpedo attack?" Nagumo asked.

He walked over to the chart table and picked up the earlier message. "Two enemy carriers with escorts," he read. He waved it at Kusaka. "Despite our attacks, we're still dealing with at least two more enemy carriers. After our losses from the previous two strikes, we have fewer than a dozen serviceable aircraft. I counted them myself as they landed on *Hiryu*. You would continue forcing battle until all of our air units are gone? What could we possibly do to compensate for such losses?"

Kusaka remained silent, knowing that Nagumo was correct in his thinking. *I am a fool. How could they even consider throwing away the remains of their air group in such a hopeless cause? Yet, the decisions that Nagumo makes now affect more than Kido Butai. Yamamoto is watching to see how Nagumo responds to the crisis. Which actions could be deemed as displaying a lack of aggression on Nagumo's part? Will any of the choices that Nagumo might take satisfy Yamamoto?*

"Sir!" A runner stood in the door extending a message. Kusaka took it and scanned the contents. His center hollowed out as he read the words. *Yamaguchi must be insane,* he thought.

"Yes, what does it say?" an impatient Nagumo asked.

"Admiral Yamaguchi says the third strike wave will take off at 1800 hours, and he wishes that our scout plane maintain contact with the enemy."

"Third strike?" The expression on Nagumo's face echoed the shock in his voice. "After everything that's happened, he would launch a third strike? Where is the logic in that? What is he thinking?"

Kusaka shrugged. "You know Admiral Yamaguchi. Attack first and ask questions afterward. He considers nothing of the consequences from his actions."

"*Hai,* he's a fool. We must save *Hiryu.* We can replace pilots and aircraft much faster than we can build another carrier. I'll not stand idly by while he sacrifices the remainder of our brave aircrews without just cause. We've suffered enough losses today."

Nagumo motioned to a runner. "Send a message to all ships. Come hard left to a due west course."

Kusaka felt the ship's motion change as it swung around and had to shield his eyes from the afternoon sun. *Nagumo's actions are correct,* he thought. *Hiryu is too valuable to gamble away on such a long shot of success against two fully loaded enemy carriers. The time has come to cut our losses. We must save something to fight with on another day.*

"Sir, a message from Admiral Ugaki." The sailor saluted and handed Kusaka a note.

Kusaka read it carefully, thinking, the insanity is spreading to Combined Fleet. They can't be serious. He felt Nagumo's presence and knew he could not delay revealing the message's contents.

"Admiral Ugaki wants to know about the progress of our attack on Midway. He particularly wants to know if we'll secure it soon enough to use the shore batteries against the American fleet tomorrow."

Nagumo's fists slammed down on top of the chart table, scattering pencils and papers. A ghostly cast tinted his face. Lack of sleep and poor nutrition are taking their toll on him, Kusaka thought. How much more can the man endure before his health breaks?

"Use Midway's shore batteries ourselves?" Nagumo seemed to ask himself. He fixed Kusaka with incredulous eyes. "Do they not understand what's happening here? Did they ignore my earlier messages saying *Akagi, Kaga,* and *Soryu* were burning?"

Kusaka held up a hand. "Please, sir, let me finish. We're to establish contact with Admiral Kondo's invasion force tonight. We will join up with Admiral Yamamoto's Main Body in the morning. This reformed Combined Fleet will press the attack against Midway."

Kusaka lowered the paper and looked at Nagumo, who was obviously trying to restrain himself. Nagumo closed his eyes and rubbed his face. A weak smirk twisted his lips.

"Now, Kusaka," he quietly said. "*Now* they finally see the wisdom of having the entire fleet combined for this operation. The Americans have extracted a terrible toll from us due to uncompromising actions taken by stubborn men . . . a toll that we now have little chance of recovering. At the loss of three aircraft carriers, hundreds of men, and dozens of aircraft, these stubborn men finally see that which was obvious from the beginning. Did you not advocate such an organization at the planning meeting?"

Kusaka could not recall his words during the few meetings they participated in. "I can't say, sir. That seems so very long ago."

"Long ago?" Nagumo's voice grew louder. "More likely you forget because we had so little involvement in the planning of this operation. *Hai!*"

Nagumo broke off. Kusaka knew that he feared saying too much. Though they were alone inside *Nagara*'s command structure, loose talk had a way of growing legs and walking off a ship.

"Sir, about Admiral Yamaguchi's desire for a third strike against the American carriers," Kusaka reminded.

"This message from Ugaki would seem to rule that out for now, if I choose to acknowledge it."

Kusaka raised his binoculars, trained them on *Hiryu*, and noticed the large vessel maneuvering into the wind.

"Yamaguchi appears to be making preparations to launch," Kusaka said.

Nagumo also focused on *Hiryu*. "She is indeed turning."

Kusaka glanced at his wristwatch. "It's not 1800 hours. He's just getting ready. Should I send him a message to halt?"

Nagumo lowered his glasses. "Not yet. Have the rest of our vessels conform to *Hiryu*'s movements."

Kusaka started to protest and then noticed the determined set in Nagumo's manner. He motioned to a runner and relayed the order. Turning back to Nagumo, he found him silently standing by the window looking out at the smoke funnels billowing up in the distance. Kusaka thought, what is going through his mind to change it so suddenly? Is his own need for revenge against the enemy overriding his concern to save what remains of the Mobile Force?

"They questioned my decision to withdraw our forces at Pearl Harbor." Nagumo again seemed to be speaking to himself. "It was whispered that I left the job unfinished . . . that I left the enemy sufficient means to strike back at us. Now Ugaki seeks the opportunity to repeat those accusations. To bury me forever."

Nagumo loudly inhaled, pulled his shoulders back, and exhaled. "No. I won't allow him the satisfaction."

Kusaka's vision dropped to the last message still gripped tightly in his burnt hand. The shadow of Yamamoto looms over Nagumo, questioning and mocking every decision that he makes. It was at that moment that Kusaka finally understood. Nagumo has made his choice. No matter what may come, Nagumo's will to fight should never be questioned again.

79. RAMSEY
June 04 – 17:00 Hours

"*Yorktown*'s been hit, sir!"

Ramsey snapped into consciousness, realizing that he had dozed off for a moment. He sat on the floor with his back against a wall and looked over at the radioman. Worry masked the young man's face, a feeling Ramsey easily shared. He thought, *Yorktown* hit? What was going on out there? He remembered the surprise and relief flooding Midway that morning when the first strays from *Hornet* had straggled in for fuel and directions. A few tense, almost disastrous moments ensued with nervous anti-aircraft gunners mistaking them for enemy planes before calmer heads prevailed. Their pilots brought the good news that two task forces had arrived from Hawaii. Admiral Nimitz did send help. Not one but three aircraft carriers to protect Midway, and now this happens.

"Is that confirmed?" Ramsey asked.

"It seems to be, sir. There's a lot of radio traffic about it between the fleet. I heard that Admiral Fletcher has moved his flag."

Brushing himself off, Ramsey got to his feet. What a waste of time, he thought. It will take a week's worth of showers and bleach to wash this place off me. I think I'll just burn the clothes . . . that is, if I can ever dry them out enough.

Simard entered the dugout and walked over to Ramsey. "Did you finally wake up?"

"How long did I sleep?"

"Not long. I noticed you dozing about thirty minutes ago and figured you could use some rest. I left orders not to disturb you unless something important happened."

"Well, it did. *Yorktown*'s been hit."

Dismay registered on Simard's face. He took off his cap and slapped his pants leg with it, raising a cloud of dust.

"Damn! Any idea how bad it is?"

"Not really. There's a good bit of radio traffic including mention that Admiral Fletcher moved his flag."

"Anything over the cable line from Pearl?"

Ramsey shrugged. Simard looked at the communications table and caught one of the aide's attention.

"See if you can get any information from Pearl Harbor about what's happening with Admirals Fletcher and Spruance."

"Aye, sir."

Simard nodded toward the doorway. "Let's get some air. You've been monitoring communications since this thing started."

Ramsey yawned, rubbed his aching eyes, and joined Simard outside. A raging inferno consumed the oil storage tanks, sending a solid tower of black smoke and curly ashes skyward. A firefighting team stood back and watched it burn, the severe heat forming an impenetrable wall denying close access. The stink of destruction and death painted the tropical scenery from a palette filled with hues of charcoal. Now I know what Armageddon in the Pacific looks like, Ramsey thought. Seeing the burnt remains of the laundry room drew a curse from Ramsey and a strange look from Simard.

"Something wrong?" Simard asked.

"My clothes were in there," Ramsey explained. "I'm wearing all I have left."

Men bustled about in every direction, making repairs and cleaning up. Ramsey noticed a line of canvas-covered forms and solemnly realized what they were.

"All I've given up is some clothing," a shamed Ramsey said. "These men gave everything they had to give."

Simard remained silent. A sudden shout caught their attention, and Ford came walking up with a movie camera in his hands.

"What a show! Hollywood couldn't dream up anything to beat that!"

"We're happy you enjoyed it," Ramsey replied. "It just a little something we call the war."

Ford glanced over at the row of bodies and his face grew somber.

"I didn't mean anything disrespectful," Ford said.

"We understand," Simard said. He pointed at Ford's bandaged arm. "How badly were you injured?"

Ford made a wave of dismissal. "Just a scratch. I've cut myself worse shaving."

"I appreciate your helping out," Simard said.

"Glad to do it." Ford looked at Ramsey. "I've shot a lot of excellent footage. Admiral Nimitz should be pleased."

"Let's hope that's all you shoot today," Ramsey answered.

Ford ignored the comment and asked Simard, "Any idea on casualties?"

"Midway wasn't hit too badly, though any casualty is one too many. It looks like about twenty killed and a few more wounded. Our aircraft and flier losses are staggering. Most of the SBDs and just about all of the torpedo planes are missing. The word is that Joe Henderson's plane went down in flames. No one observed a parachute. We've picked up a few men who ditched. I'm hoping we'll fish several more out of the water before darkness sets in. Long story short, we've two fighter planes able to take off if we need them."

"I can see what they did to this place. How much damage did we do to them?" Ford asked.

Ramsey sighed. "The only reports I've received credit the Army boys with damaging one carrier. Other than that, we've not inflicted much on the enemy. That leaves at least three Jap carriers afloat to do battle with our task forces. I have no idea how much success our carrier air groups had. The fact that most if not all of *Hornet*'s attack squadrons failed to locate the enemy leaves me concerned about the situation. Let's hope that *Enterprise* and *Yorktown* were more fortunate."

"And I doubt that the enemy has forgotten about us," Simard remarked. "When they've dealt with our carriers they'll turn their attention back to Midway."

"Those American aircraft that showed up here were from *Hornet?*" Ford asked.

Ramsey answered, "It's the first we heard about our having carrier forces in the vicinity. It appears that Admiral Nimitz prepared a surprise for the Japanese. Before I left Pearl, he had said nothing about it to me. Given *Hornet*'s results, I have my doubts as to its success."

Ford cursed and whipped off his glasses. "So what happens next?"

Ramsey pointed to a squad of busy Marines replacing sandbags around a gun emplacement. "I figure the Japs will have us under heavy bombardment by sunset. We're making preparations for it."

"That might be, but these boys are going to give them a warm reception," Ford answered. "I've never witnessed such courage under fire."

Simard smiled. "I've no doubt, but without control of the air, the best we can do is stall the enemy for a while."

"Sweeney's already taken his B-17s back to Pearl so they don't fall into enemy hands," Ramsey said. "I'm thinking about moving the PBYs out as Admiral Nimitz ordered. I'll have to put you on board one of those."

Ford's face flushed and he spat. "Nothing doing. I plan on seeing this battle through to the end."

"The end could come with the Japanese swarming onshore and killing or making POWs of us," Ramsey argued. "You're a civilian. I can't—"

"I'm an officer and am as able to fight as the next man. Give me a rifle. I intend to do my duty."

Ramsey noted Ford's clenched fists and upright posture and realized that arguing was futile. He felt a growing respect for the odd character. *This is one tough Irishman.*

Ramsey smiled. "I don't suppose we can spare the six Marines it'll take to place you on a PBY and hold you there until it lands."

Ford returned the grin.

"What about your film?" Simard asked.

"That I will allow to leave when you send those PBYs away. I want Admiral Nimitz and all of the families of these brave men to see and appreciate the ordeal they faced here today."

Ramsey looked at the row of bodies and thought, *first Pearl Harbor and now Midway. How could I have ever considered this just another job?*

"You can show them what happened," Ramsey said, "but none but the dead will appreciate the reason why."

80. BEST
June 04 – 17:05 Hours

And then there was one, Best thought, glancing down at the solitary enemy carrier. He led his flight of SBDs in following Earl Gallaher's group around to the far side of the task force, placing the sun at their rears and in the eyes of the Jap anti-aircraft gunners. Best thought, good job, Earl. Just like the book says.

"Group leaders from Earl One." Gallaher's voice whistled through the radio. "*Enterprise* groups will attack the carrier. *Yorktown* groups will attack the nearest battleship."

Clouds of anti-aircraft fire billowed up around Gallaher's flight, preceding the arrival of the combat air patrol. Zeroes tore into their ranks as Gallaher's group broke over, heading into its dive. Best screened out the incoming fighters, focused on executing his attack. Bright dots of tracer carved through the space around his SBD, threatening to disturb his concentration and throw off his aim. Refusing to yield, he reached the pushover point and opened his dive flaps. A bluish blur streaked past in front of his propeller, nearly causing a collision. Not again, Best thought. Can't anyone follow doctrine? Best slapped the dive flaps shut and wrestled his aircraft into a sharp climbing turn to avoid the other members of the errant strike group.

"Watch those Zeroes!" Gallaher shouted over the radio.

The ominous bellow of a Mitsubishi engine punctuated Gallaher's words. Best caught a fleeting glimpse of a charging Zero streaking past, the cannons on his wings winking. A flash of fire behind him and Weber's SBD collapsed out of the formation trailing smoke.

"No parachutes, sir," Murray notified from the rear seat.

"Here they come again!" someone needlessly yelled over the air.

Best dodged another attacking Zero boring in from 11 o'clock high. It skidded past, trailed by the sound of Murray's banging away with his twin .30-calibers. The rank smell of burnt gunpowder and fear-induced sweat covered the cockpit. Rubbing his itchy brow with the back of one hand, Best felt his eyes water from salty perspiration sliding into them.

He looked below at the carrier and thought, *Yorktown*'s group decided to change targets and nearly rammed me. Do I switch my attack to the battleship? No. This is the final Jap flattop. Sink her and the skies belong to us. Win the skies and we win the battle.

"VB Six from Dick One," Best radioed. "Follow me down and get hits!"

Dive flaps open, he half-rolled the SBD and plunged toward the ocean, gaining lethal momentum with each fleeting second.

"Count me off," Best said to Murray.

"Eight-thousand feet."

The SBD nearly standing on its nose, Best fought to maintain control of the dive angle. Flickers of red and yellow flames popped up on the carrier deck indicating several bombs finding their targets.

"Seven-thousand feet."

The whistle of the air rushing past his windscreen rose in intensity to a siren wail. The noisy cockpit sucked in every decibel of sound from engine, air currents, and combat. He vainly shook his head, trying to ease the pain in his ears.

"Six-thousand feet."

A nasty cough rattled his body, moistening his burning eyes. Puffs of deceptively harmless looking anti-aircraft shell bursts padded the sky around the SBD. Metal fragments rattled against the aircraft's skin. Whip crack whines like angry mosquitoes heralded near misses zipping past.

"Five-thousand feet."

The throaty roar of an angry lion announced another Zero zooming by with cannons banging away. The SBD rocked from 20-mm shell impacts and anti-aircraft gunfire concussion. Hold together, girl, Best thought. Not much farther.

"Four-thousand feet."

Best pressed his eye against the telescopic sight to line up the crosshairs and center the leveling ball in its groove. Everything looks good and on target, he thought. Just a few seconds more. Concentrate. Mind on target.

"Three-thousand feet."

The burning flight deck grew larger in the scope's view as his anticipation built. Another bout of coughing jerked his head away from the scope. Sucking in a raspy breath, he fought and stilled the racking convulsion. His sighting eye watered. A quick wipe with the back of his sleeve and his eye returned to the bombsight.

"Two-thousand feet!"

Best gripped the bomb release yoke and gave it a hard jerk. The SBD immediately felt lighter to his control hand. Closing the dive flaps, he pulled the aircraft's nose up. A brief sensation of blacking out caused by heavy G-forces disoriented him. Roaring noise and a fiery blast rocked the plane, clearing his senses. Intense heat radiated skyward, saturating his damp flight suit with more sweat.

"Bull's eye!" Murray called out. "Right on the flight deck. Nice drop, sir!"

Tracers streaking past the fuselage reminded Best the job was incomplete. His tired hands and feet worked the SBD's controls, slipping and sliding through a hail of bullets and cannon shots. Best's handling of his airplane threw off the attacking enemy pilot's aim as Murray's twin .30-calibers chattered, keeping the Zeroes at bay.

A Zero suddenly appeared crossing in front of him. Best squeezed the gun trigger on his stick. The twin .50-caliber Brownings mounted in front of his windscreen awoke to pounding life. A quick burst trailed off behind the speeding enemy plane. That was a waste of ammo, Best thought, but it made me feel better to strike back.

The lethal combination of his .50-calibers and Murray's .30-calibers served to hold the Zeroes off. The enemy fighters soon moved away in search of easier targets. Best brought the SBD around in a wide arc, heading back to *Enterprise*. He spotted Gallaher nearby and guided his plane into formation. There's safety in numbers, Best knew. We can watch each other's 6 o'clock and mass our fire. I'll make it out of this battle yet.

The flight of SBDs circled clear of the wounded Japanese fleet. Thick, choking black smoke tunneled upward from the carriers bombed in the morning's attack, covering their aircraft in a layer of sooty oil. Best eased his plane closer to gaze over at his day's efforts. Ravenous flames consumed the enemy vessels like a fiery beast with an insatiable hunger. A strange euphoria possessed Best as he reveled in the destruction. I feel like the Lord of Creation, he thought. I've never accomplished so much, nor did I ever believe revenge could be so sweet. I've done my part to protect my family. I want to remember this moment for the rest of my life. I'll never feel anything so intense again.

"Arizona, I remember you," a voice uttered over the radio.

Gallaher? Best wondered. Not that it mattered. Whoever it was spoke for us all.

81. FLETCHER
June 04 – 18:00 Hours

"Admiral, *Hughes* is carrying the fewest number of rescued passengers." A bedraggled Buckmaster, resembling a drowned cat, stood framed by the door of flag plot on *Astoria*. "I could use her to assemble a salvage team and prepare *Yorktown* for tow."

Fletcher glanced up at Buckmaster and then over at Admiral Poco Smith and Lewis seated across the table. Fletcher felt Buckmaster's desire to rejoin *Yorktown* and attempt to save her, but understood the battle had not ended. There's still a fourth enemy carrier out there, he thought. I don't want to risk placing people back on *Yorktown* until this thing is decided. She could still be attacked, and we could suffer more casualties. Caution must remain our watchword or else we'll lose much of what we have gained this day.

Fletcher searched his memory in vain before looking over at Smith. "Who is captain on *Hughes*?"

"Don Ramsey," Poco replied. "He's a good man and a fine officer."

"Harry!" Fletcher called out.

A few moments later his flag lieutenant, Harry Smith, appeared. "Send a signal to Gil Hoover, my destroyers' commander. Have *Hughes* stand by *Yorktown*. I don't want anyone going aboard *Yorktown* tonight without my permission. I'm authorizing Don Ramsey to sink her to prevent capture or if a serious fire develops again."

Harry Smith acknowledged the message and left. Fletcher turned to find Poco studying him.

Fletcher raised his eyebrows in a silent question.

"That's hard for you to say . . . sink her, I mean."

Fletcher chose not to answer. He picked up a corncob pipe and found himself fumbling to clean it.

"It's understandable," Poco continued. "*Yorktown*'s a fine ship."

"*Yorktown*'s the best!" Fletcher dropped his pipe. "That ship and crew have waged much of the fighting in the Pacific since this war began. She's done her part in every battle she's been involved in. She took a hell of a beating at Coral Sea and still made it here to Midway. *Yorktown* damn sure made her presence known today.

Massey, Leslie, Thach, hell, all of these brave fliers and support crews did us proud. I've no disappointment or regrets."

"I agree," Poco assured him. "I'm well aware of *Yorktown's* contributions. You've obviously made some plans concerning her?"

Calm down, Fletcher thought. Poco did not mean anything by his remark . . . just pointing out the difficulty for a sailor, any sailor, to destroy that which he loves.

Fletcher shifted his attention to Buckmaster. "I don't want to do anything else with *Yorktown* tonight. It's too dangerous. I want you to draw up a list of materials and personnel needed to work on her tomorrow. If the situation's stable, you can transport over at first light."

"Aye, sir. We'll get on it right away."

"Buck." Fletcher's voice stopped Buckmaster in the doorway. "I want you to get some rest, too. It's been a long day, and tomorrow could be just as long."

Buckmaster flashed a tired-looking smile. "Aye, sir."

"Message from Admiral Spruance," Lewis said as he unfolded a slip of paper. "He advises that *Enterprise* and *Hornet* air groups are attacking the fourth carrier, which *Yorktown's* scouts located. He wants to know if you have any instructions for future operations."

Fletcher smiled and thought, bless Ray for keeping me involved with what's going on, but he has the operational carriers, not I. My duty is clear. I'm not about to cause a lot of confusion by moving my flag to *Hornet*. Ray and his staff are doing a great job. I owe it to them and the rest of this fleet to follow through and finish this thing.

"Negative," Fletcher replied. "I will conform to his movements. Send that right away."

Fletcher leaned back against the seat and closed his eyes. The noise and bustle surrounding him served as reassurance . . . reassurance that his trusted staff, officers, and men were engaged in performing their duties. A good commander issues orders trusting his men to do their utmost to carry them out, Fletcher thought. Chet learned that a long time ago. It's what makes him so effective. Ray doesn't need me watching over his shoulder or questioning every decision he makes. Other people do that to me, but I'll be damned if I'll follow their sorry examples.

"Are you feeling okay? Is the head injury bothering you?"

Fletcher's eyelids popped open, and he found Poco leaning closer. His face bore a look of concern that touched Fletcher. There are some decent folks this world, Fletcher thought. I mustn't judge all of them by the actions of a few.

"I'm fine. I'm thinking about my decision to abandon *Yorktown*. I'm certain that I'll be questioned for it."

"You'll be questioned for anything you do. By now, I'd have thought that you understood that."

Fletcher stared at him and arched an eyebrow. "Thanks for reminding me."

Poco smiled and then grew serious. "There are too many unknowns out there for you to do differently. We're not sure of the Japanese's disposition or their intentions. If they should decide to engage in a night surface action, they have all of the advantages. Air power won't matter once the sun sets. We could lose everything that we've won today."

"They certainly know where *Yorktown* is located. It'd be simple for them to close in and sink anything that we leave there tonight."

"That is a fact," Poco said.

"There's been enough killing for one day. I'll not risk any more lives trying to do something without proper protection and support. When daylight comes, we'll go back over and see what we can do to save *Yorktown*."

A sudden uproar from the bridge drew their attention. A jubilant Buckmaster hurried in with a message and thrust it toward Fletcher. Fletcher guessed the contents and refused to take it.

"Go ahead and read it so everyone can hear," Fletcher instructed.

"Admiral Spruance advises that the fourth enemy carrier was struck by bombs from a combined flight of *Enterprise* and *Hornet* SBDs. Eyewitness reports indicate the enemy vessel was reduced to a mass of flames and explosions."

Fletcher grinned. "Send Admiral Spruance my regards. Communicate my thanks and congratulations to every man of these task forces."

"Admiral Nimitz gambled and won," Poco remarked. "We did it!"

Fletcher sank back into the chair, closed his eyes, and silently prayed. Dear Lord, gather us unto You and shield the souls of these brave men sacrificed in service to their country. Amen.

We did it.

82. SPRUANCE
June 04 – 18:15 Hours

"Lieutenant Gallaher reports the fourth enemy carrier burning, sir," Oliver said to a seated Spruance.

"Is it sinking?"

"No, sir, but the damage appears to be major. There are fires roaring all over the superstructure. He thinks there's a good chance it will go under."

"Relay that message to Admiral Fletcher. Make certain he's aware of the operational status."

"Aye, sir," Oliver replied.

"We need to hit it again immediately," Browning remarked. "Finish it off without a doubt."

Spruance looked out of his flag shelter and noted the setting sun casting enormous, writhing shadows of the task force vessels upon the waves. The long day draws to its inevitable, bloody end, he thought. We've no aircraft left to mount another strike, and it will take too long to prepare them. We'll not be prepared to launch before darkness sets in.

"No more attacks today," Spruance decided.

Browning flushed. "The Japs are less than an hour's flight away and are helpless. While we arm and fuel up another flight, we can close the distance until it's just a short hop. We can finish off whatever remains of those Jap carriers. Secure total victory. How can we not complete this job now?"

"Daylight is fading," Spruance replied while fighting to maintain his calm manner. "Most of our pilots have already flown two missions today. I'm not going to jeopardize them further by sending them out in the dark. They can't hit what they can't locate."

"The flames from the burning carriers will serve as beacons to home in and drop on," Browning argued.

Spruance sighed. "And how do we land our planes when they return?"

"Turn on the landing lights, sir."

"Given our present situation, that would be very risky. An enemy submarine could spot us. Submarine torpedoes can sink us just as surely as aircraft torpedoes."

"With all due respect, we have escort vessels circling the fleet, actively sonar-pinging. It'd take a long time for an enemy sub to maneuver through them in order to reach us. By then, our planes should have landed and the lights been turned off. It's worth the risk to sink that fourth carrier and finish off the others."

"Sir," Oliver said as he stuck his head back in the door, "Admiral Fletcher offers his congratulations. He says that he will conform to your movements."

Spruance remained silent, considering Browning's words and the implications. Browning is Halsey's trusted air officer. The two of them have enjoyed a good deal of success. I'm not Halsey, and this part of the operation is Browning's specialty. I'm learning on the job. Perhaps I should follow his advice one more time. Wouldn't Halsey press ahead and finish this mission? Wouldn't he make certain that success was in his hands?

An approaching SBD trailing smoke caught his attention. He stood and watched the obviously battle-damaged aircraft wobble in the wind, fighting to remain in control. Transfixed, he breathed a silent prayer as the pilot expertly brought the plane down to a bumpy landing. As quickly as it coasted to a stop, deck personnel surrounded it. Anxious hands tenderly assisted the pilot and gunner clear and then hustled both away to sickbay.

These men have suffered and given so much today, he thought. We've hit Nagumo's carriers hard, but there's a tremendous Japanese surface fleet remaining out there. What if they home in on *Yorktown* and attempt a night attack? If we steam westward to close the distance, we could sail right into an ambush from those enemy battleships and cruisers. If we loiter here to launch another attack, we run the risk of those enemy ships finding and engaging us.

"Sir?" Browning broke the silence.

"When darkness forces our CAP to land, we're ending air operations," Spruance said. "I want ideas on how to keep these task forces away from a possible enemy night engagement."

Spruance could feel the heat rising off Browning but chose to ignore it. I'm responsible for this fleet. Thank goodness Fletcher did the logical thing of turning command of the carriers over to me. I'm following the principle of calculated risk. As things currently stand, there's too much risk in a night battle. The

Japanese have the advantage in both firepower and experience in such an encounter. I'll not gamble away what we've earned today.

"Sir—" Browning began.

"Are you about to offer an idea to protect the fleet from a night engagement?" Spruance broke in.

"No sir, about ending the air attacks—"

"There's no more discussion on that point," Spruance said, cutting him off again. "We'll attend to completing that business tomorrow. How do we protect this fleet tonight?"

"We could move toward Midway," Buracker suggested. "Perhaps bluff the enemy with the threat of Midway's shore batteries."

Spruance thought about the option. There's still a chance the Japanese will attempt a landing and occupation of Midway tonight. If they do, their large ships will lead the way with a naval bombardment, catching our forces in the trap that I'm trying to avoid.

"And if the Japs decide to make a landing tonight?" Browning voiced Spruance's concern. "We'd be right in the middle of that shooting match."

Spruance walked over to the railing and deeply inhaled the salty air. A lingering odor of gun smoke combined with diesel exhaust soured the breeze. The group fell silent waiting for him to speak. He glanced up at a thinly clouded sky and thought, it promises to be a beautiful night with a full moon . . . perfect for landing troops on a beachhead. Will the Japanese take advantage of it? And if we move in closer to prevent that from happening? Our carriers' silhouettes will stand out like targets in a shooting gallery. Browning has that point right. *Midway is not your first priority*, Nimitz had said. *Destroying those Japanese carriers without excessive loss of ours is.* We've followed his instructions so far. No need to deviate now. We must be able to muster air support for Midway tomorrow without risking everything tonight.

Spruance moved back to the chart table, picked up a marker, and drew a plot. A moving target's harder to hit, he thought. We'll keep on the move tonight.

"Here's what I want," he said to Buracker. "We're going to keep this force sailing eastward and then northward before turning back to the west. We're not going to give the enemy a chance to catch us in a surface action tonight."

"Sir, we're passing up a golden opportunity to complete the job that Admiral Nimitz sent us out here to do," Browning insisted. "We can finish that fourth Jap carrier and any of the others still afloat today."

"I'm well aware of Admiral Nimitz's orders," Spruance said, carefully measuring his words. "I'm also making the command decisions and accepting full responsibility for them."

He focused his attention on Browning. The room fell silent.

"Any questions?" Spruance asked.

"No, sir," Browning answered, before glancing away.

"When our CAP lands we head east."

"Aye, sir." Browning stood and saluted. He stalked off, his footsteps solidly clinking on the metal deck.

Spruance watched him go and thought, I've had enough of these armchair tacticians forgetting about the men tasked with carrying out missions. I'm a patient man, but there's a limit to everything. I've given him too much leeway already and paid for it today with the Point Option foul up. I'll not risk these aircrews' lives with a night action. He might be Halsey's man . . . but I'm not Halsey. I'm Ray Spruance.

And I'm good enough to get the job done.

83. BROCKMAN
June 04 – 18:30

Brockman stepped off the conning tower ladder and moved over to Benson at the periscope.

"Down scope," Benson ordered. He looked at Brockman.

"How's the coffee?"

"A-1 Navy issue," Brockman announced. "You can float a mine in it."

"I'll go down in a while and see for myself. I hope you didn't drink it all."

Brockman motioned upward with his eyes. "What's going on?"

"No sign of the cruisers or any other ships for that matter. The *Soryu* is burning out of control. It looks like they've given up on saving it."

"Low in the water?"

Benson shrugged. "Hard to tell. You can't see her hull through all the smoke. She's throwing up a plume that has to be a thousand feet tall. Reminds me of how bad the *Arizona* looked at Pearl Harbor."

Brockman locked eyes with Benson. "The *Arizona*. Was this all about revenge? All of this killing and destruction?"

Benson shook his head. "No, I'd say more about self-defense. We didn't ask for this war, but we're going to see it through . . . and on Tojo's terms. I can't help but think of the biblical saying, for they have sown the wind, and they shall reap the whirlwind. I'd say the Japs reaped a whirlwind today."

They both moved to the chart desk where Brockman glanced up at the chronometer.

"It'll be dark soon."

"Good thing, too," Benson said. "Our batteries must be getting dangerously low and in need of a long charge. We've ridden them hard today."

"We've all been ridden hard today. I'm proud of everyone's performance."

Brockman turned around and leaned his elbows on the table. He observed the normal routine of the watch party and felt deep satisfaction at the way each man went about his job. Lynch had stepped away from the TDC and now stood ready to take the next periscope sighting. Woods remained fixed to his sound gear while Crenshaw made notes in the logbook. Yates and Wetmore stood at the helm softly talking.

The boat suddenly shook as a nearby explosion tore a huge hole in the ocean.

"Rig for depth charge! Rig for silent running!"

Rushing to the periscope, Brockman bumped into Lynch. He started to raise it, hesitated, and glanced at Woods.

"Sound, report!"

Woods feverishly turned his dials and position crank, but shook his head. "I don't hear anything, sir. Just that explosion—"

Another blast rocked the boat and sent men scrambling for places to brace themselves. Brockman latched onto the ladder railing and called below.

"Take her down! Make your depth one seven five feet!"

Brockman leaned back against the pull of his arms and closed his eyes. Frayed, exhausted nerves and body fought against surrendering to the fear of another round of depth charges. I've pressed the attack all day, he thought. These men have stayed with me every step of the way. We've made it through so much. Lord, shield us a while longer, please.

"Right full rudder!" Brockman ordered. "Ahead one-third!"

His eyes remained closed as he felt the boat respond to his command. We've suffered enough and done enough for one day. Let this thing end.

"Sound, anything?"

"Still nothing, sir. We seem to be the only vessel anywhere around. Those explosions came from the direction of the damaged carrier."

Releasing his grip, Brockman eased his eyes open and looked at Woods.

"Any sound of screws before the first explosion?" Brockman asked.

"No, sir. I've had my full attention on this sound gear the entire time. I've missed nothing, sir. It's just us and that burning carrier."

A stationary ship can't lay depth charges, Brockman knew. We're not under attack, nor do we have enough juice to pursue more targets. He glanced over and saw Benson watching him. He's thinking exactly what I am. A false alarm. The Jap carrier is sounding her death throes.

"Rudder amidships! Bring her up to periscope depth!"

Brockman waited until the boat leveled off and the periscope mast was extended. He rotated the head several revolutions to confirm that no other ships had joined the smoking carrier. If anything, it seems to be burning worse than before, he thought. He lowered the scope, stepped away, and motioned to Lynch.

"You're officer of the watch, I believe. Roy and I are going below to have a cup of coffee."

A surprised Lynch glanced over at a smiling Benson. Brockman could guess the young officer's thoughts: is the skipper really trusting me with the boat in a combat area?

"Aye, sir. Any orders?" Lynch asked.

"Let's stay at periscope depth until the battery runs out," Brockman answered. "We'll have a look on the surface when we recharge."

"Aye sir."

Brockman hesitated at the ladder until Benson joined him.

"Don't say it," Brockman softly remarked.

"Don't say what?"

"That we're all learning about war together."

Benson chuckled. "I don't have to say it. You just proved it."

Brockman smirked and started below.

"Bill?" Benson said.

Brockman paused and glanced up.

"Welcome to command."

84. KUSAKA
June 04 – 19:15 Hours

Kusaka read the message once more, trying to make sense of it. He glanced out a window on *Nagara's* bridge and thought for a moment about the peaceful evening sky. Have we not had enough bloodshed for one day? The adrenaline surge of a few short hours before now dissipated, his burnt hands and leg throbbed with pain, reminding him of his ungraceful exit from *Akagi's* bridge. Falling from the window had also caused him to twist both ankles. He shifted his weight, trying to relieve the numbing ache, and mentally replayed the day's events that had brought them to this miserable place. Why must there be more casualties in a foolish effort to save face? A steely resolve can overcome a battle lost. Sacrifice to no end serves no purpose. He gazed down at the page and wondered what the Combined Fleet was thinking.

"What is it?" Nagumo appeared next to him.

"Combined Fleet is ordering us to pursue and attack the enemy fleet immediately and then to occupy Midway."

Nagumo's face paled, and his lower lip trembled. He took the paper and slowly scanned its contents.

"This has to be a mistake," Nagumo said without taking his eyes off the note. "This was sent by someone who does not understand the strength of the enemy. My message detailing *Hiryu's* bombing has been ignored. Earlier, perhaps while *Hiryu* was still available to offer air support, this might have had merit . . . but now?"

Nagumo folded the page and placed it in his pocket. He walked over to the window and leaned against a binocular pedestal. Kusaka watched him carefully and noticed the heavy sag of his shoulders. Nagumo has visibly aged since this morning, Kusaka thought. And why should he not have? He's lost three and possibly four of our aircraft carriers today. Yet, he didn't lose this battle alone. Combined Fleet and Admiral Yamamoto share equal parts of the blame.

"Your hands and ankles." Nagumo was speaking to him without turning around. "You need treatment."

"It's nothing. There are more important matters requiring my attention."

They both looked over as a frail-looking Genda entered the bridge. One hand bandaged, he forced a weak smile to reassure the worried Nagumo.

"Genda?" Nagumo asked.

"Just a small burn, nothing serious."

"And Fuchida?" Kusaka asked.

Genda sighed and his mouth drooped. "Broken bones in both legs and feet. He'll be laid up for a while."

"But you are well?" Nagumo asked again.

"I'm able to do my duties, sir."

For the first time since that morning, Kusaka saw a brief flicker of relief in Nagumo's eyes. Kusaka thought, perhaps Genda can stir up some of the dying embers within Nagumo. Someone willing to truthfully communicate the situation here must respond to this message from Combined Fleet . . . not tell Yamamoto what Yamamoto wants to hear.

"Your duties?" Nagumo asked.

Kusaka could tell by the defeated tone of his voice that Nagumo's moment for regaining command was slipping away. Genda's mentioning his duties brought to mind the destruction of all of *Kido Butai's* air groups that day. Genda was an air officer with no air units to direct.

"I am here to do whatever I can to help you," Genda said, quickly amending his offer.

This time, a smile lit up Nagumo's creased features as he placed a hand on the young officer's shoulder.

"I thank you my friend," Nagumo said. He turned toward Kusaka. "And you too. It gives a man great comfort to know he has a loyal staff."

"Admiral," Kusaka said quickly to take advantage of Nagumo's mood swing, "this message from Combined Fleet must be answered."

"There has been a message?" Genda asked.

Nagumo answered, "Yes, we've been ordered to assemble the Invasion Force and prepare for a night action against the enemy."

Genda glanced at Kusaka, received a confirming nod, and looked back to Nagumo.

"This can't be serious. There must be some mistake in transmission."

376

"It is believed that our forces will have the advantage while attacking at night," Nagumo explained. "We are much more experienced at night combat than the Americans. Our expertise will lead to a great victory and make up for our losses today."

"And when daylight comes, what then?" Kusaka spoke up. "The Americans will hold mastery over the sky with their bombers and torpedo planes. Combined Fleet will face certain destruction, not just the carriers, but battleships and cruisers, too. We'll have little remaining to continue fighting this war."

"Admiral Kusaka is right," Genda echoed. "What's the latest scouting report on the enemy's strength?"

Kusaka walked over to the chart table and picked up a piece of paper.

"Four enemy carriers, six cruisers, and sixteen destroyers," Kusaka read and then looked up at the two of them. "That doesn't include Midway which still possesses a threat with its aircraft."

"Sir," Genda said as he faced Nagumo, "we must not expose our forces to this. It's insane."

"What would you have me do?" Nagumo responded. He removed the folded message from his pocket and shook it at them. "These are orders, not suggestions."

A tense silence enveloped the room. Kusaka glanced out into the darkness and inhaled deeply. The sting of salt mixed with burnt fuel oil covered him with filthy scales. The gentle rhythms of the ship's heartbeat and motion plowing through the waves reminded him of the totality of things. Logic must prevail, he thought. Nagumo must do what's rational regardless of the cost to him.

"Admiral, you know what must be done," Kusaka said, focusing back on Nagumo. "You must send a message informing Admiral Yamamoto about the facts of our situation and explaining your decision to withdraw. You must make him understand what he's committing to do. Hiryu is damaged but still moving. We still have our two large carriers Shokaku and Zuikaku back in Japan and more are under construction. We must not allow the enemy an opportunity to destroy any more of our surface forces because of a rash, uninformed decision made far away from the scene of battle. Our fortunes and the war are not lost. This is a setback . . . nothing more."

"I don't know . . ." Nagumo trailed off.

"Sir, you must," Genda implored.

Nagumo appeared to think for a moment, and then drew himself up to his full height. "Admiral Yamamoto has misinterpreted the information he has received. I will send a message explaining the need to withdraw in order to escort *Hiryu* to safety and due to the enemy's total control of the air. I'll not risk any more of the Emperor's ships against such overwhelming odds. This unconscionable folly must end."

Kusaka made to leave. "I'll draw up the message at once."

"*No!*"

Nagumo's gruff voice froze Kusaka.

"I shall be the one to write the message. This is between Admiral Yamamoto and me."

* * *

Kusaka lay his head down on the table in the wardroom and considered reporting to sickbay. Sickbay? I fear that place of pain and death. The time has not yet arrived. The agony from my burns and sore ankles has grown into a numbing ache, but it must not cloud my mind. I need to hold on for a few more minutes. I must hear the response to Admiral Nagumo's message.

The familiar smell of rice cake and tea soothed the air and reminded him of home. Was it only one short week ago that we sailed from Japan? It seems like a lifetime has passed. I yearn to surrender myself to the meditation denied me in the last several days by this evil war.

"Admiral Kusaka," a voice called from out of the distance.

Kusaka leaned back, blinked, and realized that he had fallen asleep. He rubbed his eyes, the action reminding him of the pain in his hands. Tiny electric pricks shot up his cramping arms.

"I'm sorry to disturb you, sir." Genda stood there speaking. "We've received a reply to Admiral Nagumo's message."

Kusaka read something in Genda's behavior and realized things had not turned out as expected.

"Let me hear it."

Genda swallowed. "Admiral Nagumo has been relieved of all command except for the damaged carriers. Admiral Kondo is to assume command of the rest of our forces. He has been ordered to pursue the enemy and engage them in night combat."

"It is as I feared. The folly continues. Combined Fleet would risk losing much more of our surface forces in this rash display of

378

wasted bravery. Would that common sense could triumph over ego."

Genda remained silent. He has not forgotten Yamamoto had much to do with his rapid advance, Kusaka knew. Yet, Nagumo treats him like a son. How difficult it must be for Genda, caught between two such strong loyalties to men who loathe each other.

"You've shared this with Admiral Nagumo?"

Genda nodded.

"And his reaction?"

"He appeared dismayed, but not surprised at this turn of events. I think he expected as much when he sent that last message to Admiral Yamamoto."

Kusaka used his elbows to push himself up from the table. He stood, wobbled for a few moments but refused to surrender to the pain and exhaustion. Not yet, he thought. I have much to do to atone for my part in today's misery. I share equal blame for the incorrect decisions made. His eyes closed as he centered himself.

"Let me escort you to sickbay, sir," Genda kindly offered. "You should have your burns treated. We have a great need for your wise counsel. The challenge lies ahead of us, not behind."

Genda is right. The war is not lost. There shall be another opportunity to make amends for this.

Kusaka opened his eyes and smiled at Genda. "Thank you, Genda. I would appreciate it."

85. BROCKMAN
June 04 – 21:45 Hours

The ocean exploded in a curtain of boiling spray as *Nautilus* broached the surface and settled back onto the waves. The main hatch wheel spun and halted, and the hatch clanged open. Brockman scrambled out, followed by the lookouts quickly taking their positions on the platforms in the periscope shears. A beautiful, moonlit sky provided a soft halo on a sea dotted with the wreckage and debris of the day's battle. The roar from the diesel engines' starting and then the numbing thrum of their running provided a noisy backdrop to the men's observations. The usual marine odors of salt water and fresh air combined with that of manmade oil and smoke to form a stinking mixture that clung to the skin.

It looks so normal now, Brockman thought. If not for the debris, this could be a spot in any other ocean in the world. But it's not. The sea life knows we've profaned this place. There's no sign of birds flying or fish jumping and splashing. Just the noise and wash of our boat. What did I expect?

"Permission to come onto the bridge?" Benson called from below.

"Granted."

A few moments later, Benson joined him. Both men used binoculars for several minutes to pierce the warm South Pacific night.

"No sign of the carrier?" Benson asked.

"No, but there's wreckage everywhere from the fighting. I'm thinking some of those last explosions we heard were from it going under."

Benson lowered the glasses and gathered a deep breath. "I've never known a breeze that felt so good. Although the smell leaves much to be desired."

"That's our fault," Brockman replied. "We brought the stink out here. Ordinarily there's not a more welcome odor to me than that of the sea. Not tonight. Tonight it's different. We poisoned it with our killing . . . and disregard for human life."

Benson cocked his head and seemed to study him. "That's a very profound observation. You don't look the philosopher type."

380

"Just thinking out loud," Brockman answered. "Perhaps that's the definition of philosophy, thinking out loud?"

"Another good one. You're on a roll."

Brockman heard a scratching noise and saw a brief flicker of fire cupped in Benson's hands as he lit his pipe.

"I thought you never smoked that thing."

Benson inhaled and then coughed. "I don't know . . . something about being trapped aboard an iron coffin while depth charges rain down on a fellow makes him desire a good smoke. Can you believe that's what I was thinking as those ash cans rained down?"

"No."

"Neither can I, but it's my story and I'll swear to it."

He took another puff and coughed again. "Actually, at that time, I desired to be anywhere else—no offense, mind you. The smoke was my second choice for something to do."

Brockman smiled, appreciating Roy's presence and humor. *Lead by example and attitude. Roy had that down cold. He was going to make a damn good skipper. My loss.*

Brockman glanced up at the moon. *You can almost touch the radiance,* he thought. *It's strange how peaceful this place can be after a day filled with so much violent death. Heaven knows we had our hand in the killing. Do I blaspheme with my gratitude for surviving while feeling satisfaction at the lives that we took?*

"This is one hell of a brutal business," Benson said as if reading his thoughts.

"What's that?"

Benson raised both arms and spread them wide across the junk-strewn water.

"War," Benson answered. "It's a very brutal way for people who call themselves *civilized* to act. It makes me wonder if we're as civilized as we think. What happened out here today certainly argues against it."

"True."

Benson snorted. "Listen to me. Now you've got me philosophizing."

Brockman remained silent, considering his words. *Perhaps an experience like the one we endured today makes a man reflective. There's nothing like facing one's death to make him think about his life.*

381

Benson waited a few moments for a reply and then moved toward the hatch. "I think I'll get a little shuteye and leave you with your thoughts," he said. "Okay?"

"Yes, we've both earned it. I won't be too long behind you. I just need to write up the night orders."

"Another big day tomorrow?"

"I don't know whether to wish for or against it."

"Just take things as they come," Benson said before disappearing below.

Brockman raised the binoculars to take another sweep of the area. Roy's right, he thought. I guess we shouldn't consider ourselves as civilized in the midst of so much bloodshed. But that's a matter for philosophers and priests. Regardless of what Roy thinks, I'm neither. I'm a sailor in command of a combat vessel.

My country needs me.

86. KUSAKA
June 05—07:00 Hours

Kusaka sat on a bed in *Nagara*'s sickbay and patiently waited while a hospital corpsman treated his burns. Considering the events of the past 24 hours, the soothing salve did nothing to relieve the pain welling deep inside him. Combined Fleet had transmitted several hours ago that Admiral Yamamoto had canceled Operation AF. A reprieve from execution at the last minute, Kusaka thought. Calmer heads had finally prevailed.

The corpsman finished, bowed, and left him. Kusaka slumped as all the tension and aggression of the day finally dissipated in his drained body. He leaned back against the bed's damp, warm surface and closed his eyes. The fear slowly began worming its way inside. Ignore this place of pain and suffering, Kusaka told himself. Focus inward . . . not on the confining walls surrounding me.

How badly could we have misjudged a people? The idea that the Americans lacked the will to fight . . . how had we come to that conclusion? True enough, the enemy's rapid subjugation and mass surrendering up to this point seemed proof of it. What had changed within them? Those brave pilots sacrificing themselves yesterday morning against our forces died like true samurai. No matter how many we shot down or how impossible it was to get their slow flying aircraft near the target, they kept coming.

He felt a bitter smile crease his lips as he recalled something he had overheard Genda say to Fuchida. As they made their way one at a time out the window of the doomed *Akagi*, Genda glanced at Fuchida and said, "We goofed."

We goofed, Kusaka thought. How could two such insignificant words sum up the monumental disaster visited on them? It was a disaster born out of our own blind prejudice against and misjudgment of the enemy. No, not misjudgment, but sheer contempt for the enemy's fighting heart and ability to kill. Perhaps we deserved this punishment for our grievous error in misunderstanding the art of war.

"Sir?"

Someone was standing next to him. He sighed, forced his eyes open, and found Oishi looking down at him. The solemn look on his face reminded Kusaka of a small child caught in some mischievous act.

"Yes."

"The staff has discussed the matter, and we've all decided to commit seppuku to atone for the disgrace of Midway," Oishi announced. "Will you please urge Admiral Nagumo to do the same?"

Kusaka raised himself up high enough to check Oishi for the smell of alcohol and then lay back down. Realizing the man was sober, he felt a sudden flash of anger firing his spirit. Oishi can't blame a fog of sake for clouding his thoughts, Kusaka decided. Wrestling with hot emotion, he recalled his own initial despondent reaction to the events of yesterday. He had questioned his own courage and ability to return to Japan and face the great shame of his dishonor. At the time, suicide did seem to be a logical manner in which to address the situation. Did not Admiral Yamaguchi fearlessly go down with the sinking *Hiryu* a few hours ago? No . . . fearless isn't the proper word for Yamaguchi's selfish action. The brave and honorable thing to do is to seek another opportunity to make atonement in battle against one's enemy. I'm a Zen warrior and I won't surrender so easily to my own passion.

"Your words are those of a fool," Kusaka said. He pointed a bandaged finger at Oishi. "You are to immediately round up all the staff members and bring them to me. Go!"

Oishi flushed, bowed deeply, and hurried out. Kusaka closed his eyes for a brief nap. A short time later, the sound of a throat clearing brought him to full alertness. He looked and found the staff members gathered around the bed. I must face them eye to eye, Kusaka thought, not lying down. He ignored the pain from his burned hands, pushing himself upright. Slowly looking around at the circle of faces, he noted with satisfaction that all of them stood with heads bowed.

"You remind me of hysterical women!" Kusaka shouted, the anger gripping him. He focused on his breath for a brief moment, struggling to remain centered and rational.

"First you dance around with joy at easy victories, and now you wish to open your bellies because of one defeat," he said in a more controlled manner. "You think of yourselves and forget about Japan. This is not the time for such selfish thinking. Why not learn from this opportunity and refocus your efforts to do something beneficial for the Emperor? Use the example of those Americans who kept waltzing into the midst of tigers yesterday, seeking the smallest chance to destroy us. How can you expect to defeat such an enemy if you're not willing to do as he does?"

Kusaka paused to allow himself a calming moment. The smell of medicinal alcohol and antiseptic cleansed the air . . . hopefully it would cleanse away such foolish ideas too, he thought.

"Killing oneself is the way of a coward, and I'm totally against it. You've asked me to take a message to Admiral Nagumo. Well, *that* is the message I bear."

Kusaka eased off the bed and limped out the door.

* * *

"Admiral Nagumo?"

Nagumo looked up from his desk at Kusaka.

"Come in, Kusaka," Nagumo said, pointing toward a small stool next to his bed. "Have a seat, but don't expect much in the way of hospitality. I seem to have little heart for it."

Kusaka seated himself. "That's why I'm here."

Nagumo sighed. "I've heard that the staff members all want to commit seppuku. Perhaps Yamaguchi and Kaku had the right idea by drowning along with *Hiryu*? That moment passed for me on *Akagi*, but I can still wield a knife. You wish to join me?"

Kusaka inhaled deeply to gain a moment to compose his thoughts and study Nagumo. Nagumo's body expressions and attitude bespoke one already resigned to an ignominious fate. What has become of the man who led us to such brilliant victories over the first six months of this war? Does one defeat truly mark a man forever regardless of his many triumphs? I must find the way to speak to Nagumo's head and drown out the loud chatter coming from within his heart.

"To take one's own life at such a time is irrational," Kusaka said. "You're allowing your emotions command of your actions, and that is not following the art of war. We must prepare ourselves to meet the enemy and defeat him in the next battle. This is how the Code of Bushido dictates that we perform our duty."

Nagumo seemed to force a weak smile. "I do appreciate your advice, my friend. Try to understand that reason cannot determine every action made by a commander. My honor is at stake here. There's nothing but disgrace for one who did not fulfill his duty to his master."

385

"*Hai.*" Kusaka started to make a harsh reply, bit it off, and allowed a dense silence to blanket the room. Anger will accomplish nothing now, he thought. I must choose my words wisely . . . prudently, to penetrate beyond Nagumo's despair and into his sense of pride.

"You say that you've failed in performing your duty to your master?" Kusaka asked.

Nagumo nodded.

"Who is your master, Japan or yourself?"

Nagumo's eyes flashed and his nostrils flared. I've struck a nerve, Kusaka thought as he quickly pressed on.

"Japan needs you . . . needs all of us to continue this fight against the barbarians. Would you have her reduced to the status of a lapdog to the Western Imperialistic Powers? To be like China before we liberated much of her people and territory? Is not the future of Japan more important than your own honor and pride?"

Nagumo's head dropped onto his chest, and he sighed. Kusaka held his tongue, understanding the next words must come from Nagumo. How would Nagumo respond to his challenge?

"Your words strike like a knife," Nagumo began, "because the truth whets them. This war is not lost because of one battle. I owe it to my master–Japan–to continue the fight."

Kusaka stood. "I'll leave you to rest, sir."

He walked toward the door.

"Kusaka?"

Kusaka halted and turned back.

"Thank you for your wise counsel," Nagumo said, bowing.

Kusaka returned the gesture, left the room, and pulled the door closed. He moved down the narrow corridor to his own cabin and entered. The refuge of a bed had never seemed so welcome, he thought. Too many disparate events have consumed me these past 24 hours. I have lost my path through the irrationality of the conscious world. Reflections and memory should not cloud the Zen warrior's mind. Release today and allow things just to be as they are . . . non-interference.

Sitting on the bed, he painfully removed his shoes. He lay down, stretched out, and meditated.

Life is suffering.

Yesterday bears proof of this.

I shall live in the moment.

AFTERMATH

The Battle of Midway ends on June 7, 1942 when *Yorktown*, further damaged by three torpedoes fired on the day before from the Japanese submarine *I-168*, succumbs to her wounds and slips beneath the waves. The destroyer *Hammann*, tied up alongside *Yorktown* to provide power for the salvage party, has its back broken by the first torpedo striking *Yorktown*. Within minutes, her crew hastily abandons ship as *Hammann* goes under. Compounding this tragedy, depth charges on board *Hammann* explode at their pre-set depths, killing many of the survivors in the water awaiting pickup.

Midway is immediately viewed as an unqualified victory for the United States and one of the major naval battles in history. The Imperial Japanese Navy has suffered a defeat from which it is unable to recover. The battle marks the point at which the Americans switch from a defensive strategy in the Pacific Theater to an offensive one. Though there are dark days ahead filled with death and destruction, the course is firmly set for the war's outcome. The Japanese will taste victory on a small scale on future occasions, but their time of running rampant throughout the region is past. Midway will not be threatened with invasion again for the remainder of the war.

Raymond A. Spruance

Though some immediately criticized his decision to retreat from the scene of battle on the night of June 4, later analysis of the Japanese records of their intent to force a surface action prove him correct. He returns to Hawaii and becomes Admiral Nimitz's Chief of Staff and later Deputy Commander in Chief. In mid-1943, he receives command of the Central Pacific Force and leads the campaigns against many of the islands held by the Japanese. His later life finds him President of the Naval War College and serving a stint as President Truman's ambassador to the Philippines. He dies in Pebble Beach, California on December 12, 1983.

Frank J. Fletcher

By his unselfish act of handing Spruance virtual command of the U.S. Forces after *Yorktown* is crippled, he also gives away credit for the Midway victory. Fletcher's critics, among them Admiral Ernest King, Chief of Naval Operations, continue to question every decision that he makes and every action that he takes. Despite his leading the force that turns back a Japanese attempt to retake Guadalcanal in August, he is denied a return to his command after a slight wound forces his first leave after eight months of constant battle. Instead, he is shuffled off to defend the relatively calm area of the Northern Pacific and ends his wartime service there. The personal attacks upon him continue throughout his life. Spruance is hailed by the earliest historians and students of the battle as the American commanding officer at the Battle of Midway and is labeled a hero. Fletcher is relegated to playing the role of an observer. To Spruance's credit, Spruance steadfastly maintains until his dying day that his position was subordinate to Fletcher's. A current reappraisal of Fletcher is helping to change the negative image and put him in a more positive light. He dies in Bethesda, Maryland on April 25, 1973.

John C. Waldron

He and the rest of Torpedo Squadron 8 become the symbol of American fighting men doing their duty for their country no matter the odds. After the battle, the obsolete Douglas Devastator airplanes are removed from combat service and relegated to training assignments. It is sadly ironic that only the men from Torpedo Squadron 8 are so widely known and remembered. The figures show a loss rate of *95 percent* for the TBDs engaged at Midway. In fact, all of the torpedo squadrons that participated in the battle, among these Lem Massey's Torpedo Squadron 3 from *Yorktown*, suffered horrendous casualties.

John S. Thach

Thach won a gold star at Midway to go with a Navy Cross awarded earlier in February. During the Battle of Santa Cruz in October of 1942, Lieutenant Commander James Flatley uses Thach's beam defense with great success. Flatley renames the tactic the *Thach Weave* and comments that it is "infallible when executed properly." The weave spreads throughout the American air forces in both the Pacific and European Theaters. Thach remains in the Navy as both a fighter pilot instructor and later an anti-submarine warfare specialist. He retires with the rank of full admiral and dies in Coronado, California on April 15, 1981.

William H. Brockman

The contribution of Brockman and the crew of *Nautilus* at Midway remain virtually unknown except to historians and students of the battle. *Nautilus* holds the distinction of being the only American submarine to fire torpedoes at an enemy ship during the battle. Brockman earns a Navy Cross at Midway. He continues to serve with distinction throughout the war and receives two more Navy Crosses. He dies in Boca Raton, Florida on January 2, 1979.

Frank L. Melo, Jr.

He is awarded the Distinguished Service Cross, as are all the crewmen in the B-26s. Along with Tomonaga, he is the enigma of the group. He seems to vanish after the battle, and I have found no further record of his fate. Perhaps this is because the others were all officers while Melo was an enlisted man. Researching and contacting people from his hometown turned up nothing. I would sincerely enjoy hearing from anyone that can share more light on this interesting man and will include an update in any future revisions of this novel.

Lofton R. Henderson

He is posthumously awarded the Navy Cross for his actions at Midway. His fellow Marines latch onto his example, and he becomes the first Marine hero of World War Two. This is perhaps best exemplified by the naming of the captured Japanese airfield on Guadalcanal *Henderson Field* in his honor.

Logan C. Ramsey

Per Nimitz's promise, Ramsey returns to Pearl Harbor as Chief of Staff to Commander Aircraft, Pacific Fleet. In March of 1943, he becomes the commanding officer of the escort aircraft carrier *Block Island*. He spends the final part of the war serving as Chief of Staff to the Commander Air Fleet, Norfolk. He retires from the Navy in 1948 with the rank of Rear Admiral. His later years find him serving as vice president of Spring Garden College, located in Pennsylvania. He dies on September 26, 1972 and is buried in Arlington National Cemetery.

Richard H. Best

The two bombing missions on June 4, 1942 end his career as a Navy pilot. The contaminated oxygen he inhales during the initial sortie from *Enterprise* that morning activates latent tuberculosis. He enters the hospital back at Pearl Harbor and undergoes over two years of treatment for the disease. He retires from the Navy in 1944. His success at Midway earns him a Navy Cross to go with a Distinguished Flying Cross won earlier in the war. In his civilian life, he works for the Rand Corporation and dies on October 28, 2001.

Ryunosuke Kusaka

He remains with the fleet until November before assuming the position of Chief of Staff, Southeast Asia Fleet and later serves in the same capacity for the Combined Fleet. He assumes command of the 5th Air Fleet in August of 1945 following Admiral Ugaki's death in a kamikaze plane. He retires as a Vice Admiral in late 1945 and dies on November 23, 1971.

Joichi Tomonaga

Thach's after-action report concerning the final air attack on *Yorktown* states that he shot down a Nakajima 97 torpedo-bomber with distinctive yellow tail markings. This description seems to match Tomonaga's airplane and provides enough proof that most historians believe that Thach shot him down. Though his body is lost at sea, his memory is enshrined in the Yasukuni Shrine in Tokyo. On an interesting and poignant note, Tomonaga's memorial page at www.findagrave.com is filled with graphic flowers and comments from Americans praising his brave sacrifice. I can think of no more fitting tribute for a fallen samurai warrior than kind words of respect offered by his former enemy.

AUTHOR'S NOTE

The bulk of my material is factual, and the documentation of it found in the Further Reading section. For obvious reasons, the majority of the dialogue and all of the characters' thoughts are fictitious, though many people will recognize some of the quotes. My timetable and the action are as accurate as documentary sources allow. I remind the reader that the viewpoints used stayed faithful to the descriptions of what the individual *believed* happened and what he knew at the time. Subsequent study and research revealed much of the initial reporting of the battle to be false or misunderstood. In fact, many of its aspects are still under debate today. Among these is the reason why *Hornet*'s air groups, other than Torpedo 8, did not find the enemy fleet during the morning sortie. The initial belief fostered by George Gay, the sole survivor of *Hornet*'s Torpedo 8, and others is that *Hornet*'s groups departed on and then flew a southwesterly heading, taking them too far south of *Kido Butai*. Gay asserted that Waldron led his men in a right turn towards the northeast. Recent analysis and investigation, well documented in *No Right To Win*, listed in the Further Reading section, assert an almost due west course for the HAGs with a *left* turn by Waldron. This is a particularly thorny debate due to the good arguments from both sides. The novel details my personal belief about Torpedo 8's route. The meeting on board *Hornet* that I depicted did occur, but my relating of it is mostly fictional except for the disagreement between Ring and Waldron.

A major matter of contention between the service branches was the Army Air Corps' receiving initial credit for winning the battle. The B-17 Flying Fortress crews returned to Hawaii first and reported they caused major destruction among the Japanese fleet. Many newspapers and magazines wrote articles and stories touting this version of the combat. I have addressed the facts behind these claims from both the Japanese and American viewpoints in the novel. After thoroughly examining all of the written evidence, historians now believe the B-17s bombing from high altitude scored no hits.

My scenes of conflict between Spruance and Miles Browning were mostly fictional, but their relationship on board *Enterprise* quickly soured. Browning's failure to name or follow procedure with a Point Option for the returning aircraft did happen. Spruance was angered and started taking a more active role in flight operations. The climax of their stormy time together culminated on June 5th when Spruance sided with McClusky in a heated disagreement between Browning and McClusky. A peeved Browning went to his cabin to sulk until he was coaxed back to duty. I would point out, though, that Browning served Halsey admirably. It was also Browning who convinced Spruance to launch the first strike earlier than Spruance intended. For that reason and from the way things timed out, Browning certainly deserves credit for his part in securing the victory at Midway.

I also find it interesting that *Nautilus*'s contribution is often overlooked or only briefly mentioned in most of the Midway histories. Without *Arashi* remaining behind to occupy the persistent submarine and then dashing back to the fleet with McClusky following her, the battle would have undoubtedly ended differently. Controversy also surrounds the identity of the carrier that *Nautilus* attacked, as well as the result of her torpedo shots. I have communicated with one of the remaining *Nautilus* crewmen present at the battle. He insists that *Nautilus* successfully struck the burning carrier *Soryu* with three torpedoes and ensured her sinking. Most authorities and Japanese eyewitnesses conclude that *Nautilus* fired at *Kaga*. Furthermore, two of the torpedoes missed entirely while the third struck the ship without exploding. Upon the torpedo's breaking into pieces, several of the Japanese sailors swimming nearby used some of the pieces as life rafts until they were rescued.

Hollywood director John Ford was present at Midway and did film the Japanese attack on the island. Ramsey and Simard asked him to perform the duty detailed in the book. Henry Fonda provided narration for the footage, and Ford released it 1942. It won an Academy Award that year for best documentary. Copies can be located and purchased or viewed over the internet if one searches for "John Ford and Midway." Less well known is that Ford also shot footage of the members of *Hornet*'s Torpedo Squadron 8 several days before the battle. The sight of Waldron and his men smiling and awaiting the chance at battle is particularly haunting, considering the outcome of their attack. This footage was never released to the public, but copies were given to their families. It is also possible to locate this film for watching over the internet.

Before the battle, Admiral Nimitz was aware of only three components of the Japanese Operation. He did not know about Admiral Yamamoto's Main Force composed of the giant battleship *Yamato* along with two more battleships, several cruisers, and a host of screening destroyers. Nimitz believed Nagumo's carrier strike force was the Main Body. I wonder what influence, if any, knowledge of the actual Main Force would have had on Nimitz's plans. It is also open to speculation what might have resulted had this battleship group been close enough to offer an immediate threat to either Midway or the American Fleet during the battle. Instead, Yamamoto positioned it over 500 miles away from Nagumo's forces and too distant to offer fast response support. Upon such decisions are the fates of nations hinged.

Regardless of who did what, everyone participating in the battle played an active part in deciding the outcome. From the decisions made by the officers on both sides to the fierce resolve demonstrated by each man in performing his duty, this battle was fought and won by men . . . not the whims of fate or a miracle. I believe we do a severe disservice to the memory of these brave warriors, both American and Japanese, to think otherwise.

I welcome the opportunity to discuss the novel or answer questions from my readers. I can be reached at:
www.blog.cripplecreekpress.com
or emailed at:
galvinsimons@cripplecreekpress.com.

GAS

FURTHER READING

Books:

Buell, Thomas B. *The Quiet Warrior: A Biography of Admiral Raymond A. Spruance.* Annapolis, MD: Naval Institute Press, 1987

Caidin, Martin. *The Ragged, Rugged Warriors.* New York: Bantam Books, 1985.

Cressman, Robert J., Steve Ewing, Barrett Tillman, Mark Horan, Clark Reynolds, and Stan Cohen. *A Glorious Page In Our History.* Missoula, MT: Pictorial Histories Publishing Company, Inc. 2008

Ewing, Steve. *Thach Weave: The Life of Jimmie Thach.* Annapolis, MD: Naval Institute Press, 2004.

Fuchida, Mitsuo and Masatake Okumiya. *Midway: The Battle That Doomed Japan, the Japanese Navy's Story.* Annapolis, MD: Bluejacket Books, 2001.

Gay, George. *Sole Survivor: Torpedo Squadron Eight and the Battle of Midway.* Midway Publishers, 1986.

Johnston, Stanley. *Queen of the Flat-tops.* Garden City, NY: Nelson Doubleday, Inc. 1979

Lord, Walter. *Incredible Victory.* New York: Harper and Row, 1967.

Lundstrom, John B. *Black Shoe Carrier Admiral: Frank Jack Fletcher at Coral Sea, Midway, and Guadalcanal.* Annapolis, MD: Naval Institute Press, 2006.

Lundstrom, John B. *The First Team: Pacific Naval Air Combat from Pearl Harbor to Midway.* Annapolis, MD: Naval Institute Press, 1984.

Mears, Lieutenant Frederick. *Carrier Combat.* New York: Ballantine Books, 1967.

Parshall, Jonathan and Anthony Tully. *Shattered Sword: The Untold Story of the Battle of Midway.* Washington, DC: Potomac Books, 2005.

Prange, Gordon W., Donald M. Goldstein, and Katherine V. Dillon. *Miracle At Midway.* New York: McGraw-Hill Book Company, 1982.

Russell, Ronald W. *No Right To Win: A Continuing Dialogue With Veterans of the Battle Of Midway.* New York: iUniverse, 2006.

Tillman, Barrett. *The Dauntless Dive Bomber of World War Two.* Annapolis, MD: Naval Institute Press, 2006.

Internet Sites:
The Battle of Midway Roundtable – www.midway42.org
The B-26 Marauder Historical Society – www.b-26mhs.org
Shattered Sword Discussion Group –
groups.yahoo.com/group/shatteredsword/?yguid=159792947.
Steeljaw Scribe – www.steeljawscribe.com

26801817R00226

Made in the USA
San Bernardino, CA
05 December 2015